Best Bisexual Erotica

Best Bisexual Erotica

edited by

Bill Brent & Carol Queen

Black Books
San Francisco, CA

Circlet Press
Cambridge, MA

Best Bisexual Erotica
edited by Bill Brent and Carol Queen

Printed in Canada

First Printing February 2000

ISBN 1-892723-01-8

ALTERNATIVE CATALOGING-IN-PUBLICATION DATA

Brent, Bill, editor.

Best bisexual erotica. Edited by Bill Brent and Carol Queen. Foreword by Cecilia Tan.
San Francisco: CA: Black Books; Cambridge, MA: Circlet Press, 2000.

Focus: bisexual erotic stories. Includes material on transgender persons.

1. Erotic fiction. 2. Bisexuals--Fiction. 3. Transsexuals--Fiction. 4. Short stories, American--20th century. I. Brent, Bill.

810.803538 dc-21

A Joint Publication of Circlet Press, Inc. and Black Books

Distributed to the book trade by Circlet Press through The LPC Group (800) 626-4330.

For sales to individuals, specialty stores, and mail-order catalogs, please contact Black Books at (800) 818-8823.

http://www.circlet.com
http://www.blackbooks.com

Table of Contents

Foreword

Cecilia Tan

Bisexuality, what a concept. I began identifying as bisexual back before I'd had much of what I'd now call sex. I based my choice on my desires, not on my experiences, since at that age (my teen years) I had so much of the former and not very much of the latter. I didn't have many relationships. What I had were *crushes*, the lie-awake-and-think-about-her (or him) type of crushes. At the time, though, I had this concept that only the super-famous or exceedingly eccentric could actually be bisexual. (The fact that David Bowie was my one and only role madel may have had something to do with that notion.) I figured that at some point in my life I might have to choose gay or straight.

Which just goes to show how little I knew at that age.

The other thing I knew was looming in my future was writing. I called myself a writer,in fact, just like I called myself a bisexual, based on my wishes for myself, not my actual experience. As a teenager a scribbled out a lot of hormone-driven fantasy, romance, erotica, science fiction, you name it—again with the thought that I'd eventually have to choose a more narrow definition for myself.

Fortunately, my wishes, but not my fears, have come true. About a decade ago, after I left college, I decided it was about time I really did some actual writing, and publishing. I do not think it is a coincidence that I arrived at the point where I was ready to write something that really meant something to me at the same point when I finally realized that I could in fact choose the bisexual option for myself. I had arrived at my destination identity-wise, and suddenly found myself free of "wrtiers block" for the first time. And what was it I wrote? Erotica. Lots of erotica. Lots of bisexuality-tinged erotica.

And guess what? I'm not alone. There are other people out there who identify as bi. And who celebrate their sexuality. And who write it down. And who let the rest of us read it. Mmmm...

In fact, it was at a rather sex-positive gathering that the idea for this book came into being. During the fifth International Conference on Bisexuality (ICB5) at Harvard University, many of the people involved in the publication of this book (the editors, myself, and even some of the contributors) were at a safer sex party, playing out some of our fantasies in real life. Looking out over the happy sea of bi-indentified flesh in action that night, and especially noting how many erotica writers were in attendance, we knew the time for this book had come. Please, no puns about the "cream" of the crop... the fact is that many of the best erotica writers in the modern world are bisexual. I'd like to think that isn't accidental. And the more of us write good stuff, the more others we encourage to join us...

And you know what? We may be bisexual, but we're not super-famous or exceedingly eccentric. Though some of us are working on it. Welcome to our world.

Cecilia Tan
Cambridge, MA

Introduction

Many erotic collections have been published which might be termed "bisexual erotica," in that they have included stories from a variety of erotic perspectives likely to be of interest to bisexuals (such as lesbian, heterosexual, gay male). The *Herotica* and *Best American Erotica* collections come immediately to mind, as do a number of erotic anthologies published in the leather/SM community. This, though, is the first book of its kind that is sourced primarily in the bisexual community. Most of its characters (though not all) are bisexuals, and while the sex they have with their lovers and tricks may be just like the sex gay, lesbian, and straight people have, it doesn't happen in a gay or straight context. We know that bisexual readers have been hungry for this kind of affirmation because we both write and edit our own work from a bisexual perspective and have heard the feedback from readers who are tired of buying three or four books to get the erotic charge we hope they'll find packed into this one; we know bi women find lesbian erotica compelling, but do not necessarily see themselves truly reflected there; we know bi men who enjoy straight or gay male erotic books and magazines but find them limited; and we know bi couples who see their fe/male relationships in very different terms than those portrayed in heterosexual erotica. We're compiling this book for them, but also to showcase, in an erotic context, a bit of who bisexuals are (and who we might be with a little more sexual freedom).

As activists have been telling us for a long time, cultural ideas about bisexuals are fraught with stereotypes, especially as far as our sexual practices are concerned. We'll fuck anything that moves (only one of the stories here, "The Great Blinking MacGuffin" by Charles Anders, actually comes close to embodying this one—though in fact it lampoons it). We're non-monogamous by nature, into threesomes and group sex—after all, if we desire both women and men, we couldn't possibly be satisfied with only one lover. In a way, the qualities that make a piece of erotic writing uniquely bisexual tend to play on these stereotypes: in an exploration of monogamous passion, unless the writer works in some flashbacks, how do we know the story as anything other than straight or gay? So readers who want to see the stereotypes eroded might not exactly get what they want; but they will get plenty of high-octane bi sex, because this is an anthology of explicit erotic fiction. Mostly missing from this book, but with us in other, more theoretical contexts, is discussion of all the bisexual issues that aren't specific to our sexual practices and relationship configurations. In this erotic world (sadly, often unlike the "real" one), sex is simply a given. The authors whose work appears here explore fantasy scenarios, tell you what they like (*maybe*—you can never reliably judge a book by its cover or an erotic writer's sex life by what they put into print), and together sketch out a bisexual world which is diverse, sometimes unexpected, and unabashedly sexual.

Gender politics—both kinds!—are present here. For those of us who were around in the good old 1970s, gender politics will always reference feminism and the fight against misogyny, and several of our writers take on "the war of the sexes" from an explicitly erotic viewpoint. This isn't surprising. Bisexual female-male relationships, so frequently informed by feminism and queer understandings of sex and relationship, may not offer a clean slate for these gender wars, but they do present an opportunity to inscribe new practices and patterns of relating over old ones. The male-female sex in this book is only "me Tarzan, you Jane" (that is, *traditional*) when the participants are role-playing, and it's just as often "me Jane, you Tarzan." Sometimes this is in a completely loving context, as in "Sauce for the Gander"by Hanne Blank. Sometimes it's more like another salvo in the war between the sexes ("Boy Bashing" by Raven Gildea). One thing's certain: the women and men in this collection don't take these issues for granted; they play with, flout, and fight traditional sex-role stereotypes.

But that makes it sound as though there are only men and women, and increasingly we realize there are more genders than that: the other gender politics vibrantly present here are those of the trans community. We were thrilled to receive so many engrossing stories with transgendered or transsexual protagonists (as well as by trans authors), and we think it serves to illustrate to what extent the bi community has made space for, and values the contributions and erotic presence of, transsexual and transgendered people. Bisexual folk, after all, are defined (and stigmatized) by our desire for women and men; we really should be open to the eroticism of those who have embodied both ways of walking in the world, as well as those who walk somewhere in the middle, or somewhere else altogether. (If these are new ideas for you, see Kate Bornstein's *My Gender Workbook*, a must-read primer on new gender paradigms and possibilities.)

A recent article in *Black Sheets* asks whether bisexuals are kinkier than other people, and if this collection were to be the sole evidence to settle the question, we'd have to say yes. It's not the last word on the matter, of course; it's a smut book, produced by people who love smut and all forms of playful, exploratory eroticism. But readers will notice that many of our authors don't transgress only the boundary labeled "Thou shalt not fuck and desire women and men alike," but also many others. Plenty of these stories feature sweet, old-fashioned, bisexual vanilla sex ("vanilla" is the term many kinky folk, especially in the S/M world, use for non-kinky sex, in order to remind everyone that there are many, many flavors to choose from). Many other stories, though, play with power, dominance, roles, and role-reversal. It's all on the menu.

Interestingly, we noticed in choosing which stories to use in this collection that many of the writers who sent us submissions did not get very explicit when the sex part of the story came along. This was especially true of certain vanilla stories, whose sexual content was often largely implied. That would be fine for a book of bisexual fiction, but not for erotica. And many of the authors who incorporated the explicit most seamlessly are also cheerfully kinky—at least on paper. When we chose stories, we wanted them to work as stories—with characters you'd care about or at least could get to know. But they had to be erotic, at least by someone's lights, and they had to present some recognizably bisexual element: either bi-identified characters or an obviously bisexual situation like a gender-mixed threesome or a first-time (same-sex or other-sex) initiation.

We figured this book would be San Francisco-centric, simply because there are a lot of writers in Northern California who are bisexual, who are writing erotica, and who also happen to be our friends and colleagues. We were gratified to realize that this was not the case. The authors and their characters hail from practically all corners of the United States. We don't just "celebrate diversity," we embody it. There's the trash-talking Texan femme fatale of Linda Eisenstein's "Her Mouth, in Which I Drowned," the smart Manhattan pragmatism of Marilyn Jaye Lewis' "Anal," and the transgressive midwestern high-school reunion fantasy in Lori Selke's "Max." The wily New Orleans-based protagonist of Jamie Joy Gatto's "Pissing in the Men's Room" even gets to live out her fantasy of watching two men make it in the men's room of a local bar during Mardi Gras. Like an increasingly visible number of not-so-straight women, she prefers her sex with queer men.(To realize that there isn't really a term for this phenomenon, other than the derogatory and inaccurate "fag hag," is telling in itself.) Other authors in this book hail from San Francisco, Boston, Seattle, Cleveland, Los Angeles, rural Massachusetts,

Oregon, Wisconsin, and elsewhere. And, while these stories are by no means inclusive of the amazing breadth of polymorphous perversity (31 flavors just couldn't be enough), they are a collection of enticing snapshots that point toward our erotic potential, that open us up to where our possibilities extend.

So unfasten that seat belt, and any other belts, while you're at it. Then we invite you to make yourself real comfy, and take a wild ride with us down the wide and winding backroad of polymorphous perversity.

Bill Brent and Carol Queen
San Francisco, CA

First, Hello

Madeleine Schulman

The phone woke me up right after midnight. It was dark in my room, but I knew just how far I needed to stretch to reach it.

"Hello?"

"Hi... I woke you up. I'm sorry; go back to sleep."

"No... I mean, that's okay." I didn't want him to know that I had fallen asleep waiting for him to call. "How are you?" I ask, pretty much awake by now.

"I'm good. I just got in, long story. I can just talk to you at work tomorrow. I'm sorry it's so late but I said I'd call you when I got back into town so... "

"So you just called because you said you would?" I was trying not to sound whiny.

"No... I mean, what'd you think? I was calling to try to wangle an invitation?"

"Well... I don't know, you might try," I say, flirting.

"You mean, I could get an invitation?"

"Um... yeah."

"Really? I still have to finish unpacking my car, but... "

"It's up to you, either way."

"What am I, chopped liver?" he laughs.

"No."

"So what do you think?"

"Well, I'm already in bed. I mean, is that okay?"

"Yeah, that's great," he says, his voice going a bit deeper. "So... yeah?"

"Yeah."

"I'll be over in a few minutes."

"Okay. Hey—my roommate's already asleep so why don't you come up the back stairs and I'll leave the back door unlocked for you. Just come in, okay?"

"Okay, see you in a few."

So I change into a cuter tank top and wonder whether boys think boxer briefs are dykey or not as I leave mine on and get back into bed. The whole idea of him coming up my back stairs late at night, to have a rendezvous, has been a fantasy of mine for the past few months. We've had the hots for each other, but each had a girlfriend so we never acted on it. Now I wait, listening to the August rain pouring outside my window, and trying not to be nervous about the fact that none of the sex I've had has involved people with penises. Finally I hear the screen door open and close, and I try not to think about how fast my heart is pounding or that I'm already wet and he hasn't even walked into my room.

"Hi," he whispers as he opens the door.

"Hi."

"Can I put my wet coat over here?"

"Sure... wherever." I can see him through the light coming down the hall.

He walks over to my bed and slides over the covers on top of me—kisses me hello. I can feel the heat from his body through the layers of his clothes and the cover and my clothes. It's been a little while—a week or so. My lips remember right away even though we've only kissed on two other occasions, and one was just a quick kiss good-bye in front of my apartment. His face is damp from the rain but warm and almost smooth. His tongue slides into my mouth and I pull him closer through all of the various layers in our way.

"Hello," he says.

"Hi."

"It's really nice to see you," he says, kissing me again.

I arch up to him as my tongue touches the tip of his tongue. His hand slides into my hair, tugging just a bit. My hand pulls at his lower back, bringing him closer to me. His tongue is playing with mine and a graphic image of his tongue on my clit flashes through my mind and my breathing gets faster still. He moans quietly, and the covers are too much of a barrier now.

"Okay if I take my pants off and join you in there?"

"Yeah," I breathe, not wanting to let him up for that long.

He tosses his pants on the couch, crawls up the bed, and slides into the sheets next to me. Now we're on our sides and have full access to each other. His hands slide down my back to my butt and mine do the same to him. I can feel him already hard as our stomachs and crotches line up and press into each other. I kiss down his jawline to his neck where there isn't stubble and hear him breathing harder. He touches my bare shoulders and his hands brush the sides of my breasts as he continues the movement to my waist. I kiss his mouth again, hard, sliding my hand inside his T-shirt to his stomach. He sucks in a breath and I bite his lower lip as he covers my breasts with his hands and his thumbs rub against my nipples through my tank top.

"Can I take this off?" he asks, tugging at my top.

I sit up and pull off his shirt as he yanks off mine. His mouth closes over my breast as soon as my top is off. I moan into him and pull his head closer to me as his tongue flicks my nipple back and forth. My clit is throbbing and I can feel him hard against my leg as he lies down on top of me, my breast still in his mouth. My instinct is to move one thigh up between his legs and I have to quickly remind myself that that only works with other girls. My hand roams to his stomach at the top of his boxers and I know that my hand is getting really close to the top of his dick. I like hearing him do that quick intake of breath again.

His hand is moving up my thigh as he bites and tugs on my nipple. He rubs my clit through my boxers and then starts to slide them down.

"Okay?" he asks, looking up at me.

"Yes," I stop myself from saying "please."

I am kicking my boxers off my feet as his finger slides over my clit and he groans when he feels how wet I am. I moan as he continues to touch me and moves his head up from kissing my breast so he can kiss my mouth. I press my nails into his back and move my body harder against his hand. After a bit, he stops kissing my mouth and starts to kiss down my body, and I realize his head is going past my stomach.

"Where ya goin'?" I say. "I like you up here where I can kiss you."

His eyes go darker as he looks up at me. "Just a taste," he says, kind of a question, almost pleading.

It's so hot to hear him want me like that, I completely forget why I wanted to resist him.

He moves down to the end of the bed and crouches over. My legs are over his shoulders, and his hands are on my hips pulling me towards him. He's pretty confident for a guy who knows he's going down on a woman whose only done this with other women. Then his tongue is on me, riding up and down my clit, bringing my wetness up to the tip of it. His hands are sliding over my stomach, and move up to my taut nipples. My eyes are closed and I can feel my legs starting to shake from the tension. The rhythm of his tongue gets faster and my breath is coming out in quick pants and I want it to never end. He can feel me getting close, and holds one hand out for me to grip. And then I feel it: that single point of pleasure that melts through me in waves as his tongue catches me in circles again and again.

"Good gracious," I say after a minute, when I start breathing normally again. I ease up my grip on his hand as he crawls up my body, pausing sheepishly to pull a hair off his tongue. I kiss him, laughing, tasting traces of myself still on his lips.

"That was fun," he says.

"Oh, yeah," I say, kissing him again.

Keeping my tongue in his mouth, I roll over so I'm on top of him. One hand is roaming around the top of his boxers again, and finally I say, "How am I gonna get over this shyness thing about touching you?"

He looks back at me for a long moment, then takes my hand and guides it under the band of his boxers. For a second, all I notice is the heat coming off his body, and then I move my hand a bit more and I feel him. My hand is on the base of his penis and it's all real, too fast for me to be scared about how weird it might be. His penis feels so hard that I'm surprised by how soft his skin is there. My hand is wrapped around him and I hear him gasp as I start sliding it up and down.

"Is this okay? I'm just kind of checking it all out." I say.

"Yeah," he breathes. "It feels really nice. Feel free to do whatever."

"Okay."

I'm lying over him, up on one elbow with my hand under his neck and I lean down to kiss him as my other hand moves faster on him. One of his hands is sliding over my breasts, teasing my nipples.

His breathing has gotten loud and I can feel his stomach muscles tighten. My hand is playing with the head of his dick when he whispers, "Mind if I take my boxers off?"

"Oh, sorry." I sit up and pull them off him, aware that it is not the one smooth movement that pulling underwear off a woman is. "Is there anything different you wanted me to be doing? I'm feeling kinda nervous about this whole lack of experience with boy-parts thing."

"Really. Don't worry about it. Anything you do is gonna feel good. Just do whatever you feel like doing."

"Hmm... well, do you ever use anything? Some kind of lube, I mean?"

"I've used lotion. But only by myself."

"Really?" I consider that for a second. "Want me to get some?"

"Sure." He looks intrigued.

"Kinda cool that we get to do something you've never done before."

I grab some out of my dresser and get back into bed. After I pour a bit into my palm, I lie back over him, propped up on my elbow.

"This might be cold," I say, as I start to spread the lotion on his penis. He gasps, and then groans as I move my hand up to the head and back down to the base. I keep my eyes open as I kiss him, so I can watch him watching my hand ride up and down his dick, getting faster. His hand moves down from my back to my butt and then slides down, past it, between my legs. He groans again, and I kiss him harder, grip his dick harder. Then he slips one finger in me. I moan into his mouth as he continues to touch me. I feel him pull his legs together and clench his stomach and butt muscles, thrusting up towards my hand. I watch him strain against my hand, feeling the friction of the lotion as my hand slides up and down. He grips my hips, pressing down on them as he pushes himself up against my hand. His whole torso gets tense, and I see the cum start to bead at the end of his dick so I move even faster. I feel him swell and get harder for a second and then ejaculate against my hand and on his own stomach and chest as I keep pumping my hand. After I feel the shudders stop, he moves his hand and covers mine.

"Yow." he says.

"Yeah? Did I like, do it right?"

"Um... yeah. Definitely. Would it gross you out if I sort of wipe myself off on your nice sheet here?"

"Nah, go for it."

He does, and then pulls me over to lie on top of him.

"I like you here." he says, closing his eyes. "I could fall asleep ... I'm so tired now, aren't you?"

"Yep, pretty well tuckered out. It is... " I look over at my alarm clock, "almost 2 o'clock."

"No way. But I'm having such a nice time."

"Me too... but I guess we should get some sleep soon, huh?" I ask.

"I guess that would be the wise thing to do since we need to go to work tomorrow. Think it would look suspicious if we both wander in late looking all bleary-eyed but really chipper?"

"Um... it just might. You know people are already wondering about us... . You gonna go home to sleep?"

"I don't know." He opens his eyes to look at me. "Is that okay with you?"

"Oh, yeah. You should go sleep in your own bed and all that."

"Okay. If I don't go now, I'll never make it out of your room." He kisses me and I roll off him to let him get up to put his clothes back on.

A minute later, he walks back over to the bed to kiss me good-night and says, "See you tomorrow—well, in a few hours I guess." Then he walks to my door, stops for a second, blows me a little kiss, and I smile back at him sleepily before rolling over. I fall asleep as I hear the back door close.

Madeleine Schulman is a video editor who also likes to write. She is a Smith College grad currently living in Boston and working on a children's book. This is her first erotic story.

Triplicity

Richard Steven Beck

I was living with my uncle when I met Rick. I'd been in and out of foster homes since I was ten. My stepfather nearly beat me to death during one of his drunken rages, and the state of California took me out of the home. I was always in trouble after that. During those years I wasn't at all sure about my sexuality. That happens when you are put in with older and bigger boys.

There wasn't much happiness in my life. I was released from state custody the day I reached eighteen. I moved in with my uncle. We fought and argued constantly, but at least I had a place to stay. I got a job with a local construction company and that's where I met Rick. He treated me okay when we were both new and we became friends.

I never knew much about friends. I'd never had one but I knew that's what we were. Rick listened to me and told me about his life. He was living with Maria, and they were in love. When he took me home to meet her, I couldn't stop looking at her. I didn't know much about much, but I knew I liked her. It did complicate things with Rick.

I never let on to Rick but I started hanging around their place. One Saturday Rick was out with his father, so I came over. Maria was doing laundry and I helped her carry the clothes down to the laundry room. There wasn't anyone else in there, so I kissed her. I never thought about Rick or what it would do to our friendship. I just kissed her and ran my hand up under her shirt to feel her tits. I wanted to fuck her.

I rubbed my bulging jeans against the front of her shorts while kissing her using all of my tongue immediately. My cock was so hard I couldn't stand it. I was getting out of control with lust for her, and I was afraid of what I was going to do next. At first she put her hands up, like she was going to push me away, next thing I know she was holding me on top of her and churning her hips against the front of my pants.

She fumbled with my zipper while pulling down her shorts. I felt her rubbing my cock on her cunt hair. It was like something happened to me when she was holding my hard cock. I couldn't wait another second and I shoved in all at once when she placed me at the opening. After I did that, I was so hot I thought I'd blow a nut right then. I bit my lip to hold off. She let out a loud groan, running her hands up under my T-shirt. She used her fingernails on my back and I lost all control. I rocked the washing machine as I fucked her. She just moaned and held me tight against her, feeling me all over.

It was my first piece of ass in years. Even after I shot my load I stayed on top of her. I was already thinking I needed to do it just one more time. I was lodged inside her pussy and still trying to fuck her with my limp cock, afraid if I let up, she'd tell me to stop. It had been too long between women to just let her go. I needed more than five minutes of sex to make up for the drought.

Instead of protesting, she fed me her tongue. She undid my pants and pushed them to my knees. She ran both of her hands down the crack of my ass as she kissed me like I'd never been kissed before. She dug her fingers into my ass crack and pulled my weight onto her while fingering my hole.

While she was kissing, me my cock started to stiffen right inside her pussy. In a few minutes it was like I'd never come. This was the real deal, and Maria wanted it. She moaned softly through our kisses until she realized I'd gotten hard again, and then she came alive with passion.

It was amazing to me that I could repeat the lovemaking so quickly. As much as I wanted to just pour it to her again, I also wanted to make this incredible feeling last. It still didn't take but a few minutes before I was ready to blow my second load. I broke off the kisses so I could get leverage by holding the sides of the machine as I stood up over her. While the machine rocked noisily to my thrusts, I unloaded my liquid love to the sound of her moans.

"You're a lot bigger than, Rick. He's about average length but he's thicker. Yours is so long," she said, feeling my cock with both of her hands as she examined it.

"I really like you, Maria. I want to fuck you again," I told her in a sudden flood of emotion.

"I like you, Steve."

"I want to fuck you. I need to fuck you," I said.

"You just did, twice. Let me get the clothes done," Maria said. "Then I'll have to get something out for dinner."

"I'll order pizza," I said.

"You can't be here when he comes home. He'll know something is going on."

"I told him I'd be here when he came home," I said, "He wants to go shoot pool."

"You knew he wasn't going to be home?" she asked.

"That's why I came over. He said he'd be with his father all day. I figured you'd let me fuck you. I've been waiting for a chance since I met you."

"You planned this?" she asked. "Rick's your friend."

She pushed my back against the door when we got inside the apartment. She kneeled in front of me and slowly unzipped my pants. My cock was already tingling when she put her hand in through my zipper. Once she pulled it out, she licked the head and the shaft before going down on me. She worked it until it was in her throat, and then she worked it back out until just the head was in her warm, moist mouth.

After getting me all worked up and with my cock swinging in the breeze, she pushed me down in the easy chair. She stepped out of her shorts, jumping up with her legs straddling the arms of the chair. She lowered herself down on my cock. I held her thighs while I fucked her again. She pulled off my T-shirt so she could feel my sweaty chest as I worked up to another orgasm.

I don't know why it seemed even hotter the third time, but it did. Maybe it was because I could picture Rick sitting in the very same chair and giving it to her just like I was. Maybe it was because I hadn't done anything for so long. She hopped down and put her clothes back on as soon as I shot off.

I didn't know what to do about Rick. He was this totally cool guy that brought me home, and now I was fucking his woman. When I was fucking her, it was fine, and I never thought about Rick, but then I felt like a heel. For the next week we worked all the time, so I didn't get another shot at Maria, but I thought of her constantly.

It was at the end of that week that I had the fight with my uncle. I ended up with a black eye and a bloody lip and no place to stay. Rick seemed really concerned when he saw my face. That made me feel even worse. He was a nice guy and worrying about me, and I was fucking Maria.

Out of the blue at lunch, he said, "You can stay with Maria and me until you can find a place. She likes you."

"She does?" I said too quickly.

Their apartment was one room and I slept on the couch at the foot of the bed. The bed was in the light that filtered through the window blinds beside it. It was too easy to watch them fucking. I had to jerk off while I watched them that first night. The next day when Rick got me up to go to work, I told him I had a headache and my jaw hurt from the beating I took. He told me to stay home and he'd tell the boss. After he left, Maria pulled the sheet off her and spread her legs, sticking two of her fingers in her pussy as I watched.

I was on her in a second, sliding it into her all at once, though not as roughly as the first time I fucked her. She gasped, telling me I was the biggest guy she'd been with. She said she had thought about my big cock all night.

Rick was trying to help me, and five minutes after he'd gone out the door, I was fucking Maria again. I felt guilty but something about the situation made it more exciting for me.

Especially when I kept thinking about Rick's cock being inside her right where mine was. When I'd fucked her in the chair, I'd had the same thoughts, only then I'd never seen Rick fucking her. Now I had, and I pictured it as I fucked her.

The next few nights I watched Rick going at it. I watched his technique and how much he got into it. I would jack off so I'd come when he came. He made so much noise I didn't think they could hear me since I was trying to go unnoticed.

It was on a Friday night after a really busy week that Rick decided to buy beer. He asked me to contribute since I planned to stay. I gave him fifty dollars, considering how much food I ate. Looking at the money, he said for me to stay as long as I wanted. He called me his best friend and he said he was glad I was there. I felt guilty and still had a hard-on thinking how easy he was making it for me.

That was the night things took a crazy turn. We'd all been drinking and Rick and Maria were making out in front of me. They usually waited until after we were all in bed, but Rick seemed to be getting worked up. She unzipped his pants and fondled him in front of me while he sat in the chair where I had screwed her. His cock was thicker than mine and cut really neat but it wasn't as long as mine. She started jacking him off and kept looking to see if I was watching. He stared at me as I watched her hand on his cock. My dick was forcing out the front of my pants when I got up to take a piss. He didn't miss that either. When I came back she was straddling the arms of the chair and sitting in his lap. They were both naked, and I wanted to jack off while they screwed in front of me. I wanted them to know I was jacking off while watching them.

They seemed to forget I was there as Maria dragged Rick to the bed. With all the lights on I'd get a good show, I thought. Rick was going to town, and I had my pants down to my knees, working my cock while watching them from the couch. Rick looked back at me and was watching my hand working my cock.

There was no way to hide what I was doing, and I was staring right at them. It was like being a little kid and getting caught jacking off, but this was more exciting than it was scary. I had no shirt on to pull down over it and so I raised my hips so he could see how long it was. He seemed to like watching me, but then he whispered something to Maria. He lifted his ass up and rolled off her. His dick stood straight up. It looked even bigger now that he was completely turned on.

"You want to fuck her?" he said, staring at my cock.

`"What?" I said, not knowing what to say to him.

"You're my bud, aren't you? I can tell you need it. She said, if I say it's okay with me it's okay with her. Told you she likes you."

"It's okay. We think we should share, Steve. Get undressed," Maria said, as Rick fingered her pussy.

I was a bit reluctant to strip in front of him. It seemed like I should be more modest in front of another guy, but when I checked out Maria's pussy, well, I dropped my pants and underwear to the floor. I was naked before I got to the foot of the bed.

"Damn, boy, your momma never gave you any toys. Can you take all that dick?" Rick asked her.

"Only one way to find out," she said.

He didn't move his fingers until my cock started to slide in on top of them. I felt funny at first, fucking her with him lying next to us. He just stared at my dick moving in and out of her. I wanted to do it better, but it broke my concentration thinking of him watching. It took me about ten minutes before Finally I was approaching the moment of truth. I felt him feeling my balls as I was moaning with pleasure. His fingers moved into the crack of my ass as I was fucking harder. I thought I'd freak out when I discovered how much I liked him touching me that way.

"Boy's got a dick on him," Rick said, after I rolled off her and right onto his arm and leg and cock. He put his hand high up on the inside of my thigh. It felt odd having my best friend touching me like that.

"Yeah!" Maria said, breathing heavily.

Rick climbed over me and was fucking her before I had time to figure out how to move off him. He didn't look at me but he rubbed his hand across my chest. He turned his head and caught me watching them fucking. My eyes were right on his cock, and his hand slid down across my stomach and into my pubic hair. I put my hand on his ass and felt down between his legs until I touched his tight ball sac.

"Fucker's bigger when it's soft," he said, feeling my balls while I was feeling his. "Will it get hard again tonight?"

"You keep that up, it will," I said, while moving my fingers across his hole, wondering how tight it would be.

Maria got up and turned out the lights when Rick was done. She got into bed with Rick in the middle. Rick had gotten me hard and I wanted to fuck her again, but with Rick feeling my cock, I didn't want to make waves. I was willing to share the goods in order to get what I wanted.

Sleeping with them was better than sleeping on the couch. His ass stayed against my leg and I felt it, thinking how thin he was compared to me, and yet his cock seemed so nice and fat. I had this sudden desire to find out what his felt like.

I knew Rick was always fucking Maria, and it was a little confusing that he'd feel my dick. It was more confusing now that I was fucking Maria, and I was curious about what his cock felt like. I thought I could just brush off such thoughts, but being there in bed with him made my desire stronger.

I wondered if I could fuck him since he'd felt my body and played with my dick. Rolling on my side, I let my cock rest against his rear end. I put my arm around him and took hold of his cock, letting my cock slide up and down his ass crack as I pulled on his erection. I fell asleep like that for a few minutes, only to wake up with him putting his hand on my cock and moving it off his hole. I felt embarrassed because I knew he knew what I wanted to do to him, and it was obvious he wasn't going to allow it since he was holding my cock well away from his prize.

When I woke up it was light outside and Maria was gone. I remembered she had to go to her mother's. I was on my side, and Rick was behind me now. He had his arm around me and my cock was in his hand. My hard-on woke me many mornings but not with some dude pulling on it. His cock was moving in my ass crack just like I'd been doing to him a few hours earlier. I wondered why he thought he could get away with something he wouldn't allow me to do.

"What the fuck," I said, rolling to protect my ass from his hard cock.

"Give it up, dude. I let you fuck Maria. You got a lot of my time last night," he said, breathing heavy and acting really strange.

"She let me fuck her," I said. "You don't own her. You wanted to watch me anyway."

"Like you don't watch us. You make a lot of noise when you come, dude. We always laugh at how you get so into your hand."

"What?" I said.

"You want to keep staying here, don't you?" he asked. "I'm caught short, and I hate walking around with a bone all day. Why should I go without when you're right here."

"You're nuts," I said, watching him feel his own cock.

"You want to fuck her again, don't you?" he said, feeling my cock the same way he felt his own, causing it to pulse with this wild excitement. "You didn't mind messing with my ass last night. It's my turn, dude. We either share or we don't."

I watched as his cock twitched while he used both of his hands to feel mine. My cock was pulsing and I felt really flushed all over my body. When he started to stroke it, I thought I would blow a nut on his stomach. I didn't want him to stop. He pressed his body up against mine as he tried to turn me with one hand while jerking me off with the other.

"Roll on your side. I'll use plenty of lube. I fuck you, you fuck her," he said, humping my hip. "You're so horny you're starting to drip, dude. You want me to fuck you. Roll over, man, and let's get to it before you waste a load. You know you want my dick in your ass."

Since Maria told me they both tested negative for the HIV virus, and since Rick had confessed he hadn't been with anyone but Maria since they'd met, I knew we were all safe. I was tested by the state before they cut me loose, and I hadn't been with anyone but the two of them. I knew from state lectures that taking it unprotected in the ass was dangerous, but Rick was right about my wanting his dick in my ass. I wanted him to fuck me, but at the same time I didn't want him to. He was lighting a fire in me by rubbing his skin on mine and sliding his dick up and down my leg.

He seemed to be all hands as he managed to slop on the lotion wile never letting go of my cock, and he kept poking at my hole until the cockhead broke through all at once. It hurt like hell for a minute, burned for awhile, and then it didn't feel too bad. He was like a dog fucking someone's leg. He just went at it as fast as he could. I pictured that fat cock of his stretching my asshole wide open. We were working together as soon as the discomfort left my hole.

He wrapped his arms under mine, holding both of my shoulders as he grunted and groaned while slamming his cock into me. He showed my hole no mercy, and I liked the death grip he had on my body. I liked the way our sweat made his hot skin feel like buttered silk against mine. I liked being close to him. When he shot off, he blew hot air on my neck, groaning each time he shoved his dick all the way up my ass.

When he was done, he slid his body completely against mine and held me in his arms. I couldn't believe I liked it. As he stroked my straining cock, I was thinking of flipping him over and fucking the shit out of him, but I knew it would be more difficult to get my way right after he shot his load. I could have forced him, but I didn't want to move out of his arms. I stayed still with my eyes closed and let him pump my stiff dick. I thought about feeling his cock the night before, and how it looked when he was fucking Maria, and how it felt when he was fucking me. The more I thought, the hotter I got.

"You've got me all worked up, I need to get off," I said, a little angry I was left to jerk off in front of him.

"I wondered if you were ever going to get horny. Roll on your back, dude" he ordered.

As soon as I rolled over, his mouth was nibbling and licking my cockhead. My cock felt like it was twice its normal size by the time he was sucking me off. I'd never been so horny, and he just kept at me like he really liked sucking dick. In a while he was fucking my leg as he sucked, and then he shoved a finger up my ass.

"I'm going to blow a load in a minute," I gasped.

He started jerking himself off and taking more and more of my cock in his mouth as he shoved another finger in my ass. I couldn't believe he was so turned on already. The come was churning out of my balls as soon as his finger went into my hole. Watching him jerking on that nice piece of meat of his made me hotter. I watched him down between my legs and all I could think about was how long it would take to get hard again so I could fuck him.

I never particularly liked sex with guys. It was something you did when you were really horny or when you had to. Rick got me so worked up over sex because he got so worked up over sex. The fact that he was a guy made it even better, and I didn't understand why he was so different from other guys I'd fooled around with. What he made me feel and do made me mad, but not so mad I wasn't busy planning to do it again.

I wasn't sure how Maria would feel about me fucking Rick, but that's what I was thinking about when I started to come. I wanted to ram my cock up his ass, and I wanted to do it in front of Maria. I grabbed his head and started fucking his mouth. I thought of Rick fucking me, and I pictured him fucking Maria. I fucked his face thinking of fucking his ass. The come flooded out of me.

"Fuck," Rick said, coughing and holding his throat as he slipped my hold on him. "You trying to drown me. That shit's thick."

I should have made it clear I was about to come, but he kept at it after the first warning. Rick wiped my come off his lips with his free hand while beating me off. He dropped down beside me with his leg on top of mine when I finished spraying come up on my chest. Scooping up my hot come, he thrust his cock up at a rapid clip as he moaned loudly using my come for lube. His come leaped up into his hair and onto his face and chest. He laughed as he gulped for air and pounded his dick.

"Fuck," he said, "Your come is so thick. Mine sprays."

"Man, that was hot," I said, before thinking.

"You still pissed?" Rick asked, giggling mischievously as he mixed his cum with mine on my stomach.

"Pissed about you just giving me the best blow job I've ever had?" I said, trying to get some advantage.

"I mean about me fucking you?" he said, twisting the word fucking in a way that took away any advantage I got.

"Tell you what, I'll let you know after I fuck you," I said.

"That fucker's too big to stick up my ass. No way," he said.

"Way! Paybacks are a motherfucker. You fucked me so I get to fuck you. This isn't a negotiation. It's the way things are, Rick."

"Sure, right after you eat my come, dude. Everything's negotiable."

"Okay, okay, I get the point," I said, fearing I was losing ground.

Over cereal Rick told me that he had shared an apartment with a friend and they both screwed the same girls. One guy brought home a chick one night, and she ended up sleeping with one of them and then the other. It became a contest to see how many girls they could find that would sleep with both of them.

Then they met a girl who wanted to sleep with both of them at the same time. The next morning they woke up in bed together and she had gone. They were both horny, and one thing led to another until they satisfied each other. That was one more thing they added to their routine—after the girl left, they had sex together.

Rick said that he looked forward to the girl's departure. That was the only time they were in the same bed. Rick admitted he always made sure the girls he brought home would go along with the game to ensure they'd end up in bed together.

He told me he'd had an increasing appetite for a variety of sexual experiences as he grew up, but he'd only been with that one guy. After meeting Maria, he was satisfied with just her until he met me. Since I told him about some of the things that happened to me while I was in foster care, he'd been waiting for an opportunity to get me involved with Maria and then him. Rick had planned the whole thing, and Maria had agreed to get the ball rolling. I was set up.

While Rick fucked Maria that night, I lubed up his ass and fucked him. Maria used her hands to spread his cheeks for me, and she felt my cock as it was sliding in and out of his hole. Rick complained at first but a few days later he told me that he'd blown the biggest load in his life while my big dick was up his ass, and now his dick got hard every time he remembered it.

When I screwed Maria the next night, Rick sat on the headboard trying to get me to blow him. At first I just jerked him off, but as I got more turned on by the feel of his cock while fucking her, I had to eat him. The fact it had just been in her cunt made it more exciting.

If I were honest about it, I'd say what really got me turned on was thinking about him fucking me with it. When he started getting all worked up, I thought about letting him come in my mouth. I wasn't ready for that, and he ended up jacking off and coming in my face. Later, he ate every drop of my load while he was fucking Maria. He said it took a real man to eat another guy's load; I wasn't convinced.

It excited me a lot to just have Rick sit and watch me fuck her. One on one Maria beat the hell out of him, but when we were all together, it was doing things to Rick that made for the biggest thrills and the best orgasms. Having him sit jacking off while I fucked his woman was one of the best things of all. I don't know why that turned me on so much, but it did. It worked for all of us.

We did everything possible to her and to each other. When we screwed her at both ends at the same time, we'd finger fuck each other until we were both ready to shoot. This frequently came before we screwed each other. Those were my best orgasms, being the middleman with Rick fucking me like some incensed Great Dane while I was plowing it to Maria. She seemed to be equally turned on to both of us, but I knew she did it because it was what Rick wanted.

I was never alone with Maria after that first day I was with Rick alone. Whenever Rick and I ended up alone in the morning, we had difficulty getting out of bed. Several times on the job, Rick blew me in some out of the way spot. Once I blew him, and I fucked him at lunch several times. He'd usually start it, but not all the time.

Maria came up pregnant after a few months of this wild relationship. We all agreed that the baby had to be raised in a normal home. It was obvious what had to be done, but we waited as long as we could before doing it.

Rick and Maria got married and I moved into my own place. I've been engaged twice since then, and I'm dating two girls right now. I'm learning how to be a better friend and a nicer guy, but I miss being with Rick and Maria. I know that isn't the way things should be, but I've never had so much fun, felt so loved, or enjoyed sex more.

As strange as it may sound, I look at guys when I meet them and I wonder if they could fit in with the girl I'm dating. No one has yet, but we have this new guy at work, Bryan. I was admiring his tattoos after he took his shirt off at lunch his first day. I asked if he had any more and I was surprised when he unzipped his pants to reveal he wasn't wearing any underwear—and the scorpion tattooed next to his cock.

He looked at the way I looked at his cock, and there was a knowing little smile on his face as he tucked himself away. I'm waiting for a chance to tell him about Maria and Rick. I'll let you know what happens.

Oh, yeah! It was a beautiful little girl, and no, we don't know if it's Rick's or mine.

After being disabled in a trucking accident, Richard Steven Beck wrote and submitted his first short story. It sold a month later. He has written mainstream novels and short stories, always returning to erotic literature. He write stories for the individual, using names you select, adding the desired action to taste, for birthdays, anniversaries, or just a hot personalized gift to yourself. Contact him at writersrealm@hotmail.com, or check out his Website: http://models.badpuppy.com/cstories/

Pissing in the Men's Room

Jamie Joy Gatto

It used to piss me off that it's such a hassle just to go pee at a gay bar, but the fact that I am even able to walk in the front door is enough to make up for it. As a girlie-girl in a man-on-man's world, you just have to learn to squat and hover, rely on bar napkins for toilet paper, and deal with little to no privacy. Oh sure, they'll give you a key to the ladies' room, if they have a ladies' room, that's if the bartender will wait on you, and that's if he can find it. If you're lucky enough that this exceptional event does indeed occur, the key is often attached to a chain appropriate in size for a motorcycle and hung with a huge chunk of PVC piping. It's my guess that being such a rare and specialized item, it must be protected at all cost. After a bunch of cocktails and that first pee, who's going to wait for all that nonsense? Anyway, I'd rather hang with the boys.

It's much easier to get into the front door of the French Quarter cruise bars with my obviously bi hubbby who somehow resembles a Baldwin brother: good hair, straight nose, and fervent blue eyes. No matter how glamorous I may look, rhinestones and black feather boas are simply no substitute for the power of having a cute boy attached to your arm.

There is only one place that I have a real problem getting in and staying in, The Corral. It's upstairs, above Café Lafitte in Exile—a hot little bar full of the scent of semen, man sweat, piss and beer. It's where the man-on-man action is and, of course, that's where I want to be. I can't even think of getting into the back room at Rawhide to live out my dream of kneeling before some Daddy wearing chaps, sucking him off while he shoves it down my throat, gripping my head with his huge hands, tearing out the tiny hairs at the nape of my neck as I choke on his black cock until it fills my mouth and throat with bitter come. Perhaps he'd make me take turns with my hubby, just so I could watch up close, watch my husband's pink mouth filled with meaty mocha dick, study the way he laps at it like a thirsty dog. This fantasy turned reality has somehow eluded me in the Southern city of decadence.

The problem is, no dark bar can hide the fact that I'm hopelessly a girl. When the boys see me watching, they often stop playing with one another. Sometimes they give me a hard, accusatory stare; sometimes they move on, which makes me feel like I've blown it for them. All I want to do is observe silently from my little corner, and if a miracle occurs, be beckoned to join; simply to watch would be a thrill.

We've thought about putting me in drag, but every mental attempt to plan it comes up with me looking like a short, fat dyke. My body just isn't built for jeans. My husband even suggested wearing a ZZ Top beard, to hide my tits, but I figured I would just look like a short fat dyke wearing a ZZ Top beard, and besides, what about my hips? Simply hopeless. I'll stick to my Chanel lipstick and high heels, thank you.

I'm not sure why the gay bars in New Orleans are so adamant about the unwritten "no girls" rule, but Oz, the black-lighted, thumping disco, adds to insult by charging a higher cover charge for women. Do I care? Of course I do, but at least I can get in to look for bi boys for hubby and me to play with. It's not like there's such a thing on earth as a bi bar, at least not in my world.

For entertainment, Oz has bar-top dancers, usually studly model-types with blank faces performing the same tired dance moves, a bunch of half-naked hunks going through the motions, gyrating and humping the air. One night, by some gift of fate, we happened to find a happy little dancing boy upstairs, actually smiling, adorned with a ring for the both of us in each of his perky nipples. As we both took turns sucking his pink nipples red, I whispered in his ear, "We're a bi couple into three-ways." He was so hot and bothered, he had to jump off his post to try to rid himself of the trouble we'd caused him. "Oh, man," he groaned, "This has never happened to me at work." His hard, thin cock pointed straight up to his navel and popped right out of the band of his speedos, rosy tip glistening with pre-cum. Of course, we offered to help him out, just to be nice. As Boy climbed from the bar, trying to hide his erection, Hub decided to kiss him. I couldn't just stand by and watch this time, not with that hard body and that wet, aching cock right in my face. While the two men sucked face, I liberated his dick from lime green spandex, took a hold of it and that dancer got a hell of a hand job. Some fags do appreciate a woman's touch; I'm living proof.

Instead of trying to deal with loud clubs, we usually prefer to settle for cocktails at Good Friends, a cheery little corner bar that tends to have a fun mix of people: fag hags, drag queens, vanilla boys and usually a few soft butch dykes. Around Carnival time they feature male dancers with realistic bodies in little bitty G-strings stuffed with great big cocks, wearing nothing except baby oil and boots. They're usually from out of town, so we get to see new faces each year. For a dollar and a smile, I can reach right in, and if I'm lucky enough to find a boy willing, I can pop that puppy out and give it a nice, long lick. The smell and taste of fag cock is enough to make me give up my very last buck, bouncers be damned.

Good Friends is also where we like to spend Mardi Gras night—a cool place to hang out after getting kicked off the streets at midnight. Last year it was too cold on Mardi Gras night to be wearing what we did, but we'd planned it and stuck to it, rain or shine. Hubby was dressed as Miss Cleopatra in a thin white gown trimmed in gold, a black wig, and Elizabeth Taylor make-up that made those blue eyes of his talk. I was femmed out in a flirty little French maid's outfit, black ruffles and white lace, and we both wore matching fishnets and shiny black pumps.

Good Friends had transformed from a gay version of Cheers into a street festival indoors, since it was after midnight and the cops had closed down the whole Quarter on their trained horses. "Everyone inside, Mardi Gras is over," was a mandatory order announced through police megaphones, "Anyone out on the street will be arrested." The heavy, mechanical street cleaners followed the troop of horse cops, spraying water and mist, flashing lights as we and other costumed folks scurried into the nearest Orleans Parish bar where there are no laws about closing time. Safely inside Good Friends, we hopped up on the plywood-covered pool table (drenched with spilled drinks and littered with plastic cups) in order to make sure we would have a good seat for a while. I didn't care if it made my ass sticky and wet—after wearing spike heels on uneven concrete all day, a girl's gotta do what a girl's gotta do. My husband took off a pump and groaned as if on cue, rubbing his foot through ripped-up stockings. His nipples poked through the gauzy fabric of his white gown as a gust of wind and street cleaner spray followed in through open French doors.

A look around the barroom proved that Mardi Gras after midnight is definitely for the serious, die-hard party folks. Miss Thing in the corner with her high hair cocked, leaning like the Tower of Pisa, patted a false lash back in place with fingers wearing press-on nails. Muscle men wearing golden body paint smudged with men's hand prints grinned and nearly missed tapping their cups in a toast to an Asian-boy Tinkerbell who was outfitted with chiffon wings and a tinfoil-covered dildo wand. Bead-trading boys, looking as though their layers upon layers of plastic necklaces might choke them, surrounded us with the warmth of body heat, half-naked, dropping trou, slapping ass, sucking cock, snatching up more beads they'd won for letting the world take a peek, a grope, or a suck at their cock.

My platinum white sixties-flip wig itched my scalp as my temples began to throb faintly; I started the slow descent of coming down from two weeks of nonstop parades, parties and going into work hung-over. In order to shake the latest impending hangover, I needed another rum punch and at least a handful of ibuprofen. I had been avoiding the long lines at the bar and even longer lines to the bathroom, but I already had to pee.

A shirtless college boy wearing a ball cap approached, nearly tricking my trained eye into believing he was the only straight guy in the bar going for the only biological woman in the place, until he opened his mouth, and with the peachiest of Georgia accents said, "You go, Miss Bette Midler!" I did everything I could to keep from rolling my eyes, wondering why I only got the "You-Look-Exactly-Like-Bette-Midler" line from queer boys in queer bars. It kind of made me wonder if every girl with tits and ass got it, too. He seemed sincere in impressing me, so I played it up.

"If I wasn't gay..." he said, shaking his head, "Damn!" He took off his cap, scratched his head, put it back on.

"What?" I said laughing.

"I'd woo you, young lady. You're fucking hot."

"Well, the least you can do is buy me a drink, " I smiled.

He nodded, "Will do."

"Ever kiss a girl?" I said.

"Once, in high school," he said, looking a little shocked by the question, but not disgusted, not at all.

"Want to kiss me?" I asked, getting bolder.

"Ah, shucks," he said, turnturning red and looking at the floor, "What are you drinking?" Then he left for the bar.

By the time I had sucked down the last fruity remains of my drink, Hub was dancing on the crowded pool table with two middle-aged men. They both wore matching eyeglasses with thin tortoise-shell frames, plain button-down shirts and khaki shorts. The only way to differentiate between the two men was by their size: one was thick and one was thin. I could tell they weren't locals. Natives are almost always decked out full-hilt and tourists are usually in street clothes and beads. I couldn't imagine traveling two thousand miles to a citywide masquerade party and not bringing a costume to wear, but the fact that they were getting naked with my husband made up for it. "Rhythm is a Dancer" started pumping out of the speakers and all the boys on the pool table began to stomp in unison. Drinks splattered everywhere as old cups got kicked into the crowds, spraying stale, sticky liquor. By the second stanza, Hub had both his hands in the flies of both the men's khakis as they all jumped in time with the song. That's when I noticed Mr. Thin was broad-balled huge and Mr. Thick was definitely long and thin. I was starting to get turned on, thinking about the possibilities of being with three men for the first time, but man, I had to go. A line two men wide had wound its way around the crowds from the men's room all the way back to the bar area. Of course, the ladies' room was locked with a sign on it that read "No Key." I imagined some raucous queen had made off with the sacred key chained to PVC, thinking it was some sort of leftover '80s costume jewelry. You wouldn't believe what people might wear around their necks in order to trade beads. What the fuck? I just got in line and started bouncing, trying to stave off the urge to pee: Rhythm is a Dancer....

When I was about ten feet from the bathroom door, I felt like my bladder was going to pop. The door hadn't opened in ages, and a group of three men in front started banging on it. One jiggled at the brass doorknob shouting, "Come on ladies!" When a handful of guys finally pushed their way out of the men's room, the line cheered and a few clapped. Only the two guys making out, standing directly ahead of me, were oblivious. I watched them kissing, watched as they held each other, slowly making out. To them, evidently, the rest of the world had disappeared. The dark man stopped in mid-kiss, said something into the short, white guy's ear while pointing to the bathroom door. I couldn't discern exactly what he said, but I was able to pick out a singsong Caribbean accent in the dark guy's voice. Whatever he said caused the white guy to grin and nod enthusiastically.

The line inched its way up, man by man, until it was just the two guys ahead of me, still smooching and whispering. As the door flew open, I tugged at the white guy's shirttail, "Can I come in with you guys? I'm about to die," I pleaded, dancing from foot to foot, pulling on my short ruffled skirt. He motioned as he held the door open for me, "Come on." I nearly peed myself just thinking about finally being able to go.

The urinal trough was overflowing from men pissing into a toxic stew of spent cups, toilet paper, and cigarette butts. The boys would have to use the only john in the room, framed by an open partition sans door. I stood, legs crossed patiently, back against the door, lifted my skirts, hooked my thumbs into my fishnets ready to pull them down in a moment's notice. As the Caribbean man stood before the bowl and took out his dick to pee, the short guy began licking his neck, grabbed his dick and began jerking on it steadily. "Is this what you wanted?" he asked. The dark man fell to the wall sideways, let out a long sigh, "Oh, yeah." He braced himself with his shoulder, one hand on the tile wall, the other hand on the head of his lover who was suddenly kneeling in front of him next to the toilet, sucking his fat, prominent erection. The white man slid his palm over the shaft, pumping it back and forth, alternating between a sucking rhythm with his mouth and a jerking motion with his hand. The dark man closed his eyes and leaned his head way back, appearing as if he might topple backwards, but he steadied himself and groaned. He began to pant deeply, licking his full lips in between breaths, "Yeah, that's it," he said.

My thumbs seemed to be stuck in the band of my stockings, but I carefully shoved my right hand into them, fingered through the maze of fishnet, feeling for the smooth front of my black satin thong panties: wet, so wet. I began to touch myself in time with the bobbing head of the white man on the floor, watching the heavy brown balls slap at his chin. I still had to pee so badly, but the thought of watching these men, of them knowing I was there, but caring less, was everything

I had been wishing for. Without thinking, I moved the panties aside with my fingers and felt the slick fullness of my cream, rubbing it along my lips faster as I watched the white man's head move deeper into the dark man's fur, swallowing his cock whole, spit shining on his face. The dark guy started to shout, "Oh, God! Oh, God." I touched my clit and felt a hard spasm of come start to wave, peaking, washing upward, shivering throughout my belly and through my head like a cold rush. I closed my eyes. The man moaned even louder; someone pounded at the door; the handle jiggled frantically.

I felt it coming; I could no longer contain it. I continued to come hard, waves reverberating; I squatted down, tore open my stockings, panties ripping, satin tearing, coming, coming, pissing a hard gushing stream on the bathroom floor. I steadied myself on the door knob, accidentally releasing the handle by turning it. I almost fell over onto the wet floor when the door swung open. My husband, draped arm-in-arm by Mr. Thin and Mr. Thick, staggered into the men's room, all laughing hysterically, as if they had just heard the world's funniest joke. Hub had lipstick smeared across his cheek and had somehow lost his Egyptian wig. I was still crouching down, skirts up and panties opened wide exposing my shaved pink lips, wet, in full bloom, glistening with pee.

"You are such a bad, bad girl," he said to me, slurring just a little. The two other men burst out laughing even harder. "We've come to get you," he said.

The two men grinned as my husband kneeled in the watery puddle of my piss, put his head between my legs and began to lap at my naked cunt. I watched the two men kiss, then I almost lost my balance completely, still dazed and excited from coming so hard, and then from the shock of suddenly being eaten out. Mr. Thick reached down, held me steady, lifted my chin with his chubby fingers and stuck a fat finger into my mouth. I sucked it like a candy cane then grabbed at his face, hungry to suck on his juicy tongue. I opened my eyes when I felt what seemed to be a knobby dick tapping at my neck and bare shoulder; it belonged to Mr. Thin. I reached up and grabbed hold of Mr. Thin's cock, patted my husband on the head and as he lifted his face, made slick by my juices, then I guided Mr. Thin's meat right into Hub's mouth.

Mr Thick kissed me again, then he began to finger me, bringing me to the edge, hovering just near orgasm. He played with my clit so carefully, rubbing me like he had known me intimately for years. I began to fall into a dream-like sex trance, letting myself float out of my head, focusing on each new physical sensation with my eyes closed. As we played on the men's room floor, I was barely aware of the line of men who traipsed in and out of the bathroom door, stepping over us, pissing in the toilet and the sink, laughing and talking loudly. They seemed so far away and strange, as if our little group were phantoms occupying a different plane, as if I were playing a part in a fleeting frame of film.

A vaguely familiar voice drew me back into reality and out of my euphoric daze. Somebody said, "You go, Bette Midler!" as I began to come again in spasms, I opened my eyes to see Georgia Peach winking at me. I wondered if he had wanted to kiss me earlier but was too afraid. If he didn't then, I could tell by the lust in his eyes, he certainly did now.

Jamie Joy Gatto is a New Orleans writer whose short fiction has appeared in Black Sheets, The Unmade Bed: Twentieth Century Erotica *and is scheduled to appear is several forthcoming anthologies. She writes an opinion column, "Power Principles: Kink Think for the Real World" at http://www.ScarletLetters.com and is co-founder and fiction editor of the new ezine http://www.MindCaviar.com.*

Hunting For Sailors

Robert Vickery

It's Friday night and the fleet's in. The ships sailed in a couple of days ago to celebrate Fleet Week: destroyers, battleships, and one aircraft carrier, the John F. Kennedy. All day today, the Blue Angels have been buzzing downtown San Francisco in formation, just being a general pain in the ass as they snarled up traffic and made everybody's windows rattle. By some weird kind of logic, this is supposed to be good public relations for the Navy.

The sun set a couple of hours ago, and I sit in darkness in my apartment on top of Telegraph Hill, looking down towards the wharf where the ships are docked. Light streams in from the bedroom door, and I hear Laura moving around in the other room, making herself desirable. My throat constricts with excitement, and my stomach is in knots. I desperately want a cigarette, but Laura hates it when I smoke, and so I push the urge down as best I can. "Honey," Laura calls out to me. "Have you seen my hairbrush? I can't find it."

"Try the bathroom sink," I call back. I saw it there earlier this evening. Laura has a disorderly mind. Every time I've pointed this out to her, she's laughed and said if I wanted order I should have married a geisha girl. I hear the click of the wall switch, and the room is bathed in light. Laura stands in the doorway, one hand on the jamb, the other resting on her hip. "How do I look?" she asks.

She's dressed in a black leather miniskirt, with boots to match, and a thin, white cotton blouse opened down to the third button. It's tucked in tight, and her breasts push up against the fabric. Her dark blonde hair is brushed back like a lion's mane, and her lips are bright red.

"Try the pout," I say. Last week we went to a foreign cinema that was having a Brigitte Bardot festival. Laura's been practicing Bardot's pout ever since.

Laura obliges me and pouts.

"Your eyes are too alert," I say. "Unfocus them, and lower your lids." Laura's eyes take on a dreamy, myopic quality. She's quite bright and always has been a quick learner. "Yeah, that's right," I croon. "You look beautiful. There isn't a man who could resist you." Laura laughs. "Let's not go overboard, Bobby. This is San Francisco, remember." I laugh too. "Yeah, well, I meant among the straight crowd." I nod towards the floor lamp. "Turn that damn light off, will you? And come sit here by me."

Laura flips the switch and darkness takes over the room again. She walks over to me and sits on the arm of my chair. I slip my arm around her waist. Together we look out the window down towards the ships, all lit up like floating night clubs. Laura's fingers lightly trace a path along my chest. "You feeling horny tonight, baby?" she murmurs.

"Yeah," I say, breathing the word out like a sigh. "More than words can describe." We sit in silence for a while. All those sailors, I think. All those young bucks set loose on the town after weeks stuck on board their ships. All those hot men looking for a chance to drop their pants and their loads. I look up at Laura. "You won't let me down, will you?" I croon. "You'll get me what I need, right?"

In the dim illumination from the city outside, I can see Laura's lips curl up into a smile. "Don't I always, Bobby?" she says with a low laugh.

A few minutes later she kisses me and walks out the door. Nobody here but me now. The air feels stifling and closed. San Francisco is not known for its warm summer nights, but this is a fluke. The mercury's been in the nineties today, almost unheard of around here, and even with the onset of night, it still feels like the high seventies. None of the waterfront bars has air-conditioning, and with the crush of bodies looking for good times, all the night spots will be insufferable. At least they would be for me. But Laura likes heat; she feeds off it. And she finds crowds exhilarating. I don't have to feel sorry for her, or guilty about sending her out into the fray. She wouldn't be doing this if she weren't getting her kicks from it too.

I open a window, and a slight breeze blows through. I take off my shirt and let the cool air ruffle my chest hairs. The urge for a cigarette wells up again. Fuck it, I think. Laura's not here, and I can do what I please. I go to the desk and open the top left hand drawer. From underneath a stack of bills and papers, I pull out a pack of Marlboros and light one up. I'm pretty sure Laura knows about this private little stash; she has a way of ferreting out all my secrets. But it's a game we both like to play, pretending that this is one little deception I'm getting away with.

I sit down again and luxuriate in the heady trip the smoke makes down my throat and into my lungs. The sound of traffic from the Embarcadero Freeway wafts up through the open window. Laura's somewhere down there, I think, making the rounds. The lioness on the prowl.

Eventually I get up and shower, now that I've got the bathroom without Laura monopolizing it. I look at my reflection in the full-length mirror as I towel myself dry. I like my body. It's muscular and well-proportioned, and I like the darkness and hairiness of it. My dick is my pride and joy, thick and long, with a large head. It's swelled to half-erection now, red and meaty, swinging heavily from side to side as I dry my back. But my face is a disappointment. It's a thug's face: the chin too strong, the mouth too small, and the cheekbones so high that the eyes are permanently pushed up into a menacing squint. And it doesn't help that I have a broken nose, a souvenir of my college days on the boxing team. You may laugh, but I feel that I have the soul of a poet. This dockworker's face does me little justice, but Laura has told me she loves it. When I asked her if that meant she thought I was good-looking, she just laughed. "Of course not," she said. "Handsome men don't do anything for me."

I slip on a pair of tight-fitting black chinos and a black silk shirt Laura got me last Christmas. It'll please her to see me wear it; she has the mistaken idea that I hate it. I go back into the living room, pour myself a brandy, and wait, sitting once more in the darkness. There's nothing more left for me to do.

A couple of hours later, I hear the street door slam and Laura's voice on the stairwell. She always makes it a point to make enough noise outside to give me adequate warning. I slip out of my chair and into the bedroom, leaving the door open a crack. My heart is racing and my throat's constricted with excitement.

I hear the sound of the front door opening, and Laura's laughter fills the living room. It's joined by a man's young, tenor laugh. Then there's silence. I can picture it, the two of them with bodies pressed together, kissing, without having taken more than three steps into the room. Laura is always careful to keep the fires stoked for things to come.

"Would you like a drink?" she finally asks. I can tell by her voice that she's moved over by the window.

"Sure," the man replies. "A beer if you got one."

"No problem." Her voice fades as she moves towards the kitchen. "Sit down. Make yourself comfortable."

I hear the kitchen door swing shut. A spring in the couch creaks. The kitchen door swings open and shut again. "Here you go," Laura says. "Anchor Steam. To celebrate Fleet Week."

The man laughs again. I like the sound of it. There's an excitement in it, like he knows he's on an adventure. There's nothing jaded or crude about it.

"I'll put some music on," Laura murmurs. After a moment I hear The Doors playing "Riders on the Storm." I'm not surprised. Laura has a passion for Jim Morrison that borders on the obsessive. She insisted we see Oliver Stone's movie,

The Doors, when it first came out. I thought it depraved and depressing, but she loved it. Enough to go back and see it again. Alone.

Another creak of the couch springs. Then nothing but music for a long time. Every now and then, in the interlude after one songs ends and the next one begins, I can hear sighs, moans, and soft kisses. This is the part that requires the most delicate timing. After a while, I decide the moment is right, and I walk into the living room.

The light is dim, but bright enough to take in the two figures stretched out on the couch. The young man is partially dressed in a sailor's uniform, his shirt and cap discarded on the floor, his back to me as he grinds his pelvis against Laura. His torso is well-muscled and his shoulders broad. Laura looks at me from above his right shoulder and smiles. "Hello, Bobby," she says.

The man whirls around. He sees me and jumps to his feet. "What the fuck!" he exclaims.

I keep my distance so as not to alarm him. "Take it easy, buddy," I say in a soothing voice. "Nobody's going to hurt you."

"You're damn right!" he says loudly, cocking his fist. But a lot of it's bravura; I can tell he's unsettled. He thinks he's about to be rolled. Still, he's got a tight, muscular physique, and I suspect he would put up a good fight if it came to that. It won't.

"Relax, Tony," Laura says softly, laying a hand on his arm. "Bobby's a friend."

Tony, I think. It figures. I take in the black, curly hair, the dark eyes, the smooth, brown skin. He can't be more than twenty-one. Twenty-two max. God bless you, Laura. You know my weakness for Italians. Who could ask for a better wife?

"I'm sorry I startled you, Tony," I say. "I guess Laura didn't tell you she had a houseguest."

"It's okay," Laura croons to Tony. "Sit down." She pulls on his arm. He resists at first, unsteadily. Tony appears to be a few sheets to the wind. He finally relents and falls rather heavily down beside her. Laura buttons up her blouse again.

"I don't like shit being sprung on me like that," he says, his voice lower now. "I like knowing what the fuck is going on." His tone is more plaintive than pissed. There's just the faintest slurring of words. His torso gleams with a light sheen of perspiration, and his face is flushed. He is truly a beautiful young man; Laura has outdone herself.

"Nothing's going on," I say. "Just relax. You want another beer?" Tony doesn't say anything, so I take this to mean "yes." I go into the kitchen and come back with another Anchor Steam. Tony takes it and after a long pull from it, reaches for his shirt.

"Why don't you leave it off?" I say. "It's a warm night. And we don't stand on formality around here." Tony shrugs and lets the shirt drop back to the floor. Laura's hand once more rests on his shoulder, gently kneading the flesh. A minute doesn't go by that she isn't somehow in contact with his body, keeping the urgency there, on the back burner, maybe, but still simmering. And I start talking to him, asking him questions, drawing his stories out of him. This is something I'm good at, because it's not just artifice, empty seduction. The young men that Laura brings up here fascinate me; I want to drink their life histories out of them. Tony resists at first, obviously pissed that I interrupted what looked like a sure thing. But in a surprisingly short period of time, he gets drawn into conversation with me, telling me about the ports he's visited, regaling me with stories. His face becomes animated, and once, while telling me about some exploit that happened in Subic Bay, he throws back his head and laughs, his Adams apple rising in his muscular throat. I could easily fall in love with this guy. I notice his beer is empty and I get him another one. After a while I casually lay a hand on his knee as Laura runs her hand through his hair. Tony's beautiful eyes are dilated and slightly unfocused, but I see the alarm well up inside them. He's a young man, far from home and family, and way out of his element here. I feel a surge of compassion for him, even as my hand moves up his thigh.

"I think I better go," he says thickly.

"No, baby, no," Laura murmurs. Her hand slides across his smooth chest and she nibbles on his ear. "Please stay. For me."

"I don't think so," he says, but without conviction. Laura turns his head towards her and kisses him, hard, sliding her tongue into his mouth. He responds eagerly. I take this moment to cup his crotch with my hand. I can feel his dick, hard and urgent, straining against the tight, cotton fabric of his uniform. I bend down and bite it gently. Tony moans and thrusts his hips up. He reaches over and begins caressing Laura's breasts.

I pull Tony's shoes off, unbuckle his belt, and begin unzipping his fly. Tony's face, buried between Laura's breasts, turns towards me now. "Cut it out!" he says gruffly. He pushes my hands away.

"Relax, Tony," Laura whispers. "It's okay."

I reach up and continue tugging his zipper down. Tony scowls. "Shhhh," Laura whispers, caressing his face, running her fingers through his hair. "It's all right. Trust me." She pulls his head back down to her breasts and he nuzzles his face between them. I slowly pull his trousers down. Tony offers no resistance this time. He's wearing boxer shorts, of all things, with polka dots. I pull those down too. His dick is rock hard, thick, uncut, and veined, and his balls in this summer's heat hang low and fleshy. Beautiful, I think. Just beautiful. I catch Laura's eye and nod towards the bedroom.

"Come on, Tony," she says, almost maternally. "Let's all go to bed. We'll be a lot more comfortable there."

Tony is seemingly compliant now. He gets up, a little unsteadily, and steps out of the pants and shorts bunched around his ankles.

"Get rid of the socks, too, Tony," I say. I want to see him standing in the middle of my living room without a stitch of clothing on. He pulls them off obediently. Laura begins to lead him away.

"Hold on, a second, Laura," I say, with just the slightest edge to my voice. She stops. "I just want to look at you for a while, all right, Tony?" I ask him softly.

Tony's eyes dart uncertainly. He knows he's in uncharted waters now and there's confusion and doubt on his face. He's got slightly over two decades of lower-class, straight Italian heritage sounding the alarm inside, telling him to smash my face into jelly, or, barring that, just hightail it out of there now, run down the streets of Telegraph Hill, his clothes bundled under his arms and his heterosexual cherry still intact. But he's drunk, and aroused, and confused, and lonely, and flattered by the attention he's been getting, and ready for adventure anyway. I mean, shit, why does a man join the Navy if not to see what's out there in the wide world?

He stays put. But he's not about to capitulate without some token gesture of manly pride. "What the hell is your problem, man?" he snarls. "You some kind of queer?"

"Yeah, you dago greaseball," I laugh. "Of course I'm queer. Isn't that fucking obvious?"

Tony glares at me, and I calmly return his stare, grinning. "Come on, Tony," I finally say. "Just humor me. You're goddamn beautiful. You know it. I know it. Laura knows it. That's why she picked you and brought you back here. Just let me enjoy it, okay? What harm is there in that?" Tony still says nothing. "Tony," I say softly. "Your dick is still hard. Don't tell me you're not getting off on this yourself."

Another thirty seconds go by as we stare each other down. I can see Laura out of the corner of my eye, watching us. Finally, Tony licks his lips and swallows. "What do you want me to do?" he mutters.

"Come closer," I say, my heart racing. "And start beating yourself off." Tony walks up and stops right in front of me. His dick is jutting straight out, inches from my face, the cockhead, red and flared, pushing out from its fleshy foreskin. I trace one blue vein making its way up the length of the shaft. With a slight smile, he wraps his hand around his dickmeat and begins stroking it, slow and easy.

"Faster," I say. "Really stroke that fucker."

"I'll do it the way I like it," Tony growls, not changing his tempo.

"Sure, Tony," I say soothingly. "Any way you like. Only, could you lean back a little, arch your back?"

Tony obeys. I watch his heavy ballsac bouncing up and down with each stroke, his hand sliding over that thick Italian salami. My eyes travel up his body, taking in the chiseled belly, the hard, sharply defined pecs, the broad shoulders, the face of a young Roman god. Tony seems suffused with light and I feel something elemental and profound move through the room. "Jesus H. Christ," I groan. I get down on my knees and worship Tony the only way I know how. I take his cock in my mouth and suck voraciously.

Tony's fingers entwine through my hair, and he begins pumping his hips; I twist my head from side to side, bobbing it in time with Tony's thrusts. I reach back and and squeeze Tony's firm ass cheeks, feeling their muscles tense and relax every time he shoves his dick down my throat. My hand slides around and grasps his balls; the meaty pouch fills my palm, the two nuts have a weight and heft to them that are truly impressive. They cry out to be sucked, and who am I to refuse them? My tongue slides down Tony's shaft, and I swallow his balls, first one, and then the other, rolling them around with my tongue. I look up at Tony, his scrotum in my mouth; his eyes glitter brightly as he looks back down at me, and he begins slapping my face with his dick.

The three of us retire to the bedroom. Tony continues to plow my face as he goes down on Laura. He varies his thrusts, sometimes fucking my mouth with long, slow strokes, sometimes keeping his cock all the way down my throat and grinding his balls against my chin. By Laura's soft cries I can tell that Tony is very good at giving head; Laura puts on an act for no one. But I'm an equal match. I wrap my tongue around Tony's dick, meet Tony's thrusts with an open throat, and give him the best damn blow-job a man can get. It's a special talent of mine. Tony starts groaning with increasing loudness, and he falls back on the bed, giving in to my hot mouth and skillful tongue, all but abandoning Laura. She bends down and kisses him long and hard, and he passionately responds.

I know if I keep this up, Tony will shoot a load very soon, and I don't want that to happen yet, it's too early. I give up sucking cock for the while and press my mouth against Tony's torso, feeling the ridged bands of his abdominal muscles against my lips. My mouth wanders upwards, across the smooth, defined pectorals, and I take one of Tony's nipples between my teeth and gently bite. Tony groans, his mouth fused to Laura's, his hand buried between her legs. I run my tongue around his other nipple and bite that too, harder this time, and feel Tony's body squirm beneath me. Raising his arm, I bury my face inside his pit, drinking in the taste of fresh sweat, smelling that special man smell. I join the two of them, adding my kisses to theirs. Tony is hesitant at first, and keeps his lips shut against my thrusting tongue. But I persist, and eventually he relents, letting me slide my tongue deep into his mouth. It doesn't take long before he's returning my kisses, frenching Laura and me with the same intensity.

Tony gently pushes Laura on her back, and prepares to mount her. "Just a second, Tony," I say. I reach into the night stand drawer, pull out a condom, and hand it to him.

"I don't use those," he says.

I sigh. "It's the rule of the house. No condom, no fuck."

Tony grouses but he eventually lets Laura put it on him. Laura gets on her knees, and he mounts her from behind, his hands squeezing her breasts. I watch in fascination as this young man fucks my wife. Laura skillfully meets his every thrust, pumping her hips in a way that lengthens and prolongs every stroke of his. I lean over and twist his nipples and Tony groans loudly. He looks at me with glazed eyes, and I realize that at this moment he's up for any pleasurable sensation, regardless of the source. I kiss him again and he returns my kiss energetically. I stand up on the bed, my stiff dick directly in front of Tony, and rub his face with it. When he doesn't resist, I poke his lips with my cockhead. We look into each other's eyes, and I know this is the moment of truth. After a couple of beats, Tony opens his mouth. I slide my dick down his throat and begin fucking his face as he continues plowing Laura.

It's an exciting sight, watching my dick move in and out of this young, handsome man's virgin mouth. I hold onto the sides of his head, more for guidance than for force, and quicken the pace. It's easy to see that Tony is a first-time cocksucker; he's actually rather clumsy, and there are techniques I would love to teach him. But what he lacks in finesse, he more than makes up for in enthusiasm and energy.

Laura and Tony try different positions, but each time, Tony willingly continues sucking my cock. The warmth of the evening fills the room, drugging us, and we are all drenched in sweat. I listen to the sounds of flesh slapping against flesh, to Laura's cries and Tony's grunts. It feels like we've been in this bed for days.

Tony's groans, muffled by my dickmeat, start getting louder and more frequent. I know he's about ready to pop his cork. I'm not far myself. I cram my dick deep down his throat and gyrate my hips. I feel his tongue against it, squirming over it like a live animal. Sensations shoot through my body, and I feel myself pushing rapidly towards climax. I pull out of his mouth and beat off rapidly, my dick slick and slippery with Tony's saliva. Tony's body starts shuddering and he cries out loudly, his head thrown back, and he grinds his dick deep inside Laura. Laura cries out too, holding tightly onto Tony's body, her face twisted in ecstasy. A few more strokes send me over the edge, and cum spurts out of my dick, covering Tony's face and hair in spermy gobs, one pulse after another. I wipe my dickhead across his face, smearing his cheeks and mouth with my jism. We collapse into a pile; Laura and I gently kiss and lick my load off of Tony's face.

Tony spends the night with us. The next morning, we go at it again, and he obligingly fucks us both. After we shower and eat breakfast, he announces he has to go. I call a cab, and when it arrives, I give him cab fare back; I know sailors don't make much money. I offer him more money, but Tony refuses. I do give him our address on a slip of paper. Over breakfast, he has told us that his ship sails out in two days. I tell him to look us up, next time he's in port, or to at least send us a postcard somewhere along his travels. He says he will, but I'm resigned to the fact that sailors rarely do.

After he's left, Laura and I sit on the couch and look down at the ships below. I see Tony's cab at the bottom of the hill, heading towards the wharf. What an amazing experience that was, I think.

Laura looks up at me. "You happy, Bobby?" she asks.

I smile at her and squeeze her hand. "I guess so," I say. We sit together in silence for a long time.

Bob Vickery is a regular contributor to various magazines, and stories of his can be found in his two anthologies Cock Tales *and* Skin Deep. *He also has stories in numerous other anthologies, including* Best American Erotica 2000, Best Gay Erotica 1999, Friction, Friction 2, Friction 3, *and* Queer Dharma.

Sauce for the Gander

Hanne Blank

I hardly heard the first ring, and I certainly wasn't getting up to answer it. It was a Saturday morning, and I was busy violating sodomy laws. Dan noticed more than I did, pausing momentarily, halting the exquisitely rough-edged glide of his sweet cock slowly pumping in and out of my aching-to-be-fucked asshole. I wriggled my butt backward toward him, wordlessly reminding him of what he had been doing, grinning silently to myself at his office-conditioned Pavlovian response to the electronic chirp of the telephone.

Dan murmured, pleased to feel me moving against him. The phone rang again, and as it did he pushed in slowly, burying himself slowly to the hilt in between the soft round halves of my ass, his thickness prying me open at both ends as it coaxed a gravelly moan from my throat. The third ring came, and he backed out the same way, rhythmic and measured, making me whimper as my flesh clung to the smooth tender skin of his shaft, lingering like goodbye kisses at the train station. I gasped loud when the head popped free. My hips bucked backwards reflexively, anxious that he not leave my body. His fingers dug into my hips, keeping me from fucking backwards against him, and as the phone rang a fourth time, I let my cunt muscles contract against themselves, feeling in a sudden overwhelming wave the need to be fucked, and fucked hard. But no, no such luck. He slid into me with a lackadaisical corkscrewing motion of his hips, sighing as he pushed into me, forcing my well-lubed and eager ass to yield to his hardness with an unhurried glide. It was nowhere near enough. Clit throbbing, I tightened my muscles around him, milking the base of his cock.

"Please, just fuck me," I begged hoarsely, burying my face into the pillows in frustration. "Hard, please, please?"

The phone rang a fifth time, and I prayed like hell I had remembered to turn the answering machine on as he reversed the process, withdrawing from me with gentle deliberateness, almost completely dislodging himself from the tight, almost unbearably sensitive confines of my ass. There was only so much of that I could bear.

"So, just how many rings do you have that machine set for?" my lover asked with a sardonic leer in his tone, his cock dragging out of my ass, feeling as if it were dragging my clit along with it. I groaned, pulling a pillow over my head, simultaneously loving and hating the tease, the wait, the thrilling slow satin-rasp of his motions. He had about two more seconds before I would pass that threshold where I couldn't sustain the arousal without consistent help. I needed more from him. Without something to sustain it, my desperate need to be fucked would vanish out from under me like a magician's tablecloth.

With a click like a marble falling into a metal dish, the answering machine clicked into action. Mercifully, his fingers clawed my asscheeks, pulling up and apart as if he wanted to split me like a sweet tangerine. I cried out with a high, keening whine of want, feeling his tugging at my buttocks pull the floor of my ass all that much more firmly against the fat head of his cock. Oh, fuck me, please, I thought as he teased me with little hummingbird-like thrusts, a fraction of an inch in and out and in and out, making my nerves shriek and my muscles tense reflexively, sweet hard male flesh tormenting me in the most intense possible way. I arched back, trying to press into him, wanting to take him deeper.

The answering machine motor whirred. The volume was turned almost all the way down, and all I could hear from down the hall was a faraway murmur. I wanted Dan to reach around and stroke my clit, wanted him to slam into me, craved the feeling of his hands on my breasts. Whoever was leaving the message talked for a long time, long enough that I found myself wondering who it could be. I'd long since learned that she who answers the phone during sex gets what she deserves: by the time one has hung up, the juicy rare meat of lust has often become a cold fried egg, rubbery and tasteless when forced to be reheated.

Daniel, of course, noticed my distraction. A cold glob of lube slipping down the cleft of my ass from where he squeezed it onto my tailbone brought me back into the moment, sliding down over increasingly sensitive skin to coat his shaft, paused two inches into my buzzing sphincter. My attention was riveted to that sensation, those precise bits of hot flushed flesh that felt as if they were steaming the lube into clouds. I love the sensation, tawdry and sleazy, messy and primal, gorged and sluttish, of feeling someone fucking gooey liquid into me. Lube dripped off his cock, down my crack toward my cunt, oozed in rivulets onto the towel he'd slid under us before we'd begun. Too perfect. I bit into the pillowcase, an almost-agonized wordless cry ripping out of my lungs as I was forced inescapably into my own deep need to be fucked.

My fingers clawed at the pillow when he stopped halfway into me, desperate to get it out of the way of my mouth so that I could beg him to let me have it, plead with him to pound his cock all the way into me, split me open, slam me through the futon frame and down to the floor, anything, as long as I could feel him all the way into me, balls-deep, promising the incandescent rush of thick hot viscosity yet to come. Incoherent, lube still dripping down my ass and making me insane with need, I sobbed out a heartfelt "please," only to have him stroke my hair gently, calmly.

"Unh-unh, Anna," he whispered, maddeningly in control of himself and relishing my lack of it, "Better keep that pillow right where it is. You know how loud you scream when I give you what you're beggin' for and rape that greedy little cum-slut ass of yours."

His words, the parody of a threat sugarcoated by the loving rasp in his voice, caused a sudden trembling, radioactive bubbles carbonating my engorged pussy lips, my nipples, my clit, my cunt feeling cavernous and craving something to fill it with weight and force. I heard the footsteps of a thousand soldiers in my ears, sssshthud, sssshthud, as my heart hammered. Every neuron in my ass and pussy felt like a naked wire, alive and threatening a short-circuit as the rest of my body melted away, muscles going limp, unimportant. It was the instant of want he waited for, the sudden lassitude that told him to take me over, hard and fierce, driving into me as he collapsed onto my back, his weight driving me down onto the bed, cock like a butterfly pin nailing me, going through me, unstoppable. I sobbed with the intensity and the pleasure, my body quaking, trying not to come yet, not yet, not quite yet. Powerful fingers with short sharp nails slid under me, found my nipples, pinched hard as his hips drove into my upturned grateful buttocks, fingers kneading my tits roughly, hurting me just enough to provide spontaneous-combustion counterpoint to the thick pleasure of his cock driving in and in and further into my fuck-hungry asshole.

I reared up against him, meeting his thrust, feeling myself caught on an updraft of pleasure so thick that I could barely breathe. With a slam our bodies met, hard enough to have knocked us over had we not been locked so desperately together, and I floated away, my body hammered into the bed by the torrential, relentless, pistoning fuck, my tiny tender butthole so pristinely, so roughly, so sweetly opened by that candy apple of meat and muscle that it ripped scream after scream of pleasure out of my unthinking throat. Somewhere else a part of me soared, serene and freed, clean and immaculate in the acid bath of that coruscating, perfect ass-fucking.

Nirvana. Nerve-ana. The jewel is in the lotus. *Om mani padme cum.*

Slowly, muzzily, I opened my eyes, pushing the corner of the pillow off of my face. My throat hurt. Panting softly, almost recovered, he lay on top of me, his weight as reassuring to me as the fact that his cock was still nestled inside me and still halfway hard. Gently I tightened my muscles and gave his cock a squeeze, enough to make him gasp and scold me, telling me he was too sensitive.

"Don't tell me you want more?" he asked with mock incredulity.

"Fuck it into me," I whispered, a shy, greedy little smile on my lips. "Give me one more. Let me feel you fuck your cum into me, just a little."

He knew full well what I wanted; I knew full well he just wanted to hear me say it. Pulling out to let me savor the tip of his cock slipping out of me, I felt a small trickle of sperm leaking out of my battered ass, warm, the consistency of honey. With a soft moan, he pressed his cockhead back up against the doubly-lubed ring of my ass and pushed against me. After all these years, he's never confessed that he loves this part as much as I do, but I know better.

"You like that, don't you, baby?" he purred in a loving tease as the head of his cock slipped back inside me and he began to fuck me quickly, pulling completely out of me with each stroke, words and sensations instantaneously putting me on the verge of another orgasm. "You just love feeling me fucking all that cum up into your gorgeous tight little hole, don't you?"

Convulsing with the sharp suddenness of orgasm, I didn't need to answer. I felt my sphincter gripping his cock, milking it with hard inward strokes, and heard his amazed groan as he felt an encore of his own searing its way up and out of his almost-empty balls. "God how luscious," I gasped, the words spurting as fast as his seed, savoring the clarity with which my overtaxed nerve endings could feel the few short jets of semen he pumped deep into my rear end. We both collapsed, giggling and panting, as the orgasms rolled away, careful to be still below the waist, both his cock and my hard-used but pleasantly-tingling anus too tender, too sensitive to bear even the motion of uncoupling.

Showered and shaved, buttoning the shirt my mother had given him last year for Chanukah, he came and stood in the bathroom doorway. "That was your other sweetie," he said, a twinkle in his eye. "She says she needs to talk to you, hopes you have the afternoon free. She's horny as hell, she says, and she was purring like a kitten the whole time she left the message."

"Never rains but it pours, does it?" I asked rhetorically, walking to the phone. "Why do I even bother to shower in between?" I gave him a wink as I dialed Jill's number, enjoying the gentle throbbing of my backside, a lovely reminder of how well he'd fucked me.

"Jill, it's poor manners to answer the phone when you have your fingers in your cunt," I teased. Her "hello" had been so breathy, so transparently aroused that I could very nearly smell the sweet aroma of her slippery, barenaked cunt. She had a little-girl voice at the best of times, and when she was aroused it went from Betty Boop to breathless waif, a strong contrast to the powerful, tall, well-curved solidity of her body

She stammered a hello, the redness in her cheeks seeping into her voice so thickly that I could tell she was blushing clear down to her gumdrop nipples. In short order I discovered that I had been spot on the money with my opening salvo. She had been masturbating, fantasizing, and wishing I would call her back when the phone rang.

"I crave you," she whispered in my ear. "Inside me."

"You want to be fucked, do you?" I replied, trying to sound cool as my clit tingled between my demurely crossed thighs.

"Oh yes, Anna," she sighed, a boa constrictor of anticipation squeezing breathless words out of her.

"Is it okay with you that Dan is here?" I asked, smiling slyly up at my partner, who stood watching me, his arms folded across his chest and a knowing grin on his face.

"Oh, of course," my lover agreed. She was fond of Dan, and he was fond of her. They shared their fondness for me with remarkably little friction, a fact which pleased me afresh almost every day. It wouldn't be the first time, and it certainly wouldn't be the last, that Dan was around when Jill came over with sex on her mind. I wanted something specific, though, something rather different from anything that had ever happened before when Jill came over to our house to make love with me.

"Is it okay with you if Dan is with us this time?" I ventured, less sure of her response. For a few instants, I was caught between my partners, suspended in silence. Dan's eyes had gone wide, and he pointed to himself, index finger on his chest, incredulous. Impressively, for the straight boyfriend of a bi woman, he'd never even asked me for a threesome, and he seemed to be suffering advanced mindboggle at the prospect of having one offered to him out of the blue.

When she spoke, Jill had a chuckle in her voice. "You've got something up your sleeve, don't you?" she asked.

"Sort of," I admitted. "Is that a yes?" Dan was shaking his head disbelievingly, wearing a goofy anticipatory grin. "I cannot believe this," I heard him mutter. "Un-fucking-believable."

Jill murmured agreement with a silky light purr, about as close to a growl as a soprano that high can get. "I'll be over shortly to help you with Daniel," she agreed with a luscious little chirp. "But I want you to fuck me."

The line went dead, and I hung up. A triumphant smile plastered across my face, I looked up at my lover. "She said yes."

"Holy Mother of God at the Tast-E-Freez," he replied, genuinely taken aback. "You're serious?" He'd often told me how he envied my fucking Jill, not jealous, just envious and intensely attracted to her muscular rugby-girl thighs and long-fingered hands, her small olive-skinned breasts with their almost ludicrously large nipples, her quirky half-Lebanese, half-Japanese features. I still savored the memory of his defenseless, guttural croak when I told him that she kept her pussy shaved and that she wore a small titanium hoop in one naked inner labia. Dan was far too respectful of my bisexuality and far too aware of how seriously I took my polyamory—to say nothing of my very genuine love for Jill – to importune me to let him watch, but he was far from immune to my beloved girlfriend's charms. I found his discreet, utterly politic lustfulness endearing.

"Of course I'm serious," I said as I walked toward the kitchen.

"But you've never..." he trailed, following me. "She's never... was it her idea?"

"Doesn't matter, Dannyboy, and it's none of your business anyway. We have plans for you." I smiled like a tabby with a mouthful of canary feathers.

"Plans?" he questioned, gesturing to me with a poppy-seed bagel. "What do you mean, plans?"

"You've told me that you want to know what it feels like for me when you fuck me like you did this morning," I answered as matter-of-factly as possible.

"You want to have Jill watch you fuck me?"

With a wry grin, I looked up at Dan, shaking my head. "My word, you're quick to jump to conclusions. Who said anything about Jill watching?"

"Well, color me slow, but wasn't that what you had in mind?" Now he was slightly defensive, unable to figure out what I intended to spring on him, no longer sure that this threesome was going to be what he'd thought.

"Nope, not really." I reached across the table and brushed my fingertips against his jaw affectionately. "I want to watch her fuck you. You told me once that you thought she was so hot you'd let her do almost anything to you if only she were willing."

"You want to watch *Jill* fuck me?" Dan echoed, sounding entirely stunned by the idea. I could see in his eyes that the notion of my tall, strong, slightly butch lover bending him over and making him take it for her was not entirely unattractive. He squirmed in his chair a little, his eyes a little unfocused.

Silently, I chuckled into my mug. "Of course I want to watch Jill fuck you. You told me you'd let her." He stared at me, swallowing hard, but not saying a word. "Or were you just whistlin' Dixie, Danno?"

"God, Anna, I don't know if I can take it... I've never...." He liked it when I fingerfucked him, in recent times working him up to taking three of my fingers inside him. Still, he'd always balked at letting me fuck him the way I really wanted to, with the long slim silicone dildo that I loved to work into my own asshole when I was desperately horny and he was out of town

Dan's eyes locked on mine with an astonishing look of terrified, fierce arousal. I stroked my toes up the inside of his thigh, letting them brush against his chino-clad crotch. As I suspected, he was ragingly stiff. "Ta, ta, ta," I clucked, stroking my toenail along the length of his fly as his face turned a bright embarrassed pink, "if I didn't know better, Daniel my love, I might accuse you of looking forward to this."

Dan lay on the bed, right hand idly stroking his massively stiff cock, precum dripping over his fingers like a caramel glaze over ice cream. He'd been given strict instructions not to cum, and not to disturb Jill and I until we were ready for him.

She had opened to me with her usual silent completeness, our kiss in the foyer of the house immediately wringing-wet with overtones of desire. She'd ridden to the house on her bicycle, and the slight fresh dampness of her T-shirt pleased me. I loved the grassy, woody smell of her, rubbing my face between her persimmon-half breasts, savoring the distinctly female way she made my heart beat faster, so different from what I felt with Dan. We hardly ever spoke while we made love to one another, sly games of Mother-May-I played with butterfly tongues and ravenous hands on bodies so eloquent that words were clumsy by comparison.

Her mouth found my right nipple almost immediately, pushing the lapel of my robe aside, latching on like a nursling. I unbuttoned her skirt and let it fall onto the tile floor, unsurprised to find her nude beneath. "Naughty Jillian," I chided teasingly, my lips brushing her ear through her storm system of curls, "no panties? Only tramps go around without panties." My right pinky tip parted her labia to find her little titanium hoop, tugging her pussy slightly open. I hissed with pleasure to find her already wet, my hiss resolving itself into a coo as I tugged harder on her labia ring and she gave the softest of moans, relinquishing her hold on my breast.

"Let me take my boots off," she murmured, and I let her go. Before she could straighten up, I moved behind her and slid my thumb into her cunt. The sensation of being so quickly and unexpectedly penetrated made her clutch at the doorframe to keep from falling over. It was as though I could hear her in my mind, hear her whispering, begging me to fuck her, telling me that this was exactly what she'd been wanting all day. Jill's back arched slightly, her hips pressing back against me, trying to get more of me into her, wanting so obviously just to be fucked, without fuss or fanfare or even foreplay. Immediately I pulled out of her, pulling her around by the waist to smear her own lubrication across her mouth. I kissed her, hard, and when she smiled and her mouth opened under mine, I tonguefucked between her lips just enough to make her shudder.

"I love you, Jill," I said, taking her by the hand as I looked into her pale green eyes. Jill beamed, her lipstick-tip nipples hard as erasers and poking out under her thin yellow T-shirt, and squeezed my hand, not quite able to talk. She tugged at my arm and pulled me after her, sprinting down the hallway toward the master bedroom, naked but for her shirt.

"Hi, Dan," she said jauntily as she pulled off her shirt and grabbed me by the ends of the bathrobe sash. I could feel Dan watching as Jill and I kissed, but my attention to his presence in the room faded into the remote background as my body tuned itself in to the wavelengths of Jill's response. Standing by the foot of the bed, I grabbed her wrists and held them tightly in the small of her back, bending down to take her left nipple between my lips. Jill's nipples, so disproportionately large on her barely pubertal breasts, always responded so well to a combination of tongue and sharp-edged nipping. Switching from left to right, back and forth, I intensified the pressure until I actually succeeded in getting her to moan out loud, a rarity for her. Letting go of her wrists, I ran my fingertips along the seam between her newly-shaven, eiderdown-soft cunt lips.

Gently I turned her to face the bed and bent her over, enjoying the sleekness of her strong body under my hands as I stroked her back, her hips, her thighs. Dan moaned softly, watching, as I spread her firm, sherbet-scoop asscheeks with my hands. I loved looking at her like that, bent over, spread wide, totally open and totally vulnerable, knowing how much it was making her tremble. When I bent her over like this, she was utterly mine, just the way she wanted to be.

Holding her light-tan thighs in both hands, I gave her ten of the long, agonizingly wide licks she adored, tongue painting a broad stripe from her bursting clit up and over her cunt —she contracted reflexively as I flicked the tip of my tongue just barely inside—then over her perineum to her swirling plum-blossom of an asshole. Her breath was growing ragged, more so with each swipe of my tongue. I pushed my tongue into her cunt as far as it would go, and she ground backwards against my face, hard and needful. My hand flat against her belly, I slid my palm toward her breast and clawed at it, her reactionary writhing against my tongue tattling that she was more than ready to take whatever I dished out. I snatched a latex glove from the bureau top and put it on my right hand, teasing her labia with slick rubber fingertips as I once more found her endlessly pinchable nipple with my bare hand. I tweaked it hard, and she sucked in her breath as I slid three fingers into her, filling her to the knuckles with one simple push.

Inarticulate, preverbal gasps punctuated her panting as I kneaded the walls of her cunt just the way I knew she liked it best. Slipping my pinkie into her, she shoved back against my hand so forcefully I worried that she would hurt herself, but instead she stopped, dead still. I arched my wrist and twisted my hand inside her, just enough to push her entirely over the edge. With a high-pitched squeal she shuddered and came, cunt clutching at my fingers, sweet girl-cum dripping down my forearm as I resumed fucking my hand into her.

I'd done it to her enough times that I knew I didn't need to ask what she wanted next. I tucked my thumb into my palm and began to slowly rock my hand in and out of her, fingers forming a cone, knuckles rubbing in and out, in and out against her entrance. She began to push against my hand, soft powderpuffs of sound floating from her throat as she fucked backwards into me, and I slowly, gently twisted my arm inside her until the instant came when she opened that tiny bit more and my fist slid, fingers curling in on themselves, wrist-deep into her impossibly lush cunt. The smell of her heat was overpowering, the sensation of her body wrapped around my arm so hot and wet and tight and yet so yielding that I felt lightheaded. No matter how many times I'd fucked her this way, it still seemed holy, in extremis, so rarefied and sweet as she started to come and come and did not stop until that sudden last spasm that always seemed to take her by surprise, cunt mauling my hand with contractions, and squeezed my fist completely out as she arched and screamed.

I lowered her to the bed, stripping the glove off and throwing it over my shoulder, not really caring where it went. Cradling her against me, stroking her hair back from her ruined, exhausted face, I kissed her softly. Looking up, I saw Daniel, sheer awe on his face, his cock standing stiff but unheeded. I smiled at him, and he smiled back slowly, his eyes never leaving mine, amazed by this side of me that he was just now getting to see.

As Jill recovered, I sank down between her thighs, tongue slipping easily between her hairless lips to find her clit. The taste and feel of her in my mouth would have been enough to keep me there a long time, ordinarily, but we had things to do. Somewhere in my peripheral vision, I noticed Jill and Dan making eye contact. A fuse of jealousy sizzling in the pit of my stomach, I wrested her attention back where it belonged, trilling my tongue against the tender hood of her clit. I wanted my girlfriend eager, ready, aroused again, her own hunger blunted just enough that she could give my other lover the kind of unstinting fucking he so richly deserved.

Wrapping my arms around her waist, I looked up into Jill's glowing face. We held one another's gaze for a moment, and I buried my face against her breastbone, her fingers lovingly stroking my neck, my hair. She curled around me, whispering gentle words into my ear. We kissed, and she held me to her as I whispered in her ear what I wanted her to do to Daniel, who lay at the head of the bed, transfixed by our little show.

The slow, liquid smile I love so much flowed across her eccentrically lovely face. She cleared her throat, looking directly at Daniel with suddenly predatory eyes. Dan gazed at Jill, taking in the sight of the beautiful, bald-crotched temptation he'd so often imagined from the far side of a closed door while I was on the other side of it fucking her.

"I hope you're ready for me, Dan," she rasped, her voice still high but remarkably sexy from the post-coital grittiness in her throat. "I'm really looking forward to being inside your sweet little man-cunt. I love giving someone a good ass-fucking."

I had to fight the urge to cut to the head of the line. Jill in the leather harness, eight-inch black silicone cock jutting out from her mons was a sight that infallibly reduced me to a twitching mess of estrogen and yearning. I could tell by the Mona Lisa lines of her smile that she was looking forward to this at least as much as I. All I had to do was to keep from throwing myself between the two of them and begging to be first. I sat next to Dan, stroking his side as he knelt on all fours, Jill's long hands caressing his ass and hips. He was nervous, but he couldn't resist the fact that he had two women's hands caressing his body, and gradually he began to wriggle slightly under our palms, soft little groans floating into the air whenever Jill reached down far enough to caress the undersides of his balls.

Jill leaned down to kiss me, and I opened my mouth to her as I cupped her breast in one hand and took Dan's cock in the other. Clasping Dan's shaft in my fingers and finding Jill's nipple with a gentle, rolling pinch, I shuddered happily as I got them both to moan at the same time, Jill's baby-doll murmur like cotton candy in my mouth. I cupped his balls in my hand, jostling them gently like dice before the throw, and he pressed forward to thrust his cock against my forearm, then back, pressing his ass against the sleek length of the cock that Jill wore so well. Jill's tongue was in my mouth, playful, teasing the tender spot on my lower lip, wearing her toppishness at a rakish angle. She was eager, quite aware that she held both Dan and me in the palm of her hand, not just because she was about to fuck Dan and I found it unbearably hot, but for reasons she couldn't have known, couldn't have seen.

I loved Jill, loved the way she moved inside me, loved to look up when she fucked me, my legs hugging her waist, my feet on her ass pushing her cock into me further and further. I loved to let her torment my cunt with her tongue, her fingers, with dextrous, unending fucking until my system couldn't withstand it any more and I would just start coming, enormous waves of orgasms rendering me incoherent for five, ten, fifteen minutes at a stretch. I was desperately envious and had to laugh at my own envy – of all the people in the world that I could want to allow to have the kind of pleasure I knew Jill could bring, Dan was the one I wanted to share her with. But try telling that to the stupid reptilian part of me that kept shrieking at me to grab her for myself. As much as I yearned to watch my lover working her cock into my other lover's tight, untested ass, I also wanted to take her off somewhere, mine and no one else's.

As Jill straightened, she began rhythmically rubbing against Dan's ass, her eyes locked on mine, and I shivered with the empathetic knowledge of exactly how suavely, precisely how skillfully she was capable of stroking with her silicone member. I was scalding hot, yes, but at least part of that heat came directly from the surly flames of sexual jealousy.

Jill's expertise was by no means lost on Dan, who groaned a soft "Oh, God" as he dropped his shoulders to the bed, clutching a pillow under his head, ass in the air. A wolfish conquistador smile spread across Jill's face, and she stroked his sides, fucking her hips toward his ass, letting the shaft of her cock rub up and down his buttcrack. My pussy quivered as I watched him beginning to lose control, and I thought momentarily about sliding underneath Dan and slipping his cock into my cunt as Jill slipped hers into his ass.

I couldn't bring myself to do it. I wanted Dan to experience being fucked as purely, as whitely hot, as he possibly could. Being inside me at the same time would be too much of a distraction, the cock in his ass demoted to a sideshow attraction, and I didn't want that. Jill's expert cocksman skills deserved all his attention. And mine. Incapable of forming words, Dan just groaned and arched backwards into Jill the way he wriggled against my hands when I teased his asshole during a blowjob and he wanted me to penetrate him.

"Are you trying to tell me that you want girl-cock in your boy-pussy, Dan?" I asked coaxingly, "Is that what you want? You want Jill to shove that great big tool of hers into your tight little ass?"

Jill's eyes flashed with lust, Dan's groan broke in the middle and descended two octaves into rough gravel at the bottom. Squeezing Dan's cock, letting my fingers ripple around it rhythmically, I picked up the bottle of lube from the corner of the bed and handed it to Jill with a conspiratorial smile, sharing a moment of tenderness with her as our eyes stroked one another's faces. She lubed her cock and resumed sliding it up and down between the halves of Daniel's slim-hipped ass, making him shudder so hard I thought he might convulse.

"So hot, baby," I half-purred, half-growled, my nipples starting to tingle, speaking to both of my lovers as they moved against one another. To Jill I said, "Lube him up good for that nice long cock, sugar girl. He's virgin pussy." To my surprise, Dan moaned at being called pussy, his hardness twitching in my hand. Jill opened the flip-top on the lube bottle and held it high above Dan's ass, letting a long thin ribbon of clear sticky liquid spill down onto his waiting skin. Jill wore a beatific smile, meditatively stroking lube all over my boyfriend's ass with her cock-tip, squeezing out more in an extravagant stream.

"I hope you've got more lube," she intoned seriously. "If he's anything like you are, he's going to soak it up and beg for more, and I do want to hear him beg."

"Oh, there's more where that came from," I grinned, watching the side of Dan's face. His eyes were closed, his lips slack, as he let himself be manipulated by my hands and Jill's, abandoning himself to the sensation of being painted with lube by a thick, hard cock. I stroked gooey precum up and down his shaft with my hand, encouraging and rewarding his willingness. "Plenty more lube for that pretty little boy-cunt whenever you want it. Lube him up just like you lube me up, Jill. He'll like that. What's sauce for the goose..."

"...is sauce for the gander," my girlfriend finished, catching my drift as she took three fingers full of lube and brought them directly against Dan's tight muscled ring. "Breathe," she told him, and he did, breathing deeply in, then out. On his out-breath she slid two fingers into his ass, smooth and sure. He yelped but then groaned as I gave his ragingly hard cock a few firm strokes. Two fingers inside him, she squirted lube into the groove between her fingers, letting me watch, my cunt oozing as she used her fingers to channel the lube into my boyfriend's ass, slowly working him open for her. The fires of my jealousy raged in competition with the flames of deep, unreconstructed lust. I knew precisely how it felt to have her working all that slickness into my own ass, and the thought made me shiver. It was all I could do to remember to keep gently stroking his shaft.

Without telling him she was doing it, Jill worked a third finger into Dan's butthole, her fingertips doing invisible things inside him that had him moaning almost nonstop. Soon he was pressing back against her, pushing himself down onto fingers well-versed at making me beg her to shove her cock into me, until she was in him up to her knuckles. Dan was beyond words. He had shut down the part of himself that would've told him he couldn't do it, couldn't take it, and was letting his body be taken over by sensation, by lust, by the almost incomprehensible idea that two women, one whom he loved, one about whom he had long fantasized, were working in concert to fuck him in a way he'd never been fucked before. I got onto my knees, right hand still encircling Dan's dripping member, left hand caressing Jill's satiny ass, looking into her eyes.

"Give it to him, baby," I whispered. "I want to watch you just destroy that ass."

Jill's eyes were bright, her smile devilish and voluptuous at the same time. Pulling her fingers out halfway, she squirted another good shot of lube into him. With a long slow firm shove, she slid her fingers back in, extra lube oozing out of his butt and down his ass, over her fingers. His moans were soft and vulnerable, his cock occasionally jerking gently in my grip. My lover squeezed lube onto her cock and I reached down to smear it all over the condomed surface, eager to feel the firm weight and thickness of the shaft, altogether too well aware of how good it had felt all the times it had entered me. I positioned the tip of the phallus against Dan's sphincter, waiting for Jill to pull her fingers out, but she merely winked at me and grinned. She opened her fingers like a scissors and wedged the head of her cock between them, forcing a keening wail out of Dan, whose face was still half-buried in the pillow he held under him. I clenched my fingers around his cock, thumb stroking the sweet spot just below the cleft of his cockhead.

"Kiss me, Anna," Jill croaked, hoarse with lust, and I did, twining lube-sticky fingers in her hair as she slowly began to push her way into Dan's body, fingers coming out as her cock went in. Dan's cock swelled in my hand and I pumped him long and slow, reassuring and firm, rhythmic and constant as his body went rigid, trying to cope with the invasion. Kissing Jill, I was floored by the force of her lust and the exquisite control that she kept, somehow managing not to slam her cock all the way in to the hilt even though I could tell she wanted to. Slowly, inexorably, she worked into my boyfriend's ass, until her hips pressed against his lube-painted buttocks. Only then did she break the kiss.

"Let me have his cock," she said, sliding her arm down my forearm and replacing my fingers with hers. "He's mine now. I'm going to ride him until he screams. I want you to fuck me while I fuck him."

Relinquishing my hold on my lover's aching, oozing penis, I could tell that her words had somehow penetrated his half-consciousness. Dan wriggled his ass against her, inviting her to take him. I grabbed a glove from the bureau and moved behind Jill, the split peach of her ass and cunt open to me as she knelt spread-legged behind Dan. My own cunt spasmed, aching, yearning to be fucked. Later, I told myself, later. Right now, my girl wanted me in her pussy while she fucked Dan's round narrow boy-butt, and that was all that mattered. She bent over Dan's body, supporting herself on her left arm while her right hand teased his prick, slowly building her strokes into his ass until he was groaning ecstatically to take her in from tip to base in slow, liquid strokes. I was amazed at her, amazed at him, amazed at what I was seeing, tender, intimate, and scaldingly familiar.

It was almost difficult to intrude. My jealousy had suddenly, mysteriously vanished, perhaps overwhelmed by the erotic magic of watching my girlfriend fucking my boyfriend and my boyfriend loving every last millimeter of the cock that slid into his ass. Tentatively I pressed my knuckles against her slit.

"Bitch, I thought I told you to fuck me now," she play-snarled, looking back over her shoulder at me with sheer lust in her eyes. "I hate it when you keep me waiting. I've been fucking away for five minutes here, wondering why those fingers weren't in my pussy."

"I'm sorry, Jill," I breathed, kissing her shoulder as I slid two fingers into her sopping-wet hotness. "I promise I'll make it up to you."

"You won't make it up to me, Anna," she rasped, as much for Dan's benefit as mine, her thrusts into Dan's ass picking up speed. "You'll pay for it. And so will he."

I let her thrusts time the movements I made, her withdrawals from Dan's body pushing her back onto my fingers as I wriggled them within the tight clinging walls of her cunt. Absorbed by the rhythm, by the wetness around my gloved fingers, by the mesmerizing tense and push of the muscles of her ass as she fucked, it took me several minutes to notice that Dan's moans had turned into a torrent of words.

"Anna, fuck me, Jill, Anna, please," he pleaded, lust slurring his words. "Take my ass, fuck my ass, break me open, fuck me, Jill, fuck me, Anna, please dear God don't stop fucking me take me oh Jill Anna Anna God... fuck..."

"Listen to him sing," Jill marveled, letting go of his cock and squeezing another helping of lube onto her cock without a pause in her stroke. I corkscrewed my fingers into her again and again, reaching up to pinch her nipple as she hunched with concentration over Dan's body and started to fuck him in earnest. I slipped my thumb into her asshole and she squealed, the added sensation spurring her on. Trying hard just to keep from having her wrench herself off of my fingers, I pressed closer and did my best to hang on for the ride, feeling the thudding smack of her hips as she barreled into Dan's ass in an all-out fuck that I never would've dreamt he could've taken.

Dan sobbed, pleading with her to fuck him, to break him, to split him open, to tear him apart, his knees sliding apart and his body lowering down onto the bed, cock mashed between his belly and the bedspread. It seemed as if she was trying to do just that, sweat beading on the smooth damask of her back, eight inches violating his boy-pussy with exceptional, exquisite brutality as he arched, close to the end.

Down the hall, the phone rang. I was the only one to notice, Jill grunting savagely as she clawed at Dan's shoulder and bit between his shoulderblades, ramming herself into him as his entire body tensed. With one final plunge Dan came, his harsh sharp scream echoing off the walls in between the annoying rings of the telephone. Jill lay on top of him, not moving, letting him shake off the aftershocks, panting as I slid my fingers back into her. I'd lost her as she finished Dan off, her movements too frenzied for me to manage to stay inside, but she groaned with appreciative need when I reached two, then three fingers under the harness straps and into her, filling her in time with the fourth ring of the phone. I quickly found her G-spot with my fingertips, letting my fingers dance against it until she became caught up in her own urgency and spasmed against my hand with a motion that drove her cock deep into Daniel one last punishing time. He gasped out loud, then almost immediately began laughing, his chuckling jostling Jill as she collapsed on top of him.

I heard it, too. Down the hall, tinny through the answering machine's tiny speaker, we could clearly hear a woman's voice, chatty and high-pitched. All three of us now held our breath, trying not to laugh.

"...so I was at your Aunt Cheryl's," my mother's voice continued, disembodied, slightly adenoidal, "and what she found when she was cleaning out the attic you would never guess. Now we've got all your bat mitzvah pictures all in the same album! Anyway, Anna, give your mama a call when you get a chance, and make sure you give Daniel a kiss from me. Love you, bubeleh." The machine clicked off and we lost it, caught in a gale of laughter. Dan gasped in between giggles, short and sharp, as Jill rolled off of him, her cock sliding out of his well-used ass. Lying there together on the bed, Dan on my left and Jill cozied up on my right, the three of us basked, laughter trailing off into a satisfied, comfortable silence. Jill arched her back, lifting her hips as she slipped out of her dildo harness, her motions breaking the quiet.

Dan raised himself up on his elbow to watch Jill removing the apparatus with which she'd given him such a thorough dose of his own medicine. He shook his head at the thud it made as it hit the floor, then reached across me to stroke Jill's arm as he kissed my cheek. "One of these days, Anna," he chuckled into my ear as Jill cuddled back up to my other side, "we're going to remember unplug the phone before we have sex."

"Don't be silly, Daniel," I smiled, reveling in the feeling of being sandwiched between my lovers' warm luxuriant bodies. "Where on earth would I be then?"

Hanne Blank is the author of Big Big Love: A Sourcebook on Sex for People of Size and Those Who Love Them *(Greenery Press), and editor of* Zaftig!. *A regular contributor to* Scarlet Letters, *the* Boston Phoenix, Clean Sheets, *and* Zenpride, *she invites readers to visit www.hanne.net for more information.*

Me And Jared

Hew Wolff

I worry about Jared sometimes. He's a good guy. He lives in his head too much, you can see that. His family tells him that all the time, so I try not to, but he needs to get out more. Get drunk once in a while. You don't break some glass once in your life, you don't know what you're missing.

He has had a couple of girlfriends. There was Sally Ann—she was fine, although there were some difficulties between me and her. Me and her brother had a difference of opinion over by the swamp one time after school, and it never really got resolved, as they say, but I was happy for Jared. Then there was Keesha—his folks were not too thrilled about seeing him with a Keesha, I'll tell you that. And this Keesha was a wild one, too. Till she got that scholarship, and then pretty soon she was gone. Used to have an eye for her myself.

We all figure that's how Jared'll go, riding a scholarship out of here to someplace people have heard of. Might never see him again. He is a smart one, that's for sure; he's the only one around here really knows one end of a computer from the other.

I was playing with his computer, when I was over at his place last night. But last night was different. I was trying to get him out for a cruise over to Henley or a movie or something, but he kept sitting me down and trying to explain me things, like he always does. It's not enough to read, he says, you have to know something about these machines. Well, he calls them machines, but my idea of a machine is something that has grease in it. Which I guess is the point. "Forget TV, forget Nintendo," he says. "This is the future."

So I was pointing and clicking at the future while he was peering into the printer. "Goddamn," he says, "I think I have to take this thing into town again."

"You tried sweet-talking it?" I said. "Always sweet-talk it first, even if you know you're going to have to hit it with a Crescent wrench in a minute. Pretend it's a pussy. What the hell does 'J-P-G' mean? JPG, JPG, JPG. What's that?"

"...That's an image file." And I wasn't looking at him, but I could swear I heard him blush.

"I see," I said. "So how do I look at these image files? You must have a program around here to do that, right?" My source of information was strangely quiet. "Okay, then, it looks like I just have to guess what these image files are. So what we have here in 'Download' is a whole lot of images of... baseball cards, right? Or... snapshots of your relatives? Landscape paintings?"

He kind of sighed. "You know, Bill, you're not as dumb as you look. Anyone ever told you that?"

"You tell me, all the time," I said. "Why I keep coming over here. Now it's time for you to get your ass into this chair and show me what to do here. I want to see some of that *Internet pornography* I keep hearing so much about."

It wasn't easy to get him in that chair. I almost felt bad. But we'd been together through many late nights, and I figured we'd get through this, too.

"You old horndog, you," I said. "Didn't anyone ever tell you to share with your friends? All right, let's see what we got here... that's a dirty picture, Jare. That's a picture of a girl getting fucked. This is not kid stuff. Are you sure you should be looking at this?"

He was still nervous, but he grinned. "Fuck you."

"That'll have to wait till tomorrow, when I get together with Mary Lou. Now keep going." The next one was a black girl giving a blow job. It didn't look like any Playboy picture, it looked like you were right there next to a normal cute girl who really wanted this cock in her mouth. It was pretty sexy. "Keep going..."

There was a whole bunch of fuck pictures in there. "No wonder you spend all this time typing in here," I said. I was going to go on and develop that theme a little, but then I saw the next picture.

Now, I've seen crucifixions before. Maybe there's a woman crouched there at the foot of the cross, looking up at her writhing savior. But I have never seen Jesus writhing with a big hard-on pointing up to heaven. And this woman didn't look like some sad ex-hooker out of the Bible. For one thing, she was holding something I couldn't identify made out of leather. And she was looking at this hard-on like it was her own personal property, and she was going to have a lot of fun with it.

I just didn't know what to say. I truly didn't. I guess I spent a little while not knowing what to say, because Jared piped up: "Not kid stuff, Bill."

"Shut up. You like this?" He shrugged. There was a strange feeling building inside me. I mean, I was getting horny, who wouldn't, but there was something else, too. "Well, keep going."

A big black guy fucking his woman in the ass. After that, damn if it wasn't another black girl eating cock. White cock.

"You like that, Jare?" He shrugged like his chair was getting uncomfortable. "You like to see black girls eating cock, don't you? It gets you hard, huh? Why is that, Jare? Tell me why."

"I dunno... I just... I like to see her on her knees, all... consumed by the power of it."

"I thought you were a liberal, Jare. Now I guess you're a perverted liberal... You old horndog, sitting here and... you're hard right now. I bet you wish you were jerking off. You want to do it right now, don't you?" I cuffed him in the shoulder. "Come on. Show me how perverted you are."

I couldn't believe it. He was unzipping his fly. I was frozen, but he was feverish, wanting it bad. It was incredible to see. I just wasn't sure I wanted to see it. I mean, Jared. Shit. "Hold on, bro," I said. "Is your dad still at work? You sure? Well. Why don't you just show me the rest of your pictures." He held his cock in one hand, and the mouse in the other, and clicked away.

He talked breathlessly. "I love this one, where she's spreading herself on the couch with the high-heel shoes and she's all open, she's just daring you to come in, and she's so black and her lips are all red and sticky and shiny."

I thought to myself, Mary Lou's gonna get slammed tomorrow like she's never been slammed before. Wonder if I can maybe see her tonight? Tell the truth, though, I was kind of distracted by Jared's cock. I hadn't ever exactly seen it like this. Now, don't get me wrong here. I love pussy just as much as the next guy. Ain't nothing like being on top of some warm, shiny pussy, making some girl real happy. But a hard-on, straining and twitching, standing proud: that is just pure sex. Made me nervous.

"You can do it," I said. "Just don't shoot."

He started slapping his hard-on, and went on. "Oh, God, that's good... oh, I can't help it—that one's not great... here, you see how he's holding her by the hair, not hurting her but firm, you know, and she's looking up at him—look at her eyes, they're so soft, like she was born to suck his cock—and she's his slave, and he's going to shoot right in her face....

"Here, she's vibrating herself and she's so into it, she's moaning and moaning, she can't stop, and she's grabbing her breast, and they're so big and smooth, I just wanna grab onto them and fuck her brains out... God, this is torture... Okay, wait....

"Here, here's a girl with the other girl sucking on her pussy, all wet and dripping down, and those gorgeous tits hanging down, and she's gonna scream, and cream right in the other girl's face... and here—" He looked at me for a minute, and clicked another picture.

I was just speechless again. Twice in half an hour, a new record. I was not expecting this. "What the hell is this, Jare? Am I missing something here? I don't see a girl in this picture, Jare. Find the fucking girl in this picture. Those are two guys with hard-ons." And they look like pretty good-sized ones. "Is my friend a cocksucker?"

He was still jerking off slowly, looking down. I looked down with him, and then I just lost it. I got down on the floor so I could get a good look. His cock was pointing straight up to his stomach, and the end of it was kind of small, and curved a little back toward him. Skin stretched tight over the veins. Little hairs around the base. Kind of slim, but longer than mine. "God Almighty," I said. "Now we got the cops to worry about, too." I leaned my face into him, and smelled that burning smell. God, I want to fuck, but if I can't fuck, I will have this in my mouth before I die, so help me God. Let's get hold of it. He's just sitting there panting. I'm breathing it in. I'm breathing it in. My mouth is dry, and I have to swallow to get enough saliva to lick it onto the shaft. Hold still, Jare. You can groan all you want, but hold still. Shit, is that the front door?

That was the front door. His dad was home.

I had to go.

That was last night. This is tonight. He said, "You want to get together?" I said, "You know it." I hate lying, but I told Mary Lou I was feeling poorly. Had a funny taste in my mouth. I know a quiet place near my house, and that's where we are, sitting on dry leaves in the hollow. I'm cradling him in my hands, his tough-looking little nuts, and then I'm actually licking his cock, I don't believe this. My lips are cracked. He's not saying anything, but he sure is breathing. Under my lips I can feel him shaking. Or it might be me. I'm going to take it real slow, like this was my last meal. Underneath, mmmm, that's a good place, isn't it, Jare. All around. I want you good and slick. Okay. This is what you want, isn't it. Okay. Come in. You just come right on in. Whoa, that's enough. Jesus, I'm holding him inside me. What a goddamn fucking high. No wonder Mary Lou likes it. Let's get a little in and out going here. Yes, like that, oh yes. Jesus, it's him, hard and smooth inside my mouth. His hands are on my head, bless you. Jared's a good guy. Yes you want it, yes keep going. Is this the future, Jare? Are you going away? Here, let me suck you again, just gently. This is tonight. You're here inside me.

Hew Wolff likes the shapes of things. He lives in Berkeley, CA, works in software, and can be reached at hew_wolff@post.harvard.edu.

Almost Free

Ariel Hart

I wake up long before any of the others. Always do. The pink, gold, and orange splashes across the sky silently rouse me every morning. The glow, the warmth. At this hour, Alida is still asleep, as are Marco, Fernando, and Jacinto. They sleep in their separate heaps beside the rocks on ponchos, on handwoven blankets. Everything must have at least two purposes here: a sleeping pallet doubles as a tablecloth, and so on. That's the way it had to be with us. Vagabonds. Travelers. Tramps. Gypsies.

Yes, everyone sleeps in their separate heaps except Alida, who always has to rest beside me. For comfort, I suppose. The mosquitoes aren't up yet either. The steady breeze from the Pacific keeps them away. But still, Alida has tiny, rosy bumps flecked across her body, bumps too fresh to scratch. In villages near San Cristobal de las Casas, I hear that there are shamen, witch doctors so powerful that their saliva alone can cure a multitude of ills.

With this in mind, I flatten my tongue and press it to Alida's mosquito bites, one by one. She stirs and smiles in her sleep but still does not wake. Her wispy hair, the color of the sand, forms a crown around her head. Her skin tastes of salt, of sweat, of heat. There are bites near her ankles so small I can barely feel them with my tongue. I work my way up to her thighs, so soft they remind me of quetzal feathers. The musk of her unwashed body rises like the warmth of tortillas cooking for breakfast. Today there may or not be breakfast, but there is always Alida's cunt. Moist in dreams, always ready, Alida's cunt. And with no one else awake, it is all mine.

There are a few bug bites on her belly. I pretend there are some on her mound as I spread her with both hands. It parts and makes a tiny sound, like a wet yawn. First, I trace the most delicate place, where pussy meets thigh. I move in a circle, lathering the space between her pudgy outer lips and the inner ones, so stiff and engorged that they stand out like the spathe of a calla lily. And at the top, in the center, is that minuscule button, so difficult to find at first. (In fact, the three men still have problems.) But with patience and gentleness, it comes out, it blossoms like a *dulce*, a sweet treat, on your tongue.

This is when Alida's entire body begins to tremble, when you run her clitoris between your teeth, tugging, lapping, kissing it as dearly as you would her perfect rosebud mouth. Gasps escape her lips in time with the throbbing of her button. It pounds rhymically like a heart, subsides like the sea, then stops. That's when Alida opens her eyes. "What's for breakfast, Maria?" she grins.

Though our group has no true leader, I am something of the unspoken caretaker. It is not that I'm smarter than them. It's just that I like to know what is going to happen a few moments before it does. I like to know that I will eat, that I will have a safe place to sleep before I am famished, before I am exhausted. That's why I'm glad Maca lets me help with little chores: sweeping the cement floor of her *comedor*, washing dishes, cleaning fish when the catch comes in. But never helping serve the food. I'm far too ugly for that.

So I run up to Maca's shack. There are vegetables to be cut for soup. She gestures toward them without talking, her thick, brown arms jiggling as she shapes tortillas with her palms. Before the men stir, I am back with hot, fresh tortillas and a skirtful of fruit that is too ripe for Maca to serve to the *turistas.* But it is fine for vagabonds like us. And almost free. That's what the people say when they sell trinkets on the beach. "Almost free."

Fernando is up, behind the castle of rocks, when I return. I can hear the dull, flat splash of his piss against the cool, packed sand. He and Jacinto are originally from Spain, which explains their superior attitude. They've been traveling through Mexico for a year, in Mazunte for a month. On the road they met Marco, who is from Italy but stumbles nicely through Spanish. (He's the kindest of the three and sometimes holds me, whispers to me, caresses me, when the others are asleep and it is dark.)

Alida comes from Guatemala. She is little more than a child, really. Somehow, this fragile, delicate *rubia* (blonde) toppled across the border when her family in the Western Highlands had disappeared, which generally means that they were murdered. But Alida never likes to talk about it and we never ask questions. Sometimes there are nightmares but I never bring them up in the daylight hours. I just smooth her sweaty hair from her face, caress her, and wait until the bad dreams pass.

I am the only Mexican. I was born in Mexico City and hated it as far back as I can remember. Urban poverty is so much worse than rural poverty. Having rats is worse than having a dirt floor. Now I have no floor and it suits me fine. I heard about the Oaxacan Coast like most children hear of fairy tales: clean crescents of sand, turquoise waters, palm trees, coconut trees, bougainvillea exploding with color. Before I was old enough, I left home, stealing the few pesos for the sixteen-hour bus ride, eating nothing except what people gave me along the way.

How I survived is another story. Let's just say it was due to the kindness of strangers and others who weren't so kind. Maca gives me a bed or a hammock in the rainy season, but otherwise, I prefer sleeping under the stars. If you keep watching, you can see as many as seven or eight shooting stars in a night.

Until now, I've kept moving every few weeks or months. It's better that way. You don't get too attached. You don't get too hurt. I've been to just about every beach village along this coast. Puerto Angel, which is a fishing village; San Agustinillo;Playa Santa Cruz, near Huatulco; as well as Zipolite, which means "Dead People's Beach." It bears the name because of the nasty riptide that drowns at least 18 people each year. I've never gone as far north as Acapulco or Puerto Escondido, and I've never wanted to. If I don't see another high rise for as long as I live, it will be too soon.

We get a different brand of tourist here in Mazunte: young, European or American, traveling low-budget with backpacks. But even their idea of low-budget is a lot of money for us Mexicans. The minimum wage in Mexico City was just raised to 25 pesos a day. That's almost three American dollars at today's exchange rate. And these *turistas,* they can't seem to wait to take off their swimsuits. Maybe it's the comfort of knowing no one here; they can be naked, be drunk (the beer is less than a dollar a bottle and a good agave tequila, less than two a shot) to their heart's content. No one really cares.

I love strolling along the strand of beach, topless, watching their heads turn. Some days, there's a parade of cocks, most uncircumcised. I sway past, making sure to shake my hips in my thong bottom. The dicks rise, stiffen, stir. I try to have my best side toward them. My legs are strong, muscular, firm, my ass bouncy, my belly flat. My tits are a healthy size; they jiggle with a playful mind of their own. My nipples are thick and brown; they harden at the slightest ocean breeze. I wear my long, dark hair pulled back in a tail. But when they get to my face, I can see the disappointment melting their desire. Then pity.

There's a game I play, lying in the sand. Sometimes alone, sometimes with Alida, but mostly alone. On my back, with my legs spread, I shield out the sun with a straw hat from eyes to mouth. They think I'm asleep, only I'm watching through the narrow slats of straw. I watch them watching me. I watch their pricks grow thick and wooden, purple-tipped, until there is nothing for them to do but stroke. The beach is usually empty, so this is easy, or else it isn't difficult to find a private cranny in the rock which serves as a vantage point to view the soft spot between my thighs.

There are all sorts of different styles. Sometimes a man prefers his dry fist, lingering at his cockhead with fleeting fingertips. Other times, he discreetly spits into his palm and coats his rod with his own fluid. Once I was close enough to smell the coconut suntan oil the man used. The scent seemed to grow stronger the longer he rubbed. I liked that; it made me hot and wet. If I feel like it, I'll pretend to adjust the band of my bikini bottoms, and in doing so, I'll give a peek of my pretty bush. But this time I felt especially charitable—and aroused. I slid off my thong completely.

I felt my pussy lips unfurl as I positioned myself so he could see better. Coconut Man stroked even harder and faster. I didn't touch my slit; the steady wind was doing a fine job of teasing me. I could feel the wetness slithering down the crack of my ass and knew my cunt was glistening, glowing in the noonday sun. (My best feature, I think, but Marco will tell you otherwise. "It's your eyes," he says surely. And Alida agrees.)

Coconut Man cupped his balls in his left hand and continued jerking himself off with his right. I tried a new trick, tensing and releasing my pubic muscles in an even rhythm. Alida swore a woman could cum this way, no hands, but I had my doubts. Coconut Man's dickhead was a deep red. His fist moved at a frantic pace while I throbbed and bobbed, tensed and released. My dribble of cream became thicker when all of a sudden, I felt lighter, floating, tingling. Once Fernando so delicately told me, "Ugly girls cum easier than the beautiful ones because there are so few chances."

I opened my eyes to see Coconut Man releasing streamers of sperm into the sunny air. Two, three, four jets until they subsided to a trickle. I heard a Midwestern voice calling, "Billy! Bill!" His chubby wife in a terrycloth jumpsuit, no doubt. In an instant, Coconut Man's trunks were up and he was gone. I couldn't resist visiting the spot where he'd just stood. His pools of jizm had already soaked into the sand without even a damp trace. And wedged between the rock was a crisp one hundred peso note. With the current 9.3 exchange rate, that was a little more than nine dollars. It would buy us a feast. And did.

Maca's tortillas are still warm, snugly wrapped in her cloth napkin. Jacinto is already up, preparing the rest of our breakfast. A fisherman he knew gave him a large *atún* which he has already split at the spine and flattened between two screens. A small, smoky fire threatens to go out beneath it. "More wood?" I suggest.

"Less wood, more time, better taste," he mutters knowingly.

Alida shakes the sand from her big, checkered poncho and prepares our picnic table. We crouch around her, nibbling on fruit until Jacinto places the tuna reverently on a few sheets of *The News*. "It tastes better on an English-language paper," he jokes as he squeezes lime onto the flesh. Though we are all very hungry, we are all polite, breaking off small pieces of fish with our hands, wrapping them in tortilla shells, licking our fingertips. I make sure to turn my head slightly, for I am very self-conscious when I eat, even among friends.

You see, I have a deformity. A hairlip for which I had surgery when I was very young, thanks to a charity organization. Hairlips are supposedly more common in Latin American countries than anywhere else in the world. No one knows why. It isn't that terrible, really, just a thin line which makes one side of my mouth curl upwards. It's more noticeable when I smile, so I try not to. But Alida says the crease feels wonderful on her mons, different than anyone else's mouth. And Marco agrees. The fold gives an extra sensation to his prick. He says he knows it's me, even in the dark. But perhaps it feels different because I try harder, because I know I'm... not right.

The fish is delicious, almost raw, ruby red like the Coconut Man's glans. "Almost as tasty as you," Alida whispers into my ear. We lick our fingers and pick at the flesh until there is nothing left but bone and skin. At moments like this, it's a decent life and we're all content, even Jacinto and Fernando, who are almost never happy.

For the rest of the day, we scatter. I bring the tortilla cloth back to Maca and help her with the afternoon chores. Alida goes to the hut of a German artist she is to pose for. Lars fancies himself a Gauguin but he really isn't very talented. Marco strums his guitar, singing Eric Clapton with a heavy accent. Maybe onlookers will throw coins into his guitar case, maybe not, but he plays just the same. Jacinto and Fernando toss worn, chipped Indian clubs back and forth between them, juggling absentmindedly, aloofly, seemingly unaware of the tourists who gather and observe.

Soon it is night. Dinner is warm leftovers from Maca's kitchen: *huachinango* (red snapper), *arroz,* and two brown-flecked *aguacates* which we mash into guacamole. A portion of the day's tips buys three Coronas, which we share. Only Marco and Alida will drink from mine, but I'm used to that by now.

When the fire dies out, the air is a uniform shade of black lit only by the phosphorescence of the sea. It's a light that suit me fine. Then it begins. Hands reaching out, searching, finding. Alida and I are passed around willingly, gladly, like a cool drink of cerveza. We enjoy the feel of knowing hands on our bodies, parting, probing, tasting. To be wanted, desired, cherished—if only for the brief time it takes for an erection to grow, burst, and fade—is good. At least it is something. It is better than emptiness, loneliness. But almost anything is.

Jacinto climbs on top of me. Chili pepper bites on my neck, but never on my mouth. "Even you look pretty in this light," he says into the pitch blackness. I tear at his nipples, twisting them. I know he likes this, but when I put my mouth on it, he tries to wrench free. But my cunt feels too wet, too tight for him to pull out and leave. So I watch his shadow writhe uncomfortably while the dark ribbons of Alida, Marco, and Fernando wrestle nearby like a magnificent three-headed beast. On her knees, she takes one in her pussy while the other pokes into her face. I'm not certain which is which, or where, but it doesn't matter anyway.

I grasp Jacinto's balls a little too roughly and feel them shrink, becoming sucked up inside of him. He is very close now. I balance on my elbows, taking him in deeper, rising, surging, finally cumming around the shaft of a man who almost despises me, but that's fine, because I don't like him very much either. The other three move closer. There is a wave of hands, mouth, teeth biting. Jacinto pulls out and spasms onto my belly. I reach out and tweak Alida's clit, swollen and hanging down like a ripe fruit on a branch, until she shudders, dampening my hand. Like dominoes, Marco and Fernando follow.

Sleep is always easier under the stars, once the mosquitoes stop. I lay down alone, but soon I hear Alida thrashing and whimpering. Another nightmare she can't talk about. She skitters across the sand to my side, sobbing softly and half-awake. I curl around her back like a teaspoon.

When I have almost drifted off, I feel a man's rough, whiskered face beside my own. "Ah, Maria," Marco tells me in a voice heavy with *cervezas* and shooting stars, "The most beautiful things about you can't be seen with the eyes." He makes himself comfortable behind me, hugs me close, kisses the back of my neck. Alida snuggles against my chest. Three spoons in a drawer now.

I remember a song from a very long time ago, from before I was born. "The best things in life are free," it said. But nothing is truly free. "Almost free," I concede. And I smile in the darkness so no one can see. No one but me.

Ariel Hart is the pseudonym of a freelance writer who was born and ill-bred in Brooklyn, New York. Her numerous works of adult fiction, nonfiction, and X-rated screenplays have graced porn shops across the U.S. and have been translated into German, Japanese, and "Australian." Pushing 40, she is happily married and has a newborn son.

Miss Jackson If You're Nasty

R.T. Bledsoe

This is what Janet Jackson songs do to me. Whenever I hear one—"Control," say, or "Miss You Much," or most spectacularly "Nasty Boys"—I think of Kurt.

This was in that fuzzy part of the mid-eighties that we remember, if we remember them at all, more by the music we listened to than by anything concrete that happened. The Challenger exploding. Iran-Contra hearings. Rock Hudson dying from AIDS. What were these things? But U2 played at Red Rocks, and Madonna taught us to vogue, and even Bruce Springsteen gave us a song that had us all out on the floor; and despite all this—or maybe because of it—in That Mid-Decade of Our Lord, the 1980s, and especially that winter, Janet Jackson was God, and I looked like Janet, only white and blond, I remember Kurt.

He was beautiful. Tall. Built like a clay god. Frizzy golden hair and beard that lit up his head like it was on fire. Strong and tanned. In a phrase I'd heard often in those years, I knew he was "too beautiful for me." But that was all right. No one was supposed to last back then.

Even now I miss him much. We'd met through the campus GAYLA group, one of those Pride-type organizations that littered the cultural landscape like post-Stonewall confetti. I'd become secretary, even though the president of that time had decreed, in her big, blowzy, not-to-be-argued-with way, "there are no bisexuals here." "Bisexuals," she pointed out on more than one occasion, "are confused." I didn't point out that her own lover was prone to cross the line once or twice. Often with one of us who wasn't there. Only because I was nice did I fail to say anything. And because I wanted to stick around. My sexuality wasn't ambiguous. Like art and pornography, I knew what I liked, and I knew it when I saw it.

At any rate, Kurt made eyes with me. I think it was our shared blondness that caught his eye. Most of our compatriots were dark and looked like they didn't get outside often enough. After he'd hung around the group a few meetings, I approached him and asked if he'd like to go dancing. I left it open that there might be other people involved, just so plans could change and no one (read: me) would feel rejected. He said he'd love to and gave me one of those shy but bold looks that made me understand immediately that anyone who was with us would only be deadwood.

We went to Prime Time, the only gay disco in the area. It was about fifteen minutes south of town, and was packed every night except Thursdays. I've never been certain why Thursday was the day people in upstate New York neglected their libidos, except it may have had something to do with Friday being payday. We danced the hump bump to Our Miss Janet. The dance floor was dark and hazy with sweat, smoke, and desire. Above us, on giant screens that played porn, leather boys swallowed cocks the size of tree stumps.

I was only the second man, Kurt admitted during a lull in the music, that he'd dated. This didn't come out as straightforward as I'm making it sound, but I understood him. He was still getting, so to speak, the hang of it. So I kissed him. His tongue swooped around my mouth like a bottom-feeding fish. But he was so beautiful and tasted so good—like a plum, like rum-saturated raisins—that I just wanted all of him. There's that place you reach just beyond horniness to a state somewhere to the left of wantonness. The odor of smoke and the night is a part of it, a sensual memory-prick that touches you at the base of your skull and provides the prick-hole through which everything else comes rushing in.

We got into his car and kissed awhile. Suddenly all I wanted was to be alone and naked with him. But what Our Miss Janet taught us in those days is that, more importantly than *being* in control, one must *have* control. My first name ain't "baby" nor was I too nasty a boy. But I held Kurt's face between my hands and sucked on his tongue until his mouth was fully inside mine.

We broke a lot of speed laws and some of the laws of the state of Georgia in the rush back to my apartment. I never locked my door back then. I tugged it open with one hand, holding Kurt's ass in a deathgrip with the other and my face nuzzled into his strong, manly-smelling throat, and inside, watching television in the dark, was Caprice.

Caprice was a small woman I dated sometimes. She was Mexican-born, had taken her name during her years in Manhattan, where it was the word most often used to describe her, and had entered my life at the local Laundromat. We had been the only patrons there one evening, and after she'd put her clothes and money into a machine she sat next to where I was reading a magazine, drew her long, brown, bare legs under her and asked how I'd been. Like we hadn't seen each other in a couple days. Her eyes were large and black and her smile was an electric cattle prod. We sat on the bench all afternoon, talking, and when our clothes were done and folded we went to her place and I massaged her bare back with patchouli oil until she rolled over. She was a tiny woman, two years older than me, delicate and frail as a fairy. But she fucked like a starving lion and I left there exhausted, but exhilarated for having done it with someone whose very skin gave off the pungency of myrrh.

Caprice was always welcome at my place. But another time would have been better. All I wanted was Kurt's mouth back on mine and my hands exploring topographically the landscape his body would make on my bed.

I said to her, something obviously going on in my voice, "What are you doing here?"

Caprice looked up at me, her dark, scrubbed little face moving from me to Kurt and back again. She absolutely glowed in the light of the television. "I'm having some trouble. You know, with Mohammed." This guy she'd started dating regularly. I'd met him once. A big, burly man. Forearms like iron pipes. "I was hoping I could talk to you about it. Get, you know, your perspective."

Like I didn't have enough going on. Like what I wanted right then was this *chica* with breasts like cola nuts and smelling of dark spices sitting on my living room floor watching the religious channel with the sound turned off. My perspective was that I wanted to hump Kurt like a crazed crawfish. What I was getting was an escapade on my living room floor.

I thought to myself *I am in control*. "Now," I said. "Now is not a good time."

We stood there staring at one other. A preacher with palsy was on the screen. He flashed across Caprice and Kurt's faces, his contorted face made almost normal by spreading across them, like that kid in the movie *Mask* when he finds the funhouse mirror.

Kurt solved the situation. He said, "You're busy. I'll come back later."

I said to him, "Be sure of it." At the door I gave him a kiss that must have played to Caprice, watching from the dark, like a pair of dancing eels.

I closed the door and Caprice said, half-jokingly, "I thought he'd never leave."

I said, "Oh, this better be good."

I sat on the floor next to her while she jabbered about Mohammed-this and Mohammed-that, never once coming to the point. The palsied preacher gave way to Jack van Impe, and with the sound off, he was bearable and funny rather than scary. I glanced at Caprice every few minutes, as if to assure her I was listening. But she wasn't even looking at me. She stared at the television and went on mouthing her troubles as if she were explaining herself to the Grand Inquisitor of Trinity Broadcasting.

Finally there was a break in her chatter and I glanced at her. Now she was looking at me. She expected a solution. My solution was that she shouldn't have come by in the first place, but I didn't say that. My solution was that she deal with it on her own. My solution was that she should find someone else to burden with her problems.

But that's not the way I put it. The way I put it was, "Why are you telling me all this?"

Caprice wasn't dumb. Just self-indulgent. She didn't fail to catch the tone in my voice. She said, as if to cover herself, "Oh I get it. You were going to fuck that guy. Okay, listen, I'll go. But first, can you go down on me? I really like that."

I stared at her a little longer. Not certain she'd said what I'd heard. It wasn't a request I was expecting.

I meant to say, "Listen, I wanted something hot thick and male in my mouth tonight, and you've gone and ruined that, so I'd just like you and your sweet-smelling *Chicana* vagina gone before he gets back"; but when I opened my mouth, all that came out was, "Sure."

While Caprice and I had been sleeping together for a couple months by then, she'd only recently discovered a fondness for oral sex. And that is like potato chips to me—no one can eat just one. When we eventually stopped sleeping together—because back then you always eventually stopped sleeping with someone—she'd vanished from my life lingeringly, like the odor of alcohol and cigarettes the morning after. But for now she was the hot, iron-bar smell of sandalwood incense the moment after you light it. Caprice left the television on with the sound off and stood up to shuck off her jeans and panties. She sat back on the floor and spread her legs, resting her head against the chair.

Caprice was two years older than me but built like a teenager. Her pubic hair was sparse and downy. Her pussy always smelled of vegetables or fruits. Sucking her was like sucking the water after a drenching rain in a garden.

I nibbled the light brown hairless thighs I'd first noticed about her. I was prepared to take my time, work my way up and inside. But Caprice said, "Hurry up, your friend will be back soon." She grabbed my face with both little hands and rubbed me against her lips. The hair parted and was already soaked—she'd probably been touching herself before I'd come home—and soon my face was wet like I'd been showering. Her pussy was that wrinkled, distended shape of peach skin after the meat has dried and shrunk.

She said some nice things to me, about my eyes and about my lips and about the way I used my tongue, and brushed the hair back on my forehead. I stuck out my tongue and lapped clockwise. Counterclockwise. Around and around, taking special care to lick the soft nubbin surrounding her clit. Chasing the orgasm I wanted suddenly to give her.

She tasted like lemons, as if she'd sprayed some juice there. The taste made me pucker. My mouth pursed around my tongue, which became a probe. Licking and tasting and lapping. All of it delightful. The taste of her warm and heady.

Caprice didn't last long. When she came, her legs stood straight out and shook, and she held my face so deeply into her that I was on the verge of developing gills before she let go. I came up for air, my part of the bargain done. I felt a tiny pang of regret, wanting suddenly for it not to end, wanting to take her into the bedroom and play with her all night, delighting in that fleshy female funk.

But I had something else, hot and fleshy on its own, returning. And Kurt was not expecting Caprice to still be there.

With a small sigh, but the knowledge I was doing the right thing, I backed away from her pussy. The better so she could get up, put her panties back on, and go.

Caprice had other plans.

She said, "I need more than this." In a better, less horny world, I'd have seen it coming. She kissed me until I was pressed backwards to the floor. She yanked off my jeans. I didn't fight much.

Her tiny hand clamped around my penis and she was so wet that all she needed to do was touch me to those lips and I slipped inside until she was full of me. Caprice bounced up and down on me for a minute or two. I watched the door the whole time, certain Kurt would walk in any minute and then back out of my life forever. But he didn't. And when Caprice came, groaning and calling me "darling" and "love," I said, "This has been really nice, and I'd love you to stay, but I *am* expecting company."

Caprice said, "Of course." She stood on shaky legs and slipped back into her panties and jeans and was out the door before I had even gone soft.

I lay on the floor in a daze. I wasn't entirely certain the last half hour had really happened, but the delight I took in my own funk was real enough. The religious channel had started broadcasting Dale Rogers. I wondered, vaguely, if television were a two-way street, would Dale have turned off Caprice and me?

But Kurt was unlikely to appreciate the odor and tang of Caprice on me, so I popped the television off and rushed into the shower. I came back out, clean and sweet-smelling, and sat reading on the floor until there was a knock at the door.

Kurt came in and said, "Did you two settle everything?"

I said, "Sure."

It was a little after one o'clock now. I said, "Did you want anything to eat?"

And he said, "Just you." (Yeah, I know; but he was still getting the hang of it all and the comment touched me nonetheless.) He drew me up until I was standing with him. His tongue slipped into my mouth like vinyl into a slipcase. I hugged him and ran my hands under his shirt, all over his back. Without breaking his liplock, he pressed my arms until my fingers rested on his jeans, and then they were at the front and rubbing an increasingly large hard-on.

We made a pile of discarded clothing all the way to the bed. It was winter, and dark by now, but the moon was out and lit the bedroom just enough to make him visible against my sheets. Light against light. When I was naked, and kneeling next to him, he twisted my penis in his fist. It felt nice, but it certainly wasn't about to get me off. I said, "Let me show you what I like."

I started out kissing his mouth. It was soft and warm. I moved to his face, and then the ringlets around his ears. The whole effect like kissing cotton candy. My hands made their way to his ribs and I sucked his nipples.

My fingers found his erection. It already had the heft and weight of a block of wood. Kurt wasn't very large, which was fine, as I'm not too crazy about size—all that meat and no potatoes—but he was thick and hard. Holding him was like holding a fish, with that strange uncertainty between holding him so loosely you might let him go, or so tightly you might crush him.

Kurt's body was covered with a fine golden halo, and making love with him was like making love with an ewok. I put my tongue in his belly button. That made him laugh. Then I shifted downward, and the chuckle became something guttural in his throat. He pulsed in my hand.

I put him in my mouth. Drew him in. Held him there. Let him slip out until the spongy tip brushed my upper lip. Then swallowed him whole. Kurt made contented baby noises and ran his hands through my hair, around my eyes, everywhere he could touch. He said, "I want to do this to you," but I said, "Not yet. I haven't finished yet."

I swooped up and down. Long lazy strokes that, in my euphoria, could have lasted days. His balls were soft against my palm. He smelled of nutmeg and sweat. When his hips started to buck, I dropped him out of my mouth but kept stroking him. Harder. Now gentler. I crawled up his body until I found his mouth again. We tongued like guppies, both our eyes closed, my fist around his cock, his hands going everywhere, unsure what to do, his hips making the bedsprings squeak.

Then Kurt made a low moaning sound in my mouth and his tongue was still; and then quickly, like a minnow, it was licking every crevice it could reach. He came in a slow, crazy arc that was yellow and gold in the moonlight. I saw it spew up and out and onto his belly, which quivered. He pulled me onto his chest and kissed me and said some things I couldn't hear but knew anyway. I felt his come slathered across his belly and then across mine, mixed, getting it in my navel where it would condense like glue.

The room smelled of patchouli and raw meat. We spent that night curled into one another like tender ferns. In the morning he tried with all his might to make me come. And I did. Just to please him.

Zigzagging the country grown tiresome, R. T. Bledsoe now makes his home in a western Wisconsin town of 500, not counting eagles, bears, and trout. He's joined by his wife, two dogs, and a cat. His work appears in a number of journals, and he's published two long-out-of-print books. His erotica—among which are the novels-in-progress Sally Can't Dance *and* The Last Small, Good God*—appears regularly.*

Triple Dance

Raven Kaldera

"It's no use," I said to Ian. "She wouldn't be interested. I know she wouldn't." I flopped into our battered beanbag chair, dejection in every line of my body. Okay, so I was overacting a little. Ian knows that I get over things quicker when I'm allowed to be melodramatic.

"How do you know?" he asked me from the depths of the refrigerator. "Hey, can I have the last of the Havarti?"

"Only if you split it with me. No, seriously," I moaned, "I've seen the guys she goes out with. They're nothing like me."

"That's because there is no one like you," Ian said. I could hear him smiling into the luncheon meats. Another time I would have been filled with warmth, but I was too determined to stay with my black mood.

"Don't patronize me," I grumbled.

"Would I do that?" he chuckled. "So how are they all that different from you? Are they rich or something?"

"Nope. It's not like she's a golddigger. I mean, with legs like that, you'd think she could attract a millionaire, but..." I shook my head. "No, they're all tall, for one thing. She doesn't do short guys. Her kind never does.... Always obsessed with making themselves feel tiny and petite. And they're craggy, and older. And frequently domineering. Goddamned cliché."

"You can be pretty domineering yourself, sometimes," Ian pointed out, rather diplomatically, I thought.

"Yeah, but it'd never work. She doesn't see me that way. She'd like you, though," I said. "You're tall enough."

He came over to my chair and put a companionable hand on my shoulder. "You know I'd switch bodies with you for a few days if I could," he said compassionately.

It was something he'd said many times before, and it finally broke through my gloom enough to give me that warm feeling. Bless Ian for the way he keeps on trying. "Thank you, love." I covered his hand with mine.

He squatted down next to my chair and popped a piece of Havarti in my mouth. "So maybe I'll go track her down," he said in a conspiratorial whisper, "and entice her back here to the apartment, and tie her to the bed so that you can make your grand entrance and do unspeakable things to her tender flesh." He hunched over and gave me an exaggerated leer. "I am your devoted if perverted servant, O master! Give me the word, and I'll abduct the fair maiden for our disgusting experiments in human depravity."

I spluttered with laughter around the cheese in spite of myself. Ian could always break me up with the Igor imitation. "Maybe I'll take you up on that," I giggled.

The object of my unrequited lusts was a co-worker named Shelley, the new bookkeeper at our magazine headquarters. She'd sailed into the office with résumé in hand one day, and after talking to her for five minutes, I knew I'd pull every string I could with the boss to get her into the company. It wasn't just that she was six feet tall and had legs to die for, pert little tits, and an ass I'd love to get a closer look at; and it wasn't just that she had a good résumé. It was also that I was tired of being the only transgendered person in the company.

Okay, so one could call it a bit of nepotism. It'd hoisted me good by my own petard, though. Getting her into the company had been the easy part. Working with her day after day, watching her walk past in her conservative suit tops over short skirts, hearing her talk about her dates with the big, ugly guys she dated... and figuring out, right quickly, that she never showed the slightest bit of interest in me; that was the hard part.

Ian stood up. "I have to piss," he said. "Do you want to..." He trailed off, his voice inviting. I grinned in spite of myself.

"Okay," I said getting up and stretching, and following him to the bathroom. We have this little ritual that Ian knows I like. When he pisses, he lets me hold it for him. That way I can pretend it's mine for a moment. He won't let me write my name with it, though.

That night, I thought about Shelley while Ian was eating me, his head between my legs as he pulled my testosterone-enlarged clit from its foreskin and sucked on it until I writhed and yelped. I came, but it was the sort of quick, desperate come that just takes the edge off. Ian sat up, grinning at me. "You wanna pitch or catch?" he asked.

I thought about it, visions of Shelley bent over her desk at work while I rammed into her from behind dancing in my head. I wondered if she'd had a vaginoplasty, or still had a cock. I wondered what she'd think about my ball-less, almost dickless crotch; wondered if she'd been a gay man before and was still in love with dick on her lovers. "Catch, I guess," I said. "Then I'll pitch afterwards, if you're still up to it."

"I can be, if I don't blow off right away," he said, and lay down next to me. I rolled onto my side and felt him press up against me, molding the curve of his belly to my back and ass. His hard cock pushed at my thighs as he put his arms around me, holding me tight to him, stroking my newly furry chest. The scars from my mastectomy no longer ached, just felt a little strange. "How do you want it?" he asked.

"In the ass," I whispered, wiggling against him. "Grab the lube." I used to hate assfucking, but somehow testosterone woke my asshole up. It was as if I'd gained a phantom prostate. Ian got his hand greasy and slid a finger into me; I groaned and pressed backwards into it. Ian loved my ass; he'd often said that the two things he loved most on human beings were the broad, muscular shoulders and chests of men who worked out, and large, round women's butts. I was his perfect human being, he said. He couldn't know how grateful I was to have found him.

"You're thinking about her, aren't you?" he whispered mischievously into my ear as his finger moved gently in and out of me. I'd actually stopped thinking about her by that time, but his words brought back a flush of guilty memory and I drew in my breath quickly. "I thought so," he chuckled. "Thinking about her in a tight black leather miniskirt? Or maybe just stockings and a garter belt, hmmm?" He added another finger.

"The latter," I gasped, writhing. "Definitely the latter."

"Were you imagining her on her knees in front of you, sucking your biggest cock?" he murmured. "You could grab her by the back of the head and slam it all the way down her throat; I'll bet she'd be able to take it. I'll bet she'd bend over, after you'd come in her mouth, and spread her cheeks with her hands for you." Another finger worked its way in.

"She'd better," I moaned, getting into his fantasy. "She'd damn well better bend over for me. Fuck me, babe. I'm loose enough now." I wanted him inside me, in a way I never had when I'd been a girl. I'd hated penetration then; now I couldn't wait for it. His fingers pulled out and the tip of a greased cock pushed against my pulsing asshole.

"I know you, Jack," he whispered. "You'd make her stay that way the whole time, on her knees with her hands spreading those perfect ass cheeks, while you fucked her unmercifully." The head of his cock passed my sphincter and then he was in, moving back and forth slowly. He was trying to keep himself from coming, I could tell. I grabbed my own dick with my thumb and two fingers and started jerking it off; it never took long for me to come.

"You'd slam into her ass until you drove her face into the mattress," he hissed in my ear. "You'd call her a slut, make her beg you to fuck her even harder. Make her say how much she loved it, how you were a better fuck than all those big ugly goombahs. Make her come all over the bed." As he said it, I came, grunting and humping him, contracting around his cock, yanking my own for all it was worth. He held me tightly as I strained through the long seconds of my orgasm—since my clit had grown, orgasms were about twice as long as they had been—and then gently pulled his still-hard organ out of me.

I let myself lie, limply, in his arms until my breathing had quieted, and then I said, "Nice fantasy."

"Never say never," he chuckled in my ear.

"You need to come," I commented, feeling the wet trace of his cock against my sticky buttock. "Feel like getting back what you gave out?"

"I've been wanting it all day," he groaned, a touch of the melodramatic queen in his voice. Sometimes Ian's such a girl. I laughed and got up stiffly, stretching my muscles and grabbing a fallen towel to wipe off some of the stickiness. By the time I dug out my harness and got it on, the rubber cock jutting out from my pubic mound, he was already on his hands and knees with his lubed ass facing me.

"Hey," I said, running my hand up and down the rubber shaft and feeling how the base of it rubbed my still-swollen dick. "Get over here and suck this, boy." I stepped up to the edge of the bed and Ian turned around obediently. "Get it good and wet, 'cause that's all it's getting when it goes up your ass," I ordered. Actually, I had every intention of lubing it till it dripped, but I knew the thought would excite Ian. He swallowed it up to the hilt, moaning until his breathing was cut off by its length, and pumped his hips so that his swollen cock thrust against the air.

I grabbed his head, fucking his face with the cock—I knew from his comments about Shelley that he was telling me, sideways, what he wanted. "Suck it, boy," I snarled at him. "Eat my dick. You want it just as much as that bitch-slut, don't you? Maybe I'll have the two of you, down on your knees, eating each other in a 69 while I just walk around you, sticking my cock in whatever hole I like." I pulled out and slapped him across the face with it. "You'd like that, wouldn't you?"

"Yes, sir," he gasped. "Please fuck me, sir!"

"Turn around," I ordered, and he scrambled to obey with an alacrity that made me smile. When Ian got fuck-hungry, there was no denying him. I climbed onto the bed and knelt between his spread legs, adding more lube to my cock and his crack. "Spread your ass and beg for it," I said, feeling mean and nasty. "Imagine Shelley's right here, wet and ready. Show her that you're even more of a slut than she is." I slapped his ass and he reached back, spreading his furry cheeks for me, making himself open and vulnerable. Shelley, I thought, if you only knew how your unwitting presence is making sex hotter for a couple of fags.... I guided my wet cock into his hole, slowly, leaning into it as he moaned.

Then I started to fuck him in earnest, ramming it home. "Hump it, boy!" I hissed at him. "Hump it with your ass. Make love to it. Show me how much you love my cock!" It had always been hard for me to talk dirty during sex when I'd been a girl, even though I loved it. Testosterone had loosened my tongue. Having a big furry hunk impaled on my strap-on helped, too. Ian growled and shoved backwards, banging into me; I grabbed his hips to keep my balance and pounded him the way I know he likes it. I imagined Shelley there next to us, squirming belly-down on the bed, rubbing herself against the sheets. Ian's eyes were tight shut as he groaned and jerked himself off, but I wondered if he was imagining the same thing.

The next morning I had two surprises, one pleasant and one a bit unnerving. Ian stopped in at lunchtime to see me, bringing me a Coke and a lemon pepper chicken sandwich from Au Bon Pain. It wasn't the usual thing for him to do, but I was happy to see him. Half an hour later, though, when I passed the front window, I saw him talking to Shelley in front of the building. Their heads were bent close together and I could tell she was laughing at something he was saying. He took something from her and pocketed it, and then waved a goodbye as he walked off.

"What did she give you?" I asked him as soon as I got home.

"Her email address," he said, busily stir-frying the chicken and vegetables.

"She just gave it to you?" I was incredulous. "Why did she just suddenly decide to do that?"

"I asked her. Do you think we should put red pepper in this, or just keep it meat and greens?" His large hands moved deftly as he chopped the onion Japanese style. I blinked several times.

"You just asked her, and she gave it to you? Ian, I've worked with her for three months and I don't have her email!"

"Did you ask her?" he pointed out with infuriating logic. When I didn't reply, just stood there with crimson cheeks, he reached over and patted me on the shoulder. "I keep forgetting you were raised a girl. Guys just learn to go up to someone and make the first move. You learn, or you're out of luck. Too many girls just expect to be approached, even in this day and age, because it's easier, and if they can get away with it, they'll try." He grinned. "That's why it's so much easier to be a fag, right?"

I shifted my weight from foot to foot. "So, uh, what did you think of her?" I asked tentatively.

"You were right; she is pretty." He rummaged through the cupboards looking for spices. "Nice legs."

My heart sank a little more. I love Ian, but I think I'd kill him if he ended up sleeping with someone I wanted that badly when she wouldn't even consider me. I don't know if I could touch his flesh without anger after that, knowing that he could get what I wanted by virtue of his factory-equipped body. "Are you... are you interested?" I asked quietly.

Ian shrugged. "Dunno. She certainly was. Here, this is finished. Get yourself a plate."

My ears buzzed with blood as I fetched dishes from the shelves. Maybe it hadn't been such a great idea to bring her into our lovemaking, even in fantasy. What if I came home and found them going at it? Normally Ian and I fucked other people occasionally and it was okay, but we always tended not to want the same people. I was not at all sure about my ability to sit in the next room and watch TV while the two most attractive people in my life got it on noisily on the other side of the wall.

I'm sure Ian's stir-fry was delicious, but it sat like lumps of salt in my mouth and my throat refused to swallow.

We didn't bring it up over the next few days, although I did see Shelley's name flash by on one of Ian's emails. It was an especially arduous week at work, and the hours crawled by that Friday. Shelley came up and leaned over the edge of my desk, grinning at me. "Got an exciting weekend coming up?" she asked as I shook out my coat and wrapped my scarf around my neck.

"Not particularly," I said, tongue-tied as I always was around her. I looked at her long pale hands, perfectly manicured rose nails tapping against the doorway. I didn't suppose she'd ever be amenable to cutting even one hand's worth of them short, for putting inside someone. No, they were straight girl's hands, meant to impress conservative older men.

"Well," she said, winking at me, "I do." Then she swept out.

It wasn't exactly what I needed to hear ringing in my ears as I took the bus home. I stopped off at the bookstore, but didn't find anything I could buy for the change in my pockets. Finally, feeling gray and depressed, I made my way to our apartment.

There were voices in the bedroom, and I froze. One was Ian's, and one was... Before I could figure out if my worst fears were true, he came out of the bedroom and saw me, his face lighting up into a big grin. "Jack! You're home!" he sang, pulling me into a bear hug. "I've got a present for you, honey. I worked hard to get it, and I hope you appreciate it."

"A present?" The last time he'd bought me something it had been the miniature crossbow that he'd wanted but hadn't felt justified in spending the money on.

"Come on, get your coat off, hurry up!" He helped me unwind my layers, pulled my boots off, and dragged me into the bedroom. The lights were dimmer in there, and I had to blink to make out the figure sitting on the bed, but then my eyes adjusted and I gulped.

Shelley was sitting on our bed, wearing nothing but a shiny purple bra and panties, and sheer stockings. "Hi, Jack," she said, "Told you I had a big weekend planned." Her husky voice made me instantly hard, but my stomach roiled in confusion and I turned to Ian, my mouth dropping open like a fish.

"I told Shelley how you felt about her, and she was very responsive," he grinned. "So I thought I'd arrange this little get-together for us. You are still interested, right?"

"You should have told me you liked me, Jack!" Shelley chided. "I'd have crawled into your pants that first day if I'd known, but I thought you were just a fag, that you only liked guys and I had no chance. If I'd known you were bisexual, too..."

I let out a shaky laugh. "That's one of the problems with being bisexual. Everyone thinks you're whatever your primary relationship is." I felt like collapsing with relief; my knees shook and I sat down on the bed. Shelley stretched like a cat and made a purring sound, rubbing her head of dark curls against my thigh.

"You and Ian still have all your clothes on," she crooned. "It's not fair. I want to touch you, touch you both." She wriggled her haunches and I stroked her hair, amazed at her forwardness. It was as soft as I'd imagined.

Ian was shedding his clothes. I felt a little nervous about removing mine, but then somehow Shelley had her head on my thighs and was undoing my fly. Her fingers made contact with the gel-filled pants-stuffer in my underwear and looked up at me curiously. I flushed and stood, spilling her off my lap. "It's prosthetic," I said, and stripped off my clothing, not looking at her. The small bundle of rubber and gel plopped to the floor with my underwear. "This is what's real," I said, steeling myself for whatever her reaction might be. I put one knee on the edge of the bed and spread my upper labia, showing her my clit. It was still hard for her, as if it was blithely unaware of the mental turmoil the rest of me was going through.

"Oh," she said, staring in fascination at my crotch. "Looks like it'd be real fun to suck." She flashed a grin at me, and I relaxed. I felt Ian coming up behind me, his naked chest pressing against my back, and he reached around my bent leg to grab my dick at the base and yank on it. "He likes having it pulled, like this," he informed Shelley solemnly, while I could only gasp, half-paralyzed with the sensation. Ian always knew just how to take me apart.

After a moment I pushed his hand away; it felt great, but I wasn't ready to be turned into a bowl of Jello yet. I wanted to concentrate on Stephanie, who was unsnapping her bra, revealing dainty conical tits, like those of a twelve-year-old girl. Then she slid off her panties and looked me in the eye, her legs clenched together in a last modest gesture. "This is what's real for me, too," she said, and spread her thighs.

Her pale form was scattered with freckles in the dim light. Below her small, soft dangling cock, there was only a smooth expanse of wrinkled skin, surprisingly labia-like, tight to the curve of her pelvic bone. "I had an orchiectomy two years ago," she said softly. "That means my testicles are gone. I'd like to get a box installed someday, but it's so expensive..." She trailed off and I looked up to see her flaming cheeks. My heart melted and I took her in my arms.

"You're beautiful," I told her, forgetting my own worries in reassuring her. "Believe me, I know what it's like." I brought her hand to my chest, let her fingers trace my mastectomy scars. Her skin felt very soft against mine.

She smiled and hid her face in my shoulder. "I call it my clit on a stick," she said, and we all chuckled.

Ian knelt almost reverently between her legs, stroked her empty scrotum with something like awe, and then looked up at me. "Sir," he asked, "May I?"

I could have kissed him for playing it that way, letting me know that I was in charge of this fuck. "Go ahead," I said, and he lowered his head to her crotch. He didn't go straight for her "clit on a stick", like I expected; instead he licked up and down, from her rosebud asshole to the base of her phallus, and she cried out in surprise and fell backwards onto the bed. I got off the bed and grabbed for my strap on; I don't think I've even gotten it onto my body quicker.

Shelley turned her head and saw my rubber cock just inches away from it, and her eyes lit up. I climbed back up on the bed and lowered it into her lipsticked mouth while Ian slurped between her legs, where her vulva would have been. She took the whole thing down her throat, licking it showily. I got the distinct feeling that this was not the first strap-on she'd been face-to-face with, and grinned. "You been playing with butches or something, girl?" I teased her.

She pulled back and played with the tip of it with her tongue. "Or something," she said wickedly, and then sucked it back into her mouth again. I loved watching that red mouth eat my cock, and I might have stayed there like that for an hour if she hadn't suddenly made a surprised sound, her eyebrows going up like carefully plucked black arches. I looked around and saw that Ian had the lube and was carefully inserting a greased finger into her tiny pink asshole.

I'd actually wanted to fuck her, and had put the rubber cock on in the hopes of doing so, but I suddenly changed my mind. Ian had gone to all this trouble to get Shelley into my bed; he deserved first crack at her for the thoughtfulness of his gift. Besides, there'd be time for me later. I stripped off the harness and tossed it aside; then I climbed onto the bed and straddled her, holding down her wrists with my hands, my face inches from hers. "Look at me," I said. She opened her eyes, and I saw just a hint of fear in them, and in the way her lips trembled. "You're going to get fucked now," I said. "I'm going to ream your ass until you scream."

Shelley's eyes flicked down towards my crotch in surprise; I wasn't wearing the strap-on. I wouldn't have minded doing her with it, but I had something else in mind. I bared my teeth at her in a not-smile. "You think I don't have a live cock big enough for you, don't you?" She didn't reply, just looked at me, unsure. "But I do," I said. "I've got a six-foot fucking cock, and he belongs to me, and his name is Ian. He's mine, you understand? He's my cock, and if I tell him to fuck you till you scream, he'll do it, but it'll be me fucking you." I looked back over my shoulder to the tall man behind me, who was grinning from ear to ear. "Fuck the bitch, Ian," I said.

He grabbed her ankles and spread them in one smooth movement, letting them rest on his shoulders while he found her asshole with his cock. I felt her stiffen, felt her indrawn breath and how her jaw clenched, drank in the sobbing cry as he shoved his cockhead into her perfect ass. "She's tight, Jack," Ian said, in the voice that tells me he's reporting it all to me, letting me share his experience. "She's as tight as a virgin. Her sweet little asshole is clenching down around my cock. It'll take a while before I can work it all in." Beneath me, her body was jolted back and forth by his thrusts and she keened between her gritted teeth.

"Stop," I said, and he did, freezing in place. I took her chin and forced her to look at me. "Does it hurt too much?" I barked at her. Besides checking on her, I wanted to make sure she understood that I was in control, that I could stop or start the action at any time.

"Nnn-nno," she gasped. "I'm just getting used to it, that's all! Please! Don't stop!"

"Now, Ian," I said, and her body gave another jerk as he thrust again. I could feel his furred belly against my ass now.

"I'm all the way in, Jack," he said, and then pulled back. Shelley rolled her head on the pillow, eyes closed, and moaned. Ian thrust in again, and then started a regular rhythm, bouncing against my ass. I imagined it was really my cock shoving into her, making her body move. Making her hard. Yes, I could feel something else now, poking up against my pubic bone. My borrowed cock must have been doing its job.

I reached down between my legs for a moment and adjusted myself, opening my labia so they spread wide. It was exceedingly wet down there, wet and sloppy. I squatted lower so that my cunt rubbed against the long underside of her big curved clit, my phalloclit tracing its length back and forth. Her eyes flew open and met mine, surprised, but she started moving her hips in time to Ian's thrusts.

"Faster, Ian," I grunted. He obligingly speeded up his thrusts, making her clit rub against my little cock with a nice quick rhythm. I lowered my head and sucked on one of her tiny pink twelve-year-old nipples, and she yelled and bucked, and I came like a fireworks display.

As I lay cradled on her breasts, hyperventilating, I realized that Ian had slowed down to await further orders. "Keep going," I gasped. "But don't come till she does!" Then I levered myself off of Shelley's torso and turned around, looking at her lean, smoother pink-and-white body. Her hair was damp with sweat, and her damp form gleamed under the light. It made me realize that my dick was still hard.

(Sometimes it happens that way, especially within a few days after my shot. Early on, I had one period where I was hard for three days straight with no relief—it scared the hell out of me.) I reached down to grab it, yanking on it, and Shelley's gaze followed my hand, a smile on her face. "Since I had half the plumbing taken out," she whispered hoarsely between Ian's thrusts, "sometimes it takes me kind of a long time to come. But if you'd let me eat you, it might help." Her tongue snaked out and licked her cherry-red lips.

I didn't need a second invitation. Pulling her hair out of the way, I straddled her head and shoved my wet cunt right into her face. Her lips found my phalloclit, and she sucked at it gently. "Harder," I said. "Suck it hard." Her tentative mouth became firmer around it, and she sucked it in all the way to the base, lashing her tongue across it. Yes. Perfect. I slammed my pubic bone into her chin in pleasure, but like a trooper, she kept going.

Ian was still going at her ass; it made me even hotter to watch him pistoning in and out of her tight, reddened hole. With her smooth, tight scrotum, it looked as if her hard organ grew from just above it. I leaned forward and grabbed it, stroking it, and she made a muffled, whimpering sound into my crotch and bucked, as much as she could with her legs over Ian's shoulders.

Then I came again, one final time, and rolled off her to watch her come. Her big clit jerked in my hand as she screamed, but the come was completely dry. The spasming of her ass must have set Ian off, because he made a coming sort of noise through gritted teeth and slammed into her ass so hard that she shot a foot across the bed. His cock slipped out of her and the jet of come got me in the face. "Shit!" I yelped.

Ian fell face down on the bed, but immediately realized what he'd done. "Oh, god, sir, I'm sorry, I'm so sorry," he gasped, but I could tell he was trying to hold back the snickers, and after I got my eyes clear I decided it was pretty funny myself. "Here, hold still," he said breathlessly, "I'll try to clean you off," and then proceeded to lick at my face in much the same way that I expect an overenthusiastic St. Bernard would.

"Never mind! Cut it out!" I protested, trying to fend him off. Shelley broke out laughing at the sight and I glared at her, and then started laughing in spite of myself. "You guys!" I said in mock-annoyance. "How am I ever going to face my co-workers with smutty tales of conquest if you keep being silly?"

Shelley sat straight up. "You're telling our co-workers?" she cried, horrified. "But—"

"Gotcha," I said wickedly, and she relaxed. It set Ian off again, and he fell backwards on the bed, giggling uncontrollably.

"Bastard," she muttered. "Both of you. How did I end up in bed with a couple of crazy bi-fags anyway?" Her tone was teasing, but her words sobered me.

"Because we can give you what you can't get from those other guys," I said, catching her gaze and holding it. "Don't we?"

Her eyebrows went up. "You mean great sex?"

"No. I mean acceptance," I told her. Then I added, "And great sex. While we're at it."

A slow, thoughtful smile crept across her face, very different from her flirtatious grins, and I knew at that moment we were going to be seeing a lot more of Shelley. "You know," she said quietly, "you just might be right."

Raven Kaldera is an intersexual transgendered FTM activist, organic farmer, parent, pagan minister, and pornographer whose writings are scattered hither and yon. 'Tis an ill wind that blows no minds.

Anal

Marilyn Jaye Lewis

I knew a woman who had a virgin asshole until she was in her early 30s. I never understood that kind of woman, she's not at all like me. I'd read about *Last Tango In Paris* in my mother's *Cosmo* when I was only thirteen, for god's sake—and the accompanying article, too, all about how to do it through the back door and, more importantly, why: Because a Cosmo girl is an American girl and American girls love pressure.

I don't know if it was related to that distant article or not, but I dropped out of college in a real hurry, after only about six weeks. Something about wanting to feel alive instead, and that's how I ended up in New York; at the tail-end of the disco era, pre-AIDS, a time when any self-respecting underpaid New York office worker drank heavily on his or her lunch hour and didn't have to be choosy about who he or she wanted to fuck when the work day was over because eventually you fucked everybody. And there were so many exciting cross-purposes going on! For instance, drugs. Did you fuck somebody sheerly because s/he had the good drugs? Or did you use the good drugs as bait to get somebody to fuck you? Of course, if you hung in there long enough, the inevitable descent into hell finally occurred. That's right, you remember it: You fell hopelessly in love with a completely insane person, a dangerously paranoid schizophrenic perhaps, but you were too fucked-up on the good drugs to even notice it. Maybe for a couple of years.

When it happened to me, it was with a woman. Back then, she was already twenty years older than me, so god knows, if she's still alive now she's using a cane to get around. But she was in fine form in 1980, thin as a rail of course. All bone, no muscle, but that was de rigueur in 1980. We didn't lift free weights. Every ounce of energy was reserved for lifting cocktail glasses off the wet bar (a long distance endurance process) and for raising those teeny-weeny silver spoons, over and over—all right, I won't go on. I guess your memory's a little better than I'd thought...

So I'll call her Giselle. Not that her name was anything close to that, but it was similarly unpronounceable and she possessed that quick, nervous energy sometimes, reminiscent of the leaping gazelle. And on our first date—or more succinctly—when we hit on each other in that 10th Avenue after-hours meat rack and went home together to fuck like dogs, she was in fine, lithe, energetic form. I know we were kissing in the back seat of that cab, but I don't remember how we got from the cab to her sparsely furnished living room in that huge penthouse apartment in midtown, with the vaulted ceilings and all that glass. That part's a complete blank, but what happened from that point on is clear and that's the sex part and all that matters anyway.

Giselle's husband was apparently loaded. And not one of those cash-poor types, either. He seemed to travel on business constantly—or so he said. At any rate, he was away an awful lot and Giselle had nothing but time and money to take his place. You'd think those two things—time and money—would have been enough, but when you're remarkably thin and nearly forty, and beautiful and sharp and hopelessly underutilized like my dear Giselle, it takes a lot more than time and money to get your rocks completely off. Hence, Giselle's insatiable drive toward the strange.

I'd agreed willingly from the outset, I just want that part to be clear. I had my clothes off in a hurry and was letting Giselle douche my ass, simply because she wanted it so much. I was happy to let her do it. I was on my knees and elbows in her half-bath, right off the living room, there. Completely stripped with my ass in the air, a bulb syringe squeezing warm water into my rectum while I had a lit cigarette in one hand and a nice glass of merlot in the other.

When the water had done its trick and we were through making a mess in the half-bath, Giselle led me back to the living room and she showed me the huge leather ottoman, how it lifted open for storing magazines and stuff. But she kept her bag of toys in there. It was a pretty big bag. That leather ottoman was sort of like a Playskool Busy Box for the seriously grown up. When she'd emptied out the ottoman, Giselle encouraged me to bend over it, so she could fasten my wrists securely to the wooden casters underneath. She even had specially made rubber wedges she'd shove under the casters to keep them from rolling all over the carpeting. Right away it occurred to me, when I saw the specially made rubber wedges, that it wasn't likely I was the first girl Giselle had stripped and douched and put over the leather ottoman. But I was okay with that. I drank like a fish and took a lot of drugs back then, so I was usually feeling pretty self-confident.

Once Giselle had secured my wrists, she inserted a steel thigh-spreader between my legs and buckled each padded end snugly around each of my thighs. And even though the thigh-spreader worked fine—it kept me from being able to close my legs—Giselle attached a padded ankle-spreader between my ankles, too. I guess she just wanted to be sure. And then she came around the front of the ottoman, gave me a hit off her cigarette and a couple of slugs of that great merlot.

My head was buzzing. I loved the feeling of being exposed—in fact, forcibly so. Giselle leaned over and kissed my mouth for a while. It made me feel hot. It made my naked backside squirm. When her tongue pushed around inside my mouth, it made my ass arch up and it made me want to have her tongue poking into my hole.

"Look at this," she said.

She pulled a color Polaroid from a leather envelope and placed it on the floor under my face and went away.

I studied the Polaroid picture curiously. It was a picture of a girl much like myself. Well, it was impossible to tell if her face looked anything like mine, but she was totally naked and kneeling over the same ottoman, her legs forcibly spread in the same way, and she was tied down in the same provocatively helpless position. It could have easily been a Polaroid of me.

That's when I saw the familiar bright flash coming from behind me and heard the quick grinding sound of the inner workings of the camera. In a mere 60 seconds, the color Polaroid in front of me was replaced by a color Polaroid of myself. It was uncanny, you know; the similarities and all.

We didn't talk anymore after that. Giselle gave me a couple quick swigs from my glass of merlot and gave me one last drag off the cigarette, then she slipped the gag into my mouth. Tied it pretty tightly, I must say. One of those knots where you just know your hair's in a big gnarly mess in back.

Giselle got undressed somewhere, out of my field of vision. I couldn't see her. But when she straddled my back, her slippery pussy was sliding all over my skin. It was obvious she was naked. She leaned down and spoke in my ear confidentially, as she replaced the picture in front of me with yet another one. Of the other girl again.

"She's awfully pretty, honey, don't you think? Her asshole's so tight, would you look at that? Incredible, isn't it?"

I grunted, uh-huh, and nodded my gnarly head in agreement.

"Not even a hint of a hemorrhoid, see? This girl's in great shape."

I have to admit, I was a little transfixed; I'd never owned a Polaroid camera that took such vivid close-ups! Giselle had obviously invested a fortune in her camera lens.

"She was very well-behaved, if I remember correctly," Giselle went on. "She took it like a champ, that one did. You think you're going to be a good girl, too? Huh? You've been awfully accommodating so far." Giselle began to kiss my neck slowly and she rubbed her wet pussy all over my lower back. "What do you think," she repeated. "You think you're going to be a good girl?"

Uh-huh, I grunted through my gag. I was going to be a very good girl. I was going to be stellar.

"You like things in your ass? You've had things in your ass before, right?"

I nodded my head, yes, but I confess I felt a little tripped up; what did she mean by things?

Then a different Polaroid was put in front of my face, a slightly more startling one. "Same girl," Giselle whispered, "but do you notice anything different about her hole?"

It's a huge gaping hole, I thought nervously.

"This is how her asshole looked when I was through appreciating her. Pretty remarkable, isn't it?"

Giselle brushed some stray hairs affectionately from my forehead, I guess to make sure my vision wasn't obscured in any way. I was riveted to that Polaroid, the crystal clear close-up of that well-appreciated sphincter.

"Of course, this sort of appreciation takes a few hours," Giselle explained. "You don't have to be anywhere for a while, do you?"

I don't think I really responded to that, I was a little too transfixed. She left the gaping-hole Polaroid on the floor in front of my face and then disappeared somewhere behind me.

The anticipation is always the greatest part, isn't it? Man, you're just waiting and you don't even know what the hell for. But you feel real certain that you're going to get it, that it's eventually going to come. And that's the sort of excitement I was feeling; like some mad ferret had chewed his paw free from a steel leghold trap inside me and now he tore wildly around in the darkness of my intestines, wanting very much to find his way out. But that was 1980. You know I was young. I was still excited by things like suspense and fear, and the chance to get my asshole reamed by a seriously grown up girl.

It started with a simple strawberry. A bright red one with a long stem. Giselle had straddled my back again and lowered the long stem down in front of my face. She twirled it gently, holding the stem between her thumb and forefinger. "What do you think?" she asked. "Can you take it? It's not too big but it's awfully fragile."

In an instant the bright red berry was gone and Giselle slid her slippery pussy slowly down my back, until I imagined she must have been on her knees between my spread thighs. The tip of the berry was icy cold when she pressed it against my tight hole, but I could feel my asshole clench even tighter. It was an involuntary reaction to the icy intrusion.

"I can see I have my work cut out for me," Giselle announced solemnly. "We could be at this a long time."

I felt something sticky dribble down the crease in my ass. It oozed slow, like honey. And I think that's just was it was. When the slowly dribbling drop inched toward my clenching asshole, Giselle's tongue was there to meet it. She pushed the sticky substance around and around, all over my anus. The stickiness felt strange. It was lightly pulling at my hole. But the warmth of her tongue, pushing into the tight opening now and then, felt good. My hole definitely liked that. When Giselle had licked the surface of my asshole clean, she dripped another trail of honey down the crack of my ass. Again, it oozed so slowly down I felt that this alone, this waiting on the honey business, could in itself take hours. My ass wriggled and squirmed impatiently, perhaps trying to assist the honey in its journey down, but when the honey finally reached its destination, and when Giselle's warm tongue was once again there to greet it, the honey felt even more appealing than it had the first time. I felt my sphincter muscle relax a little. I felt it eagerly anticipate her poking tongue. I moaned into my gag. And I arched my ass open for her.

"This is definitely progress," Giselle announced quietly. "But let's not rush it. You're not really ready for the berry yet."

Giselle came around in front of me and I watched her polish off my glass of wine. She sat naked where I could see her and she lit a cigarette.

"I know how to remedy this, though, so don't lose heart," she said. "It takes patience and then you'll be able to get anything you want in there. Even something like a strawberry."

I watched her as she thoughtfully smoked and even though I didn't have some long list of things I'd been trying to get in there, I suddenly felt like I desperately wanted to please Giselle. I wanted anything in my ass that she wanted to put in there. My hips were rotating restlessly against the ottoman while I watched her smoke. I could feel the wetness in my vagina beginning to drool down into a puddle on the carpeting. I didn't know what she had in mind for me, but I had a pretty good inkling that my ass was going to get fucked good by this gorgeous skinny woman who, let's face it, was technically old enough to be my mother.

When she finally stubbed out her cigarette, I watched her snap on a latex glove. I'd never been with anybody who'd worn gloves like that before, except the doctor in the examining room and it made my stomach a little queasy watching her snap it on. I wanted to ask her where she got gloves like that, but I had that gag stuck in my mouth and couldn't say a word. But when she disappeared again behind me and, without much fuss, slid a lubed finger up my ass, I wasn't thinking about buying gloves. I just gasped. Well, I moaned a little bit, too. She worked that latexed finger into me deep. And it was so slick with lube my tiny hole couldn't put up any kind of resistance. It tried to push against the intrusion, but Giselle was insistent. She worked against the pushing hole. She slid two fingers in, in fact, and pumped them vigorously in and out while I grunted a little and tried to figure out whether or not I liked it.

But I didn't have a lot of options. I was spread open for her either way. She paused for a moment and squirted the lube directly into my hole. It was an icy and unpleasant feeling, but the sensation didn't last long. It was replaced by the less subtle intrusion of three greasy fingers this time. Three greasy fingers shoved into my lubed hole. Giselle was exerting herself, I could tell; she was grunting from the effort of pumping her three fingers against the muscle that was trying to expel her.

"Jesus," I gasped into my gag. And my eyes were riveted to the picture on the floor in front of me. That gaping hole. It was going to be mine before morning came and I was sickly curious about how we were going to achieve this.

"Are you ready to pick up the pace?" she panted. "Are you ready for some action?"

Of course I couldn't answer her and I guess she didn't really expect me to, but Giselle came around the front of me then and let me watch her strap on the dildo.

"What do you think?" she asked urgently. "Can you handle this guy?"

She was referring to the dildo, to its overall size. But I was too caught up in looking at her. I'd been with girls before, and girls with dildoes, too, but I'd never been with a woman yet who had actually strapped one on. Giselle looked hot. I was eager again.

"What do you think?" she persisted, as if she'd forgotten about the gag. "You think you can take him?"

I grunted my urgent approval as I watched her lube it up. Uh-huh, I grunted several times, and I even nodded my head.

And when she climbed onto me, mounted me, pressing the greased-up head against my asshole, easing the dildo into my rectum, it was like I was fourteen again and I was with that boy. We'd skipped school and we were hiding in his father's den. It was dark and very quiet in there. Their maid was home, but she didn't know we'd skipped school and snuck back into the house. She didn't know we were hiding in the den. But we had decided we were going to do this thing, we were going to try it out. We were determined. And I'd brought my torn out article from my mother's old Cosmo and my plastic jar of Vaseline in my shoulder bag. We didn't get undressed because we were afraid of needing to leave in a hurry. So we just unzipped his fly and took his hard dick out. We smeared Vaseline all over that thing. And then I leaned into one of his father's big leather club chairs, I laid with my face pressed against the cool leather, while the boy shoved up my skirt and pulled my panties down to my knees. Vaseline makes everything a greasy mess, especially nice leather club chairs, but it sure helped that boy's hard-on slide right into me, right into my asshole. It was like we'd talked about over the phone, he was actually fucking my ass. I wasn't sure I really liked it, but I wasn't sure I didn't like it either. The pressure felt exciting, I liked the feeling of being filled up. But what I liked most was his fully-clothed weight on top of me while my panties were around my knees, and the way he smelled while he grunted and pumped away at my virgin asshole, the way all boys smelled back then; like mown grass and sweat and tobacco and spearmint gum.

That was how it felt with Giselle, like I wasn't really sure I liked it, but I wasn't sure I didn't like it either. The dildo felt huge in my ass and I was grunting into my gag. But her naked weight was on top of me. Her breasts were pressed flat against my back and she was sweating from the effort of pounding my hole. I loved all that sweat. And I didn't mind it when she pulled the dildo out and reminded me I wasn't fourteen anymore and that it was 1980: She shoved a glob of Crisco up my ass and proceeded to pump me with a dildo too huge, too heavy to even attempt to fit into the harness. Giselle didn't strap it on, she held it with two hands and shoved it clear down to its base, stretching me completely open.

I groaned like some drugged animal giving birth in a public zoo, but I was loving every minute of it. The Crisco made it easy on my hole. I opened right up and accepted every round fat rubbery inch of the fake dick that Giselle pounded so mercilessly into me.

And my eyes were glued to the photo in front of me, I was transfixed by that gaping hole. I was suddenly in love with the mystery girl in the Polaroid. I knew now what had stretched her open, I knew now how she must have felt—spread wide and securely battened down. A gag probably shoved into her mouth, too, so she could grunt over and over in it as her rectum was filled to capacity, her ears filled with the sounds of Giselle's own grunting, from all the strenuous effort...

When Giselle had worn herself out she disappeared briefly into the half-bath then re-emerged with a soaking towel. The towel was hot and felt great against my tired hole. And when Giselle had wiped away most of the grease, there was the familiar bright flash again behind me and the sound of the grinding inner workings of the camera. By the time she'd untied my gag, the new photo was ready.

"What do you think?" she asked softly, as she laid the Polaroid of my seriously opened hole on the floor in front of me. "You think you can handle that berry now?"

I'd forgotten about the strawberry. "I suppose so," I panted, although I wasn't entirely sure.

"I'll wedge it in with a little honey and then I'll eat it out of you. But I want to get a picture of it first. My husband loves these pictures," Giselle explained, "the ones with the food in the girls' asses. He carries them in his overnight case and takes them all over the world."

I wasn't sure I was particularly pleased with that idea, but I couldn't keep Giselle from wedging that sticky strawberry into my gaping hole. It took it easily this time, the berry perched right there in my puckered anus. Then the camera flashed away. I wondered what her husband looked like; would I ever recognize him on the street? Would it haunt me that somewhere in the world a man was flying from place to place with a picture in his overnight bag of me with a strawberry in my ass? And what about the mystery girl in the other Polaroid? What kind of food had ended up in her stretched hole?

But my worries melted away when Giselle's mouth found the berry. True to her word, she nibbled it out. She plucked the stem clean and then sucked the berry and gnawed it and licked it until it was gone.

"Come on," she said, as she undid all the hardware, the buckles and the restraints, "let's go to bed. Let's make a little love."

She refilled my wine glass but I didn't want it anymore. I just wanted to be flat on my back underneath her on her big bed. The sun was just coming up in all those enormous penthouse windows, so when she straddled my face for some 69 I could see her bung hole clearly. It was stretched like mine, but hers was permanent. She lowered it right onto my tongue while she shoved my thighs apart wide and buried her face between my legs. Her hot tongue licked at my tender aching worn out hole, while her fingertips deftly massaged my clit. I tried to rub her clitoris, too, but she didn't seem to want that. She seemed content to just ride my tongue with her open hole.

I licked her asshole with all the earnest attention I could give her, but after a while, I must confess I couldn't help it; the way her mouth was making me feel between my legs absorbed more and more of my concentration. I couldn't give Giselle the amount of attention I should have. While her fingertips slipped all over my swollen clit, and while her tongue licked eagerly at my played-out asshole, I couldn't help myself, I came. I dug my fingers into Giselle's gorgeous ass and clamped my thighs tight around her head and came.

And since it was 1980 I didn't sleep with her. I stumbled into my clothes and left. I kissed her good-bye and all, but then I went out alone for breakfast.

A couple nights later she called me. "My husband's in Thailand," she said. "What do you say we go at it again? Are you up for it? You're not still sore, are you?"

My bung hole quivered. "No, I'm not sore," I said into the receiver.

"I have some new things that we could try putting up there. Are you game?"

And I realized I was. It was the beginning of my inevitable descent into hell with a completely insane person. "I'm game," I confessed.

"Good," she exclaimed quietly. "Be a doll and pick up some film. Now, how do you feel about root vegetables?"

Marilyn Jaye Lewis' professional writing career began in the late '80s when underground zines such as Frighten The Horses *and* Bad Attitude *began publishing her bisexual erotica. In 1997, as head writer for RomAntics, Inc., Marilyn helped create the first bisexual CD-ROM game, the award-winning* DADAhouse, *featured on HBO. She is currently President of EroticBookSociety.com, the largest online bookstore dedicated to promoting not only erotica but books on all aspects of human sexuality from all over the world. Her first full-length book,* Neptune & Surf, *a collection of novellas published by Masquerade Books, was called "a sensational debut" by* The (London) Guardian *and reminiscent of "Sergio Leone's* Once Upon a Time in America*" by* American Review of Books.

Birthday

Jack Random

One of the best sexual experiences I ever had came about because I didn't get a birthday present for a friend. In my own defense, let me say that, normally, I'd never show up to a birthday party empty-handed, but the invitation actually had said not to bring anything. In big black type down at the bottom. "Party at seven, ritual at nine, no gifts please", followed by a handwritten note from Bonnie, "It's my 45th. Make me happy, wear your leather pants."

Still, even wearing the leather pants, I was beginning to feel just a little uncomfortable at about an hour into the party as I watched guest after guest arrive with a bouquet or a bottle of wine. Bonnie told all of them that they shouldn't have brought anything, but she did look pleased, and I was beginning to feel as if I'd made a social error of some kind as I stood in the tightly-packed living room with some other guests, discussing the large framed photograph of our host that hung over the fireplace.

The picture, recently taken, was of Bonnie, nude from the waist up and strapped to a large wooden cross with heavy leather cuffs and thick chains.

"I love the way it's lit," said a dark haired guy to my right who looked to be about 40. He was wearing one of the tightest pairs of jeans that I'd seen since the '70s and had a fantastic ass. "Whoever took this really captured her."

"Yes," I said, "She looks extremely captured, all tied up like that." And then stuck my hand out before he could become embarrassed. "I'm Tom, by the way. How do you know Bonnie?"

He took my hand and smiled. Great eyes, I noticed, to match the ass. "Jim," he said, "I used to sleep with her boyfriend Robert once in a while, and when he died of you-know-what, she and I became close. How about you?"

"Bonnie and I dated the same woman about a year ago." I noticed that he and I were still holding hands, prolonging the contact. "Also, she and I write for a lot of the same queer magazines here in San Francisco," I added quickly, wanting to get the word "queer" into my resume before he let go of my hand and looked away. It seemed to work because he put his arm around my shoulders as we both turned back to the picture.

"I had no idea that Bonnie had gotten so into all the leather stuff," he said.

"Oh, no?" I said, "Have you seen her bedroom? She's got a full rack of whips hanging on the wall, right under that display of all her Girl Scout merit badges."

"Ah, lost youth," he said letting his arm slip from my shoulders, but slowly. "No, I meant that I've been living in San Diego for the last couple of years, and I didn't know until I got here for this party."

"Oh?" I said, beginning to get what seemed to be a really good idea. "So you'll be staying here with Bonnie tonight?"

"Yeah," he said. "We always try to get together and play a little bit when I'm in town."

As he said this, a woman with a shaved head slipped through the crowd and stood between us and the fireplace looking up at the picture. I didn't know her but Jim did.

"Hi, Karen!" he said. "What do you think of the portrait? It's good art, isn't it?"

Karen turned and looked at him for a moment before returning to the picture. "Yeah, it's good art if you say so." She said, "But mostly it looks to me like a really great pair of tits. Excuse me, boys. I think I need to go find Bonnie and tell her what fantastic boobs she has."

"Well, that ought to make this a happy birthday for her," said Jim, laughing as Karen butted her way through the crowd toward the kitchen.

I laughed, too, and then excused myself, heading off to find Bonnie as well. If my really good idea worked out, Bonnie would be getting more than compliments on her boobs this year.

As things turned out, I didn't get a moment alone with Bonnie until sometime around midnight. We ran into each other in the darkened back hall as she came out of the bathroom. Since the party was starting to wind down by then, there was no one else nearby and I found myself reaching out and grabbing two of her belt loops. She grinned as I pulled her close and we kissed.

"I hope you're having a good birthday," I said when we broke our clinch.

"Pretty good," she said, running her hands across my ass. "Thanks for wearing the pants."

"My pleasure," I said. "Your friend Jim is hot."

"Oh, you two met? He's staying here tonight. I'm thinking that'll make my birthday happy."

"I bet," I said, and kissed her again. "I've got an idea that might make it even better. Do you think you and Jim might like it if I stayed as well?"

"Oooh, that is a good idea," she said, grabbing my ass and slamming my hips into hers. "Just let me check with Jim. He might be too tired after the party."

"Somehow I doubt it," I said, remembering our conversation earlier.

"Still, I need to ask him. It will have to be tonight, too, because he's leaving tomorrow afternoon. Let me talk to him first, and if he's into it, then you two can talk. That way nobody feels pressured." By this time Bonnie was actually starting to hop from one foot to another while she tried to consider every possible problem and how to handle it.

"Of course, he's into safe sex for something like this, but it wouldn't hurt if you mentioned that you just got tested. Oh! Thank God! I just remembered that I bought a new bottle of lube this week."

"Bonnie," I said gently.

"You know he has a boyfriend in San Diego, don't you? They're open—I mean he came down here to see me and we always sleep together—but I'm not sure if it's okay for him to do another guy."

"Bonnie," I said again, putting a hand over her mouth this time, "If you could just stop being such a process queen for five minutes, we can settle all of these questions by you going into the kitchen and asking Jim if he'd like to fuck me. Okay?"

"Okay," she said when I moved my hand, and, still bouncing a little, she ran off down the hall.

All of the other guests had left and I was killing time by cleaning up the living room when Bonnie led Jim out of the kitchen.

"So," she said, "I told Jim about your idea, Tom, and he's into it."

"Wonderful." I said, as Jim and I grinned at each other.

"I'm going to go get the bedroom ready. You two can do your negotiations out here," she said, and bustled off to her bedroom to light candles, turn on music, dig out the lube, find her vibrator, and do all the thousand and one things she always did to make herself feel in control of her space.

Jim and I sank down on the couch together, both knowing that we were going to have some time alone before she got back.

Tentatively we moved closer together and, smiling a little, he leaned forward. Smiling some myself, I bent my head to his and we began to kiss.

Softly at first. I loved the way his beard tangled up with mine and the texture of his lips. We opened slowly to each other, tongues probing gently, feeling the hot wetness inside the other's mouth.

Almost trembling, I reached out and touched his chest, hard muscle and bone, feeling the curve of the pecs and the tiny jutting points of his nipples.

He started to do the same to me, seeming to be surprised by my nipple rings and then tugging them gently, just the way I like.

Shifting our hips and shoulders on the couch we pressed our bodies closer together. My cock was getting hard inside the leather pants, and the tight pressure was making me even hotter. I love having a hard-on in leather pants.

Slowly I let my free hand drift down Jim's body to his thigh and then stroke my way upward to his crotch. I felt him stroking my cock at the same moment that I reached his, beautifully outlined in those tight jeans.

Moving together as we kissed, we started to develop a rhythm. We rubbed each other's cock through our clothes, tracing the shaft, softly pinching the head, getting hotter and harder, our tongues beginning to roll faster against each other. I found myself groaning into his mouth and he answered me.

The leather felt good but it was getting uncomfortably tight over my hard-on. I was just about to reach for my belt buckle when Jim and I both became aware of Bonnie standing silently over us. Watching us, she stood perfectly still except for her hard breathing and the slight movement of her right hand in her crotch.

"So," she said when we looked up at her, "I take it that you two settled everything that you needed to?"

"Oh, yes," said Jim. "Tom and I have had all the conversation that we need."

"Yes," I said, standing up and moving toward her. "We have everything settled. Now, I believe that it's somebody's birthday tonight. What do you think we ought to do about it, Jim?"

"I'm not sure." he said as he stood up, too, "but I'll bet there's some inspiration in the bedroom."

"Great idea!" I said, and scooped Bonnie off her feet and into my arms. She squealed when I did it, not out of fear or surprise, but because she loves being carried to the bedroom to be screwed.

Bonnie kept squealing and giggling as Jim and I carried her down the hall, both of us laughing our heads off and, about halfway there, we began singing "Happy Birthday" to her. Because it was a short hallway, we managed to time it so that the song ended just as her ass hit the bed and we both tumbled down on top of her.

Bonnie stopped giggling then, grabbed Jim by the hair and levered herself on top of him. She held him down and they started kissing while I slipped in next to him and wrapped my arms around them both. With a slight moan she turned her head and began kissing me as well.

We were all quiet now, passing the kiss back and forth, beginning to stroke each others arms and shoulders, letting the tension build a bit, seeing if this was going to work or if anybody was going to get weird all of a sudden.

We did that for a couple of minutes before Bonnie broke the kiss and sat up.

"God damn, this is hot!" she said, sort of wiggling back and forth on top of Jim. "Let's get naked so I can see you two together."

Jim and I exchanged a look. "So," I said, "I take it that's what you want for your birthday. To watch us fuck?"

"That'll do for a start," said Bonnie, rolling to the side to kick off her boots.

Unlike in the porno movies, where articles of clothing simply vanish at convenient times, the three of us spent the next ten minutes or so removing the various collections of straps, buckles, and zippers that we were wearing.

Bonnie watched Jim and I strip, and then the two of us undressed her. He unzipped her leather halter and started kissing her throat again while I pulled off her jeans and Calvin Klein briefs.

"God damn it, Bonnie!" I said, "You know I hate it when your panties are more butch than mine."

"Oh, baby, please!" she said as Jim began sucking her right nipple, "You know perfectly well that you are just a great big slut and you never wear panties, so you can just suck my cock."

"Tempting," I said, "but since your cock is still over there in the sock drawer, I think I'll just suck his."

I bent my head down between their hips and slowly took the head of Jim's half-hard cock into my mouth. It tasted sweet and smooth on my tongue and softer than anything else on a man's body. I felt Jim moan a little and then the shaft stiffened and lengthened, going completely hard. His hips thrust forward the tiniest bit, seeking that soft place in the back of my throat. I took him slowly, letting myself get used to it, getting my gag reflex under control and wanting to tease him a little. Bonnie started to lick his nipples, and that made him twitch, the shaft surging, the head mushrooming out against the roof of my mouth. Compulsively I noticed that he had a nice cock but not as big as mine.

Jim rolled to the side as Bonnie pushed him over onto his back, and I rolled with him, still sucking. Bonnie climbed up and straddled his head, lowering her pussy to his mouth, watching me in the big mirror above the bed.

"Oh, that looks so hot," she whispered, and then moaned as Jim began to lick her clit, and I stroked my long hair back, giving her a better view. About half the fun of group sex is being able to watch and be watched. She started pumping her hips a little, almost fucking his mouth, opening and closing her eyes as he sucked her in the same rhythm as I was using to suck him. She looked down at him doing it and then into the mirror to see me, getting herself more and more turned on until, not wanting to come yet, she slipped to the side and lay down beside Jim again.

Without speaking, I stopped sucking and climbed up to lay down on the other side of him. He and I started to kiss again and stroke each other. Bonnie lay back and watched, playing with herself.

Nobody was smiling or laughing now. We were down to the serious business of desire, the hard and wonderful work of getting each other off in the the most powerful way possible.

Jim's tough, work-calloused hand stroked my cock as I did the same to him. We lay there, chest to chest and almost nose to nose, not kissing but breathing together, looking into one another's eyes as we jerked each other off.

The only time in my life that I ever get to look another man in the eye for more than a second or two is during sex. Sometimes I do people just for that moment, just to share the sense of knowing and seeing, of being present with someone for no other reason than because we are giving each other pleasure.

Jim closed his eyes and, moaning that he was getting too close, broke contact and turned back to Bonnie, starting to kiss her again. She rolled over him and then down in between me and him, kissing us both, grabbing one cock in each hand and seeing if she could stroke us both at the same time.

Bonnie turned to me after a minute or so and said simply, "Fuck me, Tom. I need you to fuck me now."

I groaned and nodded, and started fumbling in a dresser drawer beside the bed where I knew she kept the condoms. When I found one, I tore it open with my teeth and watched Bonnie suck Jim's cock while I put it on.

When I was ready, I pulled her down onto her back and put her legs up over my shoulders. Bonnie's pussy was wet and dripping in the candlelight as she grabbed my cock and guided it up inside herself. I started thrusting, slowly at first, and then, falling forward to rest my arms on either side of her, slamming hard and fast as she grabbed my nipple rings and pulled.

"Jim," I said, "Give me your cock. Let me suck you while I fuck her."

Jim nodded and scrambled up to stand in front of me, his feet on either side of Bonnie's shoulders, one hand stretched out behind him to balance on the wall above the mirror. His cock was still hard and starting to drip pre-come. I was rocking back and forth from fucking and he just grabbed the back of my head and jammed that meat in my mouth, fucking my face just the way I was fucking her. We got the rhythm going, and Bonnie started to scream and thrash around under me.

Now I know that it would be traditional at this point to say that the three of us all exploded in a simultaneous, three-way, safer sex orgasm, but let's be honest. It's damn hard to breathe with a cock down your throat and it's even harder to fuck for a long time when you can't breathe. Aside from that, Bonnie got so excited watching Jim fuck my mouth that she started yanking my nipples way too hard and that messed up my concentration. Jim seemed to be enjoying what I was doing but even the best sexual athlete would have a hard time reaching orgasm by fucking a moving target while balanced with one hand on a rocking bed.

This a true story, or at least a mostly true story, so I'll tell you what really happened. That position was fun and memorable but we stopped when it got to be too much and, since it was about two a.m. by this time, decided to take turns getting each other off.

Bonnie lay back and used her jumbo-sized, industrial strength, post-feminist vibrator while she watched Jim and me jerk each other off and shoot hot come all over each other's chest and stomach. After that, still dripping with it and ginning from ear to ear, we each grabbed one of her nipples and sucked while she kicked that baby into high gear and sent herself rocking and screaming to the moon three times in succession.

It would also be traditional to say that, afterward, we all fell immediately into an exhausted and dreamless sleep. But, since Bonnie only has a queen-sized bed, I got up and put my leather pants back on. Then I kissed them both good-night and wandered down to Valencia Street in search of a cab.

When I made it home, I was still a little hyped up, so I sat down at the computer, wrote the first draft of this, and then emailed it to Bonnie. Then, just as the sky outside my window began to brighten and turn grey, I did actually fall into a deep but wonderfully dream-filled sleep.

Jack Random is a long-haired, pierced, and tattooed bisexual Pagan, poet, pornographer, leather daddy, and health care worker who lives a fulfilling but slee-deprived life in San Francisco. He can be reached for almost any purpose at randomj@earthlink.net, and yes, Jack Random is his real name.

Changing

Betty Blue

She used to be my lover. Maura sat on the edge of my tub, watching me in the mirror while I brushed the pale pink "snow plum" across my cheeks. We had gone to the drugstore (after finding nothing playing at the movies that we wanted to see) and tried all the testers of lipstick, eyeshadow, and blush, like two teenagers on our way home from school. She had come back to my apartment with pale orchid lips and bright lights in her ice-blue eyes from the breezy, almost-warm, spring afternoon. It had been months since I'd seen her, months since I had finally pushed away from the ambiguity of her friendship to try to heal from our long-ended affair; I had almost forgotten the sprinkling of freckles over her sharp, ivory cheeks.

"I hope you don't mind if I stay," she said, as I traced a line of blood-black over the crest of my lips. She perched her elbows on her knees and cupped her chin in her hands while I finished the outline, watching her reflection behind me. "I have an hour before I'm supposed to be downtown."

I uncapped the new lipstick I'd bought and twisted it up to look at it. "As long as you don't mind my getting ready." I glanced at her in the mirror as I leaned forward to put on the lipstick. "You might think it's a little weird the way I'm going to be dressed."

"Weird?" she asked. "Why?"

Instead of answering, I turned and handed her the lipstick. "I can never get this stuff on without looking like a clown," I said. "Do me?"

She grinned as I crouched down in front of her. "My pleasure." I braced one hand on Maura's knee while she carefully painted in my dark-lined lips. "You have great lips," she said, and grinned again. "I noticed that right away; I mean, once we'd undressed."

It was my turn to grin—difficult to do when a silky stick is moving in soft strokes down one's mouth. She polished off the center of my bottom lip with an extra double stroke and capped the lipstick. "Interesting color," she said, smoothing a stray line with her fingertip. "It's like an iridescent band of steel."

"Mmm," I said, straightening. "It reminded me of when I was a kid... 'Fembots.'"

Maura laughed. "The Bionic Woman."

"You know it." I took her hand and prompted her up from her perch, leading her with me to my bedroom.

"Um, what are we doing?" she said softly behind me.

"You're going to help me dress," I said.

My room was already a mess of clothes. I'd been trying things on for days in search of the right look. There was an art to this, like costuming for a play, and each time I'd stood before the mirror testing out "the look," I'd gotten wetter between my thighs. The last time he'd summoned me, John had included orders in his brief email note: "pull all of your hair up on top of your head in a ponytail; wear whatever makeup and underwear make you feel the sluttiest." I had been a bit dismayed; I was already planning "the look" then, and his orders derailed what I'd had in mind. I had stewed for several days, trying to decide if I should refuse; surely this one small order couldn't be as important as the scene itself; he wouldn't really care. In the end, it had made me hotter to follow the letter of his law.

"Looks like a cyclone's been through your room," said Maura, bouncing on the edge of my bed. She picked up a g-string from the bed, the one I had worn last time, and turned it around in the light. "Um, this is...almost underwear," she offered.

"It's decorative," I laughed defensively. "But I don't need that tonight." I plowed into the pile of clothes and dug out my pair of thigh-high, black woolen socks. "This is all I've got so far," I said, holding them up. Maura raised an eyebrow at me. I unbuttoned my jeans and leaned back on the bed, kicking them off, to put the socks on. I pulled the socks up tightly, my fingernails making a scritching sound in the elastic band that reminded me of grade-school. I dangled my feet in the air in front of me as I leaned back on my elbows. "The socks are perfect," I said. "I just don't know what to wear with them."

"They're cute," she said tentatively. "I had some like that when I was a kid."

I smiled. "Yeah. Me too." I picked up a black mini-skirt and held it over my lap. "I thought about this, but I don't know. Do you think it goes?"

Maura ran her hands over the slick stretch-cotton. "Actually, yes. That's a great skirt."

I dropped the skirt next to her and rolled over, dragging out shirts, skirts and shorts that had been rejected, and tossing them over my head to the floor. "Okay; socks, skirt...now I need a blouse. I want something with a button front, sort of conservative, but maybe a little too transparent."

"A crisp white blouse," she said. "Like a school uniform."

I stopped tossing clothes and looked up at her with a smile. "Exactly."

A slow smile was spreading over her white teeth. She began to help me dig through the pile. "What about this?" she asked, holding up a pale, gauzy blouse with bare blue stripes. She laid it over the skirt and we both nodded. "Let me see the whole thing together," she said. "Put them on."

I sat up and took the skirt, pulling it over my legs and standing up to zip it. Maura silently handed me the shirt, and I put it on, buttoning the front all the way up to the top, and turned around to look in the mirror. I was starting to see the image I had created in my mind. This really worked.

"Do you have a tie?" she said.

"A tie?"

"Yeah, you know, uniforms usually have a little black tie."

I was holding my hair up at the sides of my head, trying to decide what I should do with it. "I've got a black leather tie I've had forever," I said doubtfully.

Maura opened the closet and found the tie hanging on the back of the door. "Ah, '80s punk," she smiled. "I think it'll work." She came over to the mirror with the tie and looped it around my neck, and her fingers paused for a second at my collarbone. I could smell her subtle scent of soap and a sweet conditioner, something that reminded me of avocado blossom, as she stood so close to me, head bent over the tie to slip one end through the knot. I breathed in that scent that was the complicated simplicity of Maura, that quiet blossom scent that mingled with a fired spice, like the multiplicitous blending of cardamom, anise, and a dozen mysterious things.

I used to run my fingers through that soft, baby-fine hair, I thought, and tuck a buttery curve of it behind her ear. I used to let my fingers travel beneath it around the slope of her neck to the nape and stroke her there lightly, listening to her soft breathing, the understated reply of an inner, buried moan. I used to push my hands up beneath her shirt and softly pry down the curves of her bra, and smooth my thumbs over the tight nipples and their beaded steel adornment, to dip my head to taste them, hands and tongue privy to those secrets that filled my mouth with the softness of white, and the contradiction of their glossy firmness, like an erection, encircled in my palm.

"God, that looks perfect," said Maura, with a little satisfied tug on the knot of the tie.

I glanced in the mirror. "Almost," I said. "But my hair—I thought I'd wear braids."

"So that's what the little hair-bands are for. I wondered what you were doing with those."

I had picked up a package of "ponytail holders" along with the makeup, the kind with colored balls on the ends like bright plastic marbles. I started to separate one side of my hair into three, beginning the braid, and Maura took up the other half, combing it with her fingers. Her fingers were long and thin, and closely manicured for her girlfriend.

We watched each other in the mirror as we matched each other's motions—over, under, over, under. "You must have been a very bad girl," she said in a deep, quiet voice. "Is John going to punish you?"

I smiled. "Yes. He knows just what a bad girl I really am."

Maura stroked the braid as she finished, making sure it was smooth and tight. I reached over to the bed and picked up one of the ponytail holders from where I'd dumped them all when we came in, handing it to her and taking another for my side. "I was always afraid to hurt you," she said. "I guess he's not."

"No."

"Do you like it?" she asked, twisting the pink balls of the band together. "Does it make you hot?"

I laughed. "Uh, yeah, Mo. I'm a masochist, not an idiot."

She pushed me slightly with a little frown. "No, I mean it. I want to know. Do you mind? Is that rude?"

I never asked her about her lovers. I didn't want to know. Her husband didn't bother me; maybe it was the gender issue, the "competition," but I couldn't stand to think about Tracy and Maura in bed. It only made me think of my body, and how it hadn't been good enough for her. She liked to try to tell me anyway, to slip it into conversation. ("I've made other women scream since you, but none of them have screamed my name.") I never quite knew what she wanted from me, what she got from me. She loved me, she said. I had always longed to know why.

"It would be rude," I said, "if it was anybody else but me." I smiled as I let her wind the other band around my hair. "Masochist, narcissist...anything with an 'ist,' that's me."

"So what turns you on?" she asked again. "What does he do?"

"Well," I said, and I could feel the heat in my cunt already, before I'd ever said a word. "He calls me names."

"What names?"

"Bitch," I snarled suddenly, and Maura jumped. "'You like it like that way, don't you, you little bitch? You're just a little slut, aren't you?'"

Maura's breathing had quickened. "Oh. That's what he says to you."

"Yeah."

"And then what?"

"He makes me take off my clothes and get down on my knees to wait for him." I felt my own breath begin to rise beneath my breasts. I didn't tell her how I pressed my fingers between my hot lips while I waited for him, felt the nakedness of my own shaved pussy and stroked the slick, swollen center of my cunt, smearing the sticky fluid across my thighs, and rolling the hood of my clitoris against the hard, painful bob of flesh. I didn't tell her how I watched his cock growing hard as he jerked off his pants and his shirt, replacing his everyday boots with a pair of high, black, leather ones that I longed to ride with my wet, open cunt. I neglected to mention how I moaned and felt faint just at the sight of his body, firm and cruel, and about to become the instrument of my correction, while his hair fell down about his hard shoulders, caressing his deep tattoos and draping over the small rings in his own tight nipples while he adjusted his leather cap.

I told her that I swallowed his cock, but I did not mention that I took him in my mouth while balanced on my knees, and that he thrust it hot and swift past my lips, against my tongue, and deep into the hollow of my throat, as I struggled to take more. I left out the part where I pressed him into me with my supplicating hands against his ass, silently begging for him to obliterate me with his hard and angry jolting inside this hole that was my mouth, until I could not breathe, and only moaned and cried my grateful acquiescence.

Maura was still and fascinated as I told her how he took me by my hair and threw me down, and ordered me across his lap. I told her that he spanked me with his hard and open hand, but I said nothing of how his cock bobbed and nudged hungrily beneath my belly while I parted my legs against his brutal touch, of how my cunt covered him in a flood of ecstasy, ever wetter, ever hotter, ever redder, as his beating hand cut against the bruised skin of my ass, itself beating with a pulse of its own with the rush of blood—as his cock was, as my cunt was. I kept to myself how I screamed and howled like a dog to the Master Moon, shaking beneath his merciless punishment, unwilling to ask for mercy, even hoping for more when his hand would pause.

Maura was surprised that I allowed John to spank me. "I never would have thought that was what you wanted," she said, still playing with my hair. She smiled. "So what did you do that he's going to punish you for, anyway?"

"I ran into him at a bookstore, and asked to suck his cock out front, in my car."

Maura laughed and pulled my braid. "You are a dirty little slut, aren't you?" She curved the braid up underneath and looked at me in the mirror. "That's better," she said. "Don't you think? In a little loop like that?" She took out the ponytail holders and refastened them around the loops of braid behind my ears. I put on my Doc Martens and laced them up, adjusting my long socks so that enough thigh showed beneath the short skirt.

A dull, high beeping sounded, and Maura turned away to check out the number on her pager in the light. "It's Tracy," she said. "Time for me to get going."

"I'm glad you came by," I said. "Next time maybe we'll even find a movie."

She laughed and gave me a hug, and her breasts felt warm and weighty against my smaller ones. We "mushed" together, in the way that I loved about touch between women, and she kissed me—quick and soft, the way women's lips were. There was nothing hard about women, the ones I'd known, except loving them.

I watched her go down the stairs when she left, before I turned back inside to look in the mirror once more. John was so different from her; there was no comparison. His possession of me was like an upside-down kind of worship, a wonderful release. Maura was something else, untouchable, like water. I slipped off my panties and tossed them aside. He would punish me for that, parading through town with my bare cunt just inches within my hem. He'd put his hands beneath my skirt and discover that, discover me already swollen and throbbing at the thought of him. His fingers would thrust into me and make me even more wet, slipping and sliding into me, his fist against my thighs as his other hand demanded entrance to my shirt and yanked the bra out of the way, crushing my tit inside it. He would press my soaking cunt against his jeans and let me feel how hard he was at the thought of chastising me. He'd chain my wrists together and make me wait, half-naked and hungry on the floor, with pounding clit and pounding heart.

The pouty girl in the mirror was thrusting her fingers beneath her own skirt. She was a greedy, dirty little bitch.

I arched against the trembling in my clit and cried out, feeling the thunder and destruction of a desert monsoon breaking inside my thighs. The wail of the storm came from my mouth and I fell to my stockinged knees as the electricity of lightning skated over my skin. Was I coming because of Maura, or because of John, or because of myself? Maybe it was all three of us. Did it matter? I moaned John's name as I came, and the climax did nothing to ease my need, or my desire. I wanted to be taken by him.

I would be at his mercy within the hour.

Betty Blue is a dirty girl who lives, works, and subs in San Francisco. Her hobbies are collecting beautifully fucked-up ex-girlfriends and emotionlly unavailable birds. Currently involved in a doomed love triangle with her cat and her cockatiel, she also enjoys living in a state of denial about motherhood, growing strange things in her garden, and living vicariously through her self-titled hamster. In her spare time, she nurses a narcissistic obsession with growing longer hair than her leather daddy primary partner. Betty is the online moderator of Birotica *and editor of* Bay Area Bi Women *on the web.*

Max: A Sexual History, or, My 10th High School Reunion-To-Be

Lori Selke

My most important friend while I was growing up was a boy named Max.

I didn't say best friend. I had several of those, through the years. Max wasn't as intense a friendship, but he lasted longer. There was more than just "best friends" between us.

I met him first in fourth grade. In fifth grade he taught me how to French kiss. He was the first person, boy or girl, I kissed that way. (Years later, he'd come out as gay. This seems rather emblematic,considering my own later proclivities: I Was An Elementary School Fag Hag.) He backed me up against a tree in his backyard and inserted his tongue inside my mouth, clinical, inelegant, and startling.

A few years later, we began exploring sex together. I don't mean as lovers, exactly. More like fellow seekers; we made do with each other because there was no one else available, nobody we trusted enough. Instead of touching my girlfriends during sleepovers, under the sheets, playing "truth or dare, will you take off your underwear," I tried things out with Max, or at least talked about them first. We read everything we could find, from *The Joy of Sex* and its tasteful line drawings, to my father's Frederick's of Hollywood catalogs. For some reason, I was always the source of this material—I remember Max's mother yelling at us from the front seat of the car never to trust a word of *Everything You Always Wanted to Know About Sex But Were Afraid to Ask*, with its tales of lightbulbs and lesbian prostitutes that we already knew by heart, but I don't remember her offering any better alternatives. But my parents, they didn't even put the sex books on a high shelf; the *Playboys* were stocked in a closed cabinet next to the bed. Soon, we moved onto adolescent parlor games—I practiced oral sex with a pencil on a dare in my living room; we played "strip 21" in the woods behind his house.

On the last day of eighth grade, on the long bus ride home from an amusement park, Max asked me to put my hand in his lap, underneath his jacket. Did I know what was coming? I can't remember anymore. All I can remember is the dry, strange texture of his penis, larger than I imagined. Boneless and firm, but the skin, uncalloused, was fascinating, with its silky texture. So I guess I didn't mind. It remained strangely inert and unthreatening beneath my hot palm. Did I fall asleep with my hand in his lap? Was he disappointed that I wasn't more shocked?

I was disappointed, later, that that was the closest we ever came to having sex.

In high school, he had an affair with another friend of mine, a boy with a glass eye who gave me rides home from school every day in his white Toyota. Their affair was so secret, I didn't find out about it until I'd graduated, when Max told me about it over dinner. He never told me any details, just that they were now over, and that the other boy was still closeted, ashamed. Max always told me everything, eventually. I mean, he told me about the case of crabs he caught after a session at the bars, when he was still living at home, and how his mother wouldn't touch his laundry or his furniture and was hardly speaking to him anymore.

For over ten years, Max had been my secret sexual compatriot. Now it's been almost as long since I've even spoken with him; I don't have a clue as to where he's ended up. Max helped plant my sexual seeds (so to speak), but he hasn't had a chance to witness the harvest. During our childhood, he was always in the lead, physically, artistically, most definitely sexually. I was a late bloomer, always lagging behind, jealously hoping to catch up, someday.

I suspect I have. I suspect I may have surpassed his best mark.

But there's only one way to find out.

I'd always imagined that by my tenth high school reunion I'd be a famous author, or at least on my way to a Ph.D. Max would be a theater star. It didn't happen for either of us (though we do have a top-ranked professional tennis player in our graduating class).

But I've accomplished a lot. Max missed the time I cut my hair, worn waist-length since before we met; it's grown back to my shoulders now. He missed my marriage to another woman. He missed the divorce.

Now I'm a bi pervert living in San Francisco. I've even appeared as a "poster queer" in *Newsweek*. And I've been published, here and there, talking dirty in the magazines.

I used to be a shy, smart girl. Now, I'm loud, tough, and not always a girl.

If I go back to my reunion, it would be to see Max. I have this fantasy about our meeting that I can't shake.

This time, I want to be the initiator. For once, I get to take the lead. In the intervening decade, I've processed and sorted, and I've grown comfortable with my sticky, gnarled sexual self. I've even shared it with audiences of strangers. Max is the exception.

I want to turn the tables on him. On the man (well, boy) who overshadowed my sexual expression for so long. Who gave me permission to think about being queer. I want to show him how far I've taken it. How well I've come.

I want to show up at the reunion on a motorcycle, and strip down from battered leathers to fresh, pressed tux. (I don't even know how to ride a motorcycle. Yet.)

I want to show up packing a dick. Look at the new me, it would say. Look at just how much I've changed. Blossomed. Beauty to Beast, no doubt, to my former classmates, except that I was never a beauty. The Beast has grown fangs and claws and broken the cage. Surprise!

I want him and everyone else to notice the bulge in my pants. I want to take him aside and make him feel it, out in the yard, near the trees, in the cool Michigan night air. I want him to run his hand over it, slowly and with surprise. I want him to feel every curve, each ridge, and think about what they mean. What potential they hold. I want his mouth to water at the thought of that bulge and where it belongs, taken gently between teeth, nestled against the roof of the mouth. His mouth.

I want to back him against the rough brick wall, and slide my tongue between his teeth. To take his lower lip and bite it, with a smile. Watch him wince, and open wider for me.

I want to keep him off-balance, scared and in new territory. I've learned a lot in the interim, and I've got some new tricks. I want to share them.

I want to push him to his knees and pull his face to my crotch. I want to tower over him. Always taller than me, but not when he's on his knees. I want him to press his cheek against that bulge in my pants, mouth open, eyes closed.

I want his tongue, that slick, worm-like tongue that was always the aggressor before, the symbol of his drive, to wrap itself around my cock. As if it were real. I know he's done this before, sucked cock in public—he told me about doing the boys in the parking lot outside the local gay bar the last time I talked to him. I want him to hunger for a taste of me, the way he hungers for real boys' cocks. Other boys' cocks. I want to wrap my fingers in the tight curls of his hair, and I want to pull and I want it to hurt and I want him not to care because he's already deep in shock. And desire.

And I want to do this with the fear of discovery looming, someone coming out on a smoke break, or just seeking fresh air, about to walk in on us. That adrenalin shudder I lived with for ten years as I hid in the bushes, pulling up my shirt because he asked, letting him touch because I didn't want to say no, because I craved any touch so bad and I hadn't learned to ask for it yet myself, and because he was the only one who was there to ask, to push, he was the only one available to yield to.

I want him to suck me until I come. And I will, and I want that to surprise him. I want to see his throat move to swallow what isn't there, but should be. I want him to miss the taste. I want him to want more.

I don't want him to have a chance to touch me in any other way. This time, I will be the one who remains mysterious and sealed against *him*. He'll put his hand and his mouth on my dick, more than I ever did for him, and maybe, if I'm lucky, he'll spend the next decade wondering why I stopped at a blowjob. Maybe we'll have the longest foreplay courtship in history; maybe at our twentieth reunion we'll consummate our relationship in a more traditional fashion. Maybe I'll plant that seed in his head before I leave.

I want to leave him wondering. Wondering, and wanting more.

I want to pull him to his feet, spit slicked over his lips and chin, and laugh. Not in a mean way. I'll laugh with pleasure and delight.

And then I want to thank him. For those furtive touches, the pressure to explore, the fright and excitement. I want to thank him for the chance to even things up.

Then, my slate will finally be clear, my books balanced. This time, he'll be the one left with heart pounding, with unfulfilled and unexpressed desires, with a hard-on in his pants.

In ten years, maybe he'll come looking for me.

Lori Selke lives in San Francisco, but grew up in the Upper Midwest. Her erotic writing has appeared in Black Sheets, On Our Backs, *and anthologies such as* Leatherwomen 3, Midsummer Nights Dreams, Genderflex, *and* Sex Spoken Here. *She attended her 10th high school reunion without incident.*

Cartographers of Desire

Andy Ohio

I wish I could say it's about sex. I wish I could say it's about asses or thighs or breasts or anatomy in general. But it's not. It's about deceit. I have a trust fetish.

We walked down 2nd Ave. to the corner store. She went in and bought cigarettes while I waited on the sidewalk. When she came back out, she handed me a smoke, slipped one between her pouty red lips, lit it.

The rain fell lightly on her black hair. We whispered to each other like spies as we made our way back to the bar.

"I don't know what it is," I told her, "I haven't felt like this about a woman in years, or maybe ever."

"What am I supposed to think?" she said, "I mean, you're gay! Aren't you? How am I supposed to respond to this?" Her face was flushed and her eyes were alight with conviction. She was torn between anger and passion, between dismissing me or submitting to me.

"I don't know what you're supposed to think. I don't know what I'm supposed to think; it's beyond my control. I thought it was just friendship, but I have to be honest—I can't get you out of my mind. Every night, I go to bed and toss and turn, wishing you were there. I hold my pillow, wishing it were you. When I finally sleep, I dream of you, you coming to me, holding me, kissing me, making love with me. I feel like a teenager with a crush."

"Oh, god," she said, "this is all wrong."

"I'm sorry," I said, "I'm sorry, I never should have brought it up, it's just, it's eating me up inside, and I needed to get it out. I know it's not fair to burden you with this, it's not your problem, really."

"No, I'm glad you told me, but..."

"No, I shouldn't have. But I figured, since today was my last day..."

"Listen, I just... I need time to think about this."

We were back at the bar. I opened the door for her and we walked in.

"What were you two talking about?"

"Who?"

"Who do you think? Lara!"

"Oh, she's having some trouble with her boyfriend."

"Well, so am I."

"Steve, don't start."

"Zack, I can't help it, you drag me to your last-day-at-work party at some hideous yuppie straight bar, and then you leave me there with all these people I don't know, while you go gallivanting about in the rain with Lara, the ditsy goth girl."

"Don't call her a ditsy Goth girl, Steve, she's been our friend for years, I don't see why all of a sudden you're getting all possessive."

"I'm not getting possessive, I just think it was rude of you two to just vanish, and especially to leave me there with a bunch of gross straight people that I don't even know!"

I opened the door to our apartment and let Steve in, following behind him and taking off my coat.

"Okay, Steve, first of all, Lara and I were only gone for fifteen minutes. Second of all, you were the one who demanded that we start being more involved in each other's lives, and part of that life is straight co-workers. If you're not ready to deal with that, then don't ask for it!"

"I don't have a problem with straight co-workers, Zack, I have a problem with how you treat me in front of them!"

I turned to look at him. Steve standing there with his heart in his hands. After two years I knew his moods. The way he nervously tucked his dirty-blond hair behind his ear, the way he cocked his eyebrow, looking at me with X-ray vision. Steve with his heart in his hands like a gift and a threat. Steve who had been there, with whom I had so much, with whom I had come so far. I loved him, still.

"I'm sorry, Steve. You're right. I've got to do better."

"No. Stop. We shouldn't do this."

"Alright," I say, and pause; pull back, wait, breathless.

"Kiss me again," she whispers.

And I do.

"Zack, honey?"

"Steve? What is it ?" I said, as I closed the front door quietly behind me, putting my coat on the hook in the wall.

"Zack, I'm in the bathroom, and I'm soaking wet. I can't believe I forgot to bring a towel. Be a dear and bring me one?"

I grabbed a towel from the hall closet and took it to Steve standing in the shower. The shower curtain was pulled to the side, and he was revealed, naked. His hair was slicked back, and water dripped from his perfect chest to his thighs, from his chest in sleek rivulets across his downy abdomen and into his trimmed thicket of brown pubic hair. I beheld his elegant prick at rest, relaxed and attenuated like a courtesan in repose.

"Here's your towel," I said, handing it to him.

"Thanks, sweetheart," he replied, taking one end from me and pulling me to him.

He let the towel drop as he reached out with one hand to pull my face to his, and held me with a long kiss. With his other hand he guided my hand to his cock, which was already hard. I could feel his wet body pressing up against mine. While I stroked his cock with one hand I took off my now-wet clothes with the other.

"Ummm," he murmured, and began to stroke me in return.

We were both naked now. As Steve and I kissed, he backed up until he bumped into the commode, he started to lose his balance and sat down abruptly on the seat.

"Interesting," I murmured, and, grabbing my cock in hand, I gently rubbed it on his lips.

With the other hand, I tried to stabilize myself and accidentally turned the water of the shower back on.

I parted his lips with my cock head and he started to suck it. Gently at first, and then harder, taking more of it deeply into his throat, grabbing my hips until I was bucking forward and back, my eyes closed, breathing heavily, lost in passion.

Suddenly he pulled back and pushed me off of him.

"You taste funny!" he spat.

"Funny like a clown funny? What the hell are you talking about?"

"I don't know, you just taste... metallic or something."

"Well, let's wash it, then."

We climbed into the shower. I grabbed some soap and started washing my cock, in long slow strokes.

"My turn," Steve said, and grabbed my shoulders, gently moving my head down to his hips and feeding me his beautiful prick. The water rushed over us, warm and relaxing.

"I'm coming," Steve said, and I took him out of my mouth, stroking him. We stood facing each other, deeply kissing. Our wet bodies were pressed close, each of us furiously jerking off, and for the first time ever we came at the same time, covering each other's stomachs and smelling of bleach.

"Your hands," she says.

"What about them?"

"You touch me like a woman."

"Gee, thanks."

"No, I meant, you touch me like you know my body the way a woman would, like I imagine a woman would...."

"Like this?"

I move in closer to her, brushing my body lightly up against hers, aching, withholding, creating electromagnetic fields of desire between her flesh and mine. I bite her earlobe gently, softly, and kiss down her neck. I undo the buttons of her blouse, making a path down the silky skin of her chest, exploring her gentle breasts with my tongue, tasting the salt and perfume, the small blonde hairs that raise themselves in goose-flesh tribute as her nipples become erect, inviting me to suckle.

My hands are Spaniards on the high seas, Conquistadores in the New World, seeking El Dorado over the supple mountains of her body. One hand approaches her delta from the front, one from the rear. My fingers find her; she is wet and warm, inviting. I am covered with her scented oils; her body is slick with sweat and strains against my touch.

My tongue finds her cleft, and I lick until she relaxes, suck until she is soothed, bite so she is surprised and shudders. She smells gloriously like a woman, her hands in my hair.

"Fuck me," she murmurs softly in my ear. "Fuck me!"

And I do.

"Zack?"

"Hmm?"

"What are you thinking?"

I turn over, pull the covers around my ears and look at the clock that reads two a.m.

"Mostly, Steve, I was thinking that I really wish I was asleep."

"Zack?"

"Yes, Steve?"

"Do you love me?"

"Of course I do, now go back to sleep."

"I can't."

"Why not?"

"Because you're fucking that girl."

"What does your boyfriend think you're doing?"

"He knows I'm with you."

"And it doesn't bother him?"

"He thinks you're gay. He thinks we're just shopping and sharing girltalk."

She runs a finger through my chest hair, rests her head on my shoulder. I can feel the warmth of her body pressed to my side, her leg laid across my pelvis, I can feel the damp glow of where I was inside her pulsing gently on my thigh. It feels good.

"But I am gay. I guess. I don't know anymore."

"You don't seem gay when we're fucking. Well, maybe you do, I mean, I don't know. You don't fuck like a straight man, either, certainly not like my boyfriend."

"Doesn't it bother you to cheat on him like this?"

"It doesn't feel like cheating—what about you?"

"It doesn't feel like cheating either. But..."

"But what?"

"Nothing...."

To change the subject, I grab her in my arms and pull her on top of me. We kiss deeply and I rub her breasts and buttocks, slipping a finger up her now-wet cunt and a thumb ever so slightly into her ass.

"Maybe," I whisper, "If it doesn't feel like cheating, we're doing it wrong."

She grabs my cock and puts it inside her, straddles me and rises up.

She supports herself with her hands on my chest as my hands wander all over her body, famished for her, wanting to map every inch of her flesh.

I suck her nipples as she leans in, shifts her hips, washing over me like high tide, taking me in deeper.

"Come on, Zack," she says, "make it feel like cheating."

"Well, what do you want to do then?"

"I don't know, Steve, it's up to you."

"I just don't understand, I don't know what to do. Right now I feel like I never want to see you again."

"I understand that, but..."

"But what?"

I sit down at the kitchen table and reach into the pocket of the jacket hanging on the back of my chair, still damp from the rain. I pull a smoke out of the crumpled pack, and light it.

I look at Steve long and hard.

"Are you telling me you never cheated before? Look me in the eye and tell me you never cheated before."

"Well, I don't see what that has to do with it."

"It has everything to do with it—I don't feel like I'm cheating with her."

"Well, let's see, monogamous means one partner—and you're fucking two people—so that must mean somebody's getting cheated on here."

"We never said we were monogamous."

"I thought that was kind of a given when we moved in together."

"It's not that simple."

"It certainly is. It's either me or her."

"What the hell are you talking about? She's got a boyfriend, she doesn't want a relationship with me—"

"How do you know?"

"I don't, I just assumed..."

"Oh, Zack, when will you ever learn?"

"I broke up with my boyfriend."

"Wow, that's awful."

"Yeah, well, he found out about us and... I guess I didn't really try too hard to hide it from him. I think I was trying to provoke him into breaking up with me."

"But, why? You two seemed so happy?"

"Well, I wasn't unhappy. But it had gotten so—domestic. I'm not, I mean, I just need more than that. I want a family one day, sure, I want a stable home ,just like anybody else does, but I just don't want it to be only two people. Call me crazy, but I just can't, it doesn't feel right to me somehow. I feel like I'm pretending. I only feel comfortable when things are weird."

"Yeah, me too."

Steve and Lara and I are sitting in the living room, being high, watching videos. We cooked a huge spaghetti dinner, far too much for three people. We are drinking red wine. We call it our "Peacemaking Potlatch" and "The Treaty of Versailles". Steve broke up with me, Lara broke up with what's-his-name and I have been away for two weeks, working the new job.

"So, how did this happen, exactly?" I say.

"Well, Steve started stalking me..."

"I did not stalk you, exactly...."

"Alright, not stalking me, but let's just say, frantically calling me, demanding an explanation."

"Oh, Steve, how could you?" I say.

"I was out of my mind, I was so angry at you two!"

"He called me at two in the morning and called me a homewrecker!"

"I'm so sorry—"

"Anyway," Lara continues, "I told him if he really had a problem with it, then he had to tell me to my face."

"And that scared the shit out of me," says Steve, shaking his head and laughing, "And you, you passive-aggressive asshole, had skipped town!"

"Skipped town? I had to make the money to pay the rent on an apartment you wouldn't even let me back into!"

"Calm down, girls," says Lara."The point is, that when we got together, and Steve and I got to talking, we found that we had a lot in common."

"Yeah, which is kind of weird."

"And the more we talked about it, we realized that no one was benefiting from us all being broken up and apart, and it was time to make peace."

"Well, I'm glad," I say.

I want to say more, I want to tell them that I love them both, that I feel safer and more secure now than ever before, that I wish this moment would never end. I want to tell them that, for once, the thrill of cheating and transgression, the thrill of deceit, has been supplanted by something else, by a feeling of calm that is as mystifying to me as if I had suddenly sprouted wings; that for the first time in years I'm allowing myself to feel: emotionally, sexually, to really feel with my whole being, feel what it means to be alive.

But I can't speak. I'm afraid.

I lay my head down on Steve's lap and I take Lara's hand.

We lie there, listening to music from the television. Steve strokes my hair and I stroke Lara's hand. I shift from my side to my back and Steve bends down and kisses me. There is a hand on my cheek that is Lara's, and it moves to Steve's cheek. As he pulls back from me and our lips separate, her hand guides his face to hers, and they kiss as Lara helps me to my knees.

The kiss ends, and we three are on our knees, facing each other, incredibly aware, incredibly alive, unable to speak.

I look at the two of them, and slowly start to unbutton my shirt, like a ritual. As if we were mirrors, Lara and Steve do the same. And next our pants come slowly off, and then all of our clothes, as we look at each other, not touching. Layers fall, and we are revealing ourselves until we are kneeling in a circle, naked. We move together in an embrace. I kiss Steve's neck, Steve kisses Lara's, Lara kisses mine. Slowly, as if underwater, Lara lies down as Steve and I embrace, falling on either side of her. Steve fondles my erect cock, and I, his, our legs intertwined over Lara, our mouths on her breasts. Lara reaches down and runs her fingers through her wet, glistening pussy, stroking her clit, and penetrating herself with her middle two fingers. She bucks her hips as Steve and I, cocks in hand, hump her thighs like dogs in heat. The room is warm, smelling of musk and friction, electric.

Steve licks his way down Lara's chest to her crotch, where my cock is, licks her pussy once and then slides my cock in his mouth. As he pushes me onto my back and starts to lick my shaft and balls, Lara gets up and straddles my face.

I can barely concentrate as Steve goes to work on me, slowly letting my shaft out of his mouth and then squeezing it back in with perfect tension. As my hips move with the rhythm of Steve's mouth I grab Lara's ass and bring her pussy to my face. She keeps her nether hair neatly trimmed, as do I, and my tongue gently pries apart her outer lips, darting in and out of the depths of her beautiful delta. My tongue moves in circles over her clitoris, and I flick at it, feel it throb. She leans over, supporting herself with her hands on the ground, and gyrates her hips against my mouth. My hands, now free, find my way to her small but perfect, beautiful breasts. As Steve flicks his tongue up and down the shaft of my cock, driving me wild, overloading my senses, I moan into Lara's pussy, and she moans out loud: we fill the air with a cacophony of pleasure.

Suddenly I feel the cool air on my prick as Steve lets it slip out of his mouth. He has reached out to Lara and nudged her shoulder, grabbing her and pulling down my body, until my cock is inside her. She and I roll over as Steve gets behind us, and I feel his hands grab my ass and start massaging. Lara pulls away from me and turns around, I embrace her from behind, and re-enter her. As we start to get a rhythm going, Steve sticks a well-lubricated finger up my ass, and starts to rub his prick up the length of my ass crack. I'm outside myself, almost completely lost in a sea of absolute sensation. I feel Steve's strong hips on my ass as he slips his finger out of my hole and replaces it with his cock. Every time I pull out of Lara, I'm penetrated more deeply by Steve. All three of us are moving, grunting, moaning, bathed in each other's sweat, in perfect communion. We are losing ourselves in each other, becoming one.

Finally, I am completely overwhelmed; waves of pleasure—some emanating from my toes, some from my head, some from the tip of my cock, and some from my ass—all converge in my center, and I know I am going to come or else explode into oblivion. I manage to mutter, "I'm coming," and pull Lara in close, holding her to me as I am immobilized by my orgasm. All of my sensation has been focused on my cock, but now it's as if my body is one vast nerve: tingling, alive.

Steve whispers in my ear, "I'm coming," and pulls his cock out of my ass. He pulls off the condom, and I hear him jerking off and then I feel his hot cum land on my back and drip down my ass. He grunts and moans and collapses on top of me. His cum makes a squishy noise as air is displaced between his stomach and my back.

For a few moments we lie there. Spent.

Then Lara says, "Um, you guys? A little help here?" as she begins to rub herself again, working herself up.

Steve and I start to massage her all over. He starts at her neck and shoulders; I begin at her feet and calves. We use our hands and tongues to lavish attention on every part of her body. I take each of her toes in my mouth and suck; Steve takes each of Lara's fingers. As we work our way up her body, massaging, kissing, fondling, Lara jills off.

Lara starts breathing more heavily, I can tell she's getting close when she says, "Hold me, don't fuck me, hold me." And Steve and I embrace her, our stiff members up against her, not entering.

We hold her between us like a flesh cocoon as she takes her pleasure. Suddenly she gasps and shudders, and Steve and I feel her orgasm rush through her, rush through us. She lets out a small cry and tenses up; we hold her more firmly, all of our bodies tense, all of us holding our breath.

Finally, we exhale. We lie together quietly, the television playing music quietly in the background. The room is filled with contentment. I feel, maybe for the first time, complete.

Maybe there is a new way; maybe three isn't a crowd. Only time will tell. All we have is now. And in this moment we have become a symphony of hands and tongues. We are a triptych of touch and language in motion. We are explorers of undiscovered countries, cartographers of desire.

Andy Ohio is a writer/performer who's been published in Seattle's alternative weekly The Stranger, Torso *magazine and a handful of small zines and journals. He has performed his poetry and monologues all over the United States. He currently lives in Brooklyn where he is developing his solo performance piece,* radius.

Her Mouth, In Which I Drowned

Linda Eisenstein

When Katy ate a plum, you'd think you'd died and gone to heaven. Those sharp teeth biting into the purple skin, the rosy flesh bursting with juice, the pulp tender as a bruise.

When men saw Katy's mouth, their hearts and their cocks would throb in rhythm. Katy's mouth loved cocks. You could tell. She had the kind of mouth that God designed for fellatio. The biggest, hungriest, reddest lips you'd ever seen in real life, outside a magazine ad. All over campus, that mouth was legend, Davy Jones' locker, the sailor's watery grave.

Katy said things I never heard from a woman, before or since. In traffic, she could blister the paint off passing cars with her swearing. "Move over, cockbreath!" she'd yell as she cut in front of blundering jocks. She drove like a maniac, too. One winter I rode shotgun while she delivered pizzas. We careened around corners, the pizzas shimmying and sliding in the back of her VW, which she handled like a stock car, wheels squealing over the crunch of ice. Even today, the smell of pepperoni makes me imagine death in a fiery crash. As scared as I was, she made me crave it. She was my personal adrenaline pump, my roller coaster, my drug of choice.

Later, in the bar, she'd describe the color and shape of the dicks she sucked that week like market sausages. "Oscar Meyer, teeny weeny," she'd gasp, "cocktail frank," her Texas laugh whirring like a butcher's slicer. "She's as big a size queen as any faggot," our friend Buddy Ray told me, admiringly. We all laughed until we hiccupped. While my heart sank.

I never got tired of watching her mouth. She had teeth like a ferret's. I'd dream of kissing her, how I'd cover her whole mouth with my own, feel the basket of her teeth pressing behind her lips. Her mouth was a cage, and my tongue a bird, battering itself against it. Trapped, forever trying to get in.

Katy was a counter-revolutionary. She believed in make-up: foundation, two tones of blush, eyeshadow like a fading bruise, and three shades of lipstick, including lip liner. She talked me into a makeover once. I leaned back in her desk chair and bared my throat to her like a Mayan sacrifice. I'd have let her paint my eyeballs black to smell her bent over me like that. She fussed with my mouth for nearly twenty minutes, drawing and redrawing my lip line. Try as she might, we both knew it could never look like hers. "We're gonna redefine the lines here, sugar," she purred, but she was wrong. I had felt them blurring all year long.

She was tiny, 97 pounds dripping wet. She had to buy her clothes, she said, in the children's department. Where she got her black push-up bras I never did find out. I loomed over her like a Yeti, awkward and hulking. The only time we ever seemed like the same size was when we smoked dope. We'd lie on the floor, heads nearly touching, staring up at the ceiling. Then her head seemed enormous, all black hair and black eyes and red mouth. Once she decided I wasn't stoned enough and she shotgunned me: inhaling, then putting her mouth over mine and blowing the sweet smoke into me until I nearly exploded from desire. I can still taste her lipstick.

Me, I stopped wearing makeup that year. It was her makeover that did it. She made me see myself through her eyes. When Katy was done with me, she took a puff on her cigarette, and sighed. I looked, she said, like a drag queen. That's when I knew: I would never be a woman she wanted.

Later that night, she came on to me, bold as brass, in front of her latest boyfriend. Left him hanging gape-mouthed in the bar, and pulled me by the hand until we landed in her bed. For years I wondered why. At the time I assumed it was just a chess move in a game between them, me the lowly pawn suddenly advanced to make queen. But now I think she meant it as a consolation prize: for failing me in my transformation. But she was wrong. I changed, all right. With her head in my hands, drinking her mouth, the mouth I knew I'd never taste again, I drowned, I died.

She moved back to Houston soon afterward. She didn't even bother finishing out the semester. I heard from someone that she was dancing topless, making big bucks. For years I dreamed of hitchhiking to Texas, haunting strip bars until I found her, her child's body grinding under a garish light, pierced by a thousand hungry eyes. She'd feel me there in the dark, and come right to me: sit on my lap, press her lips against my fluttering throat. Fat chance.

After we both admitted we'd slept with her, Buddy Ray and I lay in bed, smoking, comparing notes. Yes, children, back in the Golden Age, those bright days before the labels. Back when we all swallowed mouthfuls of each other as easily as we downed the pills our hosts poured into our open hands, without asking what they were. "Her mouth," I sighed. "It was so...ineffable." He agreed. "I guess this makes me a lesbian, huh?" I asked him. He blew a smoke ring, considering. "It's hard to tell," he said. This was a good five years before he came out himself. "I mean, if Katy was a puppy dog," said Buddy Ray, "even the Pope would get himself locked up for bestiality."

And I took out one of Katy's lipsticks, one I'd stolen. And with it we painted each other's mouths, he and I, and blotted our lips on each other's flesh, until we stopped aching. And shared another cigarette, tasting lipstick and tobacco, dreaming, dreaming of her mouth.

Linda Eisenstein's plays have been produced on three continents. Her work has appeared in Blithe House Quarterly, Paramour, *and* Anything That Moves, *and anthologized in* The Actor's Book of Gay and Lesbian Plays *(Penguin), and* The Best Women's Stage Monologues 1997 & 1998 *(Smith & Kraus). She lives in Cleveland, Ohio.*

Boy Bashing

Raven Gildea

I don't wanna fuck straight boys, usually.

I mean, the boys I fuck are dykes, and the boys I fantasize about are fags. When I'm fucking a boy-dyke, she's a fag, 'cause she's a boy and I'm her Daddy, see? Okay. But I do have this one fantasy about a straight boy.

Not any particular straight boy. I'm not even sure what he looks like. Sometimes he's street-tough in ripped jeans, sometimes he's an expensively dressed rich kid. What I know for sure is, he's lean, he's handsome, and he's white. His hair is a little long, 'cause he knows lotsa straight girls dig that. Me, I like shaved-head fag boys, but this boy is no fag. This boy has privilege written all over him.

He's young, he's male, and he's cocky. Hell, he's probably even blond. I almost never go for blonds. Alright, he's blond. He's not a day over twenty-three and he thinks he's got it all. But I've got at least ten years on him, so I know what's up.

Okay, so I'm walking down the street, all decked out. I love walking around in leather, feeling the solid thump of my boots hitting the pavement, the way my chaps grip my thighs, the push of my dick against the crotch of my jeans. Of course I'm packing. After all, it's my fantasy.

I don't notice the boy until he yells at me. "Hey, faggot," he calls. "Do you wanna suck my dick?"

Now, usually when people yell "hey, faggot" at me I just laugh and think, "If only they knew." Straight people are so confused about gender. But there was that one time, last summer. Six redneck boys in a pickup truck, hollering, "You're a cocksucker, aren't you? Are you a man or a woman? Hey, I'm talking to you! Answer me or I'll knock your fucking motorcycle over!"

I get sick of educating straight people. I didn't see the point in explaining that I'm neither a man nor a woman, that I *am* a cocksucker but I prefer to get mine sucked, by a boy-dyke on her knees. So when I saw my opening to get past them, I yelled, "I'm a fucking dyke, assholes!" and roared away.

I got out with my skin intact, but it shook me more than I care to admit. My first girlfriend was jumped by a pack of rednecks in a pickup truck. They threw her in the back, took her into the woods, and gang-raped her. They beat her so badly that her eyesight was permanently damaged. She was fourteen years old.

So when this boy yells "Faggot" at me, something snaps. I get right up in his face. I look him in the eye. "No," I say slowly, "I don't want to suck your dick. Do you want to suck mine?"

He starts to say "I... I..." but stops when I reach for my knife.

What I love about my knife is, I can pull it out and flick it open in one smooth motion. I do. The click as the blade locks into place has exactly the effect I want. His eyes get wide and he goes all quiet. I like that in a boy.

I back him up against the wall, and look him up and down real slow. I'm sizing him up, the way boys do with each other. But he also sees that I'm checking him out, the way boys do to girls. Like I wanna know what he's got to give me. Like

I'm gonna take what I want, and it's not about him at all. This makes him really uncomfortable.

"Just kidding, man." He eyes the knife and smiles sheepishly. "It was just a joke."

"Shut up," I say, my voice pitched low. "The joke's on you this time."

I grab him by his collar and push him into the alley. Between a dumpster and a pile of cardboard boxes, there's a spot where no one will notice us.

I grab a handful of his hair and shove his face into the wall, twisting so that his cheek, not his nose, hits first. Can't have him bleeding all over my dick. On second thought, I don't mind a little blood, so I grind his skin against the rough brick. He gasps. I smile.

"So you're looking for a faggot, are you?" I growl in his ear. "Someone who can take you back here and feed you all the dick you need?" He doesn't answer, perhaps because my blade is resting at the corner of his eye. Well, you know what they say: silence implies consent.

I slip a pair of handcuffs off my belt and snap them onto one of his wrists. He stares in disbelief. I savor that for a moment before yanking the hand behind his back. It takes a sharp upward twist to convince him to give up his other arm. When he does, I reward him with a "Good boy" as the second cuff clicks into place.

Putting my weapon away, I wind my fist into his hair, push the toe of my boot against the back of his knee, and pull him to the ground. "That's where you belong, boy, down in the dirt." I push his head against the asphalt with one foot. "You're not good enough to lick my boots, are you? But you want to be a good boy, don't you? Do you need somebody who can make you be a good boy? Do you need some cock? I hope so, 'cause you just found some."

I unbutton my jeans, leaving my belt buckled, and ease my dick out through the opening. I pull the boy up by his hair, and he struggles to his knees. When I let him look up, his eyes practically bug out of his head. Maybe he didn't realize until now just what kind of pervert he was tangling with.

What I love about my dick is... well, it's my dick. What's not to love? It's shiny, red and black, and fierce. The end is sharply pointed and there are ridges along the shaft. It feels good under my hand. I wave it in front of his nose a few times, then rest it against his wet, slack mouth.

"Do you wanna suck dick, cocksucker? Is that why you're looking for a faggot? Is this what you've been waiting for? Hell, you've waited your whole life for this, haven't you? Waited to find someone who could force you to suck faggot dick. Someone who could take you down and give you what you need. Someone who wouldn't give you any choice."

Another yank on his hair and his mouth falls open. The tip of my cock slides past his lips. He tries to push away, but his hands are cuffed and I've got a firm grip on him. There is only one thing he can do.

"Suck it, bitch," I purr. "Suck it like you love it. Don't even think of using your teeth. Make my dick feel good, really good, 'cause you don't want to see what I'm like when I get into a bad mood."

His head is bobbing up and down, his throat quivering. My cock slips nearly all the way out of his mouth until just the tip rests on his shining lips, then slides deep until those same lips kiss the fabric of my jeans. The scrape on his face is red and raw. I can smell his blood and his fear. This is so beautiful it almost scares me.

When he starts to gag, I pull out and let him gulp in some air. Coated with his saliva, my cock glistens.

Just before his ragged breath evens out, I plunge back in. I've got both hands fisted in his hair, and I feel a pleasant strain on the muscles in my arms as I rock him against my pelvis, fucking his face. The base of my dick presses rhythmically against my clit, but it's the adrenaline rush, not the pressure, that thrills me.

When I pull his head back for the last time, the wet line of a tear traces down his face. His blue eyes hold no hope. He is utterly mine, and we both know it.

"You don't look so smug now, do you?" I croon. "See, you can be a good boy. You just need someone to show you how."

Unlocking one cuff, I bring his hands around in front of him. He's still kneeling, and it's easy to pull him forward until I can slip the handcuff chain around the wheel at the base of the dumpster. One boot firmly planted on the back of his neck holds him down until I've snapped the cuff back around his wrist.

He is stretched across the ground as if in supplication. He looks good like that, but I've got something better in mind. Grabbing his belt, I push my knee under his ass and haul him to his feet.

He squeals in protest as the cuffs bite into his wrists. I grab his balls with one hand and his hair with the other, and soon have him in the position I want. With his hands and feet supporting him, his ass waves tantalizingly in front of me. Sweet.

I unbuckle his belt and pull it free. Flicking out my knife, I slit open the back of his shirt, then go to work on his pants. The fabric resists, but my blade has been lovingly sharpened and before long I've exposed the soft white skin of the boy's ass. I kick his legs apart, and his balls hang loosely, vulnerable and exposed. He begins to tremble.

Dangling his belt from my hand, I draw it slowly across his butt, letting him get the feel of it, gauging my range.

Then I let him have it. The leather makes a loud, satisfying crack and leaves an angry red welt in its wake. The boy lets out a startled bellow.

I'm having too much fun to want anyone breaking this up, so I pull a couple of bandanas from my pocket. The green one gets wadded into his mouth, the black one threaded between his jaws and tied behind his head. That oughta shut him up.

"Don't you be hollering, now," I admonish him. "Be a good boy for me and you'll find out what the good boys get." He's face down and can't see me stroke my dick. He can't see my evil smile, either, but I'm sure he hears it in my voice.

I cup his balls in my hand. He can't help himself; he relaxes into my touch. He doesn't know me, like me, or trust me, but his balls say yes and he follows their orders. When he moves himself against my palm, I immediately stop touching him.

The next crack of the belt lands without warning, and his head snaps up in surprise. His anguished cry is muffled by the gag, but it's still plenty loud. "No hollering!" I snap, bringing the belt across his ass again. This time he is silent, and I praise him again. "I knew you could take it like a good boy," I whisper, softly stroking the raised welts with an open hand. "I knew you wanted to be good for me."

Now I really give it to him. The leather strap smacks down rhythmically, leaving a series of lurid marks which contrast beautifully with the paleness of his skin. The boy grunts with each stroke, but doesn't scream again. Sweat beads on his back and runs in rivulets down his arms. I don't stop belting him until his knees are shaking so furiously that I think they might give out. I'm not ready for that to happen. I'm not done with him yet.

Looping the belt around his waist and cinching it tight, I steady him on his feet. I let him lean into me for a moment, let him feel the solidness of my body supporting him. The sensation of his ass pressing against me makes my dick twitch. He's slick with sweat, and my dick slides along his crack for a moment before he notices. When he does, he freezes.

"That's right, hold still for me," I purr. He is motionless, but his body clearly conveys the depth of his panic. I step around to where he can see me and lean against the dumpster, one foot on either side of his hands. He drops to his knees and looks up at me. His relief is palpable, until he notices the condom I'm opening.

There is nothing quite like rolling a rubber down the shaft of my cock. I take my time, savoring the slick feel of the latex under my fingers and the smooth curve of red and black reflected in the boy's terrified eyes. I pull out a glove and snap it onto one hand, open a packet of lube and begin rubbing its slippery contents over the warming surface of my dick. I could get lost in this, could lean here forever letting my hand slide up and down, under and around, feeling my power. I could, but I've got work to do.

Placing the toe of my boot on the back of his hand, I slowly apply increasing pressure. When he's about to panic I bark out, "Ass up!" He lifts his ass to the sky, gratified to know what's wanted of him. I release his hand from under my boot and step back behind him.

For a straight boy, he's got a sweet ass. It's round and inviting, covered with golden fuzz. The red welts shine, and his legs fall in a long smooth line down from his hips to where the shreds of his pants bunch around his ankles. His pink, puckered asshole quivers, waiting for my touch.

I touch him where he doesn't expect it, on the back of his neck. My hand rests there until he begins to breathe again, then traces a slow, caressing path down his spine. When I reach the belt, I slide my fingers under it and pull the boy's lean body toward my own. But I don't touch his ass. I place my gloved, lubed hand on his skin just below his waist and slide it smoothly around his hip and onto his belly. His dick jumps in response. My hand makes slow circles around his navel, palm flat to his skin. His dick strains upward trying to make contact, but I stay just out of reach.

When I'm certain his dick is aching for my touch, I slip my hand away from his body. I pause before I use the belt to ease him closer. His low moan is the sign I've been waiting for. A shiver courses through us both as we make contact.

He's scared, but he's all mine. My lubed finger circles his asshole gently, while he waits for me to take him. At long last I slide a fingertip into him. I give him a moment to adjust to the unfamiliar feeling, then push the rest of the finger all the way in. I can't tell whether his groan is fear, pleasure or pain, and it doesn't really matter. "Relax, boy," I tell him. "You're gonna like this." I wait once more, until I feel the tightness in his muscles begin to ease. Then I start fucking him. He tenses again at the first movement, but soon realizes that tightening up only makes him feel more invaded. I encourage him by chanting softly, "Relax that ass, that's right, just open up for me, I'm coming to get you, you can't stop this, you know you need it, you know you want to be fucked, well I'm gonna fuck you like you've never been fucked before, that's right, you're mine, just let me take you, I'll take you where you've never been, where you've always wanted to go, just give it to me..." I can tell it hurts when I slip a second finger alongside the first, but he struggles to take it like the good boy he longs to be. I rock him forward with my hand, back with the belt, and his breathing becomes rhythmic. His ass opens up and my third finger seems to fall in.

"Look at you, you little slut!" I croon. "You need this, don't you? Well I've got just what you need, right here, waiting for your sweet little hungry ass." I pull out and he tries to follow me, to recapture my hand. I laugh and smack him on the butt. "Greedy, aren't you? You just be patient now, I'll give you what you need." I guide the tip of my slippery dick to his waiting hole, while I pull him toward me with the belt which encircles his waist. We are both amazed at the ease with which my cock slides into him. There is no question this time: the noise that escapes him is one of ecstasy. I bury myself to the hilt, relishing the pressure of his warm ass against my hips. I make him wait. It is him, not me, who makes the next move.

His wriggle grinds the base of my dick against my clit, sending an electric shock through me. Grabbing the belt with both hands, I push him off and pull him onto my cock, impaling him slowly, then gathering speed. Soon we are both grunting and panting, straining for more. His head presses against the side of the dumpster, giving him leverage to push himself back and onto me as I rock forward and into him. My excitement rises with the increasing fury of my thrusts. The muscles in my abdomen are burning, but it is the burning in my cunt which sends fire racing through my veins. My climax explodes like a white light in my brain, coursing through my body with the speed and intensity of an electrical storm. The heat fountains out through my arms and legs, leaving me shuddering, gasping, transformed.

I slump across the boy's back, wrapping my arms around his torso. His sweat soaks into my shirt as his knees gently give way and we both sink to the ground. We lie together, me covering his nakedness, him twitching and spasming around my quivering cock.

His eyelids flutter. He is breathing through his mouth, panting like a dog, and his breath quickens when I slide myself out of him. He tries to move as I rise to my feet, but his body refuses to comply.

Pulling off the condom and glove, I stand over him and drop them to the pavement beside his head. My cock wags in his face as I crouch beside him, unlock the cuffs, and return them to my belt. I leave the gag in place. His eyes are luminous as he looks up at me.

"Now remember, boy," I say, tucking my dick into my jeans and buttoning up, "Next time a faggot catches your eye, treat him with respect."

I stride down the alley without looking back.

Raven Gildea lives in Seattle. She spent her childhood trying to be a boy, her adolescence trying to be a girl, her twenties trying to be a lesbian, and her thirties trying to be a butch. She has no idea what she'll try next.

Cruising the Conference

Dominic Santi

I woke up in a distinctly het frame of mind. Not good, considering that I was a featured speaker that afternoon at WriteOUT, the queer writers' conference. I doubted I'd have much luck cruising for chicks anywhere in the hotel, and I was horny as hell.

As usual, Roger was a total pain in the ass about it. "Ooh, my little bottom boy has the hots to get some pussy of his own. Good luck *here*, pal!"

"Fuck you," I muttered, tucking my shirttails into my pants. "I didn't say I was going to *do* anything about it. I just said I was feeling het, okay? There's a difference!"

I watched him out of the corner of my eye as I quickly buckled my belt. I hadn't meant to be quite that rude. Roger's punishment spankings hurt like hell, and neither the erection I always got afterwards nor a tear-stained face would do much for my professional demeanor in the highly academic "Gender Politics in Bisexual Threeways" I was scheduled to present. I didn't want to spend the entire time I was supposed to be engaged in intelligent discourse distracted by a sore ass and trying to hide a raging hard-on.

Fortunately, Roger just snorted into his orange juice. "Remember the rules, sweet cheeks. If you want to play with the girls, you have to bring them home to meet daddy first." He set down his glass and walked towards the bathroom, pausing just long enough to grab my crotch and stroke his thumb lecherously over my cock. "And afterwards, you have to tell me every slutty little thing you did."

I moaned, rocking my hips forward as my dick immediately swelled into his warm, soothing hand.

"Now, finish getting ready for your presentation." He gave me a quick peck on the lips and a sharp swat on the ass, then sashayed into the bathroom, closing the door firmly in back of himself.

"Asshole," I grouched. I kept my voice low, though, as I started collecting my notes. Roger insisted I tell him when I was thinking about chicks. But then he wouldn't fuck me, and he wouldn't let me jack off. He wouldn't let me get my rocks off any way except by having sex with a woman—which wasn't likely to happen here. The more I thought about it, the harder my poor frustrated dick got.

Not that I was a stranger to frustration anymore. Right from the start, Roger had been crystal clear about who called the shots in our relationship. I'd been cruising the newcomers at the local writer's group. As I made a loud, smartass comment to one of my friends, Roger turned around. I froze, stunned, gawking at his drop-dead good looks. I found out later he was 35, ten years older than me, but all I saw was his smooth, slender build, short curly blond hair and expressive green eyes—a total contrast to my stereotypical Greek looks. Roger's sexy lips curled into a calm, seductive smile. I smiled back. I wanted to fuck him—bad!

I suppose I should say up front that, four years later, I still haven't had my dick up his ass. He took me home with him, my cock jutting out in front of us as it strained against the buttons of my jeans. When we got inside, he kissed me until I said "yes" to something about rope. I wasn't paying attention. In my mind, I could already see my rock-hard dick snaking up his curvy ass as I bent him over the table.

The next thing I knew, Roger was naked, my wrists were tied behind my back, and I was on my knees, licking my way down his calf. I bathed his feet until my tongue seemed to know the patterns on each of his toepads. Then I worked my way slowly back up his leg, washing his balls and cock until his smell was sealed into my face, until my mouth was hungry to kiss and suck and tease the velvety soft skin covering his stiff, hot shaft. I love uncut men, and Roger's foreskin was perfect—long and loose and easy to retract. I felt each jump and shiver against the inside of my lips as I pushed his skin back and tongued the silky flesh beneath. He tasted so good I deep throated him until he pulled out and spewed his cream all over my face. I was so turned on, my balls hurt!

That's when Roger told me I was an adequate cocksucker, but I hadn't earned the right to take my clothes off in front of him yet. He untied my wrists and told me I could sleep on the floor at the foot of his bed if I could behave myself, otherwise, to go home.

I stared up at him in total disbelief. My dick was throbbing, his spunk was dripping onto my shirt, and this yahoo was telling me I didn't get to come?!

I blew up. My whole body got hot as I worked myself into a righteous lather. I swore, shook my fist at him, screamed in his face. Roger just stood there, one eyebrow raised, looking almost amused at my tantrum. Until I threw a book at the wall. I didn't even see him move. He grabbed me by the back of my collar, put his foot on the bed, and bent me over his thigh. I hadn't even noticed the hairbrush on the nightstand, but I sure as hell felt it. Damn, I hate that hairbrush! It stings as much today as it did that first night, though now he uses it on my bare ass. That night, even my jeans and briefs didn't offer much protection. I kicked and yelled and howled as Roger thoroughly and methodically set my entire ass on fire. I was sobbing by the time he finished, begging his forgiveness, pleading with him to give me another chance.

And I came in my pants. That spanking got my ass so fucking hot, I wiggled and ground against his thigh until the friction was so intense, my dick spurted into my Jockeys. I was embarrassed as hell, but by then, I wanted him so much, I didn't care. I fell on the floor and kissed his feet.

Roger reached down and patted my head. "Good boy. Now lie down on the rug and get some rest."

I felt like I was watching somebody else move as I crawled over to where he was pointing and fell asleep, my underwear wet and sticky against my dick, my ass burning. Sometime during the night, he threw a blanket over me. I woke up warm, though I was stiff as hell from sleeping on the floor, and my ass hurt.

So I made him coffee. Actually, I brought him breakfast in bed. I'd decided I was willing to admit that my tantrum, justified as I felt it was, had been pretty childish. Roger looked fantastic sleeping under his down comforter. I still wanted to fuck him.

I walked home hungry but happy, with my cock leading the way and an order to come back in two days. Roger hadn't so much as kissed me, but I'd been inordinately pleased that he'd liked both the eggs-over-easy and the cinnamon toast I'd made for him. He'd also told me not to touch my dick until I saw him again. I had no intention of obeying him about that. I planned to go home and beat off until my dick was raw.

I'm still not sure why I didn't. I was ready to explode by the next time I saw him. It was a repeat of the previous date, though this time I avoided the spanking by saying, "Yes, sir" and going to sleep on my mat after he came. I tried to rub my dick against the floor, but the buttons were too uncomfortable. I think he was laughing, up in his warm, comfy bed. I seriously considered getting pissed at him, but the taste of his dick was still heavy on my tongue.

On the third date, he let me lick his whole body. I'd never had a thing for feet before, but his were so special, so sensitive. He wiggled when I sucked his toes, held my face to his chest as I chewed his tits, thrust against me as his cock snaked down my throat. What drove me wild, though, was when he cut a rubber open and let me tongue his ass through it. He squatted down over my face, the sound of his voice reverberating through my body each time he growled, "Dig deep, Michael, so I have a good come."

The quiet, slender man whom no one would take for anybody's daddy had me quivering like putty underneath his open ass. I wanted to fuck him! Wanted to shove my dick up where my lips and tongue were sliding into his smooth, dank heat. I arched my hips, desperately seeking some contact—some relief. I almost came when his sphincter contracted around my tongue. He groaned so loudly as his hot come gorped out onto my chest. The air was thick with the smell of his ass and his wet, sticky cream. As he purred contentedly above me, I was so frustrated I wanted to cry. I probably would have, if he hadn't petted my head and told me what a good boy I was. I fell asleep, whimpering on the rug.

The next time, there was no petting. And he didn't give me his ass. He said he was tired, so he just jacked off on my face and climbed into bed

"But I want to fuck you, sir," I grouched. The "sir" came easily now, but I was still hornier than hell. "I want to shove my cock up your ass!"

When Roger stopped laughing, he ruffled my hair and said, "Nice fantasy, boy. Go to sleep." Which is exactly what he did, while I seethed on my mat, my cock throbbing as I swore I'd never set foot in his fucking house again.

By the fifth date, I was miserably horny, and totally in love—and completely pissed off. Except for a couple of wet dreams, I hadn't come in over two weeks. So I wasn't too careful with my teeth. Roger cuffed my ears a couple time for that. I got my ass swatted when I bit his big toe. This time, he told me, I hadn't earned his come. He just stood up, tugged on a pair of slinky blue running shorts that showed every curve and contour of his mouthwateringly tumescent cock, and pointed for me to lie down on the rug.

I couldn't do it.

"Where the fuck do you get off?" I snapped. "I haven't touched my own dick since I met you, and now you say I can't touch yours! I've had enough of this shit!"

"Then leave," he said quietly, pouring himself a cup of the steaming hot tea he always kept in a porcelain pot on the nightstand. "Nobody's making you stay." He just stood there, in those crotch-hugging shorts, his still-hard dick jutting out at me as he nonchalantly sipped his tea, while I was so horny I was ready to rape the mattress.

That pushed me right over the fucking edge.

"But I haven't gotten to fuck you yet," I snarled. I climbed slowly to my feet, walked over to him, and deliberately pushed him back against the bed. I had every intention of jerking that son of a bitch around and shoving my cock up his fucking ass.

I jumped back, yelping as the scalding tea splashed over my hand and onto his chest.

"Ow!" I sucked my burning fingers into my mouth. "That's hot!" The words froze in my throat as I looked into Roger's face. His eyes had gone so cold they were like deep green shards of broken glass.

"Hey, man," I stammered, raising my hands apologetically. "I'm sorry. I didn't mean to hurt you . . ."

"Take off your clothes, Michael." Roger didn't move, but his voice was icy calm. "Now. Or walk out that door, and don't ever come back."

"I said I was sorry...." My voice trailed off as saw the bright pink marks on his chest, the dark wet spot on the front of his running shorts, and realized there wasn't anything I could say to make it better.

"One chance, Michael." Roger's voice was frigid. I could hear the controlled fury in it. "Clothes off, and bend over with your hands braced on the bed. Or get the fuck out of my life."

I'm not sure my brain was registering as I kicked my shoes off and yanked my T-shirt over my head. I was trembling by the time I slid my jeans and underwear over my hips.

"I'm sorry," I said softly, shivering as I peeled off my socks. Roger didn't answer, just picked up the belt he'd thrown aside earlier in the evening and doubled it, snapping it once against his thigh. The crack sounded like a gunshot in the sudden absolute quiet of the bedroom. I stared down in shock as my still-half-hard cock started to fill again with a vengeance.

Roger pointed to the side of the bed. I bent over, bracing my shaking hands. I jumped as he kicked my legs apart.

"Stick your butt out further. If you try to get up, I'll tie you."

"I didn't mean..." I gasped as the first crack echoed in the room. I yelled, my whole body stiffening as a wave of flame burst across my butt. Then the only sounds coming out of my mouth were yells and hollers and a long, drawn out litany of "sorry, sorry, SORRies!!" as Roger whipped my ass until I thought I'd never breathe again.

The last stroke pushed me into the bed. My arms gave out, and I buried my face in the comforter, sobbing and clenching my asscheeks, trying to ease the fiery pain. And my cock, oh god, as the heat rushed through my ass, my cock got so hard I thought it was going to burst. I stared back between my legs, stunned to see a strand of precome oozing down towards the floor.

Then Roger's firm, calm hand cupped my scalded buttcheek. I yelled and lurched forward. His touch felt like a branding iron.

"You took your punishment well, Michael. I'm proud of you."

"I really am sorry, sir," I sniffled. "I didn't mean to hurt you. I don't ever want to hurt you. Owww!"

"I know." I felt the smile in his voice, smiled in spite of myself, my eyes still blurred with tears as his fingers squeezed. "You're mine, now, Michael. Spread your legs."

I moaned as his hand slid up my crack. There was a bottle of lube on the night stand. I didn't want to admit I recognized the loud squirt as he pressed the top of the container. Then the fingers in my crack were icy cold and slick, soothing on my sore, hot, stinging skin, and Roger was playing with my asshole. One finger pressed firmly in. I quivered, my body shaking against the mattress.

"You're tight, boy. Open for me." The finger stretched from side to side in slow, lazy circles. My ass burned so badly, but my cock swayed between my legs, trying to stretch out even further, twitching in tempo to Roger's strokes.

"Feels good!" I gasped.

Something in my tone of voice must have given me away. Roger's hand stilled, his finger resting inside me as he ignored my whimper and squeezed my flaming ass. "Have you ever been fucked before, Michael?"

I didn't even consider lying to him. "No, sir." I gasped. "But I—I want you to fuck me."

Roger's laugh reverberated all the way through me. "I will, boy. Be patient."

I didn't answer. I just groaned and poked my ass out at him, wallowing in new sensations as Roger loosened my locked-tight and hypersensitive sphincter. I'd barely heard the wrapper tear when his cool, sheathed cock butted up against my virgin hole. I started to tighten, I couldn't help it, but Roger grabbed my sore strapped asscheek. I yelped as suddenly my butt had all my attention again.

"Give me your hand, Michael." A cool glob of lube squirted into my palm. "Jerk off while you press back against me. That's it. Press back more."

I moaned as my hot, familiar hand closed around my engorged shaft. The heat on my butt and in my asshole seemed to burn forward, all the way to my cock. I groaned again as my asslips seemed to reach out towards the lube-slicked head of Roger's dick. I vaguely remembered that being fucked was supposed to hurt, but the slow gradual stretching felt so good.

"More, Michael." Roger's voice was calm and soothing, and implacable. "Bear down, like you're trying shit me out."

I grunted, loudly. I felt like such a pig, but I wanted his dick so badly, I didn't care. My hand tightened on my cock. Then I gasped, like I couldn't get enough air, as the long, slow burn of Roger's shaft crawled up my ass. My "unh, unh, unhs" of pleasure echoed in my ears as my guts opened to him. He was inside of me—filling me.

He was fucking me. My whole body stiffened in shock. I tightened, crying out as the pain got sharp.

"Easy, Michael. Stroke your cock. Let me make you feel good."

My dick softened in my hand as I panted, trying to relax into his arms. Then Roger's tongue licked up my spine.

"You're beautiful, Michael." He pressed forward. "Your pussy was made for fucking." I gasped as pure sexual energy jolted deep inside me. "Your ass is so hot and red."

He squeezed my asscheeks, and I cried out at the pain. Then he licked up my back again. The tension slowly drained from my shoulders as he kissed me. My asslips tickled oddly, the new sensations echoing in my twitching dick as I smeared my cock juices up and down my shaft.

"You like being fucked, don't you, boy?"

"Unh-huh," I groaned, as my lube-slopped hand moved furiously over my shaft.

He slowly pulled out and pressed back in. I gasped as another ooze of precome leaked out of my dick. God, it felt good. I was going to come.

I realized I needed to ask permission—fast! "P-please, sir," I panted. "N-need to come. Please!"

"Let it happen," he laughed. "I want to feel you squeezing me the first time you shoot with a dick up your ass."

He grabbed my hips and slammed into me. I yelled, jerking my cock, squirming frantically as Roger's dick stretched me and he pounded into the exquisitely sensitive spot deep inside my hole. Then I threw back my head and howled as my ass clamped down around his dick and I started spurting what felt like gallons of man-cream onto my hand and my chest and the bed. Roger wrapped his arms around me and held on tight as my nuts pumped out every hot drop of semen they'd been hoarding since I'd met him.

It was the best come of my entire fucking life. I was totally wasted. I rested my head on my arms and moaned contentedly, trying to keep my balance as Roger stood back up and fucked me until my hole burned almost as much as my asscheeks. I blushed when he came, proud that I'd taken his fucking, relishing his roar, imagining what I looked like, good old Michael the Top, wallowing in being a slutty bottom boy as my new daddy's cock shot up my ass.

Two months later, I moved in. Lock, stock, bookcases and computer. I loved him. I relished the idea of finally having some discipline and order in my thoroughly chaotic life. And though sometimes I still chafed at Roger's clearly-stated rule that his word was law in our house, I'd accepted his requirement of total honesty: I agreed to tell him about everybody I slept with.

Even the chicks.

Roger laughed his fucking ass off when I told him I sometimes slept with chicks. I mean, I like women. They're soft and curvy and their pussies feel great wrapped around my dick. And they smell good.

I figured the het parts of my sex life were over, though, when he told me that from now on, he had to "interview" anybody I slept with. I mean, what chick in her right mind was going to have sex with me when I told her that before we could do anything alone, first I had to fuck her with my male lover watching, so he was sure I wouldn't forget my bottom boy place and get uppity because I'd been with her? I was mortified—and dejected. And, of course, since Roger had said I now had to tell him whenever I was even feeling het-ish, I started noticing the women around me all the time. Especially Marianne.

Marianne and I had been friends, as well as fuck buddies, for a long time. We worked together at the local bindery. She wasn't gorgeous like Roger, just smart and pretty and sexy, in a brassy Southern harlot sort of way. Her short brown hair had different color highlights, depending on her mood. She never seemed to keep the same hairstyle for more than a month. And the way she dressed drove me nuts. She wore short, clingy skirts with lace-topped stockings and no panties, and tight sweaters that showed off the way her full, naturally curvy breasts rose and fell when she breathed. I was one of the few people at work who knew why her nipples were almost always hard. They're so sensitive, she once came just from my sucking on them. God, that was hot! Marianne's also one of the only people who never bought into my Casanova routine. Even when we were screwing like hormone-crazed bunnies, she told me to just shut up and fuck her. We had a lot of fun together.

I was nervous as all hell when I finally took her to a nice restaurant, plunked down $90 for dinner and the bottle of red wine I hoped would loosen her up, and started explaining my dilemma. My squirming was only partly due to the hot ass Roger had given me earlier in the day for watching TV before I'd outlined my latest magazine assignment. As usual, Marianne's perfume was wreaking havoc with my cock. Finally, she took pity on me, picked up my hand and flashed me her heart-melting smile.

"Michael, honey, if your lover wants to meet me before we fuck, I don't mind. Hell, I'm a nineties kinda girl. I wouldn't even mind a threeway, if that's what all this hemming and hawing has been about."

"Th-that's great!" I blurted out. When her eyebrows shot up, I told her the whole, sordid truth.

By the time I was done, I figured my face was the color of the wine she'd spritzed all over the pristine white tablecloth.

"Let me get this straight, sugar," she choked, laughing as I pounded her back. "Ol' Don Juan here, the cock-waving stud of the century, has a smarmy look glued to his face because he's hooked up with a gay lover who not only whips his misbehavin' butt to keep him in line, but fucks him any time he damn well feels like saying 'drop your drawers and spread'?!!" She wiped the tears off her face. "Oh, honey, that's priceless."

I looked down glumly into my drink, mumbling something about being sorry I'd bothered her with my situation. Marianne was immediately contrite. She took my hand again and squeezed it. "Don't get me wrong, sugar. I'm happy for you. You're positively glowing." As I smiled sheepishly up at her, she added, "When do I get to meet this manly hunk of stud meat?"

I could feel my face heating again. "How about tonight? That is, if you want me to be able to fuck you. Roger insists on, you know, watching us together, so he's sure I don't get too uppity."

Marianne's hoots of laughter got us more dirty looks from the maitre d', but by then, I was beyond embarrassment, and we were done with dinner. I helped her into her coat. Twenty minutes later, I was politely introducing her to Roger. The two of them sized each other up with one glance, then shook hands as Marianne's beaming smile lit up the room.

"If you ask me, Roger, you're just what Michael needs. That boy is a born submissive, though he'd never admit it without some powerful incentive from that exceptionally fine hard-on he's always sporting."

"Now wait a minute," I protested. Two sets of upraised eyebrows turned to stare at me. I shut up and went into the kitchen to brew some tea, leaving them to discuss my well-formed endowments like I was some piece of meat at the corner market.

When I walked back into the living room, both Roger and Marianne were looking much too smug for my comfort. As I set down the serving tray, Marianne stood up and stretched her arms high over her head, spreading her legs wide as she reached for the ceiling. She'd taken off her coat. The thin silver bracelets on her wrists sparkled in the soft glow of the living room lights as her sweater moved over her obviously perked-up breasts.

"You ready for some fun, sugar?" She ran her hands seductively down her sides, rubbing first over her swollen nipples, then between her legs. "Roger says you were squirming like a cat on hot tar tonight because he'd just strapped your butt." She wiggled contentedly, still rubbing her crotch. As her skirt lifted, I could see the lace at the tops of her stocking. I sighed as my cock responded accordingly.

She didn't seem to notice. "Strip those clothes off, pretty boy, and let me see if Roger did right by you."

I wouldn't have believed my face could get hotter than it already was, but it did. The scene was definitely not going the way I thought it should, though my cock was now so hard I didn't feel like arguing, especially if cooperating meant I was going to get to fuck her. I tugged my sweater over my head and unbuttoned my shirt. Marianne sauntered over and tweaked my nipples.

"You have such pretty titties, Michael." She rubbed her cunt-scented fingers under my nose. The smell made my cock tingle. She was horny. I could smell it. I jumped as she reached down and patted my bottom. "Ooh, honey, that sensitive? I can't wait to see what he did to you."

There was nothing to do but obey—not if I wanted to come that night. When I was naked, I turned around and bent over with my hands on the edge of the couch, my legs spread, my balls hanging free, my erection pointing up hard towards my belly—overall, a now very familiar position for me.

Marianne's long, low whistle had me ready to hide my head. "He did a job on you, sugar. Those are beautiful marks." I hadn't thought it was possible to blush more than I already was, then I felt her hands tracing over the sorest parts of my butt. "I bet those still sting."

"Yes," I hissed. I couldn't believe my cock was staying hard during all of this. I wanted to fuck her. Her soft caresses and the smell of her cunt were driving me nuts. But it was difficult to feel any kind of toppish with Roger in the room. From the corner of my eye, I could see him standing placidly on the other side of the room. His hard cock was pressing out against his jeans, but he wasn't saying anything.

I groaned as Marianne started teasing the lower curve of my extremely tender buttcheek. "Roger, I think you're inhibiting our boy. Do you mind if I take over here for a while? I don't like sharing a man's attention where my pussy is concerned."

Roger's bark of laughter sounded startled, but happy. "Be my guest."

Submissive or not, I was getting annoyed at the way they were discussing me like I wasn't even in the room. Then Marianne's gentle hands pulled me upright and turned me around, hugging me close. She cupped my face with her soft, smooth palms and breathed across my lips. "Give us a kiss, sweetie. Let me feel that hard, hot, and ever so lickable cock I know and love so well."

I put my arms gingerly around her, pressed my lips carefully to hers. I was very aware of Roger's presence, but my cock was still reaching towards her.

"Forget about him, sugar," she whispered. "Think about these."

With one practiced movement, she tugged her sweater over her head, and what she had on underneath caught all my attention. I have a thing for women's lingerie. Marianne wore a black lace demi-bra, her firm, burgundy nipples resting on the open lower half like ripe cherries on a silver platter. Her scent, roses and shampoo and the faintest hint of hungry cunt, seemed trapped in her cleavage. She cupped her hands under her breasts and lifted them towards me. "Show me you remember how to make them happy, lover."

With a moan, I buried my face between her breasts. They were warm and soft, her scent thick where skin rested against skin. I licked long and slow down the upper slope, like a cat lapping up precious cream.

"Ooh, yes, baby. Show mama you like her pretty titties."

With a growl, I dragged my tongue roughly over the soft silk of her areolas. They hardened fast, poking into my tongue. I pulled her closer, tighter, my cock pressed hard against her belly, as Marianne gasped out, "Yes, sugar!"

I licked over each tip, tonguing fiercely, working the points to fierce peaks. When she was panting, I grinned up at her, then slowly and seductively, I sucked her nipple deep into my mouth—and swallowed, letting the suction pull her just that tiny bit more into my mouth.

"Yes!" she breathed. "Damn, but you know how to work a girl's tits. Do them both, lover. Make me hungry for that hot, hard dick of yours."

I love it when Marianne talks dirty. I reached in back of her, unclasped her bra. As her luscious, full breasts spilled into my palms, I started working her tits for all I was worth, squeezing, milking, pulling the sensation forward, teasing her nipples with my thumbs—and rubbing my cock against her stocking-clad thigh.

"Make me hot all over," she growled.

Laughing, I slid my hand up under her skirt. Her shaved pussy lips were slick with her juices. She trembled as I slid my fingers between her folds and pressed her clit.

"Ooh, yes, sugar. You know the magic button."

"Spread for me," I whispered. She was wet, really wet. Each time I stroked her pussy, each time I sucked her nipples, she got even juicier. I pressed into the wet velvet of her cunt, in and up, the way she always loved it, my thumb still stroking her clit. I groaned as a soft tremor shuddered through her.

"The bedroom." Her voice was husky as she kissed me, her lips opening hungrily as she sucked my tongue into her mouth. I lifted her, grasping her curvy little bottom as she wrapped her legs tightly around my waist. My cock twitched, hard and demanding against the heat between her legs.

I carried her to the bed. We fell on the mattress, the rest of her clothes—except for those gorgeous stockings with the black lace tops—flying every which way in a frenzy of stripping.

"I want you," I growled, pulling her into my arms, burying my fingers in her sopping pussy. "I'm hungry for a nice, hot cunt. I'm going to eat you 'til you scream, 'til your juices are running all over my face."

A moment later, I was flat on my back. Marianne's musky smell filled my nostrils as she straddled my face. I flicked my tongue upwards and was rewarded by her squeal as my tongue flicked over her clit.

"Work my button, Michael." She thrust against me, her swollen clit pressing hard against my lips. "Make it quiver for you."

I grabbed her hips and held her still, lashing my tongue over the exquisitely sensitive nub of woman-glans peeking out of its hood.

"Fuck, yes, Michael!" Marianne ground against me, thrusting her cunt against my face as I worked her clit mercilessly. My saliva ran down my chin as my spit-slicked tongue teased shudder after shudder out of her. Despite the angle, I worked one finger inside her, wiggling it as she squirmed. She started to pant again, stiffening and whispering my name. I sucked her swollen clit into my mouth, squeezing her bottom as she shuddered against me again. She was still quivering when I pressed one juice-slicked finger against her sphincter and slid it up. She screamed as she climaxed again, shaking as she reached back and her strong, feminine hand wrapped around my cock. "I want this, sugar," she gasped. "Right now. Fuck me."

"Yes, ma'am," I whispered. My nostrils were still filled with the smell of her climax as she moved off me. A moment later, I cried out as her hot, wet, feminine mouth closed around my cock.

"Mmmm." Her lips vibrated against me. "Just a taste, sugar. You smell good. All man." She licked slowly and carefully up my shaft, her wicked nasty tongue working the sweet spot on the underside of my shaft. She licked and sucked until I thought I was going to pass out. My cock strained against my belly, my nuts climbing my shaft. "I want this in me, sugar."

With practiced moves, she leaned over and grabbed a condom from the top drawer of the nightstand. Her well-sucked breasts glistened as she squeezed the tiniest bit of lube in the tip, just the way I liked it. Then I gasped as the tight latex engulfed my dick, wrapped inside her strong, feminine hand.

"Move down to the end of the bed, lover." She tugged my hips to the edge, then squatted over me and milked me to a rock hard peak. I was off-balance as all hell, my hips on the edge of the bed, my legs bent down to brace me as I tried to position my feet on the floor. Her soft, sexy hand guided me to the gate of her hot, wet cunt. "Give us some lovin', sugar."

I could hardly think as she slid down over me. My cock had been so hungry to fuck for so long. I gasped, trying to get enough air into my lungs, as her hot, velvety pussy wrapped around me, the soft loose walls hugging my cock. When she lifted up, I grabbed her hips and held her still.

"Slow down," I gasped. "I'm right on the edge. And I have to move my feet."

I almost jumped out of my skin as Roger's clear, strong voice said, "I have your feet." He roughly grabbed my ankles, lifted them up, spreading my legs wide as Marianne leaned forward so her cunt could catch the now-odd angle of my cock. I gasped as her talented pussy muscles squeezed me and Roger's strong fingers spread my butt cheeks. A lube nozzle slid up my butt and the cold gel rushed into me. Then Roger's hot, latex-clad cockhead was pressing against my ass.

"Don't mind me, Michael. I'm just going to rest here, with my cock kissing your asslips. You go ahead and fuck her."

My anus twitched, involuntarily kissing him back. Roger roared with laughter, the very tip of his cock sliding into me as I tried to both press back with my asslips and arch up into Marianne's cunt. I cried out with pure frustration and need—both my cock and my asshole *needed*.

"Damn, Michael. You are one hot trick," Roger laughed. "I love it when you're slutty." I shuddered as the head of his cock pressed further in. "Help him keep his mind on his cock, Marianne. He seems distracted."

A flushed, laughing Marianne rose up onto her knees and fucked herself over my cock. I glanced down, trembling, as I watched her beautiful pussy lips sliding over my cock.

"You're so hard, sugar."

I cried out as she stroked over me.

"Does having a dick up your ass always make you this much fun? Unh!"

I couldn't help it. I reached up and pulled her luscious nipples into my shaking fingers.

"Fuck, yes!" she yelled. She ground her hips against me, pressing deep as she started fucking me fast and furiously. The friction and heat screamed back to where my asshole stretched, stretched and burned, at the relentless pressure filling me. "Work my nipples, sugar," Marianne growled. "Milk them way out, like you were suckling at your mama's tits."

I was right on the edge. Marianne's face was flushed with passion, her nipples hard and straining in my fingers. She rose and fell, slamming into me, jarring me back against the huge human plug working its way into my ass. With each thumping jolt, Roger's cock moved in a minuscule amount more.

Suddenly Marianne stiffened in my arms, her voice rising in a high, keening cry. She ground against me, hard, her hips thrashing wildly as she shuddered. The spasms wracking her pussy clamped around me, jerking and pulling—a hot, wet cunt sucking me off, deep-throating me. My body stiffened. I arched up into her, my dick straining up to press her cervix, hungry, greedy to feel every minute spasm. I was at the point of no return, my orgasm overpowering my body. I stiffened, yelling, arching up deep into Marianne's welcoming cunt. As the first spurt shot through my cock tube, my legs pressed against the hard, strong hands that held them, my body opened, and Roger's cock slid all the way up my ass.

I screamed like my lungs would burst. I shot until my nuts were empty, howling and shuddering until Marianne's spasming, milking pussy and Roger's pummeling cock had pulled and pressed and sucked every last sperm cell in my body through my furiously pulsing cock tube. I stayed frozen like that, panting and shaking, unable to move, unable to do anything but look into Marianne's laughing eyes, as Roger fucked me until my eyes crossed with the pure pleasure of one really kinky, blissfully perverted, and totally overwhelming fuck. Then he shot his wad up my ass and collapsed against Marianne's back.

We stayed that way a long time, them laughing, me trying to catch my breath. Marianne rose up just as Roger pulled out. The sensations were so exquisite, I almost came again. I cried out at the almost painful pleasure, though there sure as hell wasn't anything left to shoot from my dick. When they finally stopped laughing again, we fell into one big pile on the bed.

"That was wonderful, sugar." Marianne reached up and tweaked my nipple. "The look on your face when you climaxed was pure bliss, I kid you not." I blushed as Marianne reached down and touched my sphincter. "Does my pussy purr like this after a good fuck?"

I leaned over tiredly and kissed her. "Yes, though a girl pussy shows its appreciation differently. Agghh!!"

Roger's finger had joined Marianne's. Together they were petting and stroking and playing. I moaned and buried my head between Marianne's breasts. If I hadn't been so wasted, their touching would have gotten me hornier than hell again. This time, they just made me twitch with total contentment.

Since then, Roger lets me fuck Marianne any time I want, though I always have to give him a blow-by-blow account of what we've done. And by mutual consent, we have three-ways fairly often. The feeling of being fucked while I'm fucking still blows my mind, and my dick. I've even learned to enjoy the times, now too numerous to count, when Marianne comes over to see me get my ass whipped for some infraction before we're allowed to have sex.

I still wasn't sure how I was going to discuss gender politics in bisexual three-ways that afternoon without giving my own proclivities away with a raging, leaking hard-on. The more I thought about it, the more I realized my notes were totally inadequate.

As Roger's shower stopped, I decided I didn't feel like being the only one who was frustrated at the conference. Marianne had mentioned that she was staying down on the fifth floor, with her new girlfriend. Although I hadn't met the new g.f. yet, Marianne had told me she was bi, too, and that when she saw my picture, she'd said I was a hunk.

Making up my mind fast, I left Roger a quick note. "Going to my panel, then fucking Marianne and her girlfriend. Back for dinner?"

I knew I'd come back to find Roger's belt draped over the back of a chair, mostly likely with a gag on the table as well. But I was really in a het mode, and Marianne is one hot lay. I bet her girlfriend is, too. And my ass was hungry for both a beating and a long, rough fuck. It would be worth a very uncomfortable train ride home tomorrow. After all, how often do I get to cruise the conference?

Whistling, I dumped my notes in the trash and went out the door to find Marianne.

Dominic Santi is a former technical editor turned rogue whose erotica appears in Friction 2 & 3, Best Gay Erotica 2000, Sex Toy Tales, Casting Couch Confessions, *and dozens of other smutty anthologies and magazines. Santi (along with mjc) recently edited the electronic anthologies* Y2Kinky *and* Strange Bedfellows *(http://go.compuserve.com/eroticelit).*

The Leather Daddy, His Boy, and the Dominatrix

Doug Harrison

For Mistress Cléo and Bill

Fish!" Shaun spat. "Pussies smell like fish!"

"How the hell would you know," Brad shouted across the bedroom, his anger barely masking the twinkle in his eye.

"Because my friends told me so."

"The last time one of those little fags saw a cunt was when he was born! Now finish getting ready before I really get pissed. We're due at Sherry's in half an hour."

"Do I have to go?" Shaun whined.

"Yes! We've been over this a dozen times. She wants to meet you."

"But she's your friend!"

"She's about to become *our* friend," Brad yelled as he tucked his black tank top into his 501s and strode toward Shaun. Shaun rapidly laced his black combat boots. "I know she'll like you."

"What if I don't like her?"

"We'll worry about that when the time comes. Now get your little ass in the car!" Brad smacked Shaun soundly on his bubble butt, slightly above the frayed edge of his cutoffs.

Shaun sauntered toward the door and ran his hand along the edge of the black leather sling that hung next to their queen-size four-poster. "Sure wish we were staying home and playing together," he mumbled, as his other hand massaged his crotch.

Brad ignored the remark. He grabbed a bottle of wine he had carefully wrapped in shiny red paper with a large black bow.

"You didn't pack any toys," Shaun noticed, as they got into the BMW. He scrunched into the brown leather bucket seat, head bowed, with his arms folded tightly across his chest.

"Sherry, or I should say, 'Mistress Sheryl,' has enough to satiate an army."

"But you have the best collection of floggers on the West Coast."

"She has enough. Besides, I don't expect we'll be doing that."

"Oh," replied Shaun. He wasn't sure if he was glad or not. "Aren't you horny?"

"We'll see what happens," answered Brad.

The car sped across San Francisco toward Pacific Heights. Finally Shaun spoke.

"How long have you known Sherry?"

"Since the late '70s—about ten years."

"Ten times as long as we've been together. Have you fucked her?"

"Of course."

"Yuck! You say that so matter-of-fact."

"It is. Sex just happens between us. Our real connection is through the heart."

"Oh, I thought only ours was." Brad grimaced, and Shaun continued through his smirk. "But she's a dominatrix. Doesn't that mean she does bondage and whipping and discipline and that kind of stuff for money?"

"Yes."

"So why should she go out with a leatherman?"

Brad sighed. "We enjoy each other's company. We've shared years of experiences, and friends, and lost many friends. We like to hang out and talk. And, I'm flattered to say, if she wants to get flogged, she calls me."

"Yeah, you're sure good at that. But I hope you don't want me to have sex with her," Shaun pleaded with raised eyebrows. "She must be old enough to be my mother."

"And I'm old enough to be your father."

"But that's different."

Brad tightened his hands on the steering wheel. "Forget it, enjoy the drive." The rest of the ride proceeded in silence until they entered Sherry's driveway.

"Wow! Business must be good," blurted Shaun as he took in the two-storey brick house with a small, well-manicured lawn. There were no flowerbeds, but the yard was lined with neatly trimmed bushes. Statues of Venus and David guarded each side of the small portico. It was obvious there would be a splendid view of San Francisco Bay from the rear windows.

Sherry greeted them at the door. She was about five-ten, curvaceous, with flaming red hair. Her sparkling hazel eyes accented her ready smile, and hinted at the authority that her commanding presence could easily call upon. She wore tight, black leather pants with a white, sheer, scooped-neck blouse.

"She's good looking for a woman," thought Shaun. "Even with those bumps on her chest."

Sherry stared at Shaun, slowly absorbing the young man's short, wiry frame, his flowing blond hair, and twinkling blue eyes. "He's the same age my son should be," she thought.

Brad and Sherry hugged, and she could feel his dick growing as their lingering embrace tightened. Shaun looked downward and shuffled from foot to foot.

"It feels good to hold you," she whispered into Brad's ear. "And this must be Shaun," she added, looking over Brad's shoulder. "Such a beautiful young man."

"Don't pour it on too much," Brad signaled Sherry with his eyes.

Shaun rolled his eyes, looked upward, and inched forward. He deposited his sweaty palm in Sherry's outstretched hand. Her handshake was not as firm as Shaun had expected, and she seemed suddenly preoccupied.

"Sherry? For old times." Brad handed her the red package.

"Sorry, I was taken with this cute boy. I can guess what's in here," she said as she caressed Brad's gift. "And it's wrapped in my favorite colors. Come in."

She led them to a small dining area. "Wow, look at the Bay," Shaun exclaimed as he ran to the picture window, taking in the view of Alcatraz, many small sailboats, and a few freighters.

Sherry unwrapped her present and smiled. "My favorite, Harvey's medium dry. Please open it."

Brad, Shaun noticed, seemed comfortable in the room and quickly located the bottle opener. Sherry placed three crystal wineglasses in front of them.

Brad poured the amber vintage, and he and Sherry ran their tongues along the rims of their glasses while smiling into each other's eyes.

Shaun stared at them, and thought, "I hope Daddy doesn't want something from her I don't have." His hand brushed against the open bottle, sending the remaining contents flooding across the table onto his lap. He sat frozen. Brad grabbed the bottle and used his linen napkin to stem the flow.

"Strip!" commanded Sherry. Shaun's mouth fell open.

"Take off your shorts. Quick! They need to be soaked so they won't stain."

Shaun looked at his red crotch. He stood up and lowered his cutoffs over his black boots. The stain hadn't penetrated to his white cotton jock. He sat down on the ornate red velvet chair, glad his ass was clean. Sherry took the stained pants, disappeared into the kitchen, and soon returned.

"No harm done," she said. "Would you like some pot?"

Brad nodded yes. Shaun hesitated and said, "I'll pass."

While they lit up, Sherry remarked, "It's been a long time, Brad."

"Yes, it's easy for friends to drift apart."

"I'm glad you're OK," she murmured.

"My numbers are holding steady," Brad responded.

"I'm glad you have Shaun. You two look happy," Sherry observed.

"Yes," replied Brad. "We're past arguing whether the toilet paper should unroll from the top or the bottom. Now our biggest concern is whether we go to the opera or a rock concert. We're educating each other. I take Shaun to Wagner and he takes me to Depeche Mode."

Sherry laughed. "It's good to see you so relaxed. Tell me, does Shaun have a nickname?" she asked with a twinkle in her eye as she looked at Shaun.

Brad grinned. Shaun grimaced.

"Tell her your nickname, boy," Brad ordered.

"Fuzzy-butt," Shaun scowled.

"So I noticed," replied Sherry. "I like those curls on your tight buns, and those cute little ass dimples."

"I didn't think women talked like this," thought Shaun. "She sounds horny."

Sherry turned to Brad. "He's so adorable. I could eat him up."

"You ain't having me for dessert," thought Shaun, not trying to hide his pout.

Brad cleared his throat. "I think Shaun is interested in your work. Why don't you describe it."

Sherry paused for a few seconds, brows furrowed. She turned to Shaun, and clasped her hands on the table. "Mostly, I help people realize their fantasies. As clichéd as it sounds, a lot of my clients are successful businessmen who want someone to dominate them, to tie them up, to flog them, to stick a butt plug up their ass."

A mischievous smile crossed her face. "Some of them would rather say they're interested in anal training and other kinky delights. Regardless, they want me to take them into a world where they can give up all control."

Sherry hesitated. Shaun could feel his dick getting hard.

"Sometimes, I support clients while they work through their fears and grief. My most poignant situation occurred a few months ago with a client whose son had died of AIDS. He hadn't been able to accept the young man's lifestyle, and hadn't spoken to him for years. He came to me months after the funeral, filled with self-recrimination and grief. I flogged him for over an hour. It was very intense for me, physically and emotionally. He finally let go and his crusty veneer split wide open. His anguish gushed out. I held him in my arms for a long time while he sobbed uncontrollably. I was exhausted, but I love that aspect of my work.

"I could feel what he needed, what he wanted. His longing was so palpable I could almost touch it. I put on a harness and my smallest, softest dildo. He was quivering while he watched my every move and collapsed into an accommodating heap. I fucked him gently while he whimpered. He didn't say much when he left, he just seemed calmer, but very pensive. He called me a few weeks later to thank me. He had started volunteer work at an AIDS charity and had contacted some of his son's friends."

They sat silently for a few moments. Shaun looked at Brad and reached for his hand. Sherry continued.

"My most humorous scene, especially since I'm a recovering Catholic, is with a man who dresses in a Catholic schoolgirl's uniform, complete with blonde wig, white blouse and green plaid skirt, white socks and black oxfords. He sees me every few months. I put on a nun's habit, take him over my knee, and spank him with a long, wide ruler. Sometimes I tie his hands together with rosary beads. I say, 'Naughty girl, you're being punished for playing with yourself. You know you shouldn't put your hands down there!' I make a good nun."

All three laughed, Sherry and Brad uncontrollably, Shaun somewhat guardedly.

"Don't you get tired or bored doing this?" Shaun asked while fidgeting in his chair.

Sherry grimaced. "Yes, I do. But if I don't work for a week or so, I miss it."

She glanced at Brad. "Day after day, being paid to dominate people—sometimes they get off; I never do. If it's a particularly hot scene, and that's rare, I'll use my vibrator after the client leaves. I feel lonely. Despite all these people, all this S/M, I'm frustrated. I don't go out often, a meeting here and there...." Her voice trailed off, and she looked out the window, then back at Brad.

"But enough about me; I don't want to overwhelm you. Let's go to the playroom," she suggested. They rose, and Shaun fell in behind Sherry, with Brad bringing up the rear, as Sherry led the small parade down a flight of stairs. Shaun wiggled his butt provocatively at Brad each step of the way. Sherry stopped before a locked room. Hanging on the wall to the side of the door was a large collage of photos, all men. They wore a variety of outfits, from business suits, to full leather, to jock and harness, to nothing. Some looked very emaciated. A candle was burning on a table below the display.

"This is how I remember our friends," she said. Brad swallowed hard as he scanned the array. Sherry put her arm around his waist and whispered, "I'm glad you're still healthy." They stood lost in their separate thoughts as Shaun waited patiently.

"Enough," said Sherry. "We're here to create a moment of good faith in a world filled with bad faith." She unlocked the door, flicked a switch, stepped inside, and said, with a flourish of her arms, "Voilà."

Shaun stood in the open doorway, mouth agape, oblivious to the fact that he was blocking Brad's way. Objects seemed to leap towards him, calling for attention. He couldn't possibly take it all in quickly. To the left: pegboards with coiled rope of differing lengths and colors; a shelf with leather hoods on mannequin heads ranging from slight sensory deprivation to total encasement. On the rear wall: wrist, leg, and thigh restraints, collars, and gags. In the center of the room: a heavy wooden cross and a suspension T-bar attached to a rack and pinion. In the left corner: a chef's circular black potholder, from which hung floggers and cats-o-nine-tails of all lengths with predominantly red and black handles. On the right wall:

nipple clamps, leather restraints for cock and ball torture, and a table with implements for play piercing and electrical stimulation. Towards the back: a bondage table covered in black leather with eyehooks protruding every six inches along the frame. Mirrors everywhere, including the ceiling.

Sherry took Shaun by the hand and led him into the room. Brad followed. His eyes rested on a leatherman's blemished, black leather harness with dull metallic studs hanging on the rear wall. It had wide shoulder straps joining a large, tarnished metal ring just above the navel. A vertical strap linked the ring to a leather codpiece. He went over and touched it and turned with raised eyebrows to Sherry.

"It belonged to Dan. He gave it to me just before he died. He's the last gay man I had sex with. Please put it on."

Brad removed his clothes and slithered into the harness after adjusting the straps. He was magnificent! The leather straps accentuated his broad shoulders, sculpted chest, and narrow hips. The fine, curly, brown hair on his upper body played counterpoint with his sandy moustache and close-cropped hair. He planted his feet apart, placed his hands on his hips, and faced Sherry, who had removed her clothing after turning on soft, sensual music.

She sank to her knees, and removed the codpiece. "Daddy, Dan, Brad," she sighed with moist eyes. Brad's firm dick sprang from its enclosure. Sherry put her hands around Brad's thighs. She blew her warm breath onto the tip of his dick and gently kissed it. She put the head in her mouth and teased the corona with her teeth. Brad closed his eyes and moaned. Sherry pursed her lips and slowly slid her mouth back and forth along half the shaft, making delicious slurping noises. Finally, she swallowed his dick as he ran his fingers gently through her hair.

"Sherry, you're the only woman who can give a blowjob like a man," whispered Brad.

Sherry looked up at his blissful smile. "I still remember all the practice I've had on your beautiful cock, honey," she said.

Shaun, still wearing his jock, combat boots, and tank top, had seated himself in a peculiar chair with a small hole in the seat. He stared open-mouthed at the tableaux.

"Time to slow down," cried a trembling Brad. "I'm on the edge."

"You bitch!" Shaun's mind screamed. "I should be sucking Daddy's dick. I guess I better move faster at this party! But what the hell can I do?" He looked around, strode to the small bathroom, turned on the light, and closed the door.

He leaned against the sink, breathing hard. He looked into the mirror at the tears that were slowly flowing down his cheeks. "How do I get out of here?" he whispered to his image as he banged his fists on the edge of the white porcelain sink. "Take a cab," replied his reflection. "Even if Daddy gets pissed, think of yourself."

Sherry withdrew her mouth from Brad's throbbing cock. "Go to him," she said. Brad turned questioningly, looked at the line of light under the bathroom door, and nodded. He slowly approached it, hard cock bobbing in front of him.

"Shaun, you OK?" He knocked lightly on the door and cautiously opened it. Shaun was using his forearm in a vain attempt to quickly wipe away his tears. Brad put his arms around Shaun's shoulders, his hard dick pressing against the lad's butt.

"It's OK, Buster, it's OK." This nickname and these words were always reserved for those special times when Shaun lay in Brad's arms after an intense scene. Shaun looked at Brad's dick through watery eyes. "Carpe Diem. I'll wait before calling the cab," he thought, as Brad slowly led him back into the dungeon.

Sherry smiled at Shaun and signaled him to her side with a toss of her head. He approached tentatively and knelt beside her. Brad removed Shaun's shirt. Sherry looked admiringly at Shaun and stopped herself just before reaching out to touch him. Brad lay down next to them, his still-hard dick pointing upward. He grabbed Shaun's head and guided the boy's tongue over one side of his penis. Shaun quickly lost himself in this familiar motion. Sherry licked the other side of Brad's dick, and her eyes fastened onto Shaun's. They tongued Brad in unison as his breath came in quick gasps. Sherry took Brad's large balls in her mouth, which was Shaun's signal to swallow the dick in its entirety. Brad thrust his hips.

Sherry put one arm over Shaun's shoulder. He shuddered, and the dick went sliding from his mouth.

Brad looked up, took Sherry by the arms and steered her to the floor. She lay on her back looking up at him. He knelt and put his head between her legs. Shaun rose, moved back a few paces, and turned to the wall containing Sherry's rope collection.

"Ah! Oh, yes, yes, that's it," moaned Sherry, as Brad's tongue slid slowly up her shaved lips and back down. After several passes, he sucked her clit and massaged it gently with the tip of his darting tongue.

"Fuck me with your tongue, baby," shouted Sherry. Brad thrust his tongue rapidly in and out of her moist vagina while stroking her nipples, which soon became hard. Sherry panted in rapid, guttural tones. Brad turned his attention back to her clit, which he bit, none too gently.

"I'm coming, I'm coming," cried Sherry. She arched her back and grabbed Brad's hands. He crushed his mouth into her pussy. She shuddered and threw her feet straight up, almost knocking Brad from his perch. "That's it, come for Daddy," he shouted. Her labored breathing continued for a few minutes, and gradually softened. Brad released his grip, and positioned himself beside her.

"You're beautiful," he said, as he put his arms around her. She looked at him dreamily.

"You haven't lost your touch. I was ready for that."

Shaun had tried unsuccessfully to block the sounds behind him. "Just like Mark must have sounded," he grimaced, remembering his best friend from high school, "when he was with Darlene." Driven by the similarity, Shaun's mind fled to his furtive trip to the football team's locker room several years earlier.

His eyes had quickly adapted to the room's dim light coming from the setting sun through high, dirty windows. He located Mark's locker with no dif-

ficulty; the nametag carried the prestigious title of "Captain." The door was unlocked. He immediately found the jock hanging among the shoulder and hip pads, next to the white, semi-transparent nylon training shorts.

He put the jock over his head, the wide waistband covering his eyes, with the pouch covering his nose and mouth. He reached behind his head and tied the legbands to make the pouch as tight as possible. He sat on the locker room bench and unzipped his pants. His throbbing erection sprang out and he clutched it instantly. He inhaled the jock's mixture of crotch sweat, urine, and asshole muskiness. He fantasized about being on his knees in front of Mark, his hands behind his back, while Mark grabbed him roughly by the hair and forced his hard dick down Shaun's throat.

"Oh yes, Mark, fuck my face! Make me swallow your cum," he moaned as he savagely yanked his own dick. "Oh, God, yes, here it comes, I'll swallow it all, all for me, none for Darlene." He squirted gobs of cum onto his hand. Panting, he rubbed it into the jock. He sat a few more minutes until his breathing quieted, put on the jock, licked his hands clean, and left.

Shaun glanced over his shoulder at Brad's hard-on. "Wish I could suck on that some more," he thought. He quickly turned his attention back to the rope collection, his hands intertwined in the leg straps of his jock.

Sherry glanced at Shaun. "Bondage. I think the little one likes bondage. Bring him to me." Shaun heard the comment, and his pulse increased. He felt the blood rushing to his face and crotch.

Brad went to Shaun, turned him around, and smothered him in a long, tight hug. "It's your turn," he whispered. He led Shaun to the middle of the room where Sherry was standing with a thin leather collar in her hand. She gave the collar to Brad, who put it around his boy's neck. Sherry secured it with a shiny padlock and noticed the large bulge in the young man's jock.

"Lie down," Sherry said in a soft voice that was more a request than a command. Shaun did as he was told. Sherry knelt over him and locked her gaze with his confused stare.

"Does it matter who does it, if it feels good?" she asked. She passed her hands gently over the boy's chest, so that he could almost, but not quite, feel her fingers. Then her hands gently brushed his nipples. Shaun moaned. Sherry pinched them lightly.

"Oh, yes," Shaun said with hesitation. Sherry looked into his eyes, and continued to hypnotically hold his gaze as her skilled hands put clamps on the boy's large nipples, which obviously had a history of craved abuse. Shaun sunk into the pain and blinked at the overhead light, like quickly staring at the sun on that disastrous day at the beach.

He hadn't wanted to go to the shore, especially with this crowd of jocks and their girlfriends. He always felt like an outcast. But he let himself be talked into it by Darlene. So he sat alone at the edge of the volleyball court, watching a game played by a few half-soused boys and girls groping for an elusive ball. Except for Mark, who always seemed so coordinated and together. He ran towards the net, bent over, and with one smooth swing scooped the low ball into a high arc as a perfect set-up for a bumbling teammate. He passed by Shaun, and Shaun admired the muscular, hairy legs protruding from his blue, baggy short shorts. Shaun could see the straps of Mark's jock and longed to explore its contents. Shaun's dick was noticeably straining against the red nylon of his tight Speedos. Mark smiled at him as he ran by. Embarrassed, Shaun turned away.

Darlene was leaning against a tree, watching the game. She caught Shaun's eye and staggered over. "They'd rather play with each other than me. C'mon, let's go!" She grabbed Shaun's hand and dragged him over several dunes to a secluded spot.

"You're cute," she said, standing in front of him. She looked at the bulge in his Speedo. "What you got there for me?" She knelt before Shaun, and tongued the stretched nylon. "Yum." He closed his eyes and pinched his nipples. She pulled the suit to his knees and his hard-on sprang forth. Shaun's thoughts fled to Mark, to the locker room, anywhere, anyplace, anything to keep hard.

Darlene took the dick in her mouth. "You're a mouthful, just as I thought." She sucked for a few minutes, got up, and tore off her orange string bikini. She slumped to the sand and lay back spread-eagled.

"Fuck me," she demanded.

Shaun stood over her. "I can't fantasize fast enough to keep up with this drunk slut," he thought. His hard-on wilted.

"Oh, shit. What's the matter, you a fag or something?" Shaun turned red. "Hey, I think you are a fag boy. Goddamn, just my fucking luck. Get lost! I'll play with myself!" Shaun fled with tears in his eyes.

Sherry noticed Shaun's tears and clenched fists "It's all right." She ran her fingers lightly through his hair. Slowly, ever so sweetly, she placed the boy's hands across his waist and bound them with smooth, black cord. Shaun sighed. Sherry placed her hand over his eyes. "Keep them closed," she requested.

Shaun felt a finger rubbing his asshole. It probed, and then went in, ever so gently. Was it Brad's? Was it Sherry's? It didn't matter. He was overcome with pleasure. Someone was pulling on his nipple clamps as another hand removed his dick from his jock and encircled the hard shaft. His hips began to gyrate and thrust. He felt warm lips on his cockhead, tonguing his piss hole and moving around the corona. They were soft, sensuous, caring lips. Hands and fingers were all over him and he felt as though he were floating out of his body. He stopped thrusting his hips and gave himself over to the sensations and ever-changing palette of colors his mind was mixing.

He felt a soft hand on his forehead. "Open your eyes," said Sherry. He slowly blinked himself back to an awareness of his surroundings and watched Sherry untie his hands. She put her arms around him to raise him to a sitting position. His legs were stretched straight out from his body and he was leaning on his elbows. He was still hard. She smiled at him and kissed him lightly on the lips. He didn't resist. "What a beautiful cock you have, young man," she murmured in his ear.

She instructed Brad to sit facing Shaun with his legs around Shaun's waist. Brad's dick rapidly became hard.

"You sneaky little devil, you," thought Brad, recalling a particularly hot scene with Sherry and an old friend.

"What's going on here?" mulled Shaun.

Brad snuggled as close as possible to Shaun so their dicks were almost touching. Shaun quivered with the closeness and feel of Brad's body in this unusual position, and ran his hand along Brad's thigh. Sherry placed a condom on the end of Brad's dick, leaned over, and unrolled it with her mouth.

"Wish we didn't have to use this," she whispered to him. Brad smiled.

Sherry looked at Shaun with an unspoken question. "She's not like Darlene," he thought as he nodded his head in agreement. Sherry covered his dick in the same manner, not losing eye contact as she forced the tight rubber down his shaft.

"I've never seen this done before!" exclaimed Shaun. "It feels sooo good," he moaned. Sherry stood up, admired the two dicks, and used a short piece of leather thong to tie their bases together.

Then she squatted over the two men and slowly, ever so slowly, lowered herself onto the two throbbing dicks.

"Oh my God," she gasped, while thinking, "I've been waiting years to do this again."

The two men leaned back on their elbows and smiled at each other. It was difficult to thrust, since they were stretching Sherry to her limit. Shaun liked the feel of his cock rubbing Brad's long, hard dick while surrounded by Sherry's tight moistness. She was on her knees, leaning towards Shaun. They kissed. Shaun's tongue fought to get as deeply inside Sherry's mouth as possible while his dick fought to reach up into her pussy as far as possible. He bit her lip hard.

"That's it boy, bite this bitch. Give it to me! Fuck me hard. Make me scream. Yank your Daddy's dick up my cunt. Make me come. Make me come!"

Shaun pushed his body up and down as much as possible. He twisted. He thrust. Brad tried to keep up with him, a shit-eating grin on his face.

"I'm coming, oh fuck, yes, yes, yes," screamed Sherry, dancing wildly on the dicks.

"I'm gonna squirt," yelled Shaun.

Sherry jumped up and yanked the thong off the two hard dicks. With the same motion she tore the rubber from Shaun's purple dick just in time to be rewarded by the sight of Vesuvian spurts of white droplets that shot two feet into the air, landing on his stomach and chest. Some of it even made it to his collar.

Shaun collapsed, gasping for breath. Brad smiled, and crawled over to hold his boy.

"That was beautiful," said Sherry.

"Ah, the power of youth," sighed Brad.

"Your turn will come," replied Sherry, a twinkle in her eye.

The three of them hugged. Brad rolled over, got up, and stretched.

Sherry stood up and climbed onto the bondage table. She sat with her feet dangling over the edge, silently watching Shaun. Brad was squatting next to him and stroking his hand. "You OK?" he asked.

"Sure," smiled Shaun. He took the water Brad offered. "I love you, Daddy," he said. He caressed Brad's dangling penis. Brad reciprocated, and both men slowly got hard.

"Shaun, Brad," Sherry beckoned. They stood in front of her, and she clasped their hard-ons in each hand. She gently stroked them. "Kiss me." Three mouths joined as the men hugged her tightly.

Sherry took a deep breath and placed her hands on either side of Shaun's head. She guided him to her breasts, paused a few seconds, and urged him to her crotch. He didn't resist.

"This isn't so bad," he thought, as he buried his head in her thighs. "In fact, she smells pretty good, considering the day's activities. It's kinda sweet." He was still hard.

Sherry didn't push it. She lifted Shaun's head up, and the two stood looking at each other. Shaun turned his gaze to her crotch. Sherry spread her legs, and used the fingers of both hands to open her vagina. "This is what a pussy looks like."

She touched her clit with her middle finger. "This is my clit. I'd really like it if you'd touch it." Shaun tentatively reached out with his index finger. "That's it, now stroke it." Shaun did as he was told. Sherry moaned and wiggled her hips. "You can put your finger in my pussy." Shaun put his index finger in as far as it would go. "Now fuck me!" Shaun moved his finger in and out. Sherry grasped his hard dick with her hand.

"Oh, shit, you're gorgeous! I'm gonna come again! Christ, oh,Jesus, oh, here it comes!"

"How many times can she come in one night?" thought Shaun, as his finger moved furiously back and forth. Sherry's hand kept the same cadence yanking on his dick.

"Fuck me in the ass," she pleaded. She reached behind her, and a condom and small bottle of lube appeared in her hand. Soon Shaun's dick was covered in a well-lubricated black sheath.

"You're hot!" Sherry burst out. She leaned back on the table, exposing her asshole. Shaun leaned over and tentatively probed the opening with his dickhead. He gently pushed.

"Ram it in," she ordered. Shaun did so. Sherry wrapped her legs around Shaun's waist. He started to pump, and the two rocked back and forth in a giddy embrace. He put his thumb in her mouth, just like Brad sometimes did to him, and she eagerly sucked it.

Shaun felt a finger probing his asshole. It was slippery, and soon he was lubed up. Brad entered him as Shaun opened to receive the familiar long, hard dick. He clamped his ass muscles firmly around it as Brad held his hips.

"Oh, Daddy, plow me, yes, fuck your boy while I fuck your lady," gasped Shaun.

"Give it to me, fuck me hard," ordered Sherry. "I can feel you, Brad, using your hard dick to push your boy's prick into me. Push him through me. Oh, oh, oh!" Sherry rocked back and forth in ever-increasing arcs, her legs wrapped around Shaun's waist, as Brad increased the force of his thrusting.

"Rip me apart, Sir! Yank my tits out, Mistress!" yelled Shaun.

Sherry pinched Shaun's nipples until her fingers were aching. Brad squeezed Shaun tighter and tighter around the waist with his massive forearms, as he pumped deeper and deeper. He could feel Shaun's inner sphincter opening to his onslaught.

Shaun felt something tightly covering his nose and mouth. It was the leather codpiece from Dan's jock. The odor of leather, mixed with Brad's pre-cum, which his tongue stretched to reach, pushed Shaun over the edge. "I'm coming,

Sir, I'm coming!" He reared back and let out a guttural scream as his dick spasmed again and again.

"Oh yes, let me feel you come in my ass," cried Sherry. She furiously fingered her clit. "I'm coming, coming, coming!" She dug her nails into Shaun's back, as she rode his dick and let out a long, high-pitched wail.

"I'm gonna come in your ass, boy," yelled Brad. "Oh, fuck, yes, yes, yes!" Brad locked his legs around Shaun's, dug his teeth into the boy's shoulder, and shuddered violently.

"Oh, yes, Daddy, come in me," cried Shaun through tears of pain and joy. "Oh, God, this is so great!"

They collapsed in a sweaty heap on the bondage table. After catching their breath, they looked at themselves in the mirrors and laughed.

"You'll have to come back and play some more, Shaun," said Sherry. "There's lots of toys for us to explore, especially rope."

"Sure," said Shaun. He looked into her eyes and put his hand over hers. "Maybe you'll come to our house sometime."

Doug Harrison has written book reviews, essays, and short stories for Black Sheets *and* Body Play. *Two of his short stories appear in the anthology* Men Seeking Men, *and a third will appear in* Still Doing It. *He is currently working on a book titled* Erotic Whipping. *Doug is Mr. June for the AIDS Emergency Fund's 1999* South of Market Bare Chest Calendar *and appears in straight and gay videos as Brad Chapman. He has been active for many years in the modern primitives movement and the San Francisco leather scene. Doug identifies as a bisexual top/bottom. He can be reached at puma@dnai.com.*

Rednecks and Drag Bars

Margaret Weller

Maxwell checked himself out in the mirror. So far, so good. He had done a good job on his beard; no five o'clock shadow. A careful application of foundation had covered any roughness in the skin, and now he was at work on the eyes. Just a touch of mascara, just a bit of eye-shadow. Understated lipstick—something close to his own lip color. Maxwell considered this a sort of shell game. The light touch on the makeup implied "woman" as opposed to "man in drag," and that was the effect Maxwell was after. It helped that heredity and the luck of the draw had given him fine bones and a short jaw. He smiled as he finished the eyes. Surprisingly, it also helped that he wasn't trying to look too fem. The black jeans were a challenge; Maxwell solved it by running his penis back between his legs, restraining it with snug spandex. God help him if he tried to get an erection. A corset gave him a more feminine torso, an illusion furthered by small prosthetics in a bra beneath the black turtleneck. Two-inch heeled boots and small onyx studs in his ears instead of the small silver hoops he usually wore brought the desired image closer to completion. He donned the wig, black like his own hair and only a couple of inches longer, styled with a slight curl inward at the bottom. He adjusted it and viewed the results. Good, good; very plausible. He slipped on short black leather gloves, gave himself a last inspection, then turned and went out.

As he slid onto the barstool, Jake, the bartender, raised an eyebrow, said, "Lookin' good, Jackie," and went off to get his order. Jak turned on the stool to watch the various drag efforts on parade. Some of them were more plausible than others, but he had to remind himself that what he considered plausibility might have little relevance for them. There was more than one motivation for cross-dressing, and his own was rather rare. At certain times, a total disguise had added as much to his life expectancy as a knowledge of all the exits; other cross-dressers usually had less paranoid reasons for the pastime. Some really wanted to be women; indeed, some were in the process of becoming women. Some just had a fetish for female clothing. And some, he was sure, were hostile to women and used drag as parody. His own favorite to watch, probably because it contrasted so violently with his own approach, was that of the Radical Faerie. A long-haired, bearded man dressed in a pink strapless formal, armpit and chest hair on full display, had a certain weird charm about him. None here tonight, unfortunately.

Jak felt someone slide onto the barstool next to him, then a friendly male voice said, "Hi, can I buy you a drink?" He turned, hard put not to start and stare. The fellow on the stool had to be Vic Torley, the country singer. Jak looked away, then back at the other. "Certainly, if you wish." He coughed.

"Got a cold?"

"Just getting over one." Jackie considered "her" voice the weakest spot of the imposture, and her choice of drink—whiskey, neat—was a good excuse for a husky tone. The fading cold was her other favorite. Convenient of Vic to mention it.

Jackie's admirer waved to Jake. "Bartender! I'll take scotch on the rocks. And give the lady whatever she likes." Jackie bit her lip watching Jake's carefully schooled expression.

When the drinks arrived, Jackie raised her glass. "Thank you."

"My pleasure," the other replied. "By the way, my name's Vic. What's yours?"

"Jackie."

"Well, Jackie, I'm just real pleased to find someone as pretty as you here. Some of the women in here are real dogs. Tall, too. But you, you're something else."

Yeah, and Jak thought he knew what. Jackie bore more than a passing resemblance to Vic's ex-wife, with whom he'd had a decade-long fight of a marriage. Jak's first thought was that this evening could be interesting in the extreme, if he chose to follow up on it. Vic did not seem to have a clue.

"Dunno what John was thinkin' of," Vic was saying. "He kept sayin' there'd be great cruisin'." He looked around, annoyed, then realized who he was talking to. "Sorry, I mean..." He kind of teetered there, trying to figure out what to say to extricate himself.

Jackie laughed consolingly, and added, "I understand what you're saying. Maybe he had a more specific type of cruising in mind? This is a leather bar." Her fingers swept the keys near her left pocket.

Vic looked blank. "Leather?"

Jak's wariness increased. He probably should be very blunt very quickly. "Vic, do you know what kind of a bar you're in?"

Vic had apparently just decided on a pitch and was not to be diverted. "No, and I don't care, either. I just know who I'd like to leave with."

Well, the lust was certainly genuine, though now Jak sincerely doubted it would survive the removal of clothing. "Jackie" reached over and laid her hand gently on Vic's wrist. "Vic, please pay attention to what I'm saying. Okay?"

Vic stared at her, puzzled. "Sure."

"First, a couple questions: You say that your friend brought you?"

"Yes..."

"And what did he say about the place?"

Vic shrugged. "That there would be lots of good-looking women; that I wouldn't... uh..."

"Have any trouble picking one up?"

Vic grinned, beginning to enjoy Jackie's attitude. "Yeah."

Jak increased the pressure on Vic's wrist. This was going to be touchy. He could already smell the other man's pheromones. "Vic, I want you to do something for me."

"Sure, babe." Vic was starting to chafe.

"I'm going to tell you a couple of things I think you should know. Don't move until I say you can, okay?"

"Sure, babe."

"Vic, this is a leather and fetish bar. That means that some of the people who frequent it like to wear leather. It means that some of them do S/M."

Vic looked intrigued. "You mean rough sex? I can dig it if you can."

Jak sighed. "The fetish part means it also caters to other fetishes than leather." Jackie gazed at Vic. "Haven't you figured out yet why so many of the women are so tall?" She saw Vic's eyes narrow. "Because they're men. Hold it!" Maxwell's voice came out in command mode and Vic froze. "So am I, Vic," he added gently.

Vic stared at Maxwell, stunned. "No way," he stated.

"I'm afraid there's no way I'm not. I'm very sorry, Vic. I had no intention of dropping you in the deep end of the pool. You managed to convey a very honest message of sexual attraction, but I just don't think you swing that way."

"Christ, you sure had me fooled. You're not kidding, are you?" Vic searched "Jackie's" face.

"Sorry, Vic." Maxwell pitched his voice more deeply than usual and Vic twitched.

"Why the hell do you do this?" Vic waved his hand at Jak's attire.

"To see if I can fool people. It's a challenge; sometimes I succeed."

"Well, you sure did tonight." Vic looked distinctly pissed.

"You do have my sincerest apologies, Vic. I did not expect to find anyone in this bar who didn't know the score in general if not in particular. This is a fetish bar; this is drag night. The only people I expected would try to pick me up were unattached lesbians looking for a top. I feel about your friend a bit the way I once felt about wankers who slipped acid in other people's coffee."

Vic was off on his own track again. "You're queer!"

Maxwell gave Vic a sidelong look. "Half queer, anyway. I really like women too; what I like just doesn't have much to do with gender."

Vic glared at Jak. "You're one of those bastards spreadin' AIDS around!"

Maxwell sipped his drink and gave Vic a level stare. "Not me, Vic. I use condoms." Not the entire truth, but Jak wasn't giving Vic the long form unless the man started exhibiting some brains that weren't in his dick.

"You think rubbers really work?" Vic sounded contemptuous.

"I know they do. I spent a lot of time in the gay leather scene during the years HIV was getting passed around out of ignorance. I had a real aversion to getting clapped-out, so I was pretty picky. Lucky, too. Everyone has condom failures. So did I."

"Maybe you were picky enough to pick people that didn't have the bug."

"You can't tell by looking at someone," Jak stated flatly.

Vic looked skeptical.

"Oh, you can tell if someone is starting to fail from active AIDS—sometimes. But that's years—sometimes ten or more—after a person becomes infected. Theoretically, any infected person can pass it."

"Rubbers are a bitch," Vic grumbled.

"Yea, verily," Jak agreed. "Try keeping one on when your foreskin keeps trying to jack it off."

Vic blinked. "I was thinking about the fact that you can't feel anything through them."

"Try nettles."

"*Nettles?*"

"Keep your voice down, Vic. Yes, nettles. A few on your cock, *before* you put the rubber on, makes you a lot more sensitive."

Vic stared at Jak. "I can't believe I'm havin' this conversation."

Jak grinned. "If I were more New Age, I'd say maybe that's why you're here."

"You believe that shit?" Vic challenged him.

"Not me, but as long as you *are* here, I can give you my solution. Be sure to put the nettles on before you put the condom on. Otherwise you'll be wearing a sieve. I'm sure you don't want your girlfriend telling you there's a little bastard on the way."

Vic winced. "Got one of those already."

"Rubbers help with that problem, too. Not at this point, of course. Just remember, nettles first, then the condom."

Vic shuddered. "That's perverted."

Maxwell grinned. "'I am erotically adventurous, *you* are kinky, *he* is a digusting pervert.' Well, Vic, I hate to tell you this, but perverts often have fantastic sex lives." He heard the first bleeps and noodlings as some of the band started final checkouts on the equipment. "That's my call, Vic. I've enjoyed talking to you. And thank you for the drink." Jackie slid off the bar stool, picked up her other drink and strode across the room.

Vic sat staring after the departing figure. She—*he?*—played in the band? Shit, she even *walked* like a woman. He. "Oh, Christ," Vic muttered, putting his head in his hands. Halfway through the third song, he finished his drink and walked over to John's table. John and his two buddies wore poorly disguised smirks. "What the hell are you lookin' so fuckin' pleased about?" Vic snarled.

John was too soused to be wary. "What's the matter, Vic? Couldn't you get the little dyke to fall for you?"

Vic felt a wave of relief. Shit, John didn't know she—he—shit!—wasn't a woman. When he spoke, Vic's voice was icy. "Where did you find one who looked so much like Penny?"

John jerked. "Oh, shit, Vic, I didn't—"

"Like hell, asshole. Well, if I can't fuck her, maybe I can hire her as a drummer." He gave John a poisonous look. "She's a damn sight better drummer than you are." Vic turned on his heel and left the bar.

As Jak broke down his drumkit, Lilith, the lead guitarist—and Jak's lady—sauntered over. The lights struck gold and copper highlights from her red hair. He smiled appreciatively as she approached.

"Yeah?" she asked.

"Just staring."

She grinned. "Thanks. You're good for my ego."

"As if you couldn't find that anywhere."

She shook her head. "Not without head trips."

"I try."

"You do pretty well. You, too," she turned her head toward her distant cousin Orlac, the third person in their sexual triad.

Orlac produced a friendly leer, then turned to Jak. "Who was the tourist trying to get into your pants, man?"

Jak rubbed his nose. "Er... Vic Torley, I think."

Lil cocked her head, fox face alight with speculation. "I wondered."

Jak shrugged. "Said his name was Vic."

Orrie's eyes narrowed. "And you look so much like Penny Walker."

"Done up like this, I do."

"So, he showing up later tonight?"

Maxwell went back to his work. "Don't think so; he seemed rather put off at the revelation of an extra cock in the mix."

Half an hour later, Jak stepped into the alley to open the van and get it ready for loading. He had just opened the sliding door when he was aware of stealthy movement in the alley. The movement accelerated into a rush. Maxwell turned to face his assailant and backed a couple steps down the alley. His foot came up, and his right heel took his attacker in the solar plexus. The sides of his hands slammed into the other's trapezius muscles.

"Shit—!"

Good. The voice was a choked, agonized whisper. Feel that pain, arsewipe! Jak twisted and propelled his assailant face-down onto the floor of the van. Grabbing a speaker cable, he slammed a knee in the middle of the other's back, grabbed a wrist, wrapped cable around it, held the forearm with his knee, tied the cord off and went after the other wrist. When Jak had gotten both wrists secured, he trapped the flailing legs one at a time and completed the hogtie. His assailant was now swearing nonstop. Jak laid hold of the other's hair and jerked his head up.

"Why, Vic! What a pleasant surprise!"

"Let me up, you cocksucker!"

Maxwell rolled Vic over on his side. "What was that, again?"

"I said, 'Let me up!'" Vic gritted.

Jak studied Vic's crotch in the dim glow of the van's domelight. "It would appear that you are already up, Vic," he shrugged. "So to speak..."

"You—"

"Shh, Vic. Quiet down. I'd hate to have to gag you. All I have about me is duct tape, and it's terribly hard on facial skin."

"Goddamn faggot! I'm gonna *kill* you!"

Jak reached for the duct tape, peeled off a piece, stuck one end to the back of the van seat, tore off a smaller piece and stuck it, adhesive to adhesive to the middle of the other piece. Vic was still screaming abuse. Maxwell rolled Vic onto his other side, closed his jaw with a forearm under the chin and slapped the tape on. Vic's outrage continued, much muffled. Maxwell released his hold and leaned against the seat back, waiting. Vic eventually ran down, turned himself so he could see Maxwell, and lay there, glaring.

"So. To what do I owe this unexpected pass?" That started Vic up again. Maxwell wrapped his arms around his knees and waited. When Vic ran down this time, Jak eyed Vic's persistent erection and sighed. "Either I was wrong about you, or you are quite fond of bondage." He looked Vic in the face. "Which is it, Vic?" This time, he got a reply that sounded calmer. "Will you converse like a civilized being if I take the tape off?" Vic offered a monosyllabic reply. "Nod or shake, Vic." Vic nodded. Maxwell leaned over and removed the tape as gently as he could.

"Ow! Damn!"

"Sorry, Vic. I did warn you about the tape."

Vic muttered, "Didn't think you'd do it."

"I rarely make empty threats."

"Thanks. I'll remember that." Vic grimaced and shifted.

"Do you want out of the bondage?"

Vic flushed, bit his lip. "Not yet...."

"You like it?"

"Damn you!"

"Vic, I have a whole roll of duct tape."

Vic bit his lip again. "Sorry."

"Shall we try once more?" Jak waited.

A heavy sigh from Vic. "Yeah, I like it. I loved playin' the Injun when I was a kid. Gettin' tied up was my favorite thing."

"So, could you ever get your wife to tie you up?"

"*Goddamn you fuckin'—*"

Jak pulled a length of tape away from the roll. "Quiet, Vic!"

Vic looked away and swallowed. "Leave Penny out of this," he whispered.

"Come *on*, Vic. I know why you came on so hard a bit ago. Dressed like this, I look a lot like her."

Silence.

"But I'm not terribly sure why you tried to waylay me just now."

"Me neither."

"Shall I theorize?"

Vic's whole body tensed, his head came up, his mouth opened. Then he met Jak's eyes—and deflated.

"Damn you," Vic whispered.

Jak eyed Vic's crotch. Vic's boner was harder than ever. Quite respectably sized, too.

"Look, Vic. If you really want a scene, we can do one. But under the circumstances, I must insist that you admit you want it."

"What the hell d'you mean?" Vic snarled.

"Vic, Vic. Quit wasting my time. You don't want out of the bondage; you've thrown a boner that won't quit, and the more I dominate you verbally, the bigger it gets! It seems that at some level you, or some part of you, is enjoying this. But I need to hear from you that you acknowledge that fact. I would also like to hear what you were intending when you came here."

"This is bullshit!"

"Vic, I am an experienced S/M player. I've been doing S/M and dominance/submission since I was a kid. This smells like a takedown fantasy: you come intending to take me down. If you don't succeed, then I take you down." Jak stared down at Vic. "But do you really want the consequences, Vic? I assume that you figured you could take down this little faggot and ass-fuck him just to get even with him for looking like your ex-wife, and maybe get even with her, too, somehow. But what if the faggot wins, Vic?"

Vic swallowed hard. Jak noticed, however, that Vic's hard-on was still stark against his jeans. Jak shifted and pulled a throwing knife from his boot. When Vic saw it, his eyes went wide and he started to sweat. "Hey...c'mon...put that thing away!" He started to twist in the bondage, eyes glued to the knife.

"Quiet, Vic. I do not intend to hurt you." Maxwell looked at the bound, sweating man. "Let me rephrase that; I will not hurt you deliberately. However, if you keep thrashing, something may happen that I had not planned. Do you understand?"

Vic bit his lip and lay still.

Jak swung the knife toward Vic's crotch. Vic mewled, but held position. "*Very* good, Vic." Jak laid the leaf-shaped blade flat, the knife's point between Vic's balls, and drew the knife upwards along the underside of the penis. The slight furrow made in the denim disappeared as the blade moved on. Maxwell could feel Vic's cock twitch under the knife. The knife reached the glans, and Jak drew several lines across the outlined surface. Vic groaned. His cock jumped, and a wet spot grew on the pale blue cloth. A burst of pheromones from the prisoner brought Maxwell's eyebrows up. "Vic, are you *enjoying* this?"

A groan. Jak waited.

"Damn you!" A whisper, not a roar.

"Shall I untie you, or shall I continue?"

Silence.

"Choose."

"Continue."

"Thank you. Would you prefer a blindfold?"

"No!" Vic chewed his lip again. "I wanna see where that damned knife is going!"

"I have no intention of harming you."

"So you say."

"Do you want out?"

"*No!*" Vic looked away, his mouth twisting.

Jak prodded each ball in turn with the point of the knife.

"Aaah!"

This was quite erotic, Jak thought. Too bad Vic was so conflicted about men. He ran the flat of the knife, far edge dragging, up the length of Vic's dick.

"Nnggh! Oh, yeah... *please!*"

Jak repeated the sequence.

"Ah, damn! Take it out!"

Jak carefully opened the jeans zipper, Vic's penis eagerly springing free of its prison as he did. My, my, Jak mused. Circumcised, but otherwise quite nicely shaped. With the zipper all the way down, Jak excavated Vic's balls, making a nice tight package overhanging the zipper. A gasp, then "Easy! No!" and a keening from Vic.

Jak was feeling pressure between his own legs now. "Oh, my, Vic. This is making me very horny." He knelt up and ran a hand down his jeans to free up his trapped cock. Glancing at Vic, he caught a supremely apprehensive expression on the man's face. "You needn't worry, Vic. In all my years as a leatherman, I have never discovered a practical way to assfuck a hogtied man."

"Thanks a bunch."

"You are most welcome." Jak prodded Vic's balls with the tip of the knife.

"Aahh!!" Vic strained away from the knife. A drop of precum pearled at the tip of his cock. Maxwell tapped Vic's nuts with the flat of the blade, surprising a short scream from the bound man.

"Quiet, Vic. Hardly anyone uses this alley, but I think you would not care to attract attention."

As he spoke, Jak sensed movement in the alley, then Lilith leaned around the doorway, red hair flowing.

Vic saw her too. "Oh, Jesus *Christ!*" he moaned, and turned his face away.

Lil leaned toward Jak. "You know he's gonna scream like a rabbit when he comes. I think we should offer him a gag." She looked at the bound, exposed man. "How 'bout I sit on your face?"

Vic's eyes went wide. "Oh, Christ, would you?"

"Fully clothed, of course."

Vic groaned.

"Sorry, honey, but I'm wet enough already it wouldn't be safer sex otherwise." She swung into the van and over Vic's face. "You want it?"

Vic moaned. "Yes. Please."

"Good boy." Lil settled herself over the lower half of Vic's face, her eyes on his, and pulled her T-shirt up off her breasts.

Maxwell watched Vic's glans turn a darker red, verging toward plum. "Hell, Lil, I may not have to do a thing. He may come without my touching him."

"Get in there and help, dammit. I want him to scream like a banshee when he comes." A hesitation, then a slight groan from Lilith.

Jak grinned. If she was this hot already, Vic was going to have the treat of his life. "Yes, Milady." He gathered Vic's balls and pulled them taut till the scrotal skin shone, ignoring the wails. "Don't suppose you have a hair tie?"

"Here you go." Lil dug in her pocket, then swung her hand back with a fancy black velvet hair binder.

"Do you want come all over this?"

"If he screams good for me, he can wear it home."

"Oh, Vic, you *are* privileged." Jak wound the binder tight above Vic's balls.

"Mmmph!"

Lilith looked down. "You're Vic? Hi, Vic, I'm Lilith. My daddy named me that 'cuz he, like the feminists, thought that Lilith was a right-on woman. Feel free to chew on my jeans; I want to get off, too." She smiled encouragingly down at Vic. Vic groaned, and started chewing.

Jak dug in his inner jacket pocket; gloves, lube...ah, nipple clips. He reached up and pulled open the snaps on Vic's shirt. "Breathe deep, Vic. I'm clamping your tits." He pulled up the left nipple and placed the clip. A muffled scream from Vic.

"Oh, yeah, Vic." Lil was grinding her crotch into Vic's face. Jak placed the second clip. This scream was longer, and Lil climaxed hard—and not very quietly.

"I'm not certain that this is an improvement, soundwise," Maxwell remarked.

"Too bad," Lil replied. "Besides... it's a big improvement for me...." She thrashed around on Vic's face. "Bite me, baby."

Jak grinned as he donned the gloves. His own erection matched Vic's at this point; fortunately, when Lil got into this mood, it took a lot of work to get her out of it. He drew a line of lube up Vic's cock. Vic screamed. "Easy, Vic. It's not the knife, just lube." More precum appeared on Vic's glans. Maxwell dropped a gout of lube on top of it and took it in hand. Working it with one hand, he closed and discarded the lube bottle and reached for the tit-clamp chain.

Lil shifted position, trapping his hand over the stretched chain. Vic wailed. She slid down Jak's arm far enough to present a breast to the keening Vic. "Vic! Pay attention! Lick this!" Vic opened his eyes and gasped.

"Ungh! Nice long tongue, Vic. Now the other one. Oh, yes-s-s!" She shinnied back up to sit on Vic's face again.

Jak resumed caressing Vic's penis. The groans the man emitted were glorious; Jak squirmed in his own jeans hearing them. Grinning, he lubed up the other hand and ran it over Vic's balls. A shriek from Vic; unclear whether that was pain or apprehension. Lilith muttered, "Oh, yeah, baby." Jak worried the glans and the sensitive groove just behind it. Vic's long groan brought Lil to a boil again. Her red hair flew as she put all her desires for noise into bodily motion. Jak could see Vic's cock turning purple all by itself. Too bad, no stretching it, except of course by making the experience more intense. Jak yanked the titclamps off Vic's nipples, and heard his muffled shrieks as the man thrashed. Lil grabbed Vic's hair and held his head in an iron grip where it would do her the most good. Then she peaked again, riding Vic's agony through a third climax.

Vic's load began to spurt. Jak tried to direct it onto Vic's chest, but several spots appeared on the back of Lil's jeans. Jak worked the captive cock and balls, playing them for all they were worth, so it was only a minute or so before he noticed that Vic was building for another climax. Vic's wail took on a note of surprise as it became clear to him, too, that he was experiencing a second coming. This one was nearly dry—not strange, considering the volume of semen already adorning Vic's chest. Lilith was now into aftershocks from her latest orgasm. The atmosphere in the van quieted, except for the howling erection in Maxwell's jeans. Jak smiled and rubbed Vic's load carefully into his chest hair, genitals, and the hairband.

Lil pulled herself shakily off Vic's face and pulled down her shirt. "Boy, I gotta say, you give good chew, Vic."

"Thanks," Vic croaked. "Could you untie me now? My hands are numb."

"Oh, shit!" Maxwell stripped off the gloves, flipped Vic over and untied knots. Nerve damage to a musician's wrists was something he did not even want to think about. "Be really careful unfolding, Vic. Let us help straighten you out."

"After *that*? " Vic's cackle made the double entendre clear. A gasp. "Oh, Christ!"

"Cramp?"

"No, just nothin' wants to work right. Christ, I came hard!"

"Ever come in bondage before?"

"Not like this."

"In what respect?"

"Umm." Vic stared through Lilith, rubbing a knee joint, gathering his thoughts. "I never been taken down for real before. Always had to help, y'know?" He flushed. "And I didn't know what you were gonna do...." He looked at Lil now. "And, sweetheart, I have *never* had anyone sit on my face like you just did, clothes or no."

"Thanks. I enjoyed it, too."

"Well, you can sit on my face any day."

Lilith fished a card out of her hip pocket, looked at it and tucked it into Vic's breast pocket. "Give me a call. We can talk about it. I'm interested."

Vic's eyes widened, and he gasped and clutched at the nipple Lilith's card had scraped in passing. "Uhnnh!"

Lil managed to look both concerned and amused. "Sorry, Vic. They'll probably be tender for awhile."

Vic edged over to the van door and gingerly let his legs down. "Aahhh!" The sound was half moan, half cry of relief. He flexed his shoulders carefully.

"How are the wrists?"

Vic quit rubbing his tits and considered.

"Doin' better by the minute. I think they'll be okay." Vic flexed his arms and wrists. He stood up and choked back a cry. Weaving, he reached down to tuck in his genitals and encountered the hair tie. "Uh—" He reached to remove it.

A small, strong hand gripped his wrist. "Vic. Leave it. Wear it until you get home. Do you hear me?" Vic stared, surprised.

"I can't do that!"

"Sure you can. You're not hard—"

"I will be the first time I think about that being there."

"After a double orgasm? Vic, I *do* want to see more of you." She tapped his nuts; he hissed. "Keep it on till you get home, Vic."

He stared at her a moment, then tucked in his equipment, hairband and all. "Yes, ma'am." He looked around blankly.

"I don't believe you were carrying anything when you arrived, Vic," Jak assured him.

Vic flushed. "Yeah..." He looked at Lilith again. "I'll be calling."

"Do that."

He looked at Maxwell, his face a welter of emotion. "Thanks... I think."

"My pleasure."

Vic snarled silently and tottered off down the alley.

Lil grabbed Maxwell by the hair, threw the wig it produced in a corner of the van, grabbed again and pulled toward the van's interior.

"Upstairs?" he asked, hopefully.

She shook her head. "Right here."

Margaret Weller has lived in Oregon all her life. In addition to writing, she is a metalsmith, just now getting to hot-iron work. She has stories in Western Trails *and* Leatherwomen 3. *She and her primary are celebrating 32 years in an open relationship—which keeps getting better and better.*

Ethnography

Jill Nagle

The first day of class, I christened him Biff, forever blocking out his real name. I remember the setting sun's rays penetrating the glass wall, warming the contents of the room. The students were shedding their outer layers. Biff had stood up and pulled his college sweatshirt a little too quickly over his head so that the T-shirt underneath followed suit. Elbows and head momentarily trapped in the cotton tangle, Biff struggled to both escape and remain appropriately clothed, inadvertently exposing a golden tan torso with silken skin covering rippling abdominals. I immediately looked at Randy, the instructor, who faltered almost imperceptibly mid-sentence at Biff's little blind dance, then glanced at me. I quickly looked out the window to keep from grinning too broadly.

Randy and I, old friends and occasional lovers, often bond around handsome young men. Brief glances commute detailed scenarios, past and fantasy. Remember the abandoned yacht in Point Richmond? This one looks like that one. A nod. Remember you said you wanted to make someone like him suck my cock? A smile. This one is exactly your type. A wink. A shift, a squirm.

A few brief murmurs under the breath, and, in the proper context, we move in on our prey. After a few queer play parties, our cruising technique shifted from primarily improvisational art to studied science. By the time we met Biff, we had engineered dozens of threesomes with little trouble.

But this was different. I was the teaching assistant for a class in which Biff was a student, and Randy the teacher. And potentially Biff's advisor, no less. Plus, Biff seemed awfully straight. The initiation of a straight boy would have been hot in most settings. The danger of the immediate circumstances made this particular possibility positively molten. By the end of the semester, Randy and I had exchanged many—very discreet—Biff-specific glances.

Biff could almost be Randy's brother. Deep-set light eyes, straight nose—Scandinavian stock, I thought. Despite Randy's Russian Jewish peasant background, he had somehow wound up looking very WASPy, hence the resemblance. Clean-cut Biff evoked every high school varsity football best-looking all-around hunk kind of archetype. He moved about with ease and confidence. The world was his, after all. What, I wondered, drew him to a graduate-level class in Anthropology of Cultural Deviance? He looked more like a business major.

Weeks of discussion ensued. At one point, Biff had sort of sputtered open, diffusing on many levels, about needing constructs to live his life, the importance of Truth, and how problematizing dominant discourse posed certain threats. I remember focusing on his shoulders, his thighs, watching his full lips curl around fading words. I had a strong and sudden urge to pin him down and gag him. All at once, I had loudly and involuntarily crumpled the paper I'd been toying with.

The whole class started slightly at the sharp, crispy noise. Biff had paused and looked at me. I lifted my chin, narrowed my eyes, and gave him a devious smile. Brow furrowed, he had turned away.

Thrilled, I began to plan. And fantasize.

On the last day of the last week of classes, just before the euphemistically labeled "winter break"—that just happened to neatly enclose Christmas—after most of the students had departed, I emerged from the women's room hoping to find Randy and catch a ride home with him. Just inside the classroom, I saw Biff on the edge of his seat, his small desk next to Randy's, his hand gesturing close to the teacher's face. Just inches apart, their faces seemed even more closely related; two handsome, athletic siblings having a heart-to-heart. Younger brother, head forward in earnest angst; older brother offering relaxed, open arms. Randy's hands rested on the edges of the small desk attached to his chair, and his feet spread apart just enclosing Biff's. As Biff leaned forward, the tipping desk became a cumbersome garment around his advancing torso, an institutional chastity belt.

I moved closer to the door, and caught stray phrases. Biff's voice had that familiar, grappling tone he'd used all semester, but this time with a smoother undercurrent. He had been moving toward buying, or at least making peace with the ambiguity Randy had been proffering all semester: breaking down stalwart dichotomies of good and evil, right and wrong, sacred and profane.

Embracing contradictions, honoring paradox. However, like many children of privilege, Foucauldian approaches to culture unsettled him to the core. While he obediently aped some of Randy's rhetoric in his papers, I knew that many of the fine (and crude) points of the lectures had flown over his pretty blond hetero head. I felt a certain responsibility to Biff to drive some of those points home myself.

I looked down the empty hallway. With extreme care, I quietly closed the door behind me and turned the lock. I moved closer, kneeling hidden just behind the divider. Biff was turned three-quarters away from me, and Randy could easily have seen me if he'd looked up. From my new vantage point, I recognized the specific discussion from earlier classes: can occupying a deviant position in society confer knowledge unavailable to those outside the group? All semester long, Biff had come close to baiting Randy about his homosexuality.

How could "one" have access to the information about queer life Randy claimed to possess? But Randy wouldn't bite so easily, instead enjoining Biff to take inventory of his own subjugated knowledges, his personal domain of resistant epistemologies.

Now, Biff's elbows rested on the small wedge of linoleum that bridged their torsos. He lifted his body so his face met Randy's: "I can't... I don't... understand this..." he murmured as their lips met.

Randy's hand found the back of Biff's neck, sealing their faces. Their mouths gently searched each other out for a few moments. Air filled my lungs at the sight of the four lips embracing so sensuously. Teeth appeared briefly, then a flash of tongue. They slid from the clunky barriers between them onto the floor. On their knees, stomachs pressed against each other, hands roamed asses, back, sides of face. I remembered to exhale. Then inhale. Then exhale. One, and then the other arc of hard cock appeared through jeans and sweat pants as their torsos twisted, turned and buckled. Though the room was cool, I felt my face flush.

I reached down my tight jeans to respond to my insistent clit. Moving the denim aside, my own eyes closed at the rush of feeling as blood plumped up my crushed vulva. Teasing strokes of my own fingers quickly brought me to a sharp edge. I removed my hand and ran my salty fingers just inside my lips, breathing my own scent. As I opened my eyes, Randy looked up at me, grinned, and winked. Not missing a beat, he caressed Biff's round ass, which was facing me, and gestured me toward it with his eyes. I needed no further prompting.

Randy grabbed Biff's head, as if to kiss him harshly, but instead moved past his mouth and whispered in his ear. Biff's body writhed as he attempted to turn to look at me, but instead, Randy held him fast and kept murmuring against his head. I heard only stray notes of Randy's baritone monologue, but I easily imagined the text. I remembered a post-High Holy Days episode, drunk with the high of Jewish partying, when, after driving me home, Randy had pinned me to his car and talked a long, dirty stream in my ear for about five minutes—

five minutes which had thoroughly decapacitated my capulas, and provided several months of masturbatory material besides. Watching Biff's resistant body melt into the floor, my pussy throbbed for more attention. I began to grow a bit dizzy.

Catching myself, I reached into my backpack and pulled out my big, purple rubber dick and its harness, which I'd been carrying around for weeks trusting that the right moment would present itself. Stripping down to my g-string, I quickly strapped myself in and rolled a condom over my member. The harness parted under the dildo, leaving my pussy completely exposed. I fingered myself gently, while Randy began grinding Biff's eager head into his crotch.

Biff wrapped his hands around Randy's waist, and slowly slid his pants down over his ass.

Randy's cock stretched his CK shorts like a white sail at high wind, and Biff's hands trembled at the member, rushing to release him. Randy reached into his pocket, ripped a wrapper open with his teeth, and slid a condom down his shaft. Biff ran shaky fingertips down the length of Randy's impressive prick, and in one fell motion, *siss!* Biff's hands met Randy's bare ass; *boom!* Randy's hand met the back of Biff's head; *bah!* Randy's cock met a part of Biff's throat few will ever know.

Again. And again. And again.

I mashed the heel of my hand hard against my mound to stave off my orgasm. On cue, I stole behind Biff and knelt, studying him. I couldn't catch Randy's gaze, because his eyes were half-lidded in ecstasy. Low moans trickled from his lips. Biff's cock was waving uselessly, half-hard. His hands worked the base of Randy's cock, twisting his shaved balls, squeezing the blood from his pelvis into the flesh that filled his mouth. Biff's ass cheeks were, indeed, the two round brown coconuts I'd often observed through his thin gym clothes, sometime highlighted by a dark line of sweat between the cheeks. I slipped a glove onto my right hand and squeezed a dollop of lube into my palm. With slippery fingers, I slid down into his ass crack and began working my way home, as my other hand reached around and trapped one of his nipples in my hard, dry grip.

Biff let out a low, choking groan which intensified as my fingers found his tight puckered hole and began circling him on the outside, like a vulture preparing to descend for the kill. I covered Biff's eyes with my hand and spoke softly in his ear.

"You like having that big, throbbing cock don't you? Yeah, you just can't get enough of Dr. Dick's hard stuff. You want to swallow that rod, don't you?" I surprised us all, then, by the sharpness that entered my voice.

"It isn't enough, Biff, is it, to read about it. It doesn't quite cut it to take it in through the page, through the ears, through the head...your body wants to know. Your body needs to know, doesn't it—doesn't it, Biff?" I entered him with my middle finger, thrusting upward toward his prostate. He lurched forward, gagging on Randy's cock. Randy groaned, eyes fluttering back in his head. I continued, this time louder.

"This is the language you don't speak, isn't it, Biff? Feel what's in your mouth, Biff. This is your mother tongue. This is your father tongue. This is your father cock. This is your culture. Say hello to Daddy, Biff! *This is how Rome was built!*" I added my index finger and more lube, quickening my pace. Biff began to undulate. I glanced behind me to ensure that we were truly alone. My voice filled with rage and conviction as my cunt engorged with blood. I shoved a third finger into him and shouted.

"Lots of those dead white guys had pretty boys like you sucking their cocks! Your role was to keep the ideas flowing. Can you feel that connection to the great teachers, Biff? You participate in a time-honored tradition by paying homage to the intellectual cock, Biff. Easing the stress of forging Western civilization is no small thing, little brother. We're glad we can help fill your... *role*."

Biff's voice climbed higher into a constant hum. Energy filled my body. For every one of his ilk who ever beat up a fag or even glanced at a queer sideways, I would impart the lesson of inside knowledge. If I never changed another person's point of view, I would inexorably, irrevocably, corporeally alter his. I would get under his skin. For the sins of his brothers, he would be fucked silly, and his new awareness forced to trickle down to the farthest reaches of the populace. Waves of conversion would ensue, and the masses would pay homage to this new queer icon, Biff, the christos, the anointed one. Formerly straight people would wear gold emblems of Biff impaled upon my queer fist. Priestesses would offer the body of the host in little cock-shaped wafers to the men, and vulva-shaped wafers to the women. A religion based on subjugated bodily knowledge would spring forth, carried forward by Biff, my chosen son. In white-hot fury, I jammed my four fingers toward his heart and breathed into his ear, "Through what is cast off, you enter the center! You bring the outside in, and in so doing, deconstruct the dichotomies of body and spirit, flesh and intellect, nature and culture, straight and gay. It's all one, isn't it, Biff? You understand now, don't you, Biff? Don't you? Nod if you understand!"

Now moaning in a squeaky falsetto, Biff vigorously moved his head up and down, never releasing Randy's cock with his mouth. At that moment, after many minutes of prying open his ass with my hand, I slopped on more lube and entered him slowly with my big purple dick. As I fucked him to three, four, then five inches' worth of my member, his head fell back onto my shoulder, moans lowering an octave or two. Randy finally opened his eyes and looked at me with an expression I hadn't seen: bliss, astonishment, respect, and silent raucous laughter at my inspired absurdity. I must have sounded possessed, I thought. I certainly felt that way. A husky voice came out of my throat.

"Bend over," I growled. Biff lowered himself onto his elbows, ass in the air, face back in Randy's crotch. In one in fell motion, *siss!* my hands met Biff's hard hips; *boom!* cool honeydew ass cheeks met my pubic bone; *bah!* my eight-inch rubber dick met a part of Biff's innards few will ever know. Again. And again. And again.

We remained so configured for a short eternity: Randy fucking Biff's face, me plowing the depths of his coconut grove. Biff had become a monster of the bottom, a disciple, a devotee. Gone was the shell of protection, the carefully wrought mien. In its stead was a writhing opus of orifi, homunculus of holes, a groveling gargoyle of gratefulness. I despised him. I desired him. I pitied him. I worshipped him. And, oh, yes, I fucked him.

Time became still. Spent and silent, Randy and Biff curled entwined against the far wall while I removed my hardware and placed it in a plastic bag. I said nothing to Biff, knowing we would probably never talk again. I needed to leave. I felt tired and achey inside, yet strangely peaceful, like after a good cry.

Later that night, I called Randy to debrief. Randy told me that before I walked in, he and Biff were discussing a missed class in which the students' homework had been to visit a ritual of a culture foreign to their own, hosted by a native to that culture. Randy and I had offered to help students in making these cross-cultural connections and Biff, as it turned out, had been staying afterwards to find out about the assignment. Randy thanked me for my assistance.

A lapsed bisexual activist, Jill Nagle (www.jillnagle.com) edited Whores and Other Feminists *and associate-edited* Male Lust: Pleasure, Power and Transformation. *Pir work has appeared in anthologies such as* Looking Queer, PoMoSexuals, *and* First Person Sexual, *and periodicals such as* American Book Review, moXie, *and* On Our Backs. *Pir forthcoming books include* Girl Fag *and* The Zen of Getting Laid. *Hse is currently working on several screenplays, including one about Edgar Cayce's life and work.*

The Great Blinking MacGuffin

Charles Anders

He built it. And it worked. And then the hand on my coccyx. And then everything went naked. Sorry. I should back up and slow down. Brendan (or Brenda, as I called him) built it just to show me it could be done. Brenda would do almost anything to prove a point.

The result was very impressive, I had to admit. It had lights and a satellite dish as big as my hand with a pink triangle and the word "BI" emblazoned on its center. A telescoping snout like a raygun muzzle stuck out of the front, and a big strap went around the back of your neck, so you could wear it in front of your stomach like a peanut vendor's tray at the ballpark. Brenda turned it on. The lights flashed, the dish rotated, and it made this chirping noise every few seconds that I realized sounded like the word "bi."

So that was how we ended up some time later in a pile of feathers, my left hand rubbing two cocks together while a woman with a tongue piercing licked my balls. (The piercing felt surprisingly good.) Feathers got everywhere as I French-kissed the owner of one of the two cocks and he peeled my bra off one shoulder, then the other. I looked over at Brenda, who was pumping his prick into the Kangaroo Lady in time with the Mandrill Sisters.

Sorry. Getting ahead of myself again.

So anyway, I looked at the box hanging from Brenda's denim collar. "What the hell is that thing?"

"It's a portable bi-dar unit. What do you think, silly?" Brenda pointed the nozzle at me and more lights flashed, probably as a result of the button he was pressing in the device's side. "Looks like it works perfectly, too." That was what I got for saying there was no such thing as bi-dar, that you couldn't even define bisexuals, let alone detect them.

"How exactly does it work?" I fussed with my hose. Brenda would show me something outlandish just when I was trying to get dressed up. I pulled on my skirt and started on my make-up. (While Brenda wears jeans and spends all his time building weird gadgets, I make dressing up into a full-time occupation, practically.)

"It detects bisexugenic particles in subspace, using fourth-dimensional tachyon pulse telemetry." Brenda watched way too much TV sci-fi. I concentrated on getting my wig into place.

"In other words," I countered, "you point it at someone and see how they react. If they scream and run away, they're not bi. Or at least they don't identify as bi. If they act all intrigued, they may be bi."

"Exactly." Brenda smiled. "At that point, we apply further tests."

So Brenda and I walked around the big queer conference at the local university with his bi-dar around his neck. It was being held at the Public Policy Center, a huge building full of winding staircases and hallways, and virtually no open spaces. We wandered the maze pointing the machine at people, who mostly gave us funny looks. There was no organized bi presence there, so it was probably our best shot at finding other avowed bisexuals. Anyway, the gadget was a big hit among about half the people we met, but they usually said things like, "I've never met a real live bisexual before." So we'd almost given up on detecting an actual bi person with our bi-dar until we met the Kangaroo Lady.

She took one look at the flashing lights and screamed. "I've been found out! My cover has been blown!"

She wasn't exactly dressed as a kangaroo, but she had the hood with the funny ear-flaps on it and a front pocket containing a baby doll with a spiky hairdo and a little leather jacket. "That's my baby dyke," she said, gesturing at the doll. "I'm Sasha. What's your name?"

"I'm Randy," I said, curtseying with my field hockey skirt. "And this is Brenda." Brenda bowed, careful not to damage the equipment hanging from his neck.

"We're on a mission," Brenda said. "To locate and recruit. This machine is a top-secret prototype developed by the CIA to ferret out bisexual infiltrators."

"And infiltrate bisexual ferrets," I added.

The Kangaroo Lady took only a few seconds to decide she wanted to join our crusade. Taller than either Brenda or me, she had broad shoulders supporting large breasts. Her arms and legs curved in contours of strength, but her hazel eyes were gentle. "That could be amazingly useful," she said, gesturing at the bi-dar. "In fact, I'd like to confirm a theory."

She led us to two guys whom she had always suspected of bisexuality. Sure enough, the lanky guy with unruly hair and sideburns and the short guy with a round face and glasses both reacted with satisfying alarm. The tall guy tried to run, but the Kangaroo Lady grabbed his shoulder and said, "Lane, it's no use. We've already got a positive reading on you." The bi-dar's lights went wild when Brenda trained it on the tall guy. As for the short guy, whose name was Rob, he stared at the machine and his eyes got wider and wider until finally he sank to his knees and pounded on the floor bawling, "It's true! It's true!"

So how did I end up tied up and tortured? It's a little hard to retrace. I remember I got separated from the others after we'd been talking for a while. I think I went to the men's room, drawing a few startled glances in my skirt and three-inch heels. (There was a line for the women's room.) When I got back, Brenda was nowhere to be found. But when I went looking for him, I felt a hand on the tiny bone at the apex of my butt crack. I started to turn around, but then the hand grabbed my arm and twisted it behind my back. I squawked.

"Don't try anything," I heard the Kangaroo Lady say. "You're coming with me."

She put a blindfold on me and led me out of the building, my feeble strength no match for hers. I heard conference participants muttering about godawful pantomime, then the whoosh of a glass door. Then I felt the chill of the outside air and smelled the early spring blooms. I was bundled into a car trunk and felt the sensation of motion.

Once out of the car trunk, I was carried a short way and plunked down in a big old chair with massive wooden arms. My hands were tied securely to the chair arms and my ankles to the legs. Then the blindfold was lifted, and I saw I was in a dusty room with wooden floors partly obscured by magazines, videotapes, and fast-food wrappers. Student housing. I couldn't see Brenda, but the Kangaroo Lady and her two male friends stood and smirked at me.

"You're going to tell us the secret of bi-dar," the Kangaroo Lady said, "or else."

"It could be a powerful tool in the right hands," the short guy, Rob, said.

"First of all, I don't know anything about how to make one of those machines," I said, testing the ropes on my wrists. "Brenda built it. Why don't you ask him?"

"We did," the Kangaroo Lady said. "He died under torture. And he hid his prototype somewhere." I hoped she was using "died" in the Elizabethan sense. She looked at Lane and Rob in turn. "Guys, it's time for the thumb screws." They nodded grimly.

I tried scrunching my fists, but it was no use. Soon enough Lane and Rob were each holding a thumb. Then they started screwing my thumbs—Rob sucked on my right thumb while Lane rubbed various parts of his body against my left thumb. At first it just looked silly, but soon enough I was actually moaning with pleasure. Rob's tongue caressed the space between my thumbnail and my knuckle, and I had never realized how sensitive that area could be. Then Lane got tired of rubbing my thumb against his slender ass. He unzipped his corduroys and pulled out a mostly erect cock that dwarfed the thumb against which he started rubbing it. I looked at Lane's bright carnation cock, marbled with veins and smooth convexities, and I couldn't help licking my dry lips. My own dick, whose name was Letitia, strained to escape the control-top pantyhose, and my mind imagined my thumbs as sexual organs.

"I think I should warn you," I rasped after a moment, "that I'm a die-hard submissive. By tying me up, you may actually be doing what I want you to do. Which means this is the worst way to get me to cooperate." Actually, the truth was I would soon tell them anything they wanted to hear. I go gooey in bondage. I already felt myself yearning for orders, for pain, for will-sapping stimuli.

"You'll cooperate," the Kangaroo Lady said. She shoved the great wooden chair so that it fell over and I landed on my back, with my feet in the air. My thumbs hovered in mid air, suddenly deprived of sensation. The Kangaroo Lady placed a boot on my collarbone. "But things will go very, very badly for you if you don't tell us where to find the plans for the bi-dar machine."

That was where the Mandrill Sisters came in. The Kangaroo Lady slid out of her overalls and hood, tossing them on top of a pile of Nintendo cartridges. Then she peeled off her bra and floral panties before putting her boots back on. I stared up at her strong limbs, round ass and sloping belly, and the control top pantyhose lost their battle against Letitia. The Kangaroo Lady put one boot on my frilly blouse.

"The secret of two-stepping is to put your weight forward on your right foot," the Kangaroo Lady said. Rob and Lane, standing opposite, began copying her movements as she taught them Country line dancing. My ribs seared. Her vulva passed over my line of sight. "Next we're going to learn the Achy Breaky," she added.

"No! No more!" I screamed.

"Hey, Rob," Lane said. "Do you think your roommate would mind if we trashed his down pillow? It's kinda old anyway." Rob made a verbal shrugging sound in response, and soon I felt a flood of feathers going up my skirt while the Kangaroo Lady trod on my breastbone. The mixture of sensations was wild, especially after Lane pulled my pantyhose down to my thighs.

"Cut that out!" I cried. "I'm very ticklish down there, especially when I've just shaved!" The feathers were working their way up every crevice and fold my crotch and butt offered, helped by Lane's insistent fingers. My skirt flew backwards onto my torso and promptly tore under the Kangaroo Lady's boot. Rob pulled off my shoes and then my hose, and started tickling my feet. Lane was seeing how many feathers he could cram into my butt crack with one hand while occasionally brushing the touch-starved Letitia. I punctuated my laughter with occasional yelps as the Kangaroo Lady's boot hit home.

I was enjoying the sensory overload far too much when the Kangaroo Lady drew a flat hand across her neck and it all stopped. "Now," she said. "If you want us to keep going, you'll have to tell us where the secret plans are."

I whimpered and strained against the ropes. I couldn't break free, much less make the feelings start again. "OK," I said. "I'll tell you anything you want to know. I think Brenda put the plans in the second drawer of his filing cabinet. He keeps the key to the cabinet in the base of his plaster cast of John Holmes' cock, at the head of his bed."

"Don't tell them anything!" Brenda climbed through the window, bi-dar machine still hanging from his neck. "The rescue party has arrived!"

"I don't want to be rescued!" I wailed.

Two women and another guy climbed in the window after Brenda. "Don't worry," Brenda said. "We've got them outnumbered. I feigned death, then escaped and used the bi-dar machine to find reinforcements. Anyway, the operative word in 'rescue party' is 'party.'"

"We surrender," the Kangaroo Lady said. "Do with us what you will."

Brenda was already slipping out of his jeans while his new friend Maggie (the woman with the tongue piercing) was untying me. Somebody found the stereo playing the Mandrill Sisters and turned the volume way up. Lane slid his tongue into my mouth and I found his cock and Rob's in my left hand. Rob and Lane had positioned themselves so that their cocks formed a wide V, so I could grind the two heads together lightly with my thumb and forefinger. Their cocks were warm dough one minute, juice-dribbling starfruit the next. Maggie ran her tongue over my balls. I tried to plead for more, but feathers went in my mouth.

Somehow I ended up with the nozzle of the bi-dar machine sticking into my ass, after a generous helping of Vaseline. I think Rob and Lane decided they needed to calibrate the machine more exactly. Somehow they chose me as a worthy specimen to gather a closer reading. So they positioned me on my knees. Rob offered his half-hard dick in front of my face and I obediently began licking it. Meanwhile, Maggie flicked her tongue lightly over Letitia's stem. My balls teemed with an impatient army that threatened to turn on me if it was not released. And Lane worked the raygun nozzle of the bi-dar machine in and out of my ass. "That's it," he murmured. "We're getting some very interesting readings. This is a great day for science."

I grabbed Rob's cock with one hand and wrapped my lips around the head, sucking hard until it spurted in my mouth. At the same time, I felt Maggie's lips swathe Letitia, who burst into song. Lane pushed the nozzle harder than before, and the pressure on my sphincter went insane. Letitia sighed and then spat in a most unladylike manner into Maggie's mouth. I cried out, my own tongue still coated with Rob's sperm.

"Congratulations," I heard Brenda say. I looked up to see him, naked and sticky, standing over me. "You'll be the pervert against which the machine will judge all other perverts. The next step is to invent a machine that turns ordinary people into freaks like you."

I leaned up and looked back at myself. I was face down in a puddle of various fluids. My rear stuck up in the air with the bi-dar machine still firmly attached. The machine's lights were blinking more furiously than ever as it tried to assimilate all the data it had just gathered. I shrugged. "Who are you calling a freak?" I demanded.

Charles Anders has always wanted to put two sex-positive people together to see if they repel each other. He is the webmaster of www.godhatesfigs.com and news editor with Anything That Moves *magazine.*

Soliloquy for Twig

TruDeviant

You've punished yourself for losing them. I've punished you, too.

I love the way they looked on you. The thin layer barely concealing your wet pussy. Your cunt juice made them even more revealing as you pushed up against the fabric.

Bright red.

They fit you perfectly. They were made for you. There was a way they clung to your sweaty flesh, the golden hairs matted underneath, a miniature haystack, squashed and soggy under the fine silken tarp. The lace edges accented your upper thighs, your slender waist. Your ass, encased like a flimsy lamination.

Right now, on the bed, you're showing me your cunt. Pulling it open with your fingers. Your skin is smooth now. Everywhere. This is part of your punishment. The hair on your body was particularly soft and proud. And it takes so much time for you to keep every trace of it off your body for me. Sometimes you hate me for that. Sometimes you beg me to let you have eyebrows again.

It's almost summer.

The last time you wore them, I slit them with my knife so I could fuck you while you were still wearing them. I needed to fuck your cunt that way. I can still feel the way the silk moved against me as I moved inside you. You were sobbing when I entered that sweet pussyhole, grateful to be filled after all that time, but still lamenting the ruined panties.

Tonight will be even better.

I'm ready to fuck you, but you don't know it yet. You've been working my nerves all day. You think I will beat you again or clamp things to your most sensitive areas. I know every place. I know the exact points of joy and despair. I see your body like a digital road map. It lights up for me, it tells me where to go and how to take you where I want. Sometimes I feel like there are no secrets left. But I know that can't be true. I know there's much more in there. There always is some rock unturned, some way to make everything new again.

When there are no more secrets left, I invent them.

You open your legs. Your bare foot massages the hard pole in my jeans. You love that cock of mine more than yourself right now. I've made you wait so fucking long for it. You think I will make you wait longer.

You're waiting for me to ask you. You flinch internally when you sense I'm about to open my mouth to ask you that question. The one I ask you every time. Part of you wishes I would just fuck you. Another part expects me to just use you up and toss you away, sticky and dripping with cum, like the towel crumpled under the bed. You are a mass of conflicting impulses, willing to endure anything I use to obstruct your easy goals.

Finally, I ask you if you've remembered what you did with the panties. You don't answer. You continue to thrust your cunt towards me. I slap you hard, without warning, without finesse, a slap designed to sting. You moan and push up higher. I always hit you like that. Hard. No warm-up. And where it hurts the most. That thing in my jeans is so hard against my leg.

You have no idea, as you wrack your brain and relive every moment of that night you last wore those red silk panties. Or maybe you do have some idea of what really happened. Maybe you suspect I took them. Hid them from you. Made you pay for something you didn't even do. Maybe you've gotten that far with it. It wouldn't surprise me. It really wouldn't. I've done things like that before, but not for a long, long time. As long as you were wearing those panties, I couldn't really play all those tricks on you that I like. They protected you somehow. I didn't know that then. They made everything underneath them safe from me. That's why I had to slit them open.

But I know what would surprise you. You won't ever think of it. Not when I've unzipped my jeans and pulled out that cock. It's pressing against your hot stinking cunt. This cock is so hard. I'm happy you're on your stomach as I push my jeans down to my ankles, so you can't see me. Your head smashed into the pillow.

You can't see that I'm wearing your panties. My invincible cock poking out through the slit I made when I fucked you through it before. They are too small for me. They squeeze my asscheeks together as I slowly enter your cunthole. You squeal as it worms its way into you. You need a fuck so bad. It's been weeks. You're so tight. And so are your panties as they cut into my crotch. It feels so damn good, bitch. I jab it in harder. It's starting to hurt you.

Fuck you, bitch.

It hurts me, too, as I thrust up in you good and hard. Looks like I'm going to take my time in there. I'm so consistently hard, snug up and cozy in that pussy, that sweet asspussy. It's grabbing onto my cock. And you have no idea that your panties are riding up my asscrack, rubbing hard on my pussyhole, making me fuck you harder than ever.

The crotch of your panties, which used to hold your dripping dick, is rubbing up in my asscunt, your dried jizz getting wet and merging with my asshole sweat. Your own cock is free now. I watch it stiff and poking back down between your legs while I fuck your buttpussy. Fuck, it's amazing, bitch. You know how much I love to fuck a pussyboy, his huge bloated dick lying there underneath him, twitching and unused. Especially when I'm fucking him with an even bigger dildo strapped over my wet cunt. And now with your panties cutting into my cunt and my asscunt, I know I'm going to fuck you until you can't take any more.

TruDeviant writes non-fiction for the SandMUtopian Guardian, likes to make things difficult for easy people, and sometimes quotes *Aurora Bombayalis* when she says things like, "Human perversity is greater than human heroism"—jingle jangle—"or cowardice"—th-th-thump!—"or art, for there are points beyond which we will not go in their name; but to perversity there is no limit set, no frontier that anyone has found."

Dick: A Love Story

Jaclyn Friedman

Your thigh dug into the damp seam of my jeans. It was one of those beginning nights, my lips chapped and swollen from your teeth, cunt begging audibly for one flick of your flat tongue. Back then I could come from the look in your eyes, but I always wanted more.

Tonight I was hollow. Our hips pushed and pushed and your thigh tried but I wanted something bigger than me sliding so deep inside I broke open. You bit down hard on my ear and breathed, "I wish I had a dick to fuck you with." My cunt clamped down on your words and I came in my clothes.

The next day I went shopping. The salesgirl had a cherubic face and a soft body. She wore a loose, flowered dress and did tactful paperwork while I stared at the multicolored wall of dildos. You had sent me with instructions. "Nothing that looks like a real penis," you said, "and no dolphins."

Personally, I was partial to the realistic ones. They were thicker and looked more satisfying. The cute ones were unappealing, but the neutral ones left over were a mediocre lot, curved tubes of purple or green silicone no thicker than two of your fingers. I needed your hand.

I picked up the largest of the penis variety—a black one two or three inches across and bulging with veins—walked it to the counter, and asked, "Do you have anything this big that doesn't look like a penis?" The salesgirl smiled and directed my attention to a lavender one with lovely wide ridges. It was, she said, highly recommended. I imagined you sliding it into me slowly, each ridge more persistent than the last as it spread my cuntmouth and entered. We made no small talk as she wrapped it and placed it in a bag from a shoe store, along with a leather harness and a big bottle of lube.

That night we laughed. You had not expected lavender ridges. The harness was a maze of buckles and straps—it took us fifteen minutes to figure it out. By then the sight of you standing naked with a molded purple plastic dick bobbing on your cunt gave us fits of giggles. You kissed me like that—soft and open-mouthed—while we laughed. Then your hand in my cunt, fingers sliding my lips open to find me soaking, rubbing my round clit with the flat pad of your thumb. I moaned softly, a low exhale. I had wanted this for longer than I knew.

And then you were inside of me. At first just the tip, tentatively, like you weren't sure if it would work. Then deeper, a few ridges at a time, shocking me open, until your head was pushing against my cervix and my pussy opened so wide I wanted all of you inside me, dick be damned. I wanted your whole body in my cunt. Wanted you in every crevice, so you could feel me clamp down all around you. I wanted to soak myself into your skin until you never stopped smelling like me.

You began to fuck me harder now, faster, finding a rhythm, feeling your hips slam against me as you shoved your brand new dick in up to its hilt, over and over. Your face looked soft and cruel and you were grunting like a schoolboy, like you could really feel that cock sliding against the swollen cavern of my cunt, like it felt so good you didn't care whether I got off, only that I let you keep fucking me.

I knew better. I pulled your whole body down onto me, kissed you hard, slid your upper lip through my teeth and rolled you onto your back. Now I was riding you, shoving my cunt down onto your cock and grinding. Arching back so you could see me, I slid my middle finger through my own bush and parted my cuntlips. My other hand picked up the bottle of lube and drizzled it over my clit. The cool juice dripped down my thigh as I started to rub myself, first slowly in circles, then faster. Your jaw hung open and you moaned—I knew how much you liked to watch.

I came like a seizure, gasping for breath as my cunt exploded over and around you. It felt dirty and sacred, the way I always wanted sex to feel. I only wished you could come inside me, shoot into me hot and urgent. In that moment, I wanted you to come so hard you made me pregnant.

When my breath returned, I rested in your arms, your skin sweaty against mine, your hands caressing the tangle of my hair. I swore no boy had ever fucked me better than that. Later, I ate you gratefully, savoring the faint smells of silicone and lube in your pubic hair.

It became a game between us, a language. You took out the hard-on when you wanted to be stronger. I took you in when I felt empty. Sometimes I would drop to my knees and suck you off, taking you in so deep I gagged while my fingers slid behind the harness leather and into your cunt, stroking your other erection. You loved to come like that, watching your dick slide in and out of my shining lips, holding my head by the hair so I didn't pull away. You would always make sure I swallowed after. You said the boys I used to suck didn't know how lucky they were.

We didn't even always need props. Sometimes, while I was eating you, you would tell me how you wished your clit could get so hard and swollen that you could slide it inside me. I would suck you harder then, my lips pulling your clit deep into my mouth while my tongue slowly stroked the underside of it. When you came, your cream would push past the seal of my lips and into my mouth, a briny shock to my tongue. Those times, I didn't have to be reminded to swallow.

It took a long time to realize that your dick was coming not just inside of me, but between us. It's not that you strapped on the dildo so often—maybe two or three times a month. We had all kinds of sex without it. We would make urgent love with our bodies smoldering together, fingers buried in each other's snatches, making up fantasies for each other while our wrists jerked and our clits swelled. When I was ready to cum, you would slide your thigh between my legs and I would grind into your hand until I burst. Other times it was your fist deep inside me, pushing me open, our eyes pasted to the sight of your wrist disappearing into my cunt. Many times you just ate me for hours, content to coax every drop of pleasure from me until I begged you to stop.

But your dick was different. The more central your hard-on was to our fucking, the more promises you would seek afterward. Did I ever wish you were really a man? you wanted to know. I'm better than any boy you ever slept with, aren't I? The requests for reassurance escalated. You wanted me to promise I would never leave you for a man, that I liked women better, that you were my best lay ever and no man could compare. The more you asked me, the less I found I could appease you, until I found myself asking those same questions. Did I really want a man?

I started looking at the men in my life differently, weighing my attraction for them against the way I felt about you. Every day I had a mental quickie with the burly guy three cubes down from me at work. I would bring him some papers and he would smile at me with green eyes. I would step inside his cube and before I could protest I was up against the wall, his hand under my skirt in my wet cunt. In my dreams I was never wearing panties. Then he would unzip his khaki dockers to reveal his thick and ready dick. He wasted no time as he slid it into me and started pounding, one hand clamped down over my mouth as I moaned, the other fast and light on my eager clit. It never took us more than three minutes to cum, and we never got caught.

No one was exempt from these fantasies. Waiters, delivery men, male friends both gay and straight—if they had a dick, I wanted it. I believed that if I could sleep with a man again I would know, once and for all, who I wanted more. Then I could continue with my life, secure in the knowledge that yes, I was a lesbian, or no, I was really a straight girl at heart. On the T, I would make my own Kinsey scale, rating myself on whether I was more attracted to the men or the women on the train. I always hoped the women would win. I wanted to be a lesbian more than anything, to be pure and content in the knowledge that I wanted women, I was a card-carrying cuntlicker, and all my lust for men was just patriarchal programming, residue, propaganda meant to distract me from my true sapphic nature. I knew this was the right answer, it was what you wanted, what everyone seemed to want. But more often than not the train game ended in a draw, and my heart sank as I pushed through the crowds and out into the day.

We began to use the dildo less and less. When you would suggest it, I would demur, saying I didn't want to play games tonight. If you insisted, I would hide in your desire, saying I would do anything to please you; if that's what you wanted, then I wanted it too. I never told you the truth, which is that I no longer wanted your dick—it had become too loaded.

The fights were predictable. What wasn't was the afternoon I took refuge in the local café, smarting from the words we had become accustomed to flinging at each other. I was making a beeline for the overstuffed chair in the corner when I literally banged into the tall, quiet man from your photography class. I spilled half my decaf latte down his shirt and burst into tears. He was kind, patiently letting me sop up the mess on his chest with apologies and handfuls of napkins, then fetching me another coffee while I pulled myself together.

He returned with concern in his eyes. Was I OK? What was wrong? Could he help? I remembered the night we'd had him to dinner, how we didn't stop laughing, how the pictures he'd taken in class were of people's hands—baby hands, hands covered in liver spots and wrinkles, weathered hands at work, hands entwined in other hands—he had captured so much personality and emotion in those simple shots. My throat closed up and I started crying again.

Though my better judgment argued against sharing our troubles with someone who was officially your friend, I found myself helplessly blurting out the whole sorry story. You didn't understand what you were asking, I told him. You wanted me to cut myself in half down the middle, to pick which parts of me you loved. He nodded in all the right places, told me he didn't think any less of me, couldn't imagine why you were so closed-minded. He thought I was brave. I wasn't so sure.

I didn't kiss him that night, but thought about it, and found myself at his door the next time I stormed out of the house. He was as awkward as you might have imagined, apologizing for the state of his small apartment, which was strewn with unframed photographs, magazines, and the odd dirty dish. I sank into the couch and he held me wordlessly. Maybe it was for fifteen minutes. Maybe an hour. And then I did it, the crazy, clichéd thing they do in the movies, right before the fade to black and the happily ever after—I kissed him, softly at first, like a question, then long and deep, tracing his teeth with my tongue and biting softly on his lower lip. His prick jumped to life beneath his zipper, hot against my hip.

Only that once did we hesitate. He pulled away from my mouth, his hands squaring my shoulders, his eyes a question. I didn't know how to answer, what any of it meant. "Please" was all I said, and then lips on neck, fingers on buttons, his hands sliding up the soft skin of my back to unhook my bra, my teeth on his brown nipples, my hands on his buckle, his pants crumpled to the floor, his curved cock sliding between the fullness of my breasts, my nipples purple in the tips of his pinching fingers. My heart closed up like a fist and I forgot it, knowing only this dick, this pulsing man who didn't want promises, only to comfort me, only the pleasure of our bodies combining.

He was fucking my tits faster now, pushing my breasts together against his cock, grunting softly. Before he could come, I pulled myself away from him, lay him back on the couch, straddled his face, leaned over him and took him into my mouth. He parted my lips with his tongue and lapped at my cunt like a hungry puppy. I moaned, lowered myself down hard against his mouth, slowly tongued the ridge on the underside of his dick. The brown curls of his pubic hair scratched lightly against my chin.

He started sucking me, pulling my clit against the wet flat of his tongue, over and over and over. I took his dick in deeper, faster, my lips sliding up and down against his darkly swollen skin. I had forgotten how men tasted, like bitterness and musk. My clit shuddered with rushing blood.

I don't remember who came first, if his load burned my throat before my cunt exploded, or if my cream was already dripping down his chin by the time I swallowed. Later, when we had both recovered, he made sweet missionary love to me in the dark. I cried quietly, eyes open, knowing if I closed them it would be you sliding silently into me, your lips cool against my neck, your fingers in the downy hair behind my ear. Afterward he watched me as I dressed to leave. We both knew I'd be back.

The night I kissed you with semen on my breath, you left without a word. I wanted to tell you so many things—that I still loved you, that I was sorry, that we had both made the most unfathomable mistakes. In the end I said nothing, just watched you drive off, letting the tears slide warm and silent down my cheek.

I miss you. Three years and lovers later, I still think about you and your lavender dick. It still lives under my bed with the vibrators and dirty magazines. Last night I took it out and tried to masturbate with it—it felt cold and dead inside me. I went to sleep unsatisfied. This morning I wrote you a postcard. One side had a picture of the Venus de Milo. On the other side I wrote one sentence. It read, "Sappho was also bisexual."

I sent it to your old address. I hope it finds you.

Jaclyn Friedman is a poet, performer and part-time diva. Her work has appeared in Zaftig! Sex for the Well Rounded, The Underwood Review *and* Philogyny, *and she has monopolized countless hours of mic time around Boston, including features at Culture Shock, Fluid, and Faster! Pussycat!* Write! Write! *She had hoped that writing erotica would help her get laid more often, but it hasn't happened yet.*

Like a Virgin

Carol Queen

I stand in line waiting to smooch the birthday girl. She, a former porn star, sits regally beside a table full of presents, cake, and bottles of champagne. I reflect that former porn stars must not have much trouble filling their parties with adoring friends—not like some of us ordinary mortals—but my musing stops when I notice my boyfriend missing. In this crowd he could be anywhere—or with anyone—and after glancing around a little and not spotting him, I figure I'll intensify the hunt once I've gotten to kiss the Birthday Porno Queen's cheek and gush a little. I want to interview her, and gushing seems like a promising strategy.

By the time I've homed in on my target, added a trace of my lipstick to the layers that already adorn her cheek, gushed a bit, and scheduled a tentative time to meet her the following week, Robert reappears, emerging from a curtained-off space. He has someone by the hand—I note with interest that both he and the woman who's with him wear shit-eating grins, which means they've been necking or perhaps even more. She also looks nervous, which is par for the course when he dallies with women who know me. They're hard to reassure, except the ones who were raised on married men and think they're going to supplant me—fat chance of that, so knock yourselves out, girlies.

This girlie isn't looking at all sure of herself, though she has that certain glow. She also has a serious reputation as a lesbian, so I know this is going to be fun. It's not that Robert and I go hunting for lesbians, but when we find one... well, let's just say there's more in it for me than when he picks up those cocky adulteresses.

"Did you miss me? Mona and I were just talking."

"Talking dirty, I bet," I say. Mona blushes furiously—looks really cute on her.

"A little. She was calling me Daddy." Mona turns redder by far. She clutches Robert's hand and blushes louder by the second. Yep, this will be great gossip later, if nothing else.

We don't get to follow up on this promising beginning before we leave New York. I get my interview with the Porn Queen, and Robert talks to Mona on the phone a time or two. He fills me in. Her membership in Lesbian Nation isn't just reputation—she has an identity card that hasn't, shall we say, been stamped at any other borders. She's a bona fide gold star femme, and for some reason has decided she wants to walk on the wild side. When you've already transgressed every limit in a heterocentrist, hidebound culture—most before you were twenty-one—where are you gonna go? Fucking a boy is just the nastiest thing she can think of. And my boy has been invited to do the honors.

Being my boy, Robert has the exact right mix of reactions: a hard-on complemented by an almost abashed sense of duty. Whatever else he knows, he knows when he's fucking dykes he can't fuck things up. It's not that he has to hold things up for Mankind, or anything. He knows the situation is special, that he's sort of an ambassador in the war between the sexes. He understands it's his responsibility to spread goodwill. There are other men with this sense of honor and responsibility, but mostly they're Sensitive New-Age Guys. Only trouble is, some of the dykes have been reading dirty books starring leather daddies, and a classically feminist man often can't keep up his end of the deal when he's supposed to be playing Mr. Benson.

So once in a while I get to loan Robert out to one of the dirty dykes who's looking for a new notch for her lesbian lipstick case. But mostly it's women who have a man or two somewhere back in the past—a penis in the woodwork, so to speak. It's not like they haven't ever done it before. Mona's different. Mona's a virgin, a real cherry poptart.

It takes a month of phone calls to arrange, several of which I participate in, because one of the things that makes Robert attractive to lesbians is that he comes with a built-in dyke, namely me, and sometimes I can be enticed to play too. In the case of Mona I am definitely in on the deal—not only to make it safe for her, but because this is the hottest thing that's come down the pike since we broke up with our girlfriend Jae so she could marry her girlfriend and move to a house on the lesbian side of town. It's like our bed serves as an existential revolving door. Lesbian or bisexual (or just curious)? In or out? We could start a Kinsey Scale certification service—overhaul monosexuals, tune up bisexuals, paint and lube.

Mona calls to tell us she just bought a plane ticket. She is coming to stay with us on Hallowe'en. "Oh, good," we say, "it's the perfect time to sacrifice a virgin."

When I was a virgin, back when dinosaurs roamed the earth, I hated being in that state of inexperience, a fundamental not-knowing-ness about what I already believed was one of the most important things in the world. I itched to have it over with and was grateful when it happened, even though the sex and the boy I had it with were both crummy. One of the reasons I embraced lesbianism with such fervor, a scant few years later, had to do with my assumption that I must have experienced the sum of what heterosexuality could offer.

Mona, by contrast, has been thinking about this for some time. She knows enough to be choosy about the man she wants to lose it with: choice and desire are front and center for her, as they so rarely are when virginity is lost. Our phone bills go up as she negotiates what she wants. Even before she arrives I am full of awe that she has managed to do so right what so many other women spend their lives unraveling because for them it starts so wrong. Mona knows all about her body, and how she likes it pleasured—she has explored all this with herself and with other women. The only difference between Robert's cock and a dyke dildo is emotional resonance and cultural meaning.

Well, maybe not the only difference. Mancock is soft and finicky compared to a dildo. But Robert is as queer a man as a dyke with a dick, so I think Mona has chosen well. Whatever happens, it won't feel to her like picking up a drunken frat boy in a bar, finally caving in to a boyfriend, or all the other ways it could feel. Maybe dyke virginity is (like dykes themselves must be) especially strong and sure.

Mona arrives at the airport with a suitcase full of virginity-related ritual objects. From the first kiss behind the curtain at the porno birthday party everything has been foreplay for her, including packing her bags. She takes this very seriously, yet there is a queer camp factor to her preparations: it's not a date, it's a scene; it's not something happening to her, it's something she's scheduled and scripted. On Hallowe'en, according to the schedule, Robert's cock should be sliding into her virgin pussy at the stroke of midnight. (I imagine this is the way Wednesday Addams would decide to give it up.) So at ten o'clock she insists she be given some time to get ready. It's a good thing I'm there to distract him—femme prep time is enough to make any man or butch wilt in anticipation, which is, of course, one way femmes keep a measure of control even when everyone knows they'll soon be clawing, begging, swearing, in the throes of being fucked to Jesus.

I have invited myself along, of course. Who'd want to miss it? It's the eighth wonder of the world, and it's happening in my bed—I ain't going anywhere. Besides, Mona never said she wanted a heterosexual experience. She just said she wanted Robert to be her first (who knows, maybe her only) man.

Mona emerges from the bathroom an hour later a vision in white. She brings red candles to circle us, and she cues up the tape deck with a compilation: everything from (of course) "Like A Virgin" to "My Heart Belongs to Daddy." She has made an entire 90-minute tape of losing your-virginity songs. And she is wearing the actual trousseau of one of her friends' mothers, whose wedding was in 1966. White babydoll, white peignoir, white garter belt and stockings, white high heels—high honeymoon drag. This is edgy stuff: she has chosen the unsullied and dream-laden garb of romance, the outfit you're supposed to wear to do that thing you can only do once.

I light the candles into a circle of twinkling fire. I say an invocation to Mona, her will and her courage. "East is sacred to beginnings, the first light of the dawn, the first glimmer of an idea that blooms into change. South is sacred to passion, the heat that brings you here, fiery for experience..."

Mona's eyes go wide. She, who has planned all this, set it up so it could be the way she wants it to be, now has to let go of control, or she won't get the experience she asks for. This is Robert's cue to enfold her in his arms, a deep swept-away kiss—he's very good at this, as I can attest, and he's bigger than Mona, so the effect is full-on "me-Tarzan-you-Jane"-"omigod-I'm fucking-a-man!" One of the most pronounced differences, among all the large-ish and small ones, between fucking girls and fucking boys is the size thing, at least for women who are small and men who are large. Robert appreciates this too; in fact, he likes small women best, but when he's fucking men he likes them to be large, if possible much larger than he is, so he can enjoy the same tossed-around-like-a-ragdoll thrills that Mona experiences now.

While he clasps her, I kneel behind, hold both of them, press my breasts into her back, the slight scratchiness of the lily-white fabric bringing my nipples up hard.

There are so many permutations of position in a threesome that it's hard even to describe the action. We do most of them, the special Trio Kama Sutra, but first we have a virginity to take. The idea is, from Robert's point of view, to get her so wild with fuck-lust that by midnight she already feels transported to a transcendent place: the point is not the moment cock slides into cunt, but the burning, greedy desire for it. In that sense, I suppose many of us stay virgins long after the tattered first time is over, and the most important thing about losing it is wanting the loss, not abstractly like I did but down to the hungry, clenching cunt muscles that suddenly feel empty without something to fill us up as deep as we can be.

So between that moment and midnight (we do keep one eye on the clock) we kiss Mona, stroke and suck her, play with her tits together and one at a time, and Robert talks dirty while I mostly make love-dove noises, coos and sighs and "Yes, ohhh, yes." And at the stroke of twelve, sure enough, with Mona lying in my lap so I can reach her pretty breasts and pet her, Robert lets his condomed cock nudge slowly past her virgin pussy lips while she claws his arms and clutches him and begs him to put it there, put it in! I look down at her, a vision in white, legs spread over his thighs, eyes so glittery and wide. he takes forever—he wants her screaming by the time he's fully in, the one part about penis sex that's simply different from dildo sex: Look, there's a man attached!

So then we do it this way and that way, on the bottom and on the top, my personal favorite way (nuzzling and licking her clit while Robert thrusts and fucks right under my tongue—bisexual oral). Doggy style, with her white peignoir all askew and clinging to her sweaty skin—we finally pull all her white and now-rumpled clothes from her and blow gently to cool her off. All the while Mona's tape plays, "Like a virgin, oooh!—touched for the very first time..." and Melanie's girly-girl voice piping, "I've got a brand-new pair of roller skates, you've got a brand new key..." Mona makes noise, she isn't a shy girl when she's getting fucked, more a fierce femme perpetual-motion machine as she comes again and again and again. Naked now, sweat-damp hair clinging to her face and making her look a little feral, she's not a virgin any more.

Still we fuck all night, celebrating change and risk and high heady fantasy. She came all this way to fuck; we are going to fuck 'til we drop. "This girl is a woman now," someone croons on the soundtrack, but that's ridiculous: she was a woman all the time, like all women should get the chance to be not just once in their lives but over and over.

But not a virgin. The entire trousseau has been tossed off the edge of the bed. Her skin gleams in the candlelight, her eyes shine, her hair tosses as she rides Robert's cock until nearly morning.

Carol Queen is a cultural sexologist and author based in San Francisco, who got a doctorate in sexology so she could impart more realistic detail in her smut. She has been affiliated with the national bisexual movement for over a decade, keynoting conferences in Los Angeles, Minneapolis, and Texas, and speaking at many more. She is the author of various books of erotica, social criticism, and the like, including The Leather Daddy and the Femme, Exhibitionism for the Shy, Real Live Nude Girl, *and the editor of* Switch Hitters: Lesbians Write Gay Male Erotica and Gay Men Write Lesbian Erotica, PoMoSexuals, *and* Sex Spoken Here.

September Shower

Bill Brent

for Lisa, with gratitude

Desiree Bonner stood naked in the doorway of the huge, lavishly tiled bathroom as several eager, equally naked partygoers brushed by her brown, balloon-shaped butt and into the big orgy room at the top of the mansion.

It was a famous butt, immortalized by one of her ex-lovers, a rapper. "Whenever I see a bottle of Perrier, I think of yo' butt, an' I get all *hot*," he'd panted during an amorous interlude, alluding to the shape of the famous bottle. She had laughed out loud. But then the fool had gone and written her into a rap tune (reverently ripping off a couple of riffs from old Pointer Sisters hits), which had scandalized most of the women from her old neighborhood while enticing most of the men:

When I see Desiree
I think of Perrier
I like to drink her for lunch
Sparklier than Sprite
She's my afternoon delight
She packs a helluva punch.

Most of her exes knew just how much of a punch Desiree could pack, particularly the black boys. And they really were boys, she'd soberly realized one day. That was the downside—some of the best lovers she'd ever had were macho studs who were still big Mama's boys at heart. They tried so hard—and almost always succeded—in pleasing a woman, but so often they turned out to be emotional train-wrecks.

But this dude in front of her had, *mmm, potential.* He had that Italian street-punk thing going on—defiant, like a bantamweight boxer who'd fought his way into the spotlight. And she could tell that this compact Casanova really dug the spotlight. Besides, she liked a lover who could put up a bit of a fight—till she took him down.

She was leaning against the door-jamb, which allowed her to project a cool reserve while hiding her twitching fingers, which tapped out a rhythm on the wall behind her. This was the night of the Omnivorous Orgy, billed as "San Francisco's biggest Bacchanalian bash for bad boys and bodacious girls." The moon was full and the tide was high, providing further inducement for anyone who needed the slightest excuse for going wild.

The three stories of the huge Victorian were a triple-decker threat to anyone's sense of propriety. An enormous dungeon spread across the lowest level, lit up in lurid red, featuring racks, cages, massage tables, slings, benches, and beds spilling over with writhing, moaning masses of humanity. The sprawling space was festooned with vases of fresh, fragrant flowers and bounteous baskets of latex and lubricant.

The middle level was more of a social space, lit up in soft, incandescent white, featuring as its centerpiece a pair of magenta neon lips captioned by the single and catchy commandment, "Enjoy," metronomically flashing—in green light, no less, just in case one didn't get the point. Rippling rhythm and bass tracks bathed the scene in a soft, undulating layer of sound. The kitchen featured a lavish buffet feast; the video-porn room held a huge screen depicting professional depravity of variously alternating flavors, and the bustling reception area (the "undressing room") was lit up in a frenzy, yet the glaring lights made it a practical place to fish for fresh flesh.

The top level, in whose bathroom Desiree now stood, was lit with softly glowing, multicolored globes of stained glass, which cast variously prismed hues upon the high, beamed ceiling that seemed to arch miles above the heads of the horny hedonists who slithered like serpents across the crowded cushions. The big room's airy loftiness and crackling fireplace glow evoked the mood of a ski lodge. All was framed with tall walls of glass opening onto the sky-clad redwood deck, where a dozen or so partygoers were lounging and smoking in the nude on one of San Francisco's delicious, melt-in-your-mouth September nights. Several glowing pipes were passed around. Piped-in music, piped-in water, and piped-in hash and weed provided the glue that bonded the social fabric of this fabulous fuck-fest.

The house and its grounds were awash with a watery presence. There was a massive wall of water falling down the fence, splashing into a mossy backyard garden bordering a giant, foaming jacuzzi which brimmed with the steaming, sated flesh of post-coital partygoers. There were indoor showers on every level, and a fourth outdoor shower near the jacuzzi, all blasting away to cool and cleanse the briny, raucous hordes, rivulets of suds cascading from their happy bodies while at rest between romps in a roomful of writhing revelers. Twosome or even threesome shower-sharing was commonplace and encouraged. The banner, "Save Water—Shower With A Friend!" hung near at least two of the showers. (Some especially kinky soul had cleverly sketched in the word "Golden" before the word "Shower" on the banner hanging near the outdoor stall.)

But the architectural pièce de résistance was the shower in the bathroom bordering the "ski lodge," where Desiree and Donny were now facing off. The owner of the house had commissioned a rounded wall built of rippling, translucent glass bricks which reflected tantalizingly vague, psychedelically distorted images of anyone in the spacious shower. The circular stall held three massaging shower heads, a douching station, baskets holding all manner of soaps, sponges, scrubbers, shaving and sex supplies, and room enough to accommodate up to eight bodies at once. The stall was finished in tiny tiles, psychedelic squares of crimson and navy, pink and aqua, with swirling white lines of tiny, sperm-shaped tiles set into the floor, eagerly chasing each other's tails toward the central drain, which looked like a giant ovum.

But Desiree wasn't noticing any of that just now. No, she was transfixed by the stall's lone occupant, Donny Blue (a/k/a "Rollerboy") soaping himself with lavishly extravagant handfuls of Dr. Bronner's Peppermint soap. The sensations made him squirm, especially the icy tingling on his balls. He was strongly aware of Desiree's presence; he even sensed her struggle to maintain control of her hyperkinetic hands, but he would wait a while to acknowledge her. Donny was the ultimate exhibitionist and loved to show off his body, especially to a chick as hot as Desiree Bonner. He'd make her watch him.

Donny's olive skin flashed beneath the gleam of the soapy water, like an exotic fish streaking through a tropical bay. Desiree had always had a thing for lithe, compact Mediterranean men. She'd first been seduced by the curly-haired husband of her older sister—an actual Greek fisherman—when she was just fifteen. She knew the guy was a horny, deceitful letch, but she could hardly resist him—the briny smell of the sea clung to his skin and his curls, flooding her senses, making her mouth water, making her cunt water. Her sister always did have good taste, and after one taste of that fine scoundrel, Desiree was hooked for life. She liked her black brothers well enough, she'd been with a few white guys, and she'd even dated a Japanese programmer once upon a time—but no one did it for her like those Greeks, Italians, Portuguese, and Spaniards. Desiree wasn't an indiscriminate slut, but she liked to say that she was a "an equal-opportunity enjoyer." Still, as she was quick to observe, desire isn't politically correct, and just about everyone has her preferences.

Donny nudged his growing stiffness. It was getting tough to hide how much he was enjoying his impudent display. He hoped that Perry, his date, would get sidetracked by that redheaded muscle-boy he'd been ogling all evening so that he could have a bit of time alone in the shower with this fine lady. Donny was sure that Perry suspected his bisexual tendencies, but he was loath to discuss that side of himself in the early stages of seeing a guy, particularly a catch as hot as Perry. San Francisco was full of gorgeous, unattached men who had no interest in pussy. He'd thought that even inviting Perry to this mixed-gender party might be pushing it, but Perry had just shrugged and said, "Well, might as well try something different."

Desiree was growing impatient, and she realized that she was blocking the toilet. She was afraid that someone would want to use it and disrupt this little scene. She cleared her throat and adjusted the towel atop her head.

"Hey, boy, are you gonna play ball?" Desiree demanded, "Or are you just gonna stand there playing 'soap the salami' all evening?"

The only thing Donny liked as much as a dominant stud was a commanding woman, but he still had his insolent streak. "So who wants to know, and what do you like to do with salami?"

Desiree stepped across the expanse between them. "My name is Desiree," she snapped, "And what I do with salami depends on what else is in the fridge. Like these cherry tomatoes."

Desiree reached out and began flicking his nipples rhythmically as he flexed and posed for her in sweeping, lavish strokes. The soap foamed and frothed, decorating his body like giant splashes of stucco or taffy. "Oh, yeah," he muttered, as his cock surged within his fingers. "Yeah, play with those tits."

"I will do what I please, little man," Desiree retorted, "And you had best learn to like it." Desiree stepped into the shower, moving behind him and grabbing his nipples from behind, grinding her wet pussy against his muscular ass-cheeks. The warm water felt good against her skin. She grabbed huge handfuls of his meaty pectorals and dug in her nails, which drove Donny into a lathering, frothing frenzy.

"Aren't you the dude they call 'Rollerboy'?"

"Um, yeah, that's one of my nicknames." Desiree could tell from his squirming discomfort that Donny secretly liked to be called "boy," and probably didn't mind a bit of humiliation, either.

"And the others?"

"Well, they're, uh, more personal...."

Desiree's lips curled into a smile as she suppressed a giggle. "So, I'm waiting."

Donny felt himself blush, as much as a dark-skinned Italian can blush. "Well, there's 'fuck-puppy,'" he started, "and 'cunt-lapper'—oh, man!" He groaned as Desiree dug four stenciled, bejeweled nails into the nubs of his nipples.

"I'm not a man," Desiree snorted. "And you had best remember that." She spun him around. "Does a man kiss like this?" She scraped her nails down his back and planted a deep, full kiss on Donny's mouth. He could smell the faint jasmine scent she'd dabbed behind her ears.

Perry appeared in the doorway. "Oh, I was wondering where—son of a bitch!"

Perry froze and stared at his date and the turbanned black Amazon towering above him. Donny broke their lip-lock and stared back, afraid to say a word, afraid *not* to say a word. The hushed moment hovered above them, as eye darted to eye—eyes seeking answers, then knowing, then accepting. Hours of talk packed into an instant that sparked truths beyond words—truths about fear, about power, and desire.

For once in her self-assured life, Desiree Bonner was speechless.

"Well, what the hell!" Perry shouted, stepping into the bathroom. "Sorry if I'm interrupting something, but that's just the kind of bad-mannered bastard I am."

Perry fixed Desiree with an intense stare and summed up the situation with no further questions, other than: "I think this rude motherfucker deserves a rude awakening, wouldn't you agree?"

Desiree's eyes sparkled at the mischief in Perry's. She recognized the "gay" pornstar and was pleased to see his flash of interest in her. Noting Donny's astonished expression, she surmised that the boy hadn't known that Perry liked girls, either. This was turning into quite the evening for surprises. Her heart sped up a bit as she imagined her body tangled around these two men. Perry wore his self-confidence like a comfortable, clinging T-shirt. It was different than hers—more embracing, less aloof. She wanted to know how it translated into sex. Donny would serve as their conduit. "I was teaching him a bit of etiquette when you appeared. He's got a lot to learn."

Perry flung his towel to the ground and stepped under the water. "Yeah, like how to tell his date that he likes pussy." Donny started to retort that Perry hadn't told *him*, either, but Perry waved him aside: "Yet apparently he's learned more about *that* than he let on to me. I thought he'd been taking all his, uh, lessons from male instructors. I see now that this is not the case."

"So, ah, how well do you two know each other?"

"Well enough for this," Perry said, slapping the boy's ass. Donny grunted in protest as soap suds flew off his skin like sparks. "Donny's reputation as a bad boy precedes him. And mine almost overshadows me at times. But right now, I'm about to overshadow this nasty piece of trash."

Perry spun the boy around, grasping Donny's balls in one hand while working the other hand's soapy fingers rhythmically toward Donny's pucker, pressing hard on the boy's perineum. "Oh, man," Donny gasped, as the peppermint-icy pressure forced flashing surges of fire into his fuck-stick. He bent it downward until he felt as if it would break off, then let it fly, slapping against his belly and causing flecks of foam to scatter. Perry shoved two curved digits into Donny's spasming hole and waited. Donny was always open and ready; it was one of the boy's major charms, in Perry's somewhat jaundiced eyes. Soon the boy was fucking himself on the man's outstretched fingers. Perry smiled as his dick grew long, curving upward.

"Gonna fill you up, boy," Perry grunted as he assaulted the boy's hole repeatedly with his soap-slick fingers. Donny moaned as the tingling, slightly stinging sensations from the peppermint soap made his hole feel as though it were heating over a low flame. Perry had his hardened, curving cock in his other hand and was beating off to the same rhythm as his fingers were drumming in Donny's blazing ass.

"You cleaned out, pup?" Perry asked. "Snatchurally," Donny moaned.

"Oooh, has that boy got a *mouth* on him," Desiree smirked, backhanding Donny's cock. The boy yelped.

"Yeah, he's a real 'pun' in the ass. You get used to it after awhile," Perry laughed, as he shut off the shower. "Boys are usually cocky when they need some cock."

"Makes me want to slap him *real* hard." She gave Donny's cock another stinging slap. "And me, without a strap-on. I'm traveling light tonight. But I see that your equipment can tackle the *toughest* job. "

"Well, this job looks tougher than he is," Perry smiled, his perfect teeth gleaming and wet.

This was the hottest stuff in Donny's most blazing fantasies. Perry Palmer was about to fill him with his famous cock in front of this hot, powerful bitch goddess, amidst a house full of strangers. "There's a basket of condoms hanging there," he nodded toward the shampoo rack. "Oh, man, I really want you to fuck me hard."

"Let's put one on this, too," Desiree ordered. "You're gonna have to put it somewhere, boy, so it might as well be in my snatch. '*Snatch*-urally,'" she hissed, baring her teeth.

Donny squirmed as he squeezed some lube and a rubber over his water-slickened dick. The white swirls of Dr. Bronner's looked especially delicious on Desiree's gleaming, chocolate-milk skin. Now he could feel Perry stuffing him from behind with at least three lube-filled fingers, and then that horse cock rode on home. It felt as though his hole were being stuffed with the thickest peppermint stick available, only Perry's dick had the advantage of a curve that conformed perfectly with the contours of his hungry hole. It also massaged his prostate, causing a small, trickling wetness to emanate from the head of his dick into the condom. He yelped as Perry plugged away; the tingling rhythm was driving him mad. Then his cock was engulfed with a spreading warmth as Desiree backed onto his rubber-suited cock. "Oh, man," he groaned as Desiree contracted her vaginal muscles around his thrusting cock. Perry tugged his thick nipples from behind as Donny pulled on Desiree's. Perry picked up the pace, his pelvis pounding and smashing against the boy's battered, outrageously stretched hole. The new tempo caused Perry's low-hangers to slap rhythmically against the curve of Donny's ass, causing Donnie to thrust harder against Perry and into an increasingly excited Desiree, who was rapidly approaching the first of many loud orgasms that soon had spectators crowding into the bathroom for a look.

"Yeah, fuck! FUCK!" Donny screamed, playing to his newly-discovered audience. He held still so that Perry could have even greater access to his still-hungry ass. Desiree thrust backwards onto his cock and manipulated her engorged clit with renewed intensity. Perry pulled out abruptly, his rubber-slicked cock making a loud PLOP! He surveyed the crowd. "You!" he barked, pointing at a young man, a weightlifter, who looked startled. Perry dropped his tough-guy character for a moment, his face breaking into a dazzling pornstar smile.

"What's your name, kid?"

"Leo."

"I'm Perry," he said, extending his hand. When the weighlifter grabbed it, Perry gripped his hand hard and yanked him into the shower. "You like her?" he asked. "Oh, yeah!" the guy enthused. "Desiree! You like him?"

Desiree was still breathless. "Uh...what did you have in mind?" she queried cautiously, peering over her shoulder at the hunk. "Anything you like," came Perry's response. "But I want him to hold you while we treat you like the queen you are. Move in behind her, there," he said to the weightlifter, who complied. "Good. Now press your back against the glass bricks, facing us. Desiree, press back against this hunk and face me. Let him play with your nipples, and spread your legs for me. Trust me, you're gonna like this." He grabbed the shower massage attachment and set it to maximum pulse, then he turned on the water and waited while it warmed. Then he aimed it at Desiree's clit while the hunk rocked her in his strong arms, fondling her breasts to the rhythm.

"Oh, yeah," Perry panted. "That looks so hot." He paused the attachment and took her clit between his thumb and forefinger. "You like that, honey? Is that just driving you crazy?"

"Oh, God, don't stop."

Perry's mouth was on hers, tongue betwixt tongue, salivas mingling, and then he pinched her nostrils shut. "Just let it happen," he breathed, responding to the startled look in her eyes. "Please trust me. I won't do anything to hurt you." Desiree nodded slightly, sensing that it was deeply important to this guy to win her trust. She stopped wondering why as his face merged with hers. He continued to massage her clit, breathing life into her, filling her with his air, then taking it back from her, over and over until they were both dizzy. All at once he released her nose and mouth, and each was startled by the sudden rush of fresh air, which felt very cold and invasive after all that intimate, moist warmth. "Wow," she gasped, all starry-eyed and gazing with astonishment at this white knight. "Awesome," Donny said in a low, hushed whisper. Perry backed away but continued to fix Desiree with his gaze. "Now we're gonna try something else. Donny, kneel on this bench and give me your ass while you eat her pussy." Donny, grabbing something out of his toy bag, scrambled to comply, glad he had brought his rollerblading knee-pads to this sexual soirée. He thrust his ass toward the magnificent stud as he lapped noisily at the vortex of Desiree's well-toned limbs.

Perry found the plastic tube of Aqua Lube and covered his left hand in it. He made his hand into a cone and entered Donny from behind, squeezing a generous helping of lube onto his pucker as he slowly pushed his hand into the boy. "That's it, my friend, just keep pushing out." Donny's breathing deepened as his surprisingly voracious hole expanded to accommodate the man, sucking his hand inside. The alteration in Donny's breathing communicated itself directly to Desiree's clit. The sloppy, gloppy sounds of Donny's mouth on Desiree's moist bush, and of Perry's hand easing in and out of Donny's now-cavernous hole, were soon drowned out by Desiree's delighted screams and squeals.

The weightlifter looked up from this profane trinity and noticed about half the men crowding the room were jacking off their fully-hard dicks, and a couple of the women were fingering themselves as well. Wistfully, he wished he could attend to the insistent, throbbing warmth between his own legs, but he knew that after a scene like this, he'd have his pick of anyone he chose for his postponed gratification. And the release always felt so damned good after a long, hard wait. Perry glanced up at Leo and winked, causing him to wonder if the pornstar could read his thoughts.

Perry's hand settled into a comfortable, slightly undulating shape deep within Donny's guts, and he leaned over to place his mouth once again across Desiree's trembling, parted lips. They were one of her best features, he thought. So full, so petulant at times, which only served to betray the passion concealed within. Now that she knew his game, she took one of her hands from the back of Donny's damp head and placed it over Perry's nostrils. He replied mutually, and they kissed deeply, primordially, giving and taking the precious element they shared, back and forth, air into lungs, through the throat, out the mouth, into the other, over and over, until the waning oxygen made them nearly ready to faint.

Perry and Desiree gasped rhythmically as their faces parted and they gulped the cool, stinging air, which had a—mist? Yes. One of the onlookers had picked up a spray bottle of water and was spritzing it into the air above their heads, where it settled onto their bodies and clung like the softest of laces—spider-laces, perhaps.

Now Perry's hand was slowly snaking out of Donny's innards as the boy moaned ecstatically. Then Perry was pulling a latex glove off his hand—when had he sneaked on *that*, Desiree wondered vaguely—and now he was pulling on a fresh condom and preparing yet again to assault her oral servant. Desiree felt her entire body begin to tremble from deep inside as this beautiful boy kept lashing her with his tongue, his head rhythmically smashing into her belly and crushing her pierced navel as Perry pounded him mercilessly now, causing him to cry out, which set off a whole new set of vibrations in her clit, causing her to cry out too. She thrashed against the sturdy, patient weightlifter who had never let his hands wander from her breasts and continued faithfully to ply her hardened, sensitized nipples. She was amazed at the stamina of all three of these unearthly men. She was amazed at her own.

The mist felt so marvelous, cooling their overheated bodies and mixing with their sweat, to roll off their skins in tiny rivulets that trickled down the drain with the tiniest of gurgles. Perry was really laying into the kid now, showing the assembled onlookers how he had earned the porn nickname "King Cock." Perry grunted vociferously: "Unh! Unh! Unh!" as his biceps flexed and rippled, his firm, veined hands gripping the boy's hips as he fucked his butt like it was the last thing he'd ever get to fuck. The intense pressure communicated itself through the boy's mouth to Desiree's cunt, causing it to contract involuntarily in a series of spasms as the weightlifter gripped her nipples and she screamed in terror and delight. She felt a ringing in her ears and a pounding in her chest as she came, fierce fluid gushing out of her center, spraying Donny's chin. The surprising sensation caused Donny's guts to contract around the massive cock, milking it tightly as Perry shouted at the sensation and pounded the boy's ass so ferociously that Leo was afraid for a moment that Perry would send them all crashing through the glass wall. "FUCK! Fuck! Fuck!" Perry bellowed as his cock poured its contents into the tip of the condom deep inside the boy, smashing Donny's face repeatedly into Desiree's pubes, setting off a completely new chain of orgasms which left her absolutely spent.

When she came back to earth, Perry was sitting sprawled on the tile with his arms coiled tightly around Donny's torso, in a mirror image of the brawny bodybuilder who held her still. The dazed boy's eyes were glazed and his mouth was agape as Perry buried his face in Donny's neck and rocked him softly. She vaguely remembered being lowered to the floor, but the recent moments were already a distant blur. She became aware of a tickling on her brows and nose—the woman who stood above them with the mister was still squeezing that damned trigger periodically. Desiree flinched and smeared a hand across her face to relieve the tickling. "Thank you," she said to the woman, who smiled at them and returned the spray bottle to its basket. Perry looked up and caught Desiree's glance, and mouthed a silent "Thank *you*" back at her. She wondered what was really behind that gesture. Something about trust, she recalled. She would have to ask Perry about that later.

Then she heard a thundering sound and realized it was applause. The room filled with the noise, enfolding the foursome with the sound of whistling, cheering, and clapping. "A shower would feel so good right now," she thought stickily. "Just as soon as I can remember where I left my limbs."

Bill Brent is the founder of Black Books, which co-published this anthology and produces other fine books on underground culture. He also edits Black Sheets*, a humorous magazine about sex and popular culture that he started in* 1993*. Many of his short stories and essays on sex appear there, as well as in the anthologies* Best American Erotica 1997, Eros Ex Machina*, and* The Factsheet Five Zine Reader*. He created the bisexual character, "Dick Death, Punk Detective," who appears in all three of the* Noirotica *anthologies. His stories will appear this year in the anthologies* Rough Stuff *and* Guilty Pleasures*. He has edited five editions of* The Black Book*, North America's foremost alternative sexuality resource guide. He is currently writing* The Ultimate Guide to Anal Sex for Men *for Cleis Press, and working hard on his first novel. You can stay posted by checking out* www.billbrent.com.

Acknowledgements

"Anal" by Marilyn Jaye Lewis originally appeared in *Bad Attitude, Vol 11 #1 1997-98* and *The Mammoth Book of Erotica, Revised Edition*, Fall 1999, Robinson Publishers, UK

"Her Mouth, In Which I Drowned" by Linda Eisenstein was originally published in *Paramour*, Vol. 4, Issue 1.

"Hunting for Sailors" by Robery Vickery first appeared in the December 1992 issue of *Advocate Men* magazine.

"Me And Jared" by Hew Wolff was originally published in the second "Damn Bisexuals!" issue of *Black Sheets*, issue 14.

If you enjoyed Best Bisexual Erotica, *you may enjoy these other erotica titles from* Circlet Press, Inc....

Sexcrime: An Anthology of Subversive Erotica
edited by Cecilia Tan, $14.95

Taking its title from 1984, George Orwell's dystopian novel, *Sexcrime* explores the erotic heat and intensity that can come from love under repressive conditions. In twelve stories, erotica authors and science fiction writers (including Jean Marie Stine, Simon Sheppard, M. Christian, Raven Kaldera, and more...) celebrate the ways underground love can flourish through the intimacy of secrets.

Fetish Fantastic: Tales of Power & Lust
edited by Cecilia Tan, $14.95

Top writers in today's sexual underground present tales of futuristic fiction. These lush stories transform the modern fetishes of S/M, bondage, and eroticized power exchange into the templates for new worlds. From the near future of cyberspace to a police state where the real power lies in manipulating authority, these tales are the cutting edge of both sexual fiction and science fiction.

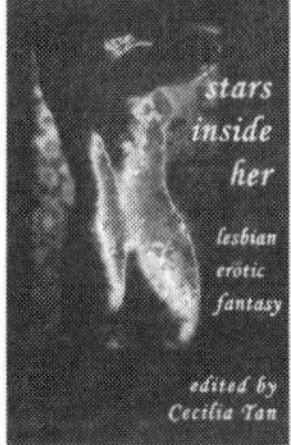

Stars Inside Her; Lesbian Erotic Fantasy
edited by Cecilia Tan, $14.95

In this anthology of erotica by queer women, the authors explore the true meaning of the word "fantasy." For in *Stars Inside Her*, any dream or wish can live at the heart of the eroticism. In these stories, women seek their pleasure through magic, from goddesses, in enchanted forests, and with fairy women.

Wired Hard 2: More Erotica For A Gay Universe
edited by Cecilia Tan, $14.95

Leap cod-piece first into wild men-on-men sexual adventures, from a gay cyberspace hacker searching for a killer to homoerotic visions of interstellar diplomats, fighter pilots, and even angels. *Wired Hard* 2 runs at high intensity—dark, hot, and heavy, and batteries are not included.

Order Online At www.circlet.com
or send check, money order, or credit card information (Visa, Master Card, or Amex only, and include account number, expiration date, and your billing address), along with your name, shipping information, and a signed statement that you are 18 years of age or older to:

Circlet Press, Dept. BBE
1770 Mass Ave #278
Cambridge, MA 02140

Include $4 shipping for the first book,
$2 for the second book, and $1 for each book thereafter,
for shipping within the US and Canada.
Massachusetts Residents Add 5% Sales Tax.

ORDER FORM

Return to: Black Books, PO Box 31155-H2, San Francisco CA 94131-0155, or call (800) 818-8823 to order with a credit card, or fax (415) 431-0172 with credit card info. We accept checks, MOs, cash, Visa, MC, AmEx, and Discover.

Hot Off The Net: erotica and other sex writings from the Internet, edited by Russ Kick
Taboo subject matter. Brutal honesty and candidness. Experimental forms and styles. From personal confessions to the most outlandish fantasies, witness the future of erotic writing.

- ❑ Please send me ____ copy[ies] of *Hot Off The Net.* Enclosed is $18 ($15 + $3 s/h), or $19.28 if I am in California (includes sales tax), or $21 US if I am in Canada/Mexico, or $24 US elsewhere for each copy ordered. ISBN 1-892723-00-X.

Best Bisexual Erotica, edited by Bill Brent and Carol Queen
Stories with a bi flavored tingle. Co-editors Carol Queen and Bill Brent have selected twenty-two stories for straight, gay, lesbian, bisexual, transgender, and fetish audiences—in short, anyone literate with a libido. Contributors include the editors, Hanne Blank, Marilyn Jaye Lewis, Jill Nagle, 17 others.

- ❑ Please send me ____ copy[ies] of *Best Bisexual Erotica.* Enclosed is $19 ($16 + $3 s/h), or $20.36 if I am in California (includes sales tax), or $22 US if I am in Canada/Mexico, or $27 US elsewhere for each copy ordered. ISBN 1-892723-01-8.

Noirotica 3: Stolen Kisses, edited by Thomas Roche
The latest release in the genre pioneered by Thomas Roche—erotic crime fiction. Contributors include Alison Tyler, Brian Hodge, Kate Bornstein, Michelle Tea, Michael Thomas Ford, M. Christian, Bill Brent, Maxim Jakubowski, Simon Sheppard, Lucy Taylor, Thomas Roche, and 14 others.

- ❑ Please send me ____ copy[ies] of *Noirotica 3.* Enclosed is $19 ($16 + $3 s/h), or $20.36 if I am in California (includes sales tax), or $22 US if I am in Canada/Mexico, or $27 US elsewhere for each copy ordered. ISBN 1-892723-03-4.

The Black Book, edited by Bill Brent
The foremost directory of sexuality resources for all orientations, gender identities, and lifestyles in the U.S. and Canada. Over 2,500 listings.

- ❑ Please send me ____ copy[ies] of *The Black Book.* Enclosed is $20 ($17 + $3 s/h), or $21.45 if I am in California (includes sales tax), or $24 US if I am in Canada/Mexico, or $28 US elsewhere for each copy ordered. ISBN 0-9637401-6-4.

Black Sheets: Our magazine of sex and popular culture. Kinky, queer, intelligent, irreverent.

- ❑ Please send me 4 issues of *Black Sheets* for $20, or $32 Can/Mex, or $36 elsewhere.
- ❑ Please send me a sample issue. Enclosed is $6 / $7 Can/Mex / $8 elsewhere.

I am 21 years of age or older. ______________________________
(signature required!)

____
Name

____
Address

____
City State Zip

______________________________ ____________
card number expiration date

In case of a question about my order:

tel. number ____________________ email address: ____________________

I heard about *Best Bisexual Erotica* or got this copy at: ____________________.

• Black Books (800) 818-8823 •